"I NOTICED YOU IN THE NET,"

Janny said. She looked away, avoiding his eyes. "System's instructed to tell me when people I like are jacked in."

He felt himself beginning to blush, and, to cover, changed his clothes to those of a rich eighteenth-century European nobleman. He bowed with an extravagant flourish; white lace swirled nicely from the sleeve of his gold silk jacket. "Milady's too kind."

She smiled, suddenly in a gown and coiffure worthy of Marie Antoinette, and curtsied. "Milady's a sucker for guys with nice legs."

"Do tell?" He flickered into sixteenth-century white tunic and black tights, and then back to metallic jeans and turtleneck. "I get embarrassed."

Janny laughed. "Silly boy. What would you have done if I'd said you had a nice butt?"

He switched to a white Greek chiton and sandals, then, blushing, back to the jeans.

Janny shook her head. "You're such a tease."

THE TANGLED LANDS

WILL SHETTERLY

ACE BOOKS, NEW YORK

This book is an Ace
original edition, and has never
been previously published.

THE TANGLED LANDS

An Ace Book/published by arrangement with
the author

PRINTING HISTORY
Ace edition/December 1989

ISBN: 0-441-79804-7

Ace Books are published by The Berkley Publishing Group,
200 Madison Avenue, New York, New York 10016.
The name "Ace" and the "A" logo are
trademarks belonging to Charter Communications, Inc.
PRINTED IN THE UNITED STATES OF AMERICA

10 9 8 7 6 5 4 3 2 1

For Terri, Val, Pat, Steve, Kara, Nate, Pamela, and Emma, who are much too good to me ... but I'm not complaining.

CONTENTS

1

In Tangled Lands

Three brothers rode into the Tangled Lands. One was clean-shaven and dressed in red leather; a sword was sheathed across his back, and he wore a wine-dark headband imprinted with a white dagger. One was bearded and dressed in magician's whites; his robes were as pale and as light as his silk headband. The third was moustached and dressed in coarse cotton; only the white headband that showed beneath his wide straw hat revealed that he was of the free caste and not the servant of the fencer or the wizard.

Something's wrong, the third man thought.

Their names were Tikolos, Thelog, and Tival. They resembled each other in that they were slim and dark and green-eyed, though Tikolos, the swordsman, was the smallest and most muscular, and Thelog, the magician, was tallest. When they had been children and the three brothers were introduced to strangers, Tival invariably said, "Tikolos is the oldest, and Thelog is the youngest. I'm Tival. I'm the middlest." Now that they were young men he would say, "This is my elder brother, Tikolos Ar, who will be Gordia's greatest soldier. This is my younger brother, Thelog Ar, who will be Gordia's greatest magician. I am Tival Ar, who will be Gordia's greatest brother."

1

Tival removed his hat to fan himself, then patted his mare's neck. Her ruddy hide was rough under his hand and felt too warm, too moist. Her breathing seemed labored. They would have to stop soon to rest their mounts, he decided, and decided too that he must have been daydreaming. Odd that he could daydream at such a time in such a place. Perhaps his mind wandered to keep him from thinking of what waited for them.

Squinting against the afternoon haze, he stood in his stirrups to look for landmarks, for a stopping place or some sign of their destination. In late summer in northern Gordia, the days should be cool and windy and clear. The green leaves of the oaks and maples should be flecked with reds and yellows impatient for the coming autumn. Blueberries and raspberries should ripen so that fall's foragers could fatten themselves for winter. Blackflies should have gone wherever blackflies go after their annual few weeks' rule of the woods.

Earlier, at the edge of Gordia's lake district, the woods had been as woods ought to be. Here, the air was hot and dry and smelled of sulfur. Something grew on the ground like grass, but it was purple and tubular and brittle; the horses did not like it. They pranced and snorted uneasily—even Tival's stolid mare—as the three brothers rode toward distorted crystalline structures that might once have been trees. Only the blackflies, the horses, and his brothers remained to remind Tival of the world he loved, the world he might lose even if they succeeded.

This is wrong, Tival thought. The wrongness seemed to include more than the Tangled Lands. He did not let himself pursue that thought. He did not trust the consequences of any thoughts in the demons' realm, which followed rules he did not know, which shaped itself to the demons' whims. Could the demons hear his thoughts to use them against his party?

Ahead of him, Tikolos slapped the back of his neck with a fencer's speed. Peering at his palm, Tikolos said, "Well, there's still life here of one form that we know."

"Damned bugs probably amuse the demons," said Thelog.

Bugs, Tival thought. *There shouldn't be bugs*. Immediately after that, almost reassuringly, came, *But what can we know of the Tangled Lands?*

"Or," Thelog continued, "the blackflies' survival may

prove that there are things even demons fear." His sparse beard, recently grown so he would look more as he thought a wizard should, twitched once as he considered this. "Hmm. Small, annoying, fearsome things. Could we offer to have you fix breakfast for them?"

"*Fft*. Have you sing. Scare off demons and blackflies both."

Tival smiled at his brothers' bickering. *Bugs? Did they come because I thought of blackflies? Or had I thought of them because my subconscious noticed the insects before my conscious mind did?* He looked around again. The scent of sulfur had been joined by something like the smell of a leviathan in decay. That, he thought, was probably the smell of the land's decay. The purple grasses rippled occasionally as if blown by winds the brothers could not feel. *I wish something would happen. I wish we would come to a cool place with kind people, and music, and ale. . . .*

The memory returned with the unreal clarity of a dream that had been forgotten—their last night at Sandiston in the lake district. The villagers had gone into their cabins to sleep, except for a young man who had passed out after the sixth pipe of mirthweed and a very quiet woman who sat by Tikolos's knee, obviously intending to accompany one of the heroes to bed and wishing they would retire soon. With an almost drunken delight, Thelog had recited:

> To banish demons, Three must try,
> For Three shall close the Demon's Gate:
> One strong, one pure, one thrown to fate,
> And two shall live and one must die.

Then he laughed once and stared glumly at the fire. After a moment, Thelog murmured words in the magician's tongue. The flames shaped themselves into tiny, perfect human figures dancing to the tune that Tival played on his flute.

The Brothers Ar said nothing for several minutes. They had known of the prophecy since they were children and the Tangled Lands were a tiny fraction of their present size. They had never spoken among themselves of its implications.

It was, Tival thought, no clearer than any other prophecy. Each of the Brothers Ar might be one of the Three mentioned

in the third line. The competitions at the Great Arena of City
Gordia had shown their strengths, certainly. If purity was a
measure of determination, the competitions had shown that,
too. Tikolos had defeated Gordian nobles, Hrotish savages,
and Dawn Isle Fencers in the Duel of Nine Weapons to prove
himself with sword, knife, bow, stave, spear, axe, iron-
rimmed shield, net, and, finally, naked body. Thelog had en-
gaged in Wizard's War with priests of the Nine, of the
Questers, of lesser and more exotic sects; he had competed
with magicians from the Nine Cities of Man, an Elf, and a
blond Hrotish shaman, all to show his mastery of the First
Language, the language that the God had used when She created the world. Tival's contests had been less flamboyant. His
opponents were the world's scholars, most much older and
more learned than he.

None of the brothers had won every contest, but Thelog
and Tikolos had won more than any other competitor in war or
wizardry. Tival had not won in any of the tests of wisdom; his
essays on history and faith and honor had been ranked sixth,
second, and third, respectively. His long poem, for which he'd
had a week to prepare, had finished eleventh, but his short
poem, for which he'd had five minutes, had taken second
place. When the judges, men and women from each of the
Nine Cities, announced his name for the third of the Three to
venture into the Tangled Lands, Tival had been the most surprised person in the Great Arena.

The judges had said that he was the best choice of all the
scholars available, being quick and flexible in his thinking,
young and healthy for the journey, and intimately aware of
those who would travel with him. Tival was not so sure.
Added to his doubts of his worth was the fear that the judges
were wrong to try to fulfill an old and ambiguous prophecy by
selecting three people as if they were applicants for a royal
position. Though he and his brothers had trained since the age
of nine in the categories that the judges had announced, the
prophecy might refer to three people as yet unborn, who might
never know of the prophecy, even if they made it come true.
The prophecy might not even refer to humans.

The silence by the village fire had ended when Tikolos
belched and said, "Don't believe in prophecies. B'lieve in my
sword and my strong right arm." They all laughed more than

the joke deserved; it was a line from a very bad play they had seen in City Gordia.

Thelog stroked his thin beard. "There's probably some truth in it. It's from *The Lore of the Wisest One*."

"Don't know if I believe in a Wisest One, either," Tikolos replied. "If I do, she's some Elf bitch who wouldn't care if the Tangled Lands swallowed all of the human countries."

"That's not fair," Tival said, setting aside his flute. Both brothers stared at him, and he blushed. "Well, even if she didn't care about humans, she wouldn't want Faerie taken by the demons. Helping us would help the Elflands." The brothers continued to stare. He said, "I'll keep playing," and did so.

"Well," said Thelog. "There's surely something to the prophecy, but I doubt we're bound to it. I think it's, well, a guideline. We can write our own program, I think, if we must."

Tival had not spoken again that night. He played folk tunes on the flute until his brothers retired, then made a bed on the ground. Restlessly watching the slow march of the constellations, he had decided. The prophecy must mean something, however vague it might be. And if it did, and if a moment came when one of them could choose to die, he would not hesitate. His brothers were strong and pure, he knew. Dying would be a small gesture of love.

Something glinted on the mottled grounds ahead of them. Without speaking, the brothers directed their horses toward it. It lay by a furry coral block that might have been a huge sponge or a rock covered with a strange mold. The block smelled too sweetly of roses, like a whore doused with the cheapest perfumes. The scent blended with the sulfurous odor of the Tangled Lands, making Tival nauseous.

He dismounted and approached the shining object cautiously, not wanting to come too near the coral boulder. At last, he reached out and picked it up. It was a book with a shiny foil cover. In luminescent red ink, it said:

Lands of Adventure
Subroutine 4, Version 3.0c:
The Tangled Lands

He stared at it and frowned. Thelog called, "What is it?"

Tival thought, *A glitch in the program.* He heard himself say, "A glyph about progress."

"About progress?" Tikolos asked.

Tival seconded the question in his mind. He looked again, and saw that he no longer held a book, but a plaque. On its pitted surface was the symbol for demons used by the scribes of Lost Sargoniom. "Yes," Tival answered, smiling though he knew he should be frightened. "We've come to the boundaries that the Tangled Lands had centuries ago. We must be within a few miles of Demon's Gate." He looked again at the plaque, shrugged, and flicked it away like a fris... like a discus. It glittered prettily in the air, disappearing into the white haze that surrounded them.

"That's true," someone said behind him. "But you will go no closer to Demon's Gate." The voice was the high shriek of a buzz saw... of chalk on a blackboard... of a fiddle played by a chimpanzee. Tival whirled and saw the coral block growing, changing its shape and increasing its size like clay worked by an invisible sculptor. The horses snorted behind him. He glanced back and saw Thelog mumbling something, probably a calming spell. The horses settled as if nothing unusual had occurred.

"Greetings," Tikolos said, his voice quiet and very assured. How was it that Tikolos could doubt the details of the prophecy, yet trust that the brothers were the Three who could succeed?

"Greetings," responded the coral transfiguration. Shoots sprouted from the primary mass and then combined with each other as if the thing could not decide how many limbs it should have, or even what shape it should keep. It finally resolved into the stocky form of a pregnant woman, a crude fertility symbol that was twice the height of Thelog, the tallest of their party, and seemingly as heavy as their three horses.

"Are you the Demon Lord?" Tikolos asked. Tival heard the tone that a cat might use to ask a chicken if it was dinner. He admired Tikolos's manner while knowing it was dangerously inappropriate.

"I?" said the demon. "Asphoriel? The Demon Lord himself, squatting all day in this dreary place, waiting for loathsome little humans to come asking stupid questions? Not very likely, don't you think?"

Too quickly to be blocked, one of the demon's arms extended itself across twenty feet of space and retracted as quickly. It drove into Tikolos's face, knocking him from his dappled gelding onto the purple grass. The near side of his wine-red headband was black with his blood.

"One down," said the demon. "Next?"

This is not right, Tival thought, then realized what a very stupid thought that was.

Thelog swung his leg over the front of his saddle and slid to the ground. "He was my brother."

The demon shook its head and laughed. "Still is. Isn't dead yet. Bandage him, make a travois to carry him, ride back to the human lands. Now."

Tival and Thelog glanced at Tikolos. The swordsman's chest moved with slow, deep breaths. Thelog said, "Quit our duty and leave?"

"Oh, you humans are a quick-witted lot, aren't you?"

Thelog spoke two syllables in the magician's language and was interrupted when the demon grunted one. Thelog frowned, then began again, more quickly. The demon again interrupted his speech, at the same point with the same harsh word.

"What's it doing?" Tival asked.

Thelog grimaced. "Whenever I begin a spell . . ."

"Yes?"

"When I get to the verb, when I say the word for 'will,' the demon says 'not.'"

The demon giggled. Its laughter seemed to make the earth shake beneath them. Its breath was hotter and more vile than the winds from the heart of the Tangled Lands. Their horses reared and bolted, but Thelog screamed a guttural word, and they became as still as statues.

The demon's laughter diminished slowly. "You humans speak the True Language so slowly, with bad accents and worse grammar! We've known the First Language for as long as we've existed. We *are* the First Language. And you hope to win a wizard's duel with the likes of us?"

Thelog shouted, "In Gordia, I could call you, bind you, bargain with you—"

"Perhaps that is true," the demon said. "Perhaps you could call me if you were in your land and made your preparations well. I doubt you could call one of my more powerful siblings. And I know you cannot defeat me here, where neither of us is fettered."

Tival stared at his brother. Thelog turned from the demon, nodded slowly, and looked toward Tikolos. "Your turn, brother," Thelog said, almost whispering. His fists were clenched tight at his side, and his body shook from the effort of withholding anger or tears.

"Mine?" Tival heard himself say.

"Do not trouble yourself," the demon said.

"No," Tival agreed. His faith, he realized, had been in his brothers, and when they were defeated, he was, too. What could he do, challenge the demon to a poetry contest?

This was a game, even if he did not know the rules. "I challenge you—" he said hesitantly.

"And I refuse," the demon replied.

He stared, then finally, petulantly, said, "There must be a way to banish you!"

"Of course there is," the demon agreed. "Do you really expect me to tell it to you?"

"No." Tival knew that the greater game had ended for the Brothers Ar. What would they do now? They could seek quieter lives in the human lands, as common people, not heroes. They could try to live ordinary lives, hoping that someone would find a way to halt the expansion of the Tangled Lands before it engulfed them all.

"We . . . may go?" he asked.

"And why not?" said the demon. "You aren't food, wealth, or entertainment. If ever you return, I'll kill you without warning. Or perhaps I will make you food and entertainment before I kill you. Take your brother and leave, if you will."

"Yes," Tival said. Hating himself, he added, "Thank you." He could snatch up Tikolos's sword, then run at the demon with the prayer that the demon would kill him. He doubted it would, not now. He suspected that the demon knew that sending them back to Gordia was the cruelest thing it could do.

He felt little more than a numb repression of failure. As he turned to help Thelog with Tikolos, he said, "I'm exiting."

He was in a tiny room without windows. The floor and walls were covered with a clean pepper-flecked gray carpet. The ceiling appeared to be the interior of a dome of frosted glass; it cast a dim, soothing white light. He was reclining in a chair of glossy black leather and burnished titanium. Next to him in a similar chair sat a beautiful red-haired woman dressed in immaculate white coveralls. Her perfume, the only smell, hinted of orange blossoms, as if someone had just carried a bouquet through the room. In Janny's voice, she said, "What function, please?"

Kevin said, "Disconnect."

"You're certain?"

"Do it."

Unjacking was an automatic process. Sit up half-blinded because no one remembered to turn down the overhead light. Reach back to yank the interface cable—and think too late that he should grip the plug instead—from its socket at the base of his skull. He heard the tiny click of the cover plate snapping over the port as he brushed his hair quickly with his fingers to hide it. The air was warm, and though it was very dry, he felt his Hawaiian shirt clinging to him. He recognized an aroma of stale cigarettes, old chocolate, ancient pizza, unwashed clothes, cat litter, and something petrochemical. The background sound was an electrical hum of piled cables with insufficient shielding, several fans, and an overworked air conditioner.

"Well?" said someone nearby. "Well?" Mad Dog's voice: gruff, quick, colored by something that Janny said was a lifetime of trying to control a stutter. Kevin had always thought Mad Dog would sound better if he let himself stutter.

Kevin blinked and shook his head. He felt a hand on his left shoulder. The grip was light; it was meant for comfort. Probably Janny. As the hand went away, he blinked again, catching the silhouette of a dark woman with red hair cut in a flapper's bob. Two dots of gold contact lenses pierced the shadow. Janny. Immediately beyond her was an old couch and the wall of massive computers that separated Bytehenge, their work area, from the clutter of Mad Dog's huge loft, a place that might be the storeroom of a museum of twentieth century technology were it arranged in a way understandable to anyone besides Mad Dog. The computers were Crays and VAXen, the best available some ten or twelve years ago, and a new Kimoda that served as the master unit. They were mostly gifts or secondhand purchases bought with Omari Corporation's advance money. Overhead were metallic-red ducts and beams, the only remnants of the building's history as manufacturing and warehouse space, and an insane spider-god's webbing of power and data cables. A yellow cardboard sign hung from one: CONTROL DATA: DON'T LET DATA CONTROL YOU.

"It's . . . good," Kevin said cautiously, his voice rough from several hours of disuse.

"Good?" Mad Dog's thin blond hair had not been washed for three or four days. Several strands fell across his watery blue eyes, red-tinged as usual from his usual lack of sleep. Oblivious to the warmth, Mad Dog wore a black tuxedo jacket over an army-green undershirt. "Good?" he said a second time, and his voice went higher. He yanked on the wheels of his wheelchair and scuttled back several feet, stopping half an inch from ramming a Cray-2 to stare at Kevin. "What's wrong with it?"

Kevin glanced at Janny. She hugged herself, tucking her hands tightly under her armpits, and looked away. *Well*, Kevin thought, *at least you have the grace to feel guilty.* She wore a faded red kimono cinched with a fatigue belt, baggy black pants, and paint-spattered sneakers. A thin blue cable ran from the main console to a point behind her right ear. Kevin wondered if she was still connected, but then she reached up, pulled her jack, and set it next to his.

"Nothing," he told Mad Dog. "I don't know. Give me a minute." He glanced at his watch. A little more than three and a half hours of real time had passed. "You got anything besides Nova Coke to drink?"

"Water."

Kevin stood, only slightly dizzy. Hurrying for the rear of the loft, he said, "Get me some. I gotta piss."

"Get him some," Mad Dog told Janny. His wheels squeaked as he followed Kevin.

Kevin stopped between two chest-high computers, breathed deeply, then turned. "Mad Dog. You coming to wipe me or something?"

"I want to know what the fuck you think!"

"I think it's good. I think it's great. I think it's completely fucked up, and Omari's gonna burn our butts if we give them that. I think if you don't let me go now. I'm going to hose the guts of this VAX and where'll the project be then?"

Mad Dog grinned. "It's good?"

Kevin looked at Janny. "Didn't I say that? Did I, or did I not, say something remarkably like that?"

She glanced at him, and her lip twitched upwards a fraction. "Remarkably like that." She owned at least a dozen different pairs of contact lenses. He wondered if he had ever seen her naked eyes. She was very thin; he could never decide if she was hideous or beautiful.

"All right, then." He hurried through a corridor of second-hand industrial computers and shelves crammed with books, toys, video cassettes, ancient appliances, arcane parts for forgotten machines, exercise weights. Somewhere in Mad Dog's maze there must have been a bed, but Kevin had no idea where it was. He had visited often enough to memorize the route to the bathroom (turn right at the mechanical gypsy fortune-teller) and the kitchen (turn left at the pachinko machine and duck under the arm of the life-size fiberglass Batman).

The wall behind the toilet was covered with mirror tile. As he pissed, he wondered whether the designer had been a woman or a narcissist. That kept him from thinking that Juan Takeda expected to see a successful test run of *Lands of Adventure* in ten days. Omari Corporation had been very generous with development funds. How would they respond when they heard that the game was not ready; it was too good?

Zipping up, he decided that was how he would tell Mad Dog: The problem is that the game is too good. Right.

Janny was waiting in the hall when he opened the bathroom door. She held out a glass of water with ice. "What'd you think?"

He bit his lip, then said, "Jesus K. Fucking Christ."

"What'll you tell Mad Dog?"

"He hasn't jacked in?"

"He says we're the program wizards, we can zip around while it's dangerous."

"It's safe enough for Mad Dog, now. Probably."

"So? You gonna tell him that?" She pushed the glass toward him.

He took it and sipped. There was a taste of lemon; either Mad Dog and Janny were keeping a water jug with lemon slices in the fridge, or someone in Enter-Tech's public relations department had heard of the project and poisoned their water supply. Kevin drained the glass. "No. Christ, Janny. What'd you do?"

She smiled. "I made it real."

"You made it real." Kevin wished he could tell whether Janny was joking or insane.

She nodded. Her hair bounced as if filmed in slow motion. "Or maybe I've only made it more real, so far. But—"

"More real?" He smiled. "I suppose that's appropriate for The Most Unique Game Ever—"

She grinned. "I don't write Omari's ad copy. You got a better way to describe it?"

"Hey, I don't even know what it is yet. Mad Dog know what you've done?"

"Sure. It was his idea. Sort of."

"You said Mad Dog hasn't been in."

She met his gaze. "No."

If he had been wearing mirrored lenses too, their reflected images would have multiplied until the images were as small as particles of light. What would the images become then? *Lovers*, he thought, and kept his face calm. "So he doesn't know what it's like now?"

"No."

"Fine. I'll quit playing Perry Mason."

She smiled. "Thank you."

"You could've warned me."

"Would you have believed me?"

"No. I'm not sure I do now. It's weird. That doesn't mean it's—"

Mad Dog's voice came from an ancient table-top radio on

the floor next to the bathroom. "I'm bored. Bored, bored, bored. Sure you don't need me to wipe you, Kid Flash?"

"We're coming," Janny said, and Kevin wondered if he heard a trace of annoyance in her reply.

"Oh. Sorry to interrupt you then, kiddies. You don't mind if I listen whi—"

Kevin spun the volume dial till it clicked. "He's such an asshole, sometimes."

"You don't understand that?"

"Just don't like it. I don't like it when he treats you badly." He set his hand on her thin shoulder to comfort her. The silk kimono felt more intimate than skin. He could not tell if the warmth under his hand came from her shoulder or his palm.

"That was just a joke to him."

"I know. A sad joke."

"Yeah. Well . . ." She shrugged, and he removed his hand. "C'mon, Kev. We got to figure out what we're going to do now."

Watching her hips as he followed, he thought, *Yeah. Don't we always.*

Mad Dog was wheeling around Bytehenge, dumping ash-trays into a plastic bread bag. He said, "Company"s coming. I called Gwen. She's bringing Brian and the new kid."

"Milo," Janny said.

"Yeah."

"Or Matthew."

"Whatever. I put coffee on."

"Bless you," Kevin said.

Mad Dog winked at him. "For you, sweetcheeks, any-thing."

While Janny gathered newspapers, comic books, and Mad Dog's dumbbells, Mad Dog did something in the kitchen. Kevin took his jacket from the back of the chair at the terminal he usually used and hung it by the door. When he returned, Janny was sitting on the bench-seat of the Cray-1. After a moment's hesitation, he sat beside her. "Anything I can do?"

"This is good enough."

Mad Dog called from the kitchen, "Want to hear some depressing news?"

"No," Janny yelled. "Thank you."

"Remember Captain Action? The nineteen-year-old who designed *Pacific Perils* a couple years ago?"

"Isn't he twenty?" Kevin said. "I read about him in—"

"Whatever." Mad Dog wheeled back into the room with a tray of cups, a red thermos, two brown ceramic bowls of sugar and honey, a small white and gold porcelain pitcher of cream, and a stainless steel mixing bowl filled with peanut M&M's. "He killed himself. Disconnected the safety timer on his rig and jacked into his temple maidens scenario on an endless loop. They figure he died of thirst, but he was grinning. What a way to go, hey?"

"Jesus," Kevin said, keeping his tone conversational. He had admired Captain Action's work, had wished he could be as good. He had thought he might someday run into Captain Action on the net, and the Captain would recognize Kid Flash's handle and compliment him on his work on *Lands of Adventure*.

"Left a note for ALL on his b.b.s., too."

Janny said, "Why're you so interested?"

Mad Dog shrugged and grinned. "It's funny. C.A. was what, four years younger than any of us? The note said he couldn't take the competition anymore. Couldn't stand watching the next generation taking over, pubescent little shits who'd jacked before they walked."

Kevin looked at Mad Dog, who lifted both eyebrows several times while wagging an imaginary cigar. Knowing he shouldn't, he laughed. "The temple maidens scenario? Poor bastard. He could've checked out with something a little more cutting edge than . . ."

Mad Dog and Janny were watching him as his sentence trailed off. Kevin shrugged. "I guess that's part of the point."

Janny put her sneaker up on the armrest of Mad Dog's wheelchair. The unpainted nail of her big toe showed through a split between the rubber and the canvas. Pushing suddenly, causing Mad Dog to spin, she said sweetly, "Thank you for sharing that with us."

2

Child of Fire and Ash

The priest was a slim and handsome man; later, the woman could not say whether his features or his light gray robe had made her so uneasy in his presence. She watched him from the woods, with her two children uncustomarily quiet by her side. He crouched in a small garden and thinned a patch of carrots. She was not a contemplative woman, but as he pulled one baby carrot and left the next with more space in which to grow, she thought of her own task.

She set her hands on her children's heads. Her son, the younger, jerked away, annoyed by a gesture for which he thought himself too old. Her daughter lifted her eyes to meet her mother's and said, "The priest?"

The man heard the girl's voice and stood. His eyes were green like her daughter's, his expression was kind, and once her husband had looked at her that way. She wished the girl had not spoken so soon, for she would have liked to watch the young man work a while longer. As she brought the children into the clearing, she dropped her gaze to the ground and said, "Lord, I come—"

"Gods, woman, do you see a white casteband?"

The angry voice was in such contrast to the expression she had seen that she glanced up. To her surprise, he was grin-

15

ning. Tapping his brow with the fingers of one hand, he said, "Priest, like the girl said. That's me. Not highborn, not low." His forehead was bare, as if he were a savage or an Elf. This seemed indecent, but the woman envied him.

"I know." She immediately looked down, wondering if he was mocking her. He enunciated quickly and clearly like most of the First Caste, with the hint of Gordian accent that many Tyrwilkan nobles affected.

He laughed. "Good. I'm called Glee. That was originally a joke, because I never was merry when I first joined the Order, but it seems to have taken. And you are . . . ?"

She knew what he saw. A woman ten years older than he, who looked twenty years older. In still water, she had seen the wrinkles in her face, the hollow cheeks that always made her man scream, "Eat more! You want people to think I'm starving you? Eat!" She did not need still water to see the white streaks in her thin hair or to know what two living children and four dead had done to her body. The narrow brown rag around her forehead told everyone that she was lowborn. The ashes that coated her rough woolen clothes revealed that she lived like most people in Korz Valley, by selling charcoal to Marganhalt Foundry.

She coughed, then stopped herself. "I'm Lu Kardeck, Lord." She set her hand on her daughter's shoulder and snatched her son's before he could jerk away. "My boy's Harj. The girl's Japhis."

"I did tell you my name," the priest said. It seemed a game with him, yet a game he took seriously.

"Yes, Glee," she said, again glancing up at him.

"Good. Why've you come here?" Stepping out of the garden, he moved his hand outward to indicate the small clearing, the gray stone house with its room of cedar shingles, a wooden outbuilding for a cow and a few goats.

"You're a priest." That wasn't an answer, she knew, but she wasn't ready to speak yet.

The man shook his head, and she stared. Her daughter looked up at her, and the boy said almost hopefully, "Go on to home, then?"

The man smiled. "Well, now. Yes, we're priests here, my companion and I, but not like you seem to think. You want a priest of the Nine, I suspect. This is a retreat of the Order of the Quest."

She continued to stare. Priests were priests; why did he say these things?

Glee's expression remained kind. "We seclude ourselves, Lu. You and your children seem healthy enough. If someone needed doctoring, you surely would've said so. We have no money, so you can't have come to beg. And we're so desperately in need of learning our own souls that we have no resources to help others learn theirs. So, whatever you may have come for, we cannot help you. For what it's worth, I am sorry." He glanced at a tiny, dirty carrot which he still held and added hesitantly, "Maybe some vegetables, if you're hungry?"

Perhaps she had been wrong to come. She answered, "No, Lord," but she did not turn away.

"There's a temple of the Nine in Tyrwilka. And isn't there an old man who lives near Marganhalt Foundry who conducts services on holy days?"

She spat without thinking. "He's a fool."

The priest wagged a finger at Lu and grinned. "That's probably true, but I wouldn't say it."

She smiled a little, meeting his gaze, and then her cough returned. When it settled, she said, "I come for the boy."

"Oh?" He glanced at Harj, who fidgeted under the priest's gaze and dug at the grass with his bare feet. "He looks—"

"No, not sick, Lord. Stupid. Like me."

The priest said quietly, "You don't seem . . ."

"Teach him," she said, suddenly imploring. "Only one child. That's not trouble, not really."

The priest stepped back, seeming as frightened as if she had threatened him with one of the forbidden weapons. Then he said kindly, "We don't teach. Even if we did, what could I do? I'm here because I know so little."

"Teach writing. Reading. Numbers. Make my child smart. Just the one." She plucked a knotted rag from her pocket and undid it before him, showing a fistful of blackened copper coins. "I'll pay."

"I don't want money, Lu Kardeck."

"These are good coins."

"I'm sure."

"My man doesn't know I have them. For each one, I said the merchant took too much, or that I lost one near the Fast-water, or that he must have counted wrong. But I did not steal these coins from my man, Glee. He hit me for every one. These are my coins."

"I . . . know."

"Then teach the boy, Lord. Please."

Glee looked back at the stone house, as if hoping another priest would come. Then he glanced at the girl, who watched impassively. Finally he said, "You don't know what you ask."

If Lu had been much younger, she would have laughed. She knew her life and she knew the life her children would live if nothing changed. "They'll both work for you. The girl's strong for her age, and a hard worker. She'll keep the boy working. Both will work, if you'll just teach one."

The priest's face was quiet, and Lu wondered if she had said too much. He stepped close to her. He had almost no scent, as if he had fallen into the river recently, and the hints were of wood smoke and damp wool and fresh earth and, under them all, something tart and healthy that was his own odor. He studied her, and only her need kept her from turning and running into the woods. When he moved, Lu flinched. Glee only knelt to look at the children. Harj seemed troubled, and the girl took her brother's hand. Harj snatched it away, saying, "Stop it, Japhis." His long hair was tangled and grimy. The girl was little cleaner, but she was calm, and Lu wished, as she often had, that her daughter had been a son.

When the priest stood, he said, "You're trying to play on my kindness."

She heard that she had succeeded, so she said, "Only so you'll teach him." When Glee failed to answer, she added, "My own mother said people who think their kindness is mis-used are not kind at all."

The priest's faint smile appeared, then fled. "Teaching's not what you think."

"Maybe not. Yet it's something."

"Reading makes no one wiser, not of itself. To tell you the truth, those who do not read wisely become more foolish."

"Reading's a skill, not a craft. I know that much."

The priest's eyes widened, then he said, "You might do better to apprentice him at the Foundry."

She wanted to spit again, and she wanted to cough, but she suppressed both. "I've seen the Foundry. They think they're big there, like the old Niner who calls himself priest. But they're little. Work the days when there's work, smoke mirthweed or drink port when there's not. They're no better than my man when he has a half-copper for mead."

"Yet you think reading will help your child, Lu Kardeck?"

"Maybe not. What else can I do? Ask a gift of Korz Demon?" Beside her, Japhis glanced up at her face. Harj had left them to squat beneath a spruce tree and dig idly in the loam.

The priest frowned. "What demon?"

Lu shook her head. "You're not Mountain, Glee. Mountain people know."

"And how'll I know if no Mountain person tells me?" He grinned, pleased with his cleverness.

She bit her lips to keep from smiling too much. "What's to tell, Glee? I've never seen it."

"Ebin Ravensdell," Japhis whispered, putting a thin hand on her mother's elbow.

The priest squinted. "What's that?"

Lu patted Japhis's hand and sighed, wanting to return to the matter of whether the priest would teach Harj. "An old story. The demon gives gifts, fools take them. Ebin Ravensdell took a horse that won many races. Then she tried to leap Asphoriel's Abyss . . ." Lu pointed, anticipating the priest's question. ". . . high in Korz Valley, where the yellow smoke always rises. It was a bet that Ebin took, and lost. The horse carried her into the abyss. Nobody saw her again."

"And Gert Trothen," Japhis prompted, a little louder than before.

The priest laughed. "Perhaps your daughter should tell this story."

Lu smiled with him. "Japhis knows all the old tales. Gert came after Ebin, when my mother was young. Gert had a magic churn from the demon. One night, people burned him and churn both. They feared the gift would curse the whole valley."

"They burned him because of a churn?"

"Because he trusted the demon. Demons win lands from us with tricks. I've heard this. Can Korz Demon be different?"

"I don't know. What's this one like?"

"Korz Demon?" Lu whispered. "Some say the demon knows everything that happens in the valley. Some say it spies on us. Say it makes itself into a squirrel or a spider or the wind. Say it hears its name wherever it's spoken and comes to hear what's said."

"You know its name?"

She stopped herself before she laughed at him. Reading had not taught the priest everything important. "Demons don't have names. Not like we do, or maybe they won't tell theirs. If you're simple enough to want this one, call—" She hesitated, then whispered, "the Demon of Korz Pass. All the stories say it answers to that."

The priest laughed lightly. "Well, I suppose if it hasn't noticed us before, it's noticed us now."

Lu rubbed her daughter's head with rough affection. "Korz Demon noticed this one long ago. Japhis doesn't think it's evil."

"No?"

"My girl's a good worker, but foolish."

The priest frowned at Japhis. "Is that so? You don't think the demon's malicious?"

The girl nodded.

"Why's that?"

"The gifts," Japhis said, as if no one had asked her before. "They're not evil."

Lu laughed nervously and nudged Japhis to be quiet. "The gifts brought evil, now didn't they?"

Japhis shrugged.

"The girl has a point," Glee said. "It's hard to believe a churn doomed the old farmer. Sounds more like jealousy to me."

"And the horse," Japhis added. "Ebin didn't have to make the horse try to leap the abyss!"

Lu nudged her again. "People hear you talk like that—" She glanced at the priest, no longer seeing a handsome man, only seeing someone who could have her family burnt for traffic with demons. "She's simple, but she does work hard. And she'll learn better. Teach her brother—"

"No," said Glee.

Lu bit her upper lip, cursing herself for speaking so easily with a stranger. "Lord, I might pay more later, somehow, if only—"

"No," he repeated, then said loudly, "Boy!"

Harj scrambled to his feet. Snot hung from his nose, which he wiped with a dirty hand, smearing grime across his already dirty face.

"What do you think of demons?"

"Demons, Lord?"

"Demons, boy."

"They're tricksters, Lord. Prey on simple folk, and high-born too. Was a highborn that gave them the Tangled Lands."

"So they say," the priest agreed. "And what do you think are the demons' motives?" Harj frowned, confused, and the priest said, "Why do they do what they do?"

"Why, Lord? Because they're evil."

"And how do you know this?"

"How?" The boy's confusion grew greater. "It's what everyone knows."

"Ah." Glee stooped again to examine the carrots growing in the small garden.

Lu waited, and finally said, "You won't teach the boy?"

"I'm not sure there'd be any point to it. But I'd teach the girl."

"My Japhis?"

The priest glanced up. "Yes."

"But she's foolish, Lord!"

"Perhaps. You've offered me money to teach a child. I'll teach one."

Lu nodded. "My man won't understand."

"I thought he wouldn't have understood anyway."

"That's true, Lord."

"Then send her every other afternoon, beginning tomorrow. The boy can come with her, if he's quiet. You may keep your coins."

Lu hefted the bag once. "No, Lord. If I kept them, I'd truly be a thief. And I will not give them back to my man."

Glee stood from his crouch and came close to her. He half-closed his eyes as though he was very weary, then held out his hand. As she set the tarnished copper coins in his palm, he said, "Now you've paid twice. I'll try to teach them both."

As soon as she was out of the priest's sight, she let her cough have its way. In spite of that, she smiled for most of the afternoon's walk to their hut, even after she had to stop and spit out the black bile that her cough brought her. It was the coal-burner's cough, she knew. Perhaps her children would never have it.

The girl, last of the Kardecks to leave Glee's sight, paused where the path turned, and glanced back. He smiled at her, wondering what sort of fool he was to accept the children as students. As he lifted his hand to wave goodbye, he realized that he was a lonely and sentimental fool. Japhis's eyes widened at his wave, and she turned and fled. He snorted a half-laugh at her shyness.

"Trying to convert the squirrels to our ways, Glee?" Felicity called.

He turned in time to see her dark robe disappear from a window of the house. "I thinned half the patch!"

The door opened, and she came into their yard. Blinking in the sunlight, she said, "And the other half will thin itself?" The sun reflected on pale streaks in her brown hair.

He shook his head. "Do you know why I love you?"

She nodded, her narrow face still, one eyebrow raised. "Because you love all living things as though they were your family."

"Did I ever mention my Mad Uncle Rix?"

"No." She came closer and hugged him. "Just your brothers."

He nodded. "Well, yes." Thinking of no proper preparation for the news, he added, "I've agreed to tutor two of the local children."

"And they agreed to tend the garden for you?"

He slapped his hand against his forehead. "Thank you! I was wondering, and now I know. I'm a shockingly stupid fool!"

"I didn't say that."

"No, but—"

"I would, if you'd like me to."

"Thank you, but—"

"You're a shockingly stu—"

He kissed her.

". . . pid fool," she finished, laughing, so he kissed her again. "Is this any way for two priests of the Quest to behave out of doors?"

"No," he replied. "Let's go indoors."

"And the carrots?"

"They can go indoors, too."

"Glee . . ."

"Did I tell you that I hate carrots?"

"Did you know that in southern cities, carrots are served to incite libidinous thoughts?"

Glee nodded and stooped in the garden. "I'll finish this shortly."

"I made that up."

"About the carrots? Damn." He continued working, and she crouched near him to help. Her hands were narrow and dark, perhaps stronger than his. When their fingers brushed together as they dropped young carrots in a pile, she smiled. He said, "What do you know about demons?"

"I know what everyone knows about the Tangled Lands. How they'll consume the world, if—"

"No." He brushed off one baby carrot, rubbed it clean against his robe, then took a bite. "Near here. Korz Pass."

"There are stories. I have trouble believing them."

Glee nodded. "The Tangled Lands are—" He frowned, then said, "alien. Something only a demon could love. But these mountains—"

"Perhaps there is a tiny place like the Tangled Lands up here."

He offered her a bite of the carrot. As she took it, he said, "I hope not. And I find it hard to believe. The local woman talked as though this demon is near, but she said nothing about an abode."

Felicity put one hand on his forearm. "You're not Tival Ar anymore, Glee. Not for years now."

He shrugged. "I've accepted that. But if there's something here to be learned, something that the true saviors of our world should know, whoever they might be . . ."

"It is curious," Felicity agreed. "One demon, alone in the world. A scout for their kind?"

"Or an outcast," Glee said. "What would that say about its nature?"

The next day, Japhis and Harj followed the ridge paths to the Questers' retreat. A cold rain fell, soaking their thin

woolen ponchos. Japhis felt an odd mixture of mistrust and
cheer when she saw chimney smoke hanging low above the
priests' shingled roof. In the yard, Harj stopped and said, "We
go in?" The house was gray in the rain, with its bleached
shingles and slatted shutters and an unadorned oak door apparently built to withstand the assault of axes or battering
rams.

Before Japhis could decide, a brown-haired woman in
robes of charcoal gray opened the door. "Ah, Glee's folly.
Come in!"

Harj glanced at Japhis, who nodded, and they hurried in.
Leather hinges squeaked as the woman closed the door behind
them. This outer room seemed to be half the house. An oven
was built into the side of the fieldstone fireplace, and the
smell of baking bread mixed with that of the burning poplar
logs. (Lu baked bread in an iron pot that she set into their
family's firepit.) The Questers' floor was made of oak planks,
darker than their door. (The Kardecks' floor was packed earth
covered with rushes, and a leather apron hung over their low
doorway in winter.) A tapestry on one wall showed many
different animals and a naked man and woman, all standing in
a field of blue and red and yellow flowers, while towering
over them a giant dark woman smiled smugly. (Japhis had
drawn animals on the rough planks of their hut with a burnt
stick one afternoon and her father had hit her.) Other strange
things filled the room; the smaller strange things occupied a
set of shelves on the inner wall. (The Kardecks' hut was
filled, too, but it consisted of a single room that was smaller
than this room, and the things that sat about were chickens
and dogs and furniture that their father swore he would fix
someday.) Japhis recognized a loom half-again as large as
Lu's, and the boxlike things on one shelf were almost certainly books.

"Wait by the fire," the woman said. "I'll fetch your
teacher."

As soon as the woman left, Harj whispered, "What's that
mean, that *gleezfolly*?"

"Means we're students."

"Oh."

The inner door opened again, and Glee grinned at them. "I
hoped you'd come." He still looked strange to Japhis. She was

not used to men who were neither fat nor muscularly lean, who did not wear a full beard or the traditional Tyrwilkan sideburns or even a moustache, whose hair did not hang to the shoulders or longer, who did not dress in jacket and trousers.

"We came," Japhis said quickly. "We're going to be gleez-folly."

The priest stared, then laughed. "Who said that?"

Harj pointed at the next room. "The woman."

Glee nodded. "Felicity's like that."

"We're not gleezfolly?" Japhis asked.

Glee shook his head. "I hope not."

Harj yelled, "What's *gleezfolly*?"

"Glee's folly," the priest enunciated. "Felicity thinks I'm foolish to teach you."

"She does?" Japhis said.

Glee nodded.

"You should hit her," Harj said.

"You shouldn't hit anyone," Glee answered. "It always means that you're stupider than the person you've hit." As Harj frowned, Glee added, "Besides, she's my superior in the Order. You can tell because her robe is darker than mine."

"She is?" Harj asked.

"She is," Glee said. "And I begin to suspect that the greater part of education is repetition."

"It is?" Japhis asked.

"Fortunately, I don't have to teach as though it were. You will both pay attention?"

The children nodded.

"Good. I am Glee, whom you may call Brother or Father or Uncle, if you wish. Felicity may be addressed as Sister or Mother or Aunt."

"Yes, Lord," Japhis said.

Glee sighed. "That's a joke?"

"Yes, Lord." She giggled.

Glee glanced upwards and sighed more loudly. "My. This is going to be fun." Then he said, "So. I will tell you a small secret. One of the tenets of our Order is that facts and lies may be taught, but wisdom must be learned. This means," he said, raising a hand to silence Japhis before she could speak, "that I will not punish you if you do not try to learn. I will only send you away. But your mother will be very disappointed."

Felicity's voice came from the next room. "Brother Glee, you're hardly letting them discover their own need for knowledge."

Glee laughed. "Are you listening?"

Felicity looked out the door. Her hair was shorter than Glee's, cut almost to her skull, and her accent was like that of the trader from Winterberry, more familiar than Glee's yet not quite Mountain. "You're hardly quiet. Are you going to warp all of our beliefs in the course of your teaching?"

"Well, I thought I'd leave the most important ones alone, so I'd have some to warp later in the year."

"Hmmf. You'll never rise to the Inner Circle." In spite of her words, her voice was fond. Harj and Japhis smiled knowingly at each other before Felicity closed the door again.

"What's she mean?" Japhis asked.

"That I've broken our rules a bit. We don't seek converts, and we only teach those who ask us. But your mother didn't ask me to teach you about the Quest. She asked me to teach you to read, so I think I may use more conventional means with you."

"Oh." Japhis nodded. "Teach us about the Quest."

The priest tucked his chin and squinted at her. "You want me to?"

"Yes," Japhis replied.

"If she says so," Harj said.

"Very well. The full name of our order is the Order of the Quest of Truth. It's not terribly profound, I fear. It's more a philosophy than a religion. You understand that?"

"No," Japhis said calmly.

Glee laughed. "Then I won't bore you." He took a pail of sand from near the fireplace and scattered it on the floor. Drawing a figure with his forefinger, he said, "We begin with the alphabet. The first letter..."

Japhis and Harj studied with the priests for several years, until their mother became too sick to leave her bed. When she died, Japhis cried, not knowing if she cried because she had lost her mother or her earlier life. She expected life to become intolerable without her mother to stand between them and their father's anger, but something happened to the old man when Lu died. He became quiet, and he no longer worked and rarely drank. Harj and Japhis took over the task of making charcoal. They no longer had time to visit the priests and read.

Her father came to Japhis's bed one night and stood near her until, frightened, she said, "Go away, Da. Go away." He never spoke of the incident. A year and a half after Lu's death he wandered into the woods and did not return. A few weeks later, searching for deadwood for their fire, Harj found their father's body in a clearing. Japhis and Harj buried him where he had fallen, and only afterwards wondered if they should have brought him back to be buried beside his wife.

3

___

Courtly Manners

Kevin, sipping his coffee, watched Janny raise both arms to rake her hair back from her face with her fingers. As she turned to accept a cup from Mad Dog, he glimpsed the tiny silver plate at the back of her neck and glanced away, wondering why he should be embarrassed. The sexual symbolism seemed too obvious, but that might be part of it. Socket plates meant wealth or privilege; perhaps he thought displaying them was gauche. Perhaps his father's belief in the purity of the body still bothered him. *"Where's your soul when you send your mind into a machine, son? You tell me that, and I'll trouble you no more 'bout what you do."*

Someone with a British accent shouted, "No one expects the Spanish Inquisition!"

Startled, Kevin almost spilled his coffee. Meeting Mad Dog's grin, he realized that his embarrassment came from watching Janny during a private moment. Mad Dog said, "Company, old boy." The button by Mad Dog's front door activated a program which generated dialogue or sound effects from old films, radio shows, and videos. It never repeated itself and always surprised Kevin.

Before any of them could leave Bytehenge, the front door squeaked and banged into plastiboard boxes stacked near it.

Kevin heard Gwen call, "Don't shoot, hombres, we're on your side!"

Footsteps approached through the maze. Mad Dog sighed, saying, "It's open, don't stand on ceremony, come right in."

Gwen circled the Cray-1 first. Her dreadlocks were purple enamel that day, surprisingly attractive against her espresso skin. She wore fire-engine red riding boots and tan jodhpurs without a shirt. She'd had plastic snaps implanted about her body, every two inches in two lines from her ear lobes down each arm and in two more lines down her torso in a V from her shoulders toward her crotch. She wore different ornaments on each snap; today, they were all small and golden, except for a pearl at her left ear. The line of the snaps on her body crossed each blue-black nipple, making them seem decorations, too. Her muscles had been built up with exercise and steroids. Her biceps were thicker than Mad Dog's.

"I like the pants, Miss Cassady," Mad Dog said.

Gwen blew him a kiss. "You just like what's in them, Hound Dog." She hugged Janny, then winked at Kevin. "How you?"

He shrugged, smiled, and greeted Brian and the new kid with a show of his palm like an aborted hand wave. Brian swaggered toward a high cushioned stool patched with duct tape. The new kid followed him, glancing at the people and the daisy-chained computers with equal shyness. Brian was bald and dressed all in black: cowboy boots, jeans, wide leather belt, long-sleeved shirt stretched over his belly. He propped one foot on the stool rung, leaned forward to rest his elbow on his raised thigh, and grinned at Kevin.

"Yul Brynner," Kevin said. *"The Magnificent Seven."*

"Damn." Brian reached with both hands to peel the Caucasian-tone Medipatch from his head. As Gwen ruffled his short black hair, Brian said, "You should be into Poseur, Kev. You'd be good."

Kevin shrugged, then laughed. "What do you mean? Look at me." He pinched his Hawaiian shirt. "I'm Don Johnson."

"Who?"

"You know. *Hawaii Five-O.*"

Brian shook his head in amused disgust. "No way, Kev. That was Tom Selleck."

"See? I guess I'm just a bum." Kevin smiled to be sure that

he did not sound bitter. On two occasions, Brian had seemed depressed for several days, and then had apologized for things that Kevin had never noticed.

Janny nodded to the new kid. "You must be Miles."

"Michael," the kid said, looking at the floor. He wore creased khaki slacks, mauve topsiders, and a navy polo shirt. "Michael Hong." His skull was partially shaved. His remaining hair fell in a long queue down his back.

"Michael. Hi. I'm Janny Laias—J. Laias on the net. That's Kevin Fikkan, a.k.a. Kid Flash. He's the resident gamesmaster."

Kevin said, "It's a silly handle, hey? I've had it since I was fourteen. Nice to meet you."

"I hear you earned it."

Kevin shrugged. The only replies that occurred to him would have sounded vain or self-pitying.

"And that's Mad Dog O'Neill. Gwen already introduced you to Brian Cohn?"

As the new kid nodded, Mad Dog wheeled forward, extending one hand. "Jeez, Mike. You and Gwen make me think I ought to paint myself blue."

Gwen shook her head. "It's just the hair, Hound Dog. For your people, you need a little more grease and some head lice."

Janny crossed her arms. "Don't give him any ideas. Please."

"So, Mikey," Mad Dog said, "how do you like the place?"

The kid looked to either side as if he were about to cross a street, and Kevin wondered what he saw when he looked at Bytehenge. A junkyard? A playpen? A workplace for mutants? The kid said, "You do good work here."

Mad Dog laughed. "Okay, so we can't afford a supercooled hairy golf ball. All this big old shit hooked together has enough memory for what we need. Almost."

"The power bill must be, ah, impressive."

"I just transfer it to Omari," Janny said. "Contract includes expenses."

The kid nodded. "That's me. An expense."

"You joking?" Mad Dog said, clapping his arm. "You're the new head of research, Miguel. Want Nova Coke, Ancien Pepsi, or hot black speed?"

"Excuse me?"

"Coffee," Kevin said. "Choice of a hyper generation."

"Oh. Please."

"Ditto," said Brian.

"Tea," Gwen said. As Mad Dog winced, she added, "I'll fix it," and headed toward the kitchen.

"We got Lapsang Soochong for you," Janny called. "On the shelf over the sink."

"Thanks!"

Janny took the seat on the Cray-1, so Kevin sat on the arm of the couch near her. Brian perched himself on the stool, his black cowboy boots on the top rung. Mad Dog wheeled over to the coffee thermos, which was on an army locker that took the place of a table in front of the couch. Michael brushed once at cat hair on Janny's favorite overstuffed chair and sat. "Uh, what happened to the last head of research?"

"I got tired," Janny and Brian said in unison, then both laughed.

Brian pointed at Janny. "She got tired. She's the program god. She needs to spend most of her time jacked into the game now, or we'll never finish on time."

To Mad Dog's look, Michael said, "Cream and a scoop of sugar, please. So I cruise the data libraries and flag anything that looks useful?"

Janny nodded. "Volcanoes, right now. I've just added these Dawn Isles, sort of a Japanese-slash-Samoan culture with maybe a hint of Ursula Le Guin's Earthsea, too. They ought to have volcanoes. But they're fairly close to the mainland, so does that mean there're volcanoes there, too?"

"Probably," said Brian.

"Almost certainly," said Kevin, reaching in the aluminum bowl of M&M's.

"That's what I figure. But I'm not sure I want volcanoes on the mainland. Not active ones, anyway. If we have to have active ones there in order to have active ones on the Dawn Isles, the ones on the mainland can't have been active recently."

"Isn't this a little late for basics like geography?" Michael sipped from a cup labeled IBM: IT'S NOT JUST A COMPANY. IT'S YOUR JOB DESCRIPTION. "I don't mean to criticize, but—"

"Not really," Janny said. "You ever jack into Enter-Tech's *Treasure Realm*?"

"Uh, I'm not big on—"

"Sex, slaughter, and the mindless accumulation of wealth?" Mad Dog shook his head. "Don't know if you'll work out with us, Mikhail."

Janny ignored Mad Dog. "You haven't missed much. *Treasure Realm*'s geography is a real mishmash. Which is pretty much true of every aspect of the game. Real pop culture pseudo-medieval Conanesque barbarian shit with an elfy-welfy gloss. It's the wet dream of a some semiliterate kid programmer who's read all of Tolkien's imitators and none of the real thing."

Brian said, "We, on the other hand, have read everything we're imitating," while Mad Dog said, "Hey, if you enjoy sex, slaughter, and greed, *Treasure Realm*'s great."

"*Treasure Realm* is sota," Gwen said, returning from the kitchen with a large mug emblazoned BORN AGAIN AND AGAIN HINDU. "That's all it is."

"Sota?"

"State of the art," Kevin explained. "You'll hear it a lot if you stick around."

Gwen said, "Yeah. Sota, and shut the fuck up, Mad Dog."

"Did I say a thing wrong in the last thirty seconds?"

Gwen sat on Mad Dog's lap and put her free hand around him to loudly kiss the side of his head. "No, you did not, you dear, dear boy. It's a new record."

"Watch the tea!" Mad Dog shouted.

Kevin tossed an M&M to Michael. "We pride ourselves on our businesslike working atmosphere."

Michael caught it and smiled. "I noticed."

"Anyway," Janny said with a trace of impatience, "*Treasure Realm*'s success is the reason we're getting so much money from Omari to do a—"

"Quick rip-off," Mad Dog said.

"Great rip-off," Brian corrected.

Janny closed her eyes. Gwen got out of Mad Dog's wheelchair and sat on the army locker between Kevin and Janny. "Ignore the peasants, kid."

"Yeah," Janny said quietly.

Kevin, unsure what to say, said nothing. Mad Dog wheeled

over to Janny and took her hand in both of his. When she glanced at him, he said, "It's great, Janny. No shit. And it's no rip-off."

Janny nodded and squeezed Mad Dog's hand. Kevin looked away from them, then back.

Janny told Michael, "That's the problem. Omari wants something that'll compete with *Treasure Realm* by the end of the month. We want to give them something no one's ever seen before. A fully realized world that anyone can live in, so long as you pay your access bills. Not a place to run around getting treasure, drugs, and sex—though you could do that too, if you wanted, I suppose. But a world. Only one that follows different rules than ours. And maybe one that's a little fairer than ours."

Brian nodded. "The only characters who die from stupid accidents that they couldn't possibly avoid are supporting characters run by the computer, never player characters. Though players can get maimed badly." After a second, he added, "There's no AIDS." Kevin wondered if anyone else thought the pause was significant.

"No sexual diseases at all," Mad Dog said with a grin. "Just like in *Treasure Realm*."

"But," said Janny, "female player characters can get pregnant if you aren't careful. We fought about that a lot. We fought about most of the details."

"I had this great idea for a cult of teenage cheerleaders—" Mad Dog began.

"Shut the fuck up, Mad Dog!" Gwen and Janny yelled, laughing.

Several of Gwen's ornaments tinkled like bells when she moved suddenly. She said, "I wanted a world populated by hermaphrodites, but I was outvoted. Everyone decided it'd scare Omari's publicity folks. It sure wouldn't be the quasi-traditional fantasy scenario they're paying for."

Brian said, "Maybe if we do a sci-fi game someday, we can have hermaphroditic aliens."

Janny giggled. "Sexually insecure aliens from outer space! Let's tell Omari they can have that instead of *Lands*!"

Michael frowned. "I'm still a little worried about filling in your geography this late in the programming."

"It's not late," Kevin replied, not wanting to hear Janny

sounding defensive. "Janny's got most of the world sketched in."

"I'm fine-tuning the Elflands," Brian said cheerily. "And a lot of the religions."

"And as the house nigger, I'm doing the Africanoid nations," Gwen said cheerily.

Mad Dog said, "Her degree in cultural anthropology has nothing to do with that. She's also doing the plains tribes, the northern barbarians, you name it."

Kevin nodded. "Much of the tweaking can wait until the game's open to the public. We've just got to get one continent fleshed out fast and have basic details available about the rest of the world. So long as you're jacked into the game, you only know as much about the world as your character does. The characters don't know any more about their world than the Europeans knew about theirs in thirteen hundred or so. The far continents probably won't be important to the game until Omari's got millions of players and needs more room. So right now, we need to fill out the details that've already been established." He glanced at Janny and wondered if it was time to mention the Tangled Lands.

She smiled. "It's probably more accurate to say we need to rationalize details that've already been programmed."

Kevin shrugged, thinking, *That's it exactly. What did you program into your world for us to rationalize now, goddess?*

"That seems . . ." Michael said.

"Sloppy?" Mad Dog suggested. "No time to change things."

"Hey," Brian said. "If it's intelligently rationalized, the players won't notice. But it has to be consistent. That's part of what sold the proposal to Omari."

"So that's my job," said Michael. "Rationalizer."

"Yeah," said Mad Dog. "And justifier. And scapegoat, maybe."

Michael shrugged. "Could be fun. What if there's something I find that's really screwed?"

Gwen said, "Don't worry about it. Say there's some god or something that made things that way."

Janny frowned. "No. Worry about it. We've pulled the god excuse once already. There are hardly any guns in spite of the world's level of technology because their main god—which is me"— She smiled —"has made sure that every faith and every government has forbidden them as demoniacal and unethical. Sort of like Japan did during their three hundred years of seclusion."

"That's because the V.P. at Omari in charge of our project thinks people don't want guns in fantasy," Brian said. "Superficially, *Lands of Adventure* has to be a lot like *Treasure Realm*. But if we're lucky, it won't be quite as stupid."

"Okay. Even so, what if I fail to find an excuse for something?"

"Don't," Kevin said. "We're doing all our programming on the jack."

Michael stared.

"Only way we'll finish in time," Gwen explained.

"But it's fun," said Janny. "I jack into the interface and say, 'Let there be light. . . .'" She laughed.

"Janny's World is an amazing tangle of code in there," Kevin said, thinking that was the greatest understatement he had ever uttered. "We can add layers to what Janny does without much problem. But trying to cut out something that she's already established . . ." He shook his head. "It'd unweave the entire world. We'd have to start all over again. No way in hell we could do that now."

"Janny's World?"

"That's what we call it," Brian said. "The world in *Treasure Realm* is named Dirt, which is cute—"

"And appropriate," Gwen said.

"—but we figured—"

"Janny figured," Kevin corrected.

"—it'd constantly jog the player's suspension of disbelief if you're referring to a supposedly real world by a funny name. So in *Lands of Adventure*, it's just the world. Outside of the game, it's Janny's World. Which is doubly appropriate, since it's ultimately her vision."

"Oh?" Michael looked at Janny, and she looked away.

"Yeah," Kevin said. "We figure one person has to be God, or the game'll become a cobbled collection of committee-designed flaws. Janny is God."

"I have this theory—" Mad Dog said.

"Shut up, Mad Dog," said Gwen.

"—that the game'll be more intense because it's one per-

son's vision. That's why *Treasure Realm* is great for those
who like it. 'Cause it was put together by some crazy little
wimp who spent all his time inside creating barbarian heaven.
Janny's just taking the world-building one step further."

"One step to the n*th* power," Gwen said.

"The important thing," Janny said, "is it's got to seem real.
No. It's got to *be* real."

"Actually," Gwen said. "The important thing right now is
what the fuck is wrong with the Tangled Lands scenario?"

The loft in Davin's home was warm all year around.
Smoke clung to the timbers, mixing with the scent of the pine
wall planks to form something his father thought unpleasant,
but Dav thought nice. On winter nights the entire family
would sleep there, sometimes shoving their cotton pallets together and sleeping like the dogs in the kennels outdoors. In
summer, the loft was Dav's alone. He lay still, listening to his
parents talk in the room below.

"We should all go," his mother said. "It's a call for everyone of Torion's First Caste."

"I'll make excuses. The baby's too young to travel," his
father replied. For an instant, Dav blushed, thinking they
spoke of him instead of his new sister. "And you shouldn't
travel in your condition, either. Besides, someone needs to
stay to oversee the field work."

"Too pregnant to travel, but not too pregnant to work," his
mother replied. "Heh!"

"I'd take your place, if—"

"I'd like to see that!" his mother said, giggling, and Dav
snickered, imagining his short, bearded father with his
mother's belly.

His mother said, "You'll just take Grae, then?"

"Davin, too. They'll expect it."

"He's second-born and only seven!"

At seven, he was wiser than most of the adults he had met,
Dav thought.

"Seven's old enough. If Grae dies, he'll be heir. The trip
will only take a week, at most. He'll enjoy it."

His mother said more softly, "I'm not worried about Grae.
She seems much older since she returned from school. But
Davin—"

In the loft, Dav frowned, suddenly understanding what they discussed. On Midsummer Day, all of the First Caste would pledge themselves to Torion's new Queen. He did not want to kneel on the ground and promise to serve this girl; Grae had told him so many times of the wonderful new Queen that he was certain the Queen must be as stupid and spoiled as his sister.

His father laughed. "Davin'll be more eager to go, and better-behaved too, I suspect, when we tell him the Unicorn Riders will come to salute the Queen."

His mother laughed with his father. "Were you as obsessed with the Riders when you were a boy, my Hule?"

"Probably more so. Maybe I've told him too many stories." During the following silence, Dav hoped his father would say more about the Riders, or about his own childhood. Instead, Hule said, "You're sure you'll be all right here?"

"Of course, my silly. But I'll miss you."

Dav heard them kiss, and he quit listening. He thought of what his father had said about the new Queen's celebration. Dav would have lain naked in the mud and promised to serve a gnat while all the world laughed, if that was the price to see the Unicorn Riders.

His excitement carried him through a week of preparation. He stood, he thought, quite patiently while his mother measured him for new pants and a shirt, and didn't understand why she dismissed him with a swat on the bottom and an amused, "Perhaps we'll have you study with dancers, next year." When the day came to hug her farewell, he said, "Don't cry, Mommy. Next year you can see the unicorns, too." The five days' walk to the Queen's Grand Picnic was frustratingly slow. He thought Hule and Grae and the horse should run all morning and carry him all afternoon, and they disagreed with both propositions.

Every Midsummer Day, Torion's court made the Grand Picnic in fallow fields outside the city. On this Midsummer Day, the site was a field bounded on three sides by the Night Woods and by the Elf King's Road on the fourth. Dav stared; he had never seen so many people at once. Many wore the thin white headband of the First Caste and dressed in pastel silks or Faerie moonthread. At home, only Dav's family had worn the white band, and their clothes had never been finer than cotton in spring or wool in fall. The lowborn raced about in dark headbands and tunics of Torionese green. They were more interesting than their masters, for the servants carried trays laden with cold meats or berry cakes or delicate porcelain goblets that held mead or water. Dav took three cakes from a smiling woman. Grae whispered, "you greedy little chipmunk," then took four.

Under nine open pavilions, each the traditional color of one of the Cities of Man, servants arranged benches and tables for the evening's feast. At the center of the pavilions stood tall flower sculptures of the nine greater gods. Hule pointed out wolf-faced Ralka, patron of Gordia, in blue violets; eagle-headed Eirara, patron of Bakh, in wild roses; and, larger than the others, bat-eared Skelth, patron of Torion.

Several circuses had pitched smaller, multicolored tents nearby. Dav saw merchants in dark castebands, different from their servants' in that they were thinner and of finer cloth. The circus folk wore a miscellany of headbands—leather thongs, red or blue or green scarves, beaded or jeweled cords—that were similar to each other only in being moderately dark.

A sausage vendor passed in one direction, a woman selling halves of grapefruit and pineapple passed in the other. Chicken and venison and trout were roasting over one seller's grill, chestnuts and peanuts and almonds over another. It seemed that half the people had doused themselves with perfumes, some subtle, some sickeningly potent. Dav saw Grae watching him, so he lifted his head higher, sniffed even louder, and said, "I'm a dog." They both giggled.

For half the day at the Grand Picnic, Dav thought that this happy place must be Torion itself and wondered why his parents said cities were ugly, bitter-smelling things. At noon, the Queen and several richly dressed adults sat on a canopied stage in the open ground between the pavilions and the circuses, and a line of Torion's First Caste moved slowly past them. The Queen was a girl smaller than Dav, though he knew she was a year older. She had the dark skin and wiry black hair of most Torionese. Her hat was a cloth-and-wire construction that made it seem as if a swan with wings extended were resting on her head. Her long robes were white like the hat, and cloth feathers hung from her sleeves like limp wings. He would feel very foolish in those clothes, though the Queen did not seem to mind them.

When at last they came before her, Dav prostrated himself as he had been taught, then stood when the Queen said quietly, "Rise." She smiled at Dav's sister, then glanced at his father. "Who are you?"

"Hule Greenboots, your loyal subject, Highness." His father bowed low.

"Grae Greenboots, your loyal subject, Highness." His sister bowed lower than his father had.

"Davin Greenboots, your loyal subject, Highness." Blushing, Dav bowed so low that he almost stumbled.

"Greenboots?" said the Queen, covering her mouth as she giggled.

Slightly behind her, a handsome young man in a short, pale yellow tunic leaned forward to say, "A northern county, Highness. When your great-grandmother rode through it in the spring after a rain, several of the people had been working in wet fields, and the grass had stained their legs."

The Queen's face grew solemn. "She was most amusing, my great-grandmother."

"Indeed, Highness."

The Queen looked at Dav's father. "I should not have laughed." Then she clapped her hands and smiled. "We must give you a present!"

Hule glanced at the man who had spoken to the Queen, then said quickly, "Highness, it is not necessary."

"No, no." The Queen nodded to herself. "You will have a pair of green boots with emerald buttons. And Grae may have any of my dresses that she wishes." She looked at the young man, who seemed perplexed. "Except for the one I'm wearing. And the red one embroidered with cats." The young man showed the palms of his hands, either in helplessness or agreement. The Queen pointed at Dav. "And you, boy, will have a pony."

"I don't want a pony," Dav said. Hule squeezed his shoulder, so he added, "Highness."

"No? And what do you want, boy?"

His father hissed a quick, soft inhalation, and his fingers probed deeply into Dav's shoulder. He did not understand what danger his father warned him of. Without thinking, Dav said, "I want a unicorn."

The Queen stared. Then the young man beside her began to laugh, and soon everyone on the raised stage was laughing. When Dav turned toward his father, he saw that he laughed, too.

The young man said, "A statue? Or a tapestry?"

"I have a unicorn doll," the Queen said, though she did not sound as if she wanted to give it up.

"I want to be a Unicorn Rider, Highness," Dav said.

Before his father's grip on his shoulder could signal anything to Dav, the young man on the stage smiled in sudden relief. "Then he shall be a Unicorn Rider, eh, Highness? And find his own unicorn, if he can."

The Queen nodded absently. His father said, "Thank you, Highness," and the push of his fingers told Dav to bow and move on. Off the field and in the crowd, out of sight of the Queen's court, his father tugged him behind a tent where they had some privacy. Dav expected to be punished for speaking out before the Queen, and was content since he also had his greatest wish. Instead, Hule knelt and hugged him fiercely. When at last Hule released him, Dav's embarrassment became confusion. Tears flowed down his father's reddened face.

"Father?" Dav frowned. "What is it?"

Hule shook his head in quick jerks, and Grae watched in puzzled sympathy.

After a moment, Hule took the children's hands. "Come. I'll buy you watered apple wine and honey bears, and then we'll see the Unicorn Riders." His tone was almost subdued. Suddenly he smiled. "You'll like that, eh?" As they walked through the crowd, Hule whistled "The Elf, the Wolf, and the Cat," a children's tune that Dav had not heard in months, and he wondered why it sounded so sad now.

He asked, "When the Unicorn Riders come, will I get my unicorn?"

"No," Hule said softly. "Not today. You have to train for a long time. Then you'll go to find your unicorn."

"Ah." Dav smiled, thinking what a wonderful place the Grand Picnic was, and what a wonderful Queen the small girl was, and what a wonderful family he had, even his sister who was so uncharacteristically quiet. Certain that Grae was jeal-

ous of the Queen's promise, he grinned. Grae frowned and
turned to watch a somersaulting clown. Hule put his arm
around his daughter's shoulders as if to console her, which
Dav did not understand. Then a vendor of honey bears appeared, and the rest of the day at the Grand Picnic was the
happiest that Dav had ever known.

The Unicorn Riders appeared at dusk. The entire crowd of
First Caste and performers and servants became so quiet that
Dav could hear a baby crying across the field. Everyone studied the woods and the road, wondering where the Riders
would enter the Grand Picnic. The Queen would give a crown
of scarlet poppies to the first person to sight them; Dav
thought that winning the crown would be a suitable end to a
day which had already won him a place among the Unicorn
Riders. The Queen's crown of flowers went to a boy far from
them, who pointed to the west and whispered, "There!"

The three Riders were very old, older than Dav's grandfather. The eldest was a stout, dark Southerner with curly
white hair. The next was a bald, bearded man of medium
height. The last was a short, thin woman whose white hair
hung to her waist. All three wore the bleached tunic of the
Unicorn Rider and the white headband of the First Caste,
but each wore pants and arm ribbons of bright colors which
matched the ribbons and blankets of their mounts.

The unicorns were almost as small as ponies. Only one, the
Southerner's was pure white—and its horn was thick, stubby,
and ochre. The bald man rode a dun with a curved yellow
horn. The small woman's mount was the red of oak leaves at
the height of autumn, and its horn was black. Dav felt as if he
had been lied to. His first thought was that these were shaggy,
misshapen horses or large, freakish goats. As he watched
them approach, his awe returned. The Riders had no reins to
direct the unicorns nor spurs to prod them. Something in the
unicorn's manner said that they carried the Riders because
they chose to. The Unicorns moved with a grace like that of
cats, but more perfect. Their small, careful steps told that they
could battle bulls, if they were ever so foolish as to want to,
and outrace basilisks, if they were ever so foolish as to need
to.

The Southern woman bowed from the back of her unicorn,
crying, "The Queen!" Every voice at the Grand Picnic echoed

her, and Dav heard a thousand human voices united in joy on a perfect summer day. The moment was forever tinged in his memory by the enigmatic glint of one unicorn's green eye, and another's blue, and the third's red, as they watched this human celebration with expressions like boredom or disdain.

When the shouting stopped, Hule led the children from the field in search of a feast table. Before they had gone ten feet, he stopped. Dav looked up to see two of the three Riders standing impassively before them. "So soon?" his father said. The smaller Rider nodded and held out her hand to Dav. Without knowing why, he wrapped his arms around his father's waist and began to cry, and Grae began to sob as though she were the one the Riders wanted. "Oh, Dav!" Grae said, over and over again.

Hule knelt again, as he had behind the tent, and hugged Dav. The Riders continued to watch, smiling in condescension, or perhaps nervousness. Hule said, "You have to go. I hoped it wouldn't be so soon. You have your wish, Dav. I hope you're happy with it."

Dav cried, "But I don't want to!" Though people in the crowd glanced at him, he did not care. "I don't!"

His father's hand slid from the small of his back to the back of his head, pressing Dav's face into his bearded neck. He could smell his father's hair, his sweat, the rose soap he had washed with. Hule's rough hands pried Dav's grip apart, and he said, "You'll be a Rider, Dav. It's your wish. And the Queen's." A little more quickly, a little more softly, he added, "Your mother and I love you. Ride well."

Dav stared as Hule stood, not knowing what he could do to stop his father from leaving. The short female Rider clapped Dav's back and said, "Buck up, boy. It's a better life that awaits you."

Dav kicked her. The male Rider laughed. Then he looked directly at Dav and said, "You'll never see your father again, nor your sister either. How do you want them to remember you?"

Hule said, "That's not fair. He's only—"

"He's an apprentice to the Riders." The bald man's tone was so final that Dav snuffled, trying to stop crying. The man laughed again. "Don't worry about stopping your tears. They'll stop themselves soon enough, and few parents are troubled by the thought that you're sad to leave them. But don't fight us, eh? They'll hate to think you didn't want to go."

Dav glanced from the Rider to his father and sister. "Bye?" he said.

"Bye," his father agreed, and Grae snuffled.

4

Demon Gifts

Toxic Moxie was tending bar at the Silver Socket. An indigo
cable ran from her half-shaven skull to a trackball hidden in
the ceiling, where a multitude of antiquated mechanical ob-
jects were attached without regard to logic or gravity. Moxie's
eyes were, as usual, closed. Kevin remembered her pale,
steady gaze; were her irises blue or green? He gave her a
quick nod and said, "Mox. I need all four food groups in
diabetic suicide quantities." Overhead, between a pink micro-
wave oven and a red neon MEN'S sign, one of several tiny
cameras and one of many microphones swiveled to follow
him.

"Coffee, alcohol, chocolate, and whipped cream?" Her
voice came from a speaker hidden in the bar.

Kevin nodded.

"One Coffee Moxie, coming up." As she reached for
crème de cacao and rum, Kevin glanced around the room. He
spotted three Poseurs: two decent Bogarts, one from *Casablanca* and one from *The Maltese Falcon*, sitting with either a
bad Marilyn Monroe or a good Madonna. The only Neotrad
was a Viking whose beard was braided with ribbons of the
same cloth as his three-piece suit; the suit and the braids
glowed dimly, changing from cobalt to violet while Kevin

watched. The majority of the thirty-five or forty customers seemed to be Serious Jackers, slightly pale and slightly unhealthy-looking people in the comfortable clothes that undoubtedly were closest to hand when their wearers woke.

Almost everyone was plugged into the retractable cables that hung from ceiling tracks. A short Asian man in a plumed top hat that made him appear even shorter was standing on a raised platform at the back of the room, jacked into a glistening new Kimoda 7X. Behind him, chalked onto a large blackboard in phosphorescent green, was the announcement: "Tonight's Programming by Salami D'Amour. Disco Dungeons begins at 9. Be there or who cares?" Several dancers were on the floor, all on the jack. Kevin had decided that three were on a Regressive Rock channel and possibly on the same one, two had completely turned their bodies over to an Astaire-Rogers program, and one was either doing Infoverload or had a bad tic.

Moxie set a large brown mug before him. It dripped whipped cream and cinnamon onto the polyurethane bar. "How's your dad?"

"The same." Below the polyurethane, computer chips and logic boards and key caps and monitor cables and other artifacts of the dawn of the electronic age were preserved for a generation that would not recognize them.

"Still working for Omari on Project X?"

He nodded.

"Goin' all right?"

He shrugged. "I think so. I don't know."

"It's not like the old days."

"No." He smiled at her. They had been lovers for two weeks, when they were both sixteen-year-old jackstars. "I think you did the right thing."

"Getting out of it?" Her eyes flicked open and closed in a negative blink. Light green.

"Yeah."

"Well . . ." She picked up a rag and swiped at the counter. "The AI's make better testers than we did. Least, they can't go hothead when they hit a bad program."

"How do you know when an artifical intelligence has gone hothead?"

Moxie's laughter slipped into stereo as she moved closer to

a second speaker. "When it chooses to stay in the business."

"The biz isn't bad," Kevin said, suddenly uncomfortable. Moxie's laugh was not like Janny's, but he wondered why he had never noticed before that Moxie, thin and blond, was Snow White to Janny's Rose Red. "AI's will never replace human testers. Not if the program's intended for human jackers."

Moxie shook her head. "AI's make the first run. There's not nearly the danger in it anymore. Never will be."

"That's why you quit?" Kevin gestured at the Asian in the top hat. "Why you opened this place?"

"No. I just got tired of jacking."

"Yeah, right, Toxic."

Her voice hardened. "Look, Flash. You got no credits in the net; I checked. The drink's on the house. Be nice, okay?"

He glanced at the dancers. There were more now; the Viking had joined them, and they all moved to the same beat. Either Salami D'Amour was a success, or they were all jacked into this week's edgiest net channel.

"Okay, Moxie. I'm sorry."

"It's not going well, is it?"

"No."

"Deadline hassles?"

"Aren't there always?"

"Yeah. Another reason I got out."

He nodded. Moxie had left the business four years ago after testing some preliminary synapse-crossfire entertainment software. Her convalesence had taken fourteen months. She still wore a modified hothead rig when she was not at home or in the Silver Socket, where the monitors and the microphones fed information about her environment directly to her mind. Kevin did not know whether she had programming to sort out touch, taste, and smell, or whether she had learned to control those well enough through therapy. Rumor had it that all her jacking now was of the tourist sort, visits to the net and the occasional use of an extremely popular—and therefore, well-tested—piece of entertainment software.

Moxie left him to draw two pitchers of Leinenkugel's, then returned while he was sipping his drink. "'S good," he said.

"You know how to drink 'em, I know how to build 'em."

He nodded again. He wanted to talk to her, tell her about the afternoon, but he couldn't. She understood, he knew;

business was business. Finally, he said, "You and Linc still together?"

"Yeah. He's home studying. Should get his Ph.D. this year."

"That's great," Kevin lied, not disliking the man but being uncomfortable envying him.

"You still seeing that girl with the haircut?"

"Not seriously."

"You ought to find someone, Kev. You know. Seriously."

"Yeah, I know." The coffee had cooled enough that he could drink half in a gulp. "Listen, if you liked someone who was happy with someone else—"

Moxie's eyes blinked open twice. "You hittin' on me after all these years? You're cute, Kev, but—"

"No." Talking about it had been a bad idea. "I think I'm gonna jack now."

The only free table was in the smoking section, but once he jacked, he wouldn't notice unless he wanted to. He snatched a dangling cable as he sat and began access while the jack snapped in.

The office was all black and silver, and lit by ten thousand tiny lights that floated within a foot of the ceiling. A door irised shut behind Kevin, mimicking the closure of the jack. The red-haired woman wore black satin coveralls and a string of tiny pearls at her neck. She smiled. "There's a message—"

"Wait. Prompt control."

He floated, intellect without body, in a space without up or down, without horizon. Uncountable silver shafts came from an infinite distance that he dubbed *down* and traveled toward an infinite point that was therefore *up*. On each shaft, a single area glowed. He selected one shaft up from the multitude, and thought that the glowing area should descend half its height. It responded so quickly that he could not tell if the glow had slid from the one spot to the second, or if the one had gone dull when the second had brightened.

Prompt, he thought.

"—from your mother." Prompt's voice seemed deeper and more like Janny's. Or was it too husky now? "And a second from Deiter Frohn."

"Mom's."

A screen rose from the front of Prompt's desk. Within it, his mother appeared. "Kevin? I hope you can come home this weekend. I know your work's important, but your father—" She frowned, glanced off-camera, glanced back. "Your father isn't feeling well, and he'd like to see you."

His mother looked off-camera again as his father's voice interrupted. "Damnation, woman, I'm fine." And then his father coughed several times, the smoker's cough that made Kevin close his eyes and want to stop the message there. "Turn that camera here," his father said.

"Do you think—"

"Turn that camera here!" The camera panned across his parents' living room and stopped on his father, sitting in a plaid silk robe in a wing chair of red leather, a Bible in his lap. "Look, boy. Your mother'd like to see you this weekend. And so'd I. But you're busy, and we know that, so you just do what you think is best." His father coughed again. "That's all we ever expected of you."

The picture faded to white, and the screen disappeared into Prompt's desk. Prompt said, "Save it?"

He nodded.

"Do you want to reply?"

"Later."

"Do you want to read the other message now?"

He shook his head and lay on his back on a sofa that faced Prompt's desk.

"Should I leave?"

He shook his head again. Prompt sat primly at her desk and watched Kevin. After a moment, she said, "Do you want to talk?"

"Not to an AI."

She nodded, and he wondered if it was possible to hurt her feelings. "I'll hear the other message now."

"It's text. I could read it to you."

"Give it."

A paper airplane floated over his head, hovered briefly, then settled onto his chest. In spite of himself, he laughed. "Too quick for real time. And you better check your aerodynamics files if you thought that flight was convincing."

"Query," she said.

"'Question' would be good enough."

"Question."

"Until I say otherwise, just ask when you need to know something, okay?"

"Okay. Do you demand the appearance of reality?"

Kevin laughed again. "Are you kidding? I don't even demand it in the real world." Then, feeling simple for conversing with an AI, he unfolded the paper airplane. The letterhead was Enter-Tech's; the address was Satellite New Brazil. The text was brief.

> Dear Mr. Fikkan,
> We expect a report tonight.
> Sincerely,
> Dieter Frohn
> Vice-President, R&D

"Send to Frohn," Kevin said. "Tell him—" *That I don't need fucking e-mail with Enter-Tech's name on it, no matter how private e-mail's supposed to be. Only reason for it is if it's a threat—* And it was a threat, he realized, a threat to expose him to Omari if he did not produce something useful immediately. There was nothing personal in it; Enter-Tech expected a return on its investment, even if that return was only to embarrass Omari by revealing a spy.

"Yes?"

"I'm ready to conference whenever he is."

One rainy midnight in midsummer, when Japhis was seventeen and her childhood was many years behind her, she slept uneasily, dreaming of chasing something beautiful through the woods. The thing stayed far ahead of her, slowing sometimes so she could see a glint of gold or silver, then disappearing, leaving a trail of laughter to make her run faster. Something snatched her from the chase. Waking, she realized that she had heard her brother repeating her name. "What—" she began, then stopped. The darkness above her was the sodden canopy of blankets that they had pitched near their fire, so one might sleep while the other tended the coals. The darkness beside her was her brother's form as he waited for her to wake. And the reason for the thorough darkness . . .

"The fire's out!" she cried, standing. A quilt fell unnoticed to her feet.

"Not quite," Harj replied in his stolid way. "Almost."

"Why?" she asked more calmly. Their fire consisted of a wavering flame on a half-consumed log. With this fire would go several days work, which meant several more days of turnip soup, another week before she could buy cloth to mend her best shirt, and perhaps a hungrier winter than the one before. Japhis hurried to their small pile of firewood.

As she put her hand on a slick branch, Harj said, "It's all soaked. I saw another fire." He pointed across the valley. "Over there, somewhere. I went to find it."

Where he pointed was within the area recognized by the local people as her family's territory. Other colliers worked the woods to the east and west, but Japhis did not want to think they would trespass on Kardeck domain. "Travelers?" She set the branch next to the log, hoping it would be dry enough to catch. The rain had stopped. If the branch burned, she could prop a wet log over it, and when that caught, another. But the branch did not look like it would burn.

"No. More like a bonfire."

She whirled, and was surprised to hear anger in her voice. "Who was it?"

"Don't know," Harj said, moving toward his bed. "Couldn't find it. You better find some dry wood."

"You couldn't find a bonfire?"

"Nope. You see it?"

She scanned the woods. "No." After a moment, she called, "You hoarded some mirthweed, and now you're seeing bonfires. Serves you right for not sharing, goat head."

"It was there," he called back sleepily. "Find some dry wood."

"I know that." She listened, and only heard wind among the leaves and the mocking cries of a whippoorwill. She adjusted the rope belt that cinched her poncho about her, then wandered into the woods, knowing that she would find nothing.

Heavy gray clouds rolled across the full moon. Few stars shone through to light her way. She knew these paths well enough to walk blindfolded, but she could not remember every low branch or puddle. She stumbled over several roots, which only made her wish for new boots. Whenever she brushed a bush or a bough, it spattered her, and soon her poncho was as wet as if she had slept in the rain.

She found a few branches that were less damp than most. When she returned to the camp, she saw that their fire had died entirely. She let her armfull fall to the muddy ground. She could taste turnip soup as she stared at the cold ashes. They would never save enough money to marry Harj to a woman with land. They would never have enough to pay their debt to the Marganhalt storekeeper. She and Harj would grow old here, speaking less and less to each other, perhaps coming to hate each other as their parents had hated each other.

She stared about her in frustration, then saw the flames of a camp across the dale. Her first thought was to chase away these trespassers, whoever they might be, and she smiled grimly, hoping they would be as inconvenienced this night as she had been. But as she reached for a staff, she realized that the strangers might offer the solution to the evening's difficulties. Taking the shovel instead of the staff, she set out to beg or barter coals to rekindle the Kardeck fire.

Her trek through the dark hills gave her time to wonder who had built such a large fire in these hills so late at night. Travelers between Gordia and Tyrwilka would have stopped earlier, either at Marganhalt or closer to the Elf King's Road. Bandits would not build so conspicuous a fire. She could not remember any Niner festivals that fell in this month; solstice was still several weeks away. The Questers had never told her that they celebrated any special day. She wondered if she or Harj had done something to anger their neighbors. She could think of nothing more than their reclusiveness, which might annoy but would surely never offend. She wished she had wakened Harj, then resolved to approach the bonfire cautiously. If she saw rival colliers or armed strangers, she would keep her presence a secret.

The fire burned steadily before her. She could not understand how Harj had failed to find it. Even if the trespassers had banked it before he could come near (which would explain why she had not seen it from their camp when she woke), he should have been able to remember its position. She smiled;

she would tease him in the morning for getting lost in the woods like a city child.

She stepped carefully as she came near the bonfire. Strangers might set guards, or traps for game or intruders. Her fears were soothed by a distant music, lilting and strange, and she saw that shadows danced about the fire in harmony with the song. The night suddenly seemed warmer; the woods, brighter and almost benevolent. Perhaps the Marganhalt villagers had decided to hold a summer dance. If so, they would offer her a cup of mead, and the handsome foreman from the forge might dance with her.

She expected the dancing shadows to resolve themselves into folk she knew, but they became odder and more elongated. They were like actors in strange costumes, some of whom seemed deformed by birth—dwarfs and narrow-skulled freaks—and others by artifice, as though they wore cloth wings or pranced on stilts or on their hands. A bearded giant in a tunic of oak leaves stood with his back to the fire, watching and laughing. He was half-again as tall as a human, though his proportions were perfectly manlike, and he held an uprooted sapling in one hand for a staff. Japhis stared from her place in the darkness, remembering the tales of the Korz Demon and the Tangled Lands.

An owl flew to the giant's shoulder. A moment later, the giant turned and looked into the woods, directly at Japhis. His eyes were in shadow, yet firelight or an inner light made them glint with a suggestion of brown, then green, then blue, changing constantly in no discernible pattern. "A visitor!" he cried with delight. "Come! Join us!"

The impulse to run immediately returned, then faded as quickly. How did she know the demons were evil? Even if they were, all the stories said that they only offered gifts, which then betrayed those who accepted them. And the gift that she needed was a more innocent one than any told of in stories. "Sir!" she called as she stepped into the firelight. "Are you the lord of these woods?"

"I've been called that," he answered with a laugh, as if pleased by her courage.

Oddly, the dancers remained shadows. Her eyes would not focus on them, though the demon was perfectly distinct. She bowed awkwardly, remembering her studies with the priests and hoping that the ways to address members of the First Caste were appropriate here. "Might I borrow some coal, Lord? For our fire."

"Take what you will," the giant said in a voice that brimmed with kindness. "For whatever purpose."

"Thank you, Lord." She filled her shovel blade and backed away, bowing as she left the ring of their camp. She heard no laughter, yet something made her think all the dancers were amused.

Harj's snore was the only music that came from the Kardeck camp. No light greeted her. The coals in her shovel had darkened as she hurried home. When she threw them into the firepit, they became as black as the shadows under the distant trees.

She kicked the ground, thinking this must be some trick. Angry, she turned to go back to the demon's fire. As she walked, she asked herself if she was foolish to do this and answered that her life was a boring and troublesome thing that she would gladly wager. Calming more, she decided that the night was cold and the trip between the two camps took long enough that the ashes must have cooled naturally. When she saw the dancing forms a second time, she stopped out of reach of their firelight, breathed deeply, then marched forward. "Your pardon, Lord," she said to the demon. "Your coals died just as I put them on my wood. May I borrow more?"

The giant's brows furrowed as he stared at her. She did not fidget under his gaze, and thought that her calm was very strange, as if this were a dream. She felt as she had when she was a child and her father stared at her, and she had stared back, thinking that the worst he could do was hit her over and over, and she would not cry no matter how many times he struck her.

The demon said, "How will you repay me?"

"With gratitude, Lord."

He laughed. "Remember that, Japhis Kardeck." She glanced at him when he used her name, but she took her second shovelful and left at a run.

These coals died more quickly than the ones before. She nodded to herself, not angry at all. She listened to Harj's steady snore. She looked from their makeshift tent to where their house stood farther up the ridge, and she could not see it in the night. She clenched the shovel and turned back into the woods.

When Japhis came a third time, the giant frowned. "You are greedy, mortal." He exhaled two gouts of steam from his huge nostrils.

Her voice quavered as she said, "Sir, the coals died again."

"Then take more," the giant answered, laughing. "But do not return a fourth time."

"I won't, Lord. Thank you for your coal."

"You thank me?"

She halted by the fire and stared at him. "But of course, Lord!"

"And will you?" He grinned. His teeth were like moss-encrusted boulders.

She stepped back with more confusion than fright. "What, Lord?"

"Hurry, mortal." He waved his staff toward the Kardeck camp. "And go."

Japhis nodded, took a last scoop of embers, and fled. She told herself that she ran quickly so these coals would not die like the others. When this effort failed, she looked again for the demon's fire and felt something like relief when she saw that it was gone. With that relief came exhaustion. Their camp was silent. Nothing stirred in the woods. Japhis went to her bed to fall immediately asleep.

At dawn, she heard Harj call, "Japhis! The fire's out!"

"Go 'way," she murmured, opening an eye. In the light of early morning, their firepit was a pile of muddy ash and cold, scorched sticks.

Harj clutched his blankets around himself and raced barefoot to their shovel, then stirred ash and burnt wood in the hope that some glow lingered, that a tiny piece of their night's work might be saved. Japhis sighed and closed her eyes again, and did not open them when Harj gasped, "Japhis! What've you done?" His tone was a mixture of joy, fear, suspicion, disbelief, and bafflement.

Curious, she looked again. Harj knelt in the middle of the firepit, brushing away ashes. Before him were three lumps of gold, each the size of a human head. Japhis scrambled to touch their rough sides, then hoisted one to lift it awkwardly. Harj stared at her. "A gift," she whispered.

"Ours?" Harj said, echoing her tone.

She nodded, letting the heavy lump fall.

"All ours?"

She nodded again, and began to grin.

He looked around their camp, at the patched tent and the tree where cooking pots hung, and his face was fearful.

"It's ours." Japhis squeezed his arm and smiled. "Or mine. I don't know, Harj. But no one's coming to take it away."

"But how could—" He looked again at the gold as if afraid it might have rolled away.

She laughed. "I'll tell you."

Harj's jaw dropped as she spoke of her three trips across the valley. His only interruption was a whispered "How could you go back?"

"I don't know. I felt, well, perfectly sober. The way you do when you're just becoming very drunk. It all made sense, somehow."

"To you, maybe."

When she finished the story, he whispered, "Demon's gifts."

Wanting to hit him, she tapped the nearest lump of gold. "Gold, Harj. Solid, pure, beautiful gold. What do you want to do? Carry it back to the clearing and leave it for the demon?"

He nodded, then pursed his mouth and shook his head, then held his hands before him as if expecting her to set something in them. "I don't know, Japhis."

"I do."

Japhis bought land and a title from Yenzla, King of Tyrwilka. She had a manor house built where their hut had stood. She studied fencing and etiquette and dance. She bought the Marganhalt Foundry and the store, and preparations for the fourth War Against Faerie meant increased business for her investments. She fought in that war with a troop maintained at her expense, and her spoils from Elfin cities more than tripled her growing wealth. The flattering attentions of poor nobility and her casual dalliances with the wealthy made her believe she had been accepted as Lady Japhis Kardeck, a full member of Tyrwilka's highest caste.

In the second month of her good fortune, shortly after buying the forge and the store, she gave a party for the Marganhalt villagers. She had musicians come from Tyrwilka, but their music did not sound half as wonderful as the music at the demon's fire. She had casks of Lyrandol wine set out to be drunk like water, yet it did not taste half as good as a cup of mead after haggling over the price of a cartload of coal. The villagers danced, but their movements never meshed with the music, being too inhibited early in the evening and too free much later. All of the lowborn addressed her awkwardly as "Lady," then whispered after she passed them. The hired Tyrwilkans seemed to sneer at her accent or her dress. She drank too much and invited the forge's handsome foreman to her new bed. The next morning, he smiled smugly at her, and she expelled him from the valley.

5

Dreams of Purity

The conference grounds were a smooth, gray-carpeted plain that extended hundreds of kilometers to meet a twilight sky. Something like a sun either rose or set to Kevin's left; he wondered if Frohn expected him to know which was meant.

A chair hovered before him, two black curved planes floating in space to make a seat and a back. A larger, white plane existed in front of that, and a second conceptual chair was behind the naked desk. Kevin touched the desk with two fingers, noting cool metal, then looked at the sky. The details were as good as any conventional programming he had done or seen. He thought there were no smells in this clean, alien place; then he smiled as he recognized the tang of an ion air-cleaner. He liked programmers with a sense of humor.

He was about to sit, when a brass doorframe rose from the carpet behind the desk. A man came through the door, smiling at Kevin and extending a hand. As Kevin returned the smile and reached for the hand, he forced himself to hide his recognition, though he knew he was supposed to know what had met him. Or perhaps, he hid his recognition because he was supposed to know what had met him.

The man's teeth were white parabolas within a poreless face the color of peach ice cream. The dark hair and eyebrows

were molded onto the skin in smooth plastic curves. The neck
met the collar of the white shirt and blue suit and joined the
body as a single unit; its tie and its shirt were only details of
shape and color, not substance. It moved with the implausibly
perfect grace of the most expensive graphics animation programs.

"Mr. Frohn?" Kevin said, thinking this appearance could
be the executive's whim, but knowing it was not.

"No, Mr. Fikkan, I am his aide. He calls me Hugo." The
handshake was momentarily disconcerting. The entire conference room flickered briefly from Kevin's reality. *That's great*,
Kevin thought. *Met by a secretary in the interface. The powerful are weirder than you or me, F. Scott.*

He realized that this meeting served at least two purposes,
and probably more. The first was to see that no tracers,
snoops, bugs, or bomb programs accompanied him to his
meeting with Dieter Frohn. The second was to remind him
that when he accepted Enter-Tech's funds, he became their
creature, to be scanned or detained as his new masters
pleased.

Hugo released Kevin's hand and gestured toward the doorway. "This way, please."

The analogy was teleportation; Kevin stepped out of one
conference room and into another. The effect was far more
distressing than the secretary's handshake had been. He remembered his father wheezing, "Where's your soul, son? Tell
me that, and I'll trouble you no more."

He could not sense his way out of the interface. He did not
worry about his body dying of shock; it was healthy. He did
not worry about his body dying of thirst; Moxie would notice
him at closing time, if not sooner. He only had to trust Enter-
Tech to restore his control of the interface before then, or he
would occupy a bed in the hothead wing of the local hospital,
his mind endlessly seeking to untangle the command programs
of his jackware, endlessly trying to reach his body.

He was tempted to shout "Out!" to see where it would take
him, but he did not think he wanted to know. He supposed that
as soon as Enter-Tech's security program had shifted him, he
had become a ghost in the machine, regardless of the fate of
his body.

"Kid Flash!" said a man who must be Dieter Frohn. His

manner was like Hugo's, but more ebullient. He appeared to be a human, paunchy, aging version of his servant. He wore a conservatively cut suit of shimmering gray threads over an unbuttoned paisley shirt, and his thinning hair curled about his ears and his neck. "This is a pleasure!" His out-thrust hand was decked with ornate silver rings; the most obvious was inset with an eye, its blue pupil and slightly bloodshot cast making it an apparent clone of Frohn's eyes. A tiny silver skull in a top hat dangled from Frohn's left ear.

Frohn's hand, during the moment their hands clasped in greeting, was cool and soft. The grip was strong. Kevin showed his teeth in a careful smile. "Pleasure's mine, Mr. Frohn."

Frohn shook his head delightedly, displaying the magnanimity of kings. "Please. Call me Dieter. I had my day on the net, too, back before the jack. Perhaps you heard of me? Hammer von Tod?"

"Yes, I think so," Kevin lied.

"We renegade hackers had a game of our own, much like your mind-wars," Frohn said, and Kevin wondered if he was supposed to think the subject came up by coincidence. "In its way, the results were as disastrous. We couldn't affect each other's sanity, but we could change credit histories, bank balances, marital status, these things. One of my opponents thought our bout was a draw, until he found the world's records showed him to be female." Frohn laughed self-deprecatingly. "Ancient history; I bore you. Please, sit, sit." He gestured toward a chair that appeared to be nineteenth-century Shaker work.

Kevin sat and glanced around. The room was tiny and remarkably crowded with shelves crammed full of books, music boxes, and ceramic figurines. Electronic memory was cheap, especially for an Enter-Tech vice-president, but whether the details were scanned or programmed, someone had spent a remarkable amount of time in creating a comfortable abode for a jacker's cybernetic self. Kevin glanced back at Frohn, suddenly wondering if all the detail was because Frohn had given up his body to live in the net. Perhaps Frohn had an AI wife in an electronic house in the cybernetic suburbs, with a little-dog program and digitized grass to be mowed by a gardening subroutine.

The idea was not amusing. *The powerful are weirder than you or me.*

"Something to drink? Or smoke, perhaps?"

"No," he said, suddenly despising this thorough illusion of the world. He wanted to ask Frohn to cancel the gravity, to invert all the colors and exaggerate the smells, to have their bodies change form randomly every millisecond—Something like a frown was appearing at Frohn's eyes, and if that was true, it was no accident. "Thank you," Kevin added politely.

"You don't mind if I do?"

As Kevin shook his head, a crinkled cigarette appeared between the tips of Frohn's right thumb and forefinger. Kevin thought *Lighter!* but nothing came into his palm.

The end of Frohn's cigarette began to glow as Frohn drew on it. Holding the smoke in his lungs, he rasped, "Tell me about *Lands of Adventure*."

"I sent in a report."

Frohn exhaled. The smell was not as pungent as true marijuana smoke; Kevin wondered if that was a bug or a feature. Frohn said, "Reports. I have a report on your report. It says Omari's funding a group of has-beens to do a rip-off of *Treasure Realm*. It says that if the project is successful, there's an eighty-seven point six per cent chance that Omari's rip-off will not take away any of our business. It says there's a sixty-one point two per cent chance that Omari's rip-off will serve as advertising for *Treasure Realm* and increase Enter-Tech's business by as much as four points. It says there's a two point seven per cent chance that your report was intentionally incomplete. It recommends that I credit you with the second half of what we promised and waste no more time on you."

"Then why'm I here?"

"Because you don't stay an E-T V.P. by depending on reports." Frohn smiled and offered his cigarette to Kevin.

Kevin shook his head. *Out*, he thought, with no intensity of emotion.

"You a hothead? I could nudge up your pleasure centers, if you want."

"What do your reports say I am?"

Frohn guffawed. "I figured you still had some guts, somewhere."

"Reports tell you that?"

"Told *me* that," Frohn said. "I know what you are."

"You want to give me a hint, I'd appreciate it."

Frohn nodded lazily. "You need credits, for your father and for that kid you mind-fried. You need a sense of purpose. World's changing around you, too fast for you to keep up. You've got a bit of Lancelot in you, or maybe Don Quixote."

"And to think I paid for my own copy of a Freud Four."

"You also have a self-destructive streak, Mr. Fikkan. That's why we approached you."

Out, Kevin thought. *Fucking out, fucking now!*

"I won't detain you much longer," Frohn said.

"You're a saint."

"There could be a place for you in Enter-Tech, Mr. Fikkan. I don't know where, and I don't know what; that depends on how useful you prove. But I can guarantee your salary'd be half-again what Omari's paying, regardless of what we have you do."

"This is a one-time deal," Kevin said. "I told your boy as much at the beginning."

"Fine." Frohn hissed in the last of his smoke from the marijuana analog. "Fine, fine, fine. The offer will be open, should you change your mind. Tell me about *Lands of Adventure*."

Nothing Kevin could say could possibly matter now. "All right. It's no rip-off of *Treasure Realm*. It's the next generation of games." He paused, expecting Frohn to laugh or grow angry, but the man only nodded gently for him to continue. "Part of it's the attention to detail. That's Janny's contribution. Part of it's the hardware. Nothing radically new, but Mad Dog and the programmers are working with each other in mind. A lot of it's the extrapolation programs that Brian and Gwen came up with."

"They're sota?"

Kevin shook his head and smiled with tight lips. "Gigasota, Dieter. Janny's World makes this place look like an afternoon vid cartoon." Kevin stood and walked to Frohn's bookcase, saying, "May I?" as he snatched a copy of *The Unabridged Mark Twain* and flicked through it. The print shimmered as he did so, as if the writing appeared and disappeared with each page. "I'm impressed," Kevin said. "I thought this'd be a white brick."

"I like to read," Frohn said.

"My point's still valid. In Janny's World, there wouldn't be that unreality as the text fills each page." Kevin replaced the book on the shelf and sat. "This chair is beautifully done. Too beautifully done for conventional programming. Someone scanned an antique, right?"

Frohn nodded.

"You have a knife or a scissors?"

Frohn shrugged; a commando knife appeared on the desk between them. Kevin stood, picked up the knife, and turned toward the chair.

Frohn said, "I beg your—"

Kevin stabbed the back of the chair as hard as he could, then hacked downwards at its seat. The blade slid from the wood as though it had encountered steel. "You see?" The knife had left no marks on the chair. "In Janny's World, I'd have just damaged an heirloom."

"It wasn't intended to receive that sort of treatment."

"In Janny's World, we don't anticipate the kind of treatment anything's likely to get."

"It sounds like a lot of niggling attention to—"

Kevin nodded. "Yeah. That's why people will love it. Next generation. Like sound and color coming to the movies."

Frohn squinted. "Omari doesn't have the memory to store a world filled with that much detail."

"'Course not. That's why Gwen and Bri have done the extrapolation programs. The detail's subjective, only in existence while an outside observer is jacked in. But things continue to happen in Janny's World when players aren't present, 'cause the programs direct the characters when no one else is running them. It's like a tree falling in the woods: if someone's present, it'll make a sound; if someone's not, it'll still fall."

"Thank you," Frohn said. "Now tell me about the problems."

"What chance did your report say we had of succeeding?"

"Three point two. Reassure me."

Three point two. It really doesn't matter. "We're not going to make our deadline."

"Deadlines can be extended."

"I don't think so. Juan Takeda's sponsoring us. If we succeed, he's a star at Omari. We fail, he's out, and no one wants a part of us."

"Enter-Tech might."

"You'd support Janny's World?"

Frohn clasped his hands and sat forward. "Frankly, no. We make our profit from games that provide instant gratification. *Treasure Realm, Pacific Perils, Psi Spy . . . Lands of Adventure* may be interesting, but it doesn't have a hook to grab the kids. It's too quiet, too specialized, it's . . . " Frohn shrugged. ". . . not for us. But it sounds like your team could contribute to improving *Treasure Realm*."

Kevin shook his head. "None of them would. Well, maybe Mad Dog, if you had an interesting hardware problem. It's a labor of love for all of them. They have too much integri—" He stopped himself.

Frohn laughed. "No desire to work for a shlockmeister? I respect that, Mr. Fikkan. But they delude themselves if they think Omari's better because it's smaller. Do you know the other two projects your principled patrons are developing? *Atlantic Evils* and *ESPeeper*."

Kevin shrugged. "Takeda's willing to take a chance on us. Omari's share of the net—"

"Point three per cent as of noon Greenwich."

"—is enough to give the thing a chance."

"That's true," Frohn conceded. "If the thing has a chance. You were telling me it did not."

"All right. Second problem is that to make the deadline, we're designing on the jack. The world has to remain consistent unto itself, or it'll crash of its own logical failures. But as we work faster, we get sloppier."

"You must keep backups."

"Of course. But we barely have enough memory to keep one backup, so we only save at the end of each work session, writing over the previous copy. And because we're designing on the jack, the code's a mess. For all we know, something that may be the final necessary development will contradict some of the programming Janny did on her first day."

"There's a third factor?"

"Yes. We have a built-in bug. To prove the program to Omari, Janny designed a problem that's integral to her world's history. Only now we can't solve it. Even if we make Omari's deadline, they'll just have the chance to watch a world destroy itself."

Frohn leaned back in his chair and gestured; a second cigarette appeared in his hand. "The Tangled Lands scenario?"

"Yes."

"It sounds like this project would be easy to sabotage."

"Why bother?"

Frohn nodded. "Exactly. You'll find you're a richer man when you jack out. Twenty per cent richer than you expected to be."

Kevin squinted. "Why the bonus?"

"Maybe we've been too conservative in our approach to *Treasure Realm*'s development. Our R&D'll look into your team's approach."

"I see. Thank you," Kevin said without thinking, then kept himself from wincing. Frohn had done him no favors.

Frohn stood to shake Kevin's hand. Behind Kevin, a door that he had not noticed whisked open, and Hugo waited to escort him back to the outer conference room. "If the situation changes," Frohn said, "let me know. You'll find me grateful."

"Of course." He turned to follow Hugo.

"And regarding the Tangled Lands problem . . ."

Kevin looked back at Frohn. "Yes?"

"I'd be very pleased if you made sure no solution was found. It'd be in your best interest. You understand?"

Kevin shifted his gaze from Frohn to study Hugo's passionless face. What did AI's know about loyalty, honor, or duty? They executed commands. *As do we all*, Kevin thought. He glanced back at Frohn and nodded.

For ten years, Dav lived with the three Riders in the Night Woods, seeing only them and a farming family who worked a nearby plot. Each year at the Grand Picnic, the Riders left him to tend the house and lands, and each year he considered running home, and each year he remained. If his family ever wrote him, he never received their letters. He learned the unicorn lore from the Riders and the small collection of manuscripts written by Riders of earlier generations. He learned that the Riders had been a large force at their founding in the time of the present Queen's great-grandmother, but that the unicorns rarely came to Torion now, or to any of the human lands. Herds ran free in Faerie, or so the Southerner said. No one truly knew if this was so.

The three unicorns had no names. The Riders called them White and Red and Gray when speaking among themselves, and never called them by any name that Dav could hear when the unicorns were present. They only came to Rider House late each spring, and then visited the House irregularly until fall, when they left to winter in some unknown place. The Riders rarely rode them; Dav could not tell if this was because the unicorns did not wish it, or because the Riders thought unicorns should only be ridden on momentous occasions.

The small woman died when Dav was thirteen. He was surprised that this saddened him, for she rarely spoke to him unless she had a fault to mention or a punishment to bestow. She was the one who had noticed the crusted spot on his sheets and had made him stand naked in the rain, reciting the prayers to the Nine. "The unicorns are only ridden by the pure," she said, striking his bare thighs with a switch. "The pure."

"The pure!" he had screamed. "I'll be pure! I will be, forgive me, I will!"

He never understood his desire to ride a unicorn, and he never noticed when that desire changed. First there had been stories, told by his father and the occasional wanderer who stayed at their home for a night or two. Then there was the sight of the unicorns at the Grand Picnic. And then there was his stay with the three Riders.

Before the Grand Picnic, his dream had been to ride through County Greenboots on a slender white unicorn while everyone cheered. But the dream changed during his stay at Rider House, and by the time the smallest Rider switched him, he dreamt of a huge dark unicorn with red eyes, and the people who cheered tried to cover their fright by cheering louder. At night, Dav treasured the dream. He lay sleepless in his bed with his hands clenched firmly at his sides, thinking that he would find his unicorn, the first to be ridden in two generations. The Queen would kneel before him and call him Saint Davin. She and he would marry—a chaste marriage, so the unicorn would not leave him—and all of Torion, perhaps all of the world, would recognize his greatness.

He wondered what the Unicorn Riders had been in their

prime. He could see their faults too well, even if he could not understand those faults, yet he wanted to learn what they knew and be what they were, and more. The three survivors were filled with stories of how the Riders had routed the Elf Lord's legions at Castle Thramering, had found the late king when he was a boy and lost in the Night Woods, had driven basilisks from the hill country. Yet these three Riders were a woman who drank too much each evening, a man who would have been pitied as a halfwit had he not been a Rider, and a woman who delighted in tiny pains inflicted to better the sufferer.

But most, he wondered about the unicorns. Why did they come each spring to Riders who were not worthy of them? Why did no more unicorns come to be found by Riders who were? He listened to stories about other apprentices who, like him, had wished to be Riders. While all three Riders agreed that these apprentices had given up their quests, none of these Riders could agree on the reasons for the apprentices' failures and their own success.

The spring of his seventeenth year saw him grown to something slightly below the common height for Torionese. His hair and his eyes were black, and his skin was tan and his muscles were well-developed from his duties at Rider House and the nearby farm. He had no sense of his own looks, or rather, he had a contradictory sense: The old man had said that if it were not for his vow to the unicorns, he might be tempted by such a pretty boy; the Southerner called him Milk-and-tea when she was pleased with him and Hawknose when she was not. The truth was that Dav's mien was more pleasant than not—though this was because his isolation and his studies and his feeling that Fate had selected him to restore the Unicorn Riders and Torion had left him with the evident sense of self-sufficiency that most people find attractive.

The Southerner was drunk on the morning of Dav's departure. Dav waited before Rider House, knowing that he was to leave to find his unicorn now and wondering if he should just go. He wanted to say farewell to someone. His life was changing, and he wanted to mark that change somehow, with a speech or a gesture. The old man came out while he waited. "Still here, boy?"

He almost left in anger then; he wore his only clothes and

carried the traditional spear, which with a loaf of sourdough bread, a leather water flask, and a round of farmer's cheese were the only things he would take from Rider House. He said, "Just going," and turned.

"Eh," said the old man. "So I see. Luck go with you! Return a Rider, or not at all!"

Dav set out on the path toward the Elf King's Road, since he had no clues as to where to find a unicorn or how to find one. The road was dry and bluebonnets were in bloom, and a robin called merrily. He felt worse than he had when he had been seven and learned that gaining all he wanted meant losing all he loved.

He carried the spear at his side, then rested it over his shoulder, then tried using it as a walking staff. He wanted to throw it away, but it was his only protection from wolves and bandits, and he remembered that the Southerner had said when she gave it to him, "Can't show anyone you come in peace if you don't have a weapon to lay aside, Milk-and-tea!" And after she had laughed, she said, "Besides, a unicorn'll expect you to come with a spear or a sword, and to set that down and hold out your empty hands." Then she barked another laugh. "And if the unicorn doesn't approve of you, it'll gut you with its horn while you stand there, or maybe it'll just run. Either way, you'll never see it again if you fail it."

When the Riders' path joined the Elf King's Road, Dav did not hesitate. Everyone said the unicorns had abandoned Torion. He walked away from the capital city he had never seen, though the road toward Torion would take him to the road to County Greenboots. He did not realize that he was humming "The Elf, the Wolf, and the Cat."

He wandered for a year, through the Night Woods to Torion's border. In his own country, his bleached vest and his quiet, educated manner told everyone what he was. Torionese gave him bread and soup, straw to sleep on, a place near the fire. All they asked was a blessing, for which he always answered, "There's nothing to prove my blessing is worth anything, but it's yours."

When he crossed the border into Gordia, his vest and his manner meant nothing. The Gordians laughed at his accent and at his quest, but he did not let this deter him. Some shared as freely as the Torionese had, and some asked for aid at a task as payment for a meal and shelter, and some snarled and re-buffed him. The worst were those who pitied him as a madman, and gave him hospitality with extreme expressions of sympathy.

No one had seen a unicorn. Almost everyone had heard that one had been seen, but the sighting was always far to the south or the west. These unicorns were magnificent beings, with manes of silver thread and horns and hooves of pearl. Still, Davin wandered on, certain that the great black unicorn waited for him. He was willing to travel into Faerie if necessary. He spent a rainy winter in Gordia, where a dishmaker gave him work. He almost gave up the quest, for the dish-maker said Dav had a sense of patience and of beauty that would take him far in that art. Yet when spring came, he took his few coins and set out again, north toward the lake district and skirting the Tangled Lands, where nothing but demons were known to live, and then south again.

A unicorn showed herself at the border of Gordia and Tyr-wilka, near a village called Winterberry. She was small and bluish-white with pale green eyes. Her horn was gray and very slender, and it hooked upwards and slightly to the left at its tip. Dav was washing a handleless kettle in which he had boiled rice and corn for dinner, and he sloshed the rinse water toward a bush. And there, beyond the bush, under a flowering apple tree, in the blushing light of the setting sun, with an expression of curiosity and vanity that was far coyer than that of any farmgirl or noblewoman that Dav had met in his travels, was the unicorn.

He stared. He had expected that rumors would lead him to a trail or a spoor which would finally bring him to a unicorn. He had not expected to be crouched by a small lake with a dented kettle in one hand and the damp corner of his cloak in the other. Catching himself staring, he glanced away, then glanced back immediately for fear that the unicorn would flee or would prove to have never stood before him. When he saw that she waited, he set aside the kettle, hoping that it was weapon enough for her expectations, and held out his hands.

The unicorn remained motionless. Dav stepped forward, smiling with anticipated triumph, yet disappointed because the quest was already over, disappointed also because this was such a small and homely unicorn. He said, "I come in—"

Something seemed to brush his mind, and he stumbled. When his vertigo settled, he looked for the unicorn. She was gone. For a horrifying instant, he was sure she had never been there.

He ran to the apple tree, and under the scent of the flowers was a hint of something like musk or smoke, the smell of the unicorn. In the dirt was the hoof print that a city dweller would have mistaken for a pony's. He felt an instant of relief that he had not been wrong. That relief fled as he realized that the unicorn had come, and she had rejected him.

His pack and his spear were close to hand, so he snatched them and ran into the woods. A distant flash of white might have been a fawn's tail, but he knew it was not. He followed, deeper and deeper into the woods, up into the foothills of the mountains called The Wall. Night came, and he stumbled on until he knew he was lost without hope of finding his way back, without hope of finding the unicorn.

The moon was bright and the sky cloudless. He wandered through the night, not caring where he went. Sometime after midnight, he saw a fire in the distance. If it had been far to either side of his path, he would have ignored it, for he did not care to see people then. The fire was directly before him. Veering from it would be as much an acknowledgment of its presence as seeking it out. If this was a holidayer or a charcoal burner or a band of thieves celebrating a robbery, he would ask if a unicorn had passed this way, and continue on while they laughed at him.

He heard music as he approached. It was not like the melancholy tunes the Southerner had played on her *bandurria*, nor like the jigs and reels of the pipers and drummers at the Grand Picnic, nor like the folk ballads his mother had sung. It was gay and intricate and slow, as if the wind played the high notes through leaves and twigs and the low notes through hollow trees, as if owls and robins were the chorus and woodpeckers kept the rhythm.

The flickering that he perceived was more than the dance of flames. Two rings of slender children or midgets capered in opposite directions about the fire. Their faces were astonishingly intricate masks of bird and animal and reptile and insect; he recognized a badger and a rattler on either side of an egret, then a bear, a pigeon, a turtle. . . .

The dance master was a stout middle-aged woman who sat

cross-legged before the fire. Had she stood, she would have been three heads taller than Dav. Her brown hair was loose about her dark face, and she wore a kirtle of green oak leaves. A hollow log lay across her lap, and, laughing, she beat the palms of both hands against it to the rhythm of the music.

He forgot the unicorn and his despair while he watched. The dance ended abruptly as a black squirrel raced up to the woman, bounded up her kirtle to her shoulder, and placed its head next to her ear. The woman threw her arms wide, almost dislodging the squirrel. The music halted as, setting aside the hollow log, she stood and cried, "A visitor! Come forth, Rider!"

At another time, he would have felt foolish. He would have apologized for intruding and hoped that they did not think he meant to spy on them. But the music's cessation brought his failure back to him, so he walked into the firelight and said, "I'm no Rider."

"You wear the tunic over your shirt."

He glanced down at himself, saw this was true, and propped his spear against his shoulder to rip the tunic with both hands. The pieces fell to the ground, and the huge woman laughed.

She said, "You sought the unicorn, and you failed."

He looked at the ring of watchers and marveled at the detail of their costumes.

"True?" she said.

Dav nodded, suddenly bored with her and these masquers. The richness of their furs and feathers and skins could only mean they were First Caste celebrants. He wondered if the woman was leader or caretaker for the others, then did not care. The world they had was one of trivialities and frivolities. The world he had lost was one of purpose and truth.

"The unicorn could come again," the woman said.

He stared at her. She laughed more loudly than before, and the others laughed with her. "That's not in your lore," she said. "But your lore is a collection of speculation and lies. You know nothing about unicorns."

"Please," he whispered with desperate hope.

"Please?" she asked, mocking him.

"The unicorn. Please. If I had one more chance . . ."

"You wish it?"

"Yes!"

She smiled and shrugged. "Then you have it."

The music began. A raccoon in the shape of a girl held out a jug from which he drank a wine that tasted of honey and wildflowers. The raccoon-girl smiled at him, and then he was dancing, more awkwardly than any other present, though this did not matter. He realized that these were not children in costumes, and he did not know what they were, but this did not matter either. The unicorn would return to him.

Several hours after dawn, something woke him, perhaps a sound, perhaps a shadow. He lay alone in a small clearing on a bed of moss, not far from a cold pool of cinders. Beyond the fire site, the unicorn watched him. He closed his eyes immediately in hopes that she did not know he was awake. A rustle of grass told him that the unicorn had seen or did not care; she was departing. He stood in time to see the unicorn glance back at him, and her expression was one of amusement or dismissal.

The spear was in his hand and flying from it almost before he knew he had snatched it up. He had practiced on the road; one of his few amusements was to choose a leaf or a branch in the road ahead of him when he could see there was no one beyond. He threw well: his aim was sure, his cast was strong. Afterwards, he told himself that he had only meant to frighten the unicorn into turning back toward him, but as he threw, he did not imagine the quivering spear embedded in the trail before the unicorn and her rearing in fear and he leaping astride her to claim her as his own. He did not imagine anything, and felt only a fury that grew from his frustration.

The spear caught the unicorn in the ribs, behind the shoulder. She fell, looked over her shoulder, kicked several times, and died. Her last expression was not pain, Dav knew, though he could not tell if it was surprise or pity.

He stared at the unicorn and then at his hand. Here was the hand, there was the unicorn. The spear jutted from her side like a mockery of her horn. The blood had stained and matted the unicorn's bluish-white coat. The sea-green eye still seemed to watch him.

He wanted to cry or rage, but the sound caught in his throat and would not come. He wanted to take the spear and drive it ten thousand times into the unicorn's body until she was shapeless and ugly. Before he could act, he dropped the spear and vomited, uncertain whether he was disgusted with what he had done or with what he had considered doing. He wanted to blame the woman who had given him this second chance or the unicorn that had rejected him twice, but he could not. He stared at his hands and rocked back and forth on his knees in the dirt. When he realized that he was humming "The Elf, the Wolf, and the Cat," he began to cry.

He blunted, then broke the spear on the rocky earth of the foothills while desperately trying to carve a grave for the unicorn. He succeeded in scratching a hole barely a foot deep. He wanted to burn the unicorn, then thought of the smell of charred meat, then thought of the danger of a large fire in the forest. He thought of dismembering the unicorn and burying the pieces, and that disgusted him more than his first urge to mutilate the unicorn's corpse. At last, he left it there for scavengers.

6

Reaching for Redemption

Janny opened the front door of Mad Dog's loft. "Kevin. Welcome to the madhouse." As usual, he could not tell if her greeting smile was shy or aloof. Her contacts were matte black, surprisingly unsettling. The reddish cloud of her hair hovered over a green cashmere sweater that emphasized the thinness of her shoulders. A Celtic Revival tune played in the background, the music overlaid by Mad Dog's and Gwen's angry shouts, which meant they were either furious or delighted. He heard Brian add something in a reasonable tone. "It's deep tech-talk," Janny said. "And I'm starving. You hungry?"

He stopped unsnapping his corduroy jacket and shrugged. "Sure." He had microwaved a burrito and eaten it topped with salsa and a fried egg before he left his apartment. "Well, coffee, anyway."

"Jakeeno's?"

"Sounds good."

Janny grabbed a copper metallic cape from an overburdened coat rack and slipped it on as she walked back toward Bytehenge, calling, "The boring designers are going to Jakeeno's while you argue about maximizing interface efficiency."

73

"Bring back a pizza," Gwen said.

"Deep-dish!" Brian added. "Extra cheese! Pepperoni! Mushrooms!"

"Oh, all right," Mad Dog said. "But it's got to have onions. All good food has onions."

"Oh?" said Gwen. "Wait'll I make you my next cheesecake."

Kevin leaned around the Cray-2 and nodded. "Hey, guys." Brian, in dark pants and white shirt and a thick black moustache, lay on his stomach on the couch. Gwen, in a large furry white pullover and a bikini bottom in a checkerboard pattern, sat cross-legged on the worn Navajo rug. Mad Dog had parked his chair in the aisle to the kitchen; he wore yellow jeans and a sleeveless JACK-OFF! sweatshirt.

Brian said, "The Kev! Man, you should've seen me with the coat on, before Gwen mussed my hair—"

"Groucho?" Kevin guessed.

Gwen shrugged as Brian shook his head. Gwen said, "Would you believe anyone could say 'Frankly, my dear,' six times in three minutes? Mussing the costume was self-defense."

Janny leaned over and kissed Mad Dog's forehead. "See you."

"Yeah, yeah, yeah." Mad Dog swiveled away to stab a finger in the air toward Gwen. "Look, I'm not talking about *that* much extra work, and it'll be worth—"

"You're ignoring the legal questions," Gwen answered.

Kevin looked at her, then away. Brian raised one eyebrow in a *What do you expect of Mad Dog?* expression. Kevin shrugged, wanting to hear this but preferring to follow Janny. Her cape was waist-length; it rode against the top of her black harem pants. He said, "Mad Dog's got a new brainstorm?"

"Yeah. I think he's convincing Gwen. He thinks the best fix for the memory shortage that'll result if too many people jack into the game is to use the brain cells they're not using."

"Can we do that?" As they clattered (his boots, her clogs) down the fire stairs, Janny slipped a brown beret onto her head, and Kevin turned up the collar of his jacket.

"Legally, morally, or practically?"

"D. All of the above."

She grinned. "We're pretty sure about practically. The

jack's effectively a two-way connection as it is. This just calls for some fancy software to make use of the existing hardware."

"Mad Dog's specialty."

"Yeah. He might be looking for extra work since hardware's the only thing that's on schedule."

Kevin shrugged. "What about morally and legally?"

"Mad Dog thinks legally isn't a problem. Signing onto the net is an act of consent, he thinks. Gwen isn't so sure. Morally?" She shrugged. "We're not talking about damaging anyone, just about using some short-term memory that they're not using at the moment. What do you think of it?"

Kevin looked away. A few drops of rain fell from the sky. A cool autumn breeze came from Minneapolis skyscrapers half a mile to the south; a gum wrapper lurched along the sidewalk like a drunk hunting a place to sleep. "I'm not too good at ethically gray areas."

Janny nodded. "You walked?"

"'Bout the only exercise I have time for."

"Then we'll take the Scarlet Hussy." She strode toward her red Lotus.

"I didn't see Michael."

"He's cruising data libraries, I imagine. He said he'd call or drop by later." She unlocked the passenger door and held it open for him. He got in, unlocked hers. Reaching for her seat belt as she slid into the driver's seat, Janny said, "He seems like a nice kid. I wish we'd added him when we started."

"Didn't know we'd need anyone else. And I'm still curious to see how he fits in. The group has its quirks."

She laughed as she looked over her shoulder, then drove onto the street. "Right. You mean Mad Dog's total lack of discretion, Gwen's tendency to interpret anything as a challenge, Brian's fear of offending anyone, or my need for reassurance that I haven't messed up everything?"

"You don't mess up things," he said, hearing his voice as a little too serious.

She glanced at him. "Well . . . Thanks."

"You're dead on about everyone else. What about me? Brash and vain—"

"You?" She grinned and squeezed his knee, then returned her hand to the steering wheel. "You're a sweetheart."

"Oh." He exaggerated his disappointment.

She laughed again. "Okay, you're brash and vain. But you're also a sweetheart."

"Well." He wondered if he was blushing. "Nice car."

She nodded. "You bet. Zero to eighty, two seconds before you turn the key."

They drove the rest of the way in quiet. At Jakeeno's, they ordered a Pizza Florentine for themselves and a deep-dish pizza to take back to Bytehenge.

"You getting any sleep?" Kevin said.

"Five hours last night," she replied. "A luxury." Her eyes were lined from fatigue.

"You shouldn't spend so much time on the jack."

She nodded. "You and Mad Dog."

He didn't like being included with Mad Dog in any context, though he wasn't sure why. "We worry about you."

"Hardly anyone else is working less."

"Except me."

She touched the back of his hand and shook her head. "C'mon, Kev. You're always the first one in on the player level. You've got to be rested. If the rest of us screw up, we're out a little work, maybe. You screw up, you get your own bed with the hotheads. I remember your first run."

He quirked his lips as though it didn't matter. "First one's almost always weird."

"I felt so guilty. I thought you'd come out drooling."

"I've got a powerful faith in objective reality." *Not much faith in anything else . . .*

"What's it like?"

"Jacking into a buggy program?"

She nodded as she sipped her coffee.

"Every time's different. I suppose what's most common is the program locks up, and so does your mind. If you've got decent safeties, you get yanked out just fine. But if the program works partially or weirdly—" He shook his head. "Sometimes you get a flicker effect, where the program works in starts that are spaced between complete disruptions of anything understandable. Synapse misfires, things like that. Sometimes you get bits of your memory thrown at you. Sometimes your memory gets distorted, tangled in with the program. Sometimes all of that seems to be happening simultaneously." He lifted his coffee mug, saluted her, and finished dryly, "It's fun."

"Right." She sipped again from her own mug. "I suppose everyone asks why you haven't retired?"

"I will. After this one." He laughed. "Maybe I enjoy the work too much. Not enjoy, exactly. But I'm good at it. That's something. And I've got expenses."

"Yeah." She smiled sympathetically.

"I mind-fried a kid three years ago." He hadn't meant to say it. He could have told her about his father, his apartment, or a few of his worst investments. If he had planned to say it, he would've brought it up more carefully. He'd only told one other person, a woman he had known for two weeks and had never seen again.

"I heard. They say it wasn't your fault."

"I didn't even know her. She challenged me on the net. I don't even know what she really looked like. Her net self was a pink bunny wearing a derby. I mind-fried a pink bunny wearing a derby." He glanced up; Janny's matte black lenses told him nothing of what she thought. "Sorry. You need food, and I'm treating you like a Freud Four."

"That's all right. If you want to talk about it . . ."

He frowned, wondering why he had mentioned it. Maybe he wanted to give Janny a piece of his past, something that would give her a fairer sense of what he was. Maybe he was trying to give her an explanation for why he spied for Enter-Tech, in case she ever learned of it.

"Here's food," she said as the waiter set the Pizza Florentine before them. Janny ate two slices without saying anything more than, "God, this is great!" and, while taking her second slice, "You think we can put this kind of food in *Lands of Adventure*? Somewhere?"

"All you need are hot, narrow ovens."

"I'm going to do it this afternoon. We'll make a fortune just from people jacking in to eat." Taking a big bite, she said, "And without gaining weight, yet. Tell Omari to advertise in all the gourmand groups: Hate fantasy, love food? *Lands of Adventure*, an adventure in eating!"

She began her third slice while he was midway through his second. She said, "You didn't finish. About the pink bunny. Unless you don't want to."

He shrugged and pushed his plate away. "She'd left these messages about me on the net. That my rep was because I was one of the first jackers, not because I was one of the best. That I was afraid to take her on. Like that. I wasn't really insulted by it. I was more amused."

Janny nodded around a bite of pizza.

"And mind-wars aren't like the media has them. Maybe someone got fried every now and then, but no one I knew ever got into gigatrouble. Well, Danger Rat had serious problems with claustrophobia after a bout he lost, but he knew the risks. Hell, I had one game that I won and still had to keep a night-light on for months after. But that was all. You don't play mind-wars more than once if you're dancing on the edge of sanity. Thing was, the bunny had only played with amateurs, and she had a trick that caved them all in fast."

Janny set her crust back onto her plate. Kevin said, "I'm sorry. You should eat."

"Go on," she said, watching him as she sipped her coffee.

"I don't know if I can make it sound as ugly as it was. I probably shouldn't. She'd hit you with a double-shot that didn't so much disorient you as make you despise yourself. She'd fire your memories of your family and your feelings about sex at the same time, and intensify them while twisting them. My family—" He paused, not having realized that one revelation might lead to others, then decided to finish what he had begun. "My family's probably like many, but—" He shook his head.

"Kev." She put her hand on his arm and left it there. He wanted to cover it with his own hand, but he didn't dare. She said, "You don't have to."

"No. What I'm trying to say is that I love my family, my mom and my dad and my sisters, even the oldest, who's a gigabitch. That shouldn't be hard to say, but it is. I've got as many repressed feelings as anyone.

"I don't think the bunny knew exactly what happened when she did her tricks. That's probably why it was so effective. Mind-wars is usually about controlling an environment, creating one that you can last in and that'll drive your opponent out. Danger Rat had this great triple whammy, where you were suddenly crammed into a tiny dark box, apparently hanging from a cord that creaked as if it was about to break while the box whirled around in what seemed like typhoon winds.

"The bunny went straight for the emotions. Sex and family. She made you create a fantasy for yourself that she could probably observe, and maybe heighten, if she wanted to. I found myself—" He hesitated, wishing he hadn't begun. Some expression flicked across her face then, and he hurried, wanting to finish. "What's important is that the cast of characters were people I'd loved for as long as I've been alive, and the bunny made me enjoy—" He swallowed and began again. "The bunny showed me that there was a part of me that could enjoy—" He shrugged. "Oh, hell. You get the idea."

"Yeah. She sounds like a sweetheart."

"I don't know. I keep wondering if she knew what she was doing. For the kids she'd gone against before me, it might've happened so fast that she didn't really see the effects, she just saw that she won. I doubt they told her much afterwards about what it'd been like. All she probably ever heard was, 'Don't do that to me again, or I'll kill you.' I don't know." He tapped his thumbnail against the side of his coffee mug.

"So what did you do?"

"What I usually do when things get weird on the jack. Instead of fleeing, I withdrew into myself. I said, *what I'm perceiving isn't me, it's only what I'm perceiving.* That didn't work very well, because I couldn't escape knowing that this time what I perceived came from me, even if I didn't know what she was doing with my feelings. So I lashed back the way she had. Exactly the way she had, hitting the same emotional centers, shoving them high, and twisting them. And she tried to withdraw, but I kept hitting her with that combination of all her fears about sex and love and family and trust and self-worth, all tangled together." After a moment, he said, to say something, "And she went mad."

"Did you know that then?"

"I suspected it. All I knew for sure was that she left suddenly. Her safeties pulled her out, just a tiny bit too late. I didn't know the truth until I found I was being sued by her parents. Irresponsible behavior resulting in mental damage, like that. We came to an agreement out of court. I'm paying her board in a hothead ward."

"I'm sorry."

He lifted one corner of his mouth into a smile. "So'm I."

"It probably means something, that the things she chose to attack were her own weaknesses."

He glanced at Janny. "I hadn't thought of that."

"It's an easy profundity. Maybe it's true, maybe it's not. It sounds good."

"I suppose."

They sat in silence. Janny said, "You do it anymore?"

"Mind-wars? No. Or maybe that's what jackware testing is. A game of mind-war where it's just me and the program."

"And no one can get hurt."

There was something too sympathetic in her voice. He shook his head. "It's not like I've got a problem about mind-wars now. I tried it a couple of times after the suit was resolved, but it wasn't fun anymore. I couldn't push to win. Maybe I just got too old." He swirled the coffee in his mug, then looked up. "There was only one more incident like that in North America before they made mind-wars illegal. Kids still do it, of course." He shrugged. "I read an article about the bunny on the morning I got sued. She wrote poetry. Very bad poetry, but still, there it is. The news had a picture of her father crying with a battered toy bunny that must've inspired her net appearance. I wanted to write him, or call, but—" He swallowed, glanced away. "Fuck." He could feel Janny watching him.

The waiter said, "Would you like to see the dessert tray?"

Janny said quietly, "No, thanks."

Kevin made himself smile and said, "You sure? They're great here."

"Well—"

"Eat, eat. Trust me."

"All right. The triple-layered chocolate thing with all the whipped cream. Since you insist."

As the waiter left, Kevin said, "Sorry about that."

"Don't apologize. You're a nicer person than you think."

He shook his head. "I'll bet you say that to all the murdering swine you know."

She frowned, then laughed explosively. "You know what's wrong with men? You don't know how to be comforted."

Kevin grinned and felt himself blush. "We get bored. Well, embarrassed, like somebody'll notice that Mommy's kissed our knee and made it better." He met her eyes. "Thank you."

She nodded solemnly. "My pleasure, sir." The waiter came with her cake then. As it was set before her, she said, "You know I can't finish that by myself. Someone'll have to help me."

"Damn," said Kevin, reaching for his fork. "Into the briar patch again."

Seven years passed as seven years will. Japhis did not marry; the only First Caste man who interested her chose to wed a woman Japhis knew to be poorer, uglier, stupider, and far more badly educated than she. That woman's parents were both of the First Caste, as were their ancestors for generations before them. Harj did not marry either, though he carried on dalliances with most of the attractive lowborn women between Tyrwilka and Winterberry.

In the fall of the seventh year of Japhis's good fortune, she and Harj sat after dinner by the fieldstone hearth (which was three times as large as that of the Questers). She lounged on a low couch, still wearing a riding suit of brown wool trimmed with marten fur. He sat on a stool, his elbows propped on his knees, and tamped mirthweed into a pipe. She frowned at him, thinking that the drug was becoming a habit, noting that his hair was thinning and his stomach was not.

He had set the end of a long stick into the fire. As he reached to draw it out, he said, "Did you hear, Japhi? Lord Lessanor's having a feast in honor of the new Queen of Gordia."

"No," Japhis replied, not really caring. Her thoughts moved lazily from her disapproval of Harj to her plans to begin a free school in the village, to her disappointment with their new cook who had served turnip soup as the first course that evening. It had been a much richer soup than she had eaten in her youth; those soups had not been laced with cubes of beef and ham, nor served in a broth thick with cream. Yet it had been turnip soup, and she had only eaten it because she thought it would be a sign of indulgence to send it back to the kitchen.

Harj put the glowing end of the stick to the bowl of his pipe and puffed it alight. Throwing the stick into the fire, he spoke around the pipe stem. "He is. It'll last a week, they say,

with hunting and games and a circus. Some say he hopes to
wed the Queen. His lands are close to the Gordian border.
And Glynaldis of Gordia is an attractive woman, I hear."

"You hear of an amazing number of attractive women,
Harj."

He glanced at her, then smiled. "Well. We all have our
weaknesses."

She thought that he was chiding her, but she could not
imagine what her weaknesses might be. Realizing that he was
speaking affectionately and not sure how to respond, she said,
"I remember Lessanor. Seemed rather arrogant."

"He was in the war?"

"Yes. Always spoke about the obligations of soldiers, that
we should be careful only to sack the Elfin forts and rob the
Elfin nobles and leave the common people alone. Yet he
didn't seem to have much sympathy for the lowborn in his
own forces, and his men were always among the first to go
wherever there was plunder. I think I'll enjoy drinking his
wine."

Harj set his pipe aside. "Japhi. We aren't invited."

"What's that?"

He shrugged. "We aren't invited. The announcement's
clear. All those born to the First Caste. That's hardly us."

She laughed without humor. "I bought a birth as good as
his."

"Japhi. You can't be serious."

"Can't I?"

She arrived at Lessanor's estate with twenty of the most
handsome of Marganhalt's men, all equipped with polished
bronze helmets, breastplates, and lances. Their horses were
bay chargers, all larger than the finest plow horses, all covered with identical black and gold blankets. Her hair billowed
about her, and her iron and silver breastplate was more elabo-
rate than her men's. Slung across her back was an ornate
sword of Faerie steel that an Elfin commander had surrendered
to her. Her shirt and britches were of a moonthread so fine it
seemed to glow. A thin casteband of silver cord circled her
brow.

Harj, riding beside her, said, "Japhis, let's pass by them.
They can all see that your company's beautifully equipped.
Better than any of theirs. That's enough, eh?"

"You worry too much." She touched her heels to her mare's side, hurrying it up the slight hill to Lessanor's fort. Multicolored striped and checked circus tents stood before the walls. People in bright robes and tunics, wearing masks or face paint, wandered lazily among tents and open wooden stages. The air carried festival music and the smell of wine and popped corn and roasting beef. Painted faces turned in their direction as the Kardeck troop approached.

Lord Lessanor's son met her at the gate. He was probably five years younger than she, with the thin beard of a fair-haired youth. He wore a long tunic and tight pants of scarlet silk, with only a silver dagger at his side. The left half of his face was painted to match his clothing. The other half was white, and there a tiny painted eagle flew up his cheek to seize his right eye. "Who are you?" he called, his voice merry or mocking.

"Japhis Kardeck," she answered proudly, aware of the people watching from the fields where the tents stood. She recognized Young Lessanor from the war and was certain that he remembered her.

"You have business with us?"

"You could say that." She smiled. "The business of pleasure." One of her men laughed as she spoke, but the others were silent. The music had stopped. Behind her, someone shifted nervously in his seat; she wondered if it was Harj.

Young Lessanor turned slightly to call, "The guest roll!" A clerk, conspicuous in his functional brown suit, hurried to bring Lessanor a wide roll of buff paper. Lessanor took it in his red-gloved hand, smoothed it with the white glove, glanced at Japhis with a smirk that told her what he would say, then scanned the list. "I do not see your name."

"The festivities were announced for all of the First Caste," she said quietly.

"Let's go," Harj whispered.

She ignored him. Young Lessanor smiled. "That's true, it was. And I have here the list of all the noble families in Tyrwilka, Gordia, and Torion."

"I bought—" Japhis began, then stopped, realizing she had erred.

"Yes," Young Lessanor said, playing to the revelers who drew near as they talked. "You bought. Anything might be *bought*, eh? As for earned . . ." He turned his red-gloved hand dismissingly. "Birth will tell, I suppose."

She drew her Elfin sword and struck him with the flat of the blade. Harj gave a quick inhalation, but Young Lessanor did not cry out. The crowd gasped, and, behind Japhis, so did several members of her retinue. Lessanor stood slowly and touched the white silk glove to his cheek. When it came away stained with his blood, the young man smiled. Only then did Japhis begin to suspect her fate.

Harj whispered, "Sheathe it!"

"No!" She whirled toward him and saw him flinch. At the sight, Japhis said, "Oh, gods, Harj!" and dropped her sword onto the ground.

As Lessanor's soldiers gathered around, Harj brought his horse beside hers and rested his hand on her shoulder. She could not meet his eyes, but she placed her black leather glove on the back of his hand. Her own company moved nervously as Lessanor's men came nearer. She could tell her retinue to flee, which they certainly would, or to fight, which they might. In either case, they would be guilty of obstructing royal justice, so she told them nothing.

"I regret that I must arrest you for disturbing the King's Peace," said Young Lessanor.

Harj squeezed her shoulder; she shook off his hand in silence. As Lessanor's troops led her unarmed, alone, and on foot toward the festive castle, the youngest of her company called, "Cat protect you, Lady!" She paused in the midst of her grim-faced guards, and they waited while she looked back at the boy in her livery. At last, she saluted him, then marched into Castle Lessanor.

The members of the First Caste gathered together that afternoon. The next day, the Lady Kardeck was deprived of her title, her lands, her wealth, and her right hand. Expelled on foot from Lessanor's gates, she might have been beaten or stoned by the soldiers and the villagers, but they permitted her brother to take her away. This was from amusement, not kindness. The only wagon that Harj was allowed to buy to carry her was a battered two-wheeled collier's cart drawn by a spavined mule.

• • •

They returned on the Elf King's Road. Japhis, delirious, thrashed about in the back of the straw-lined cart. Harj had put a damp cloth on her forehead and a blanket over her body, but she threw them off. She woke occasionally and screamed sometimes, and sometimes whimpered.

A brisk wind whipped the oak leaves till they rustled like laughter. Japhis raised herself on one elbow to shake her only fist at the woods. The wind ceased. A distant voice seemed to call, "Do you still think my gifts are free?"

She lunged forward, shrieking wordlessly. Harj turned from the old mule to push Japhis into her straw bed and pull the blanket over her. He glanced all about him, gazing into the shadows beneath the trees. His eyes were wide and fearful. The mule plodded stolidly onward. Japhis struggled, hitting weakly at Harj with her left hand and the rag-bound stump of her right while she screamed incoherent curses into the air. Exhausted, she slumped into the straw, and Harj shook the reins to hurry the mule. The wind laughed late into the evening.

Midnight brought them to the Questers' house. Harj pounded its door, calling, "Felicity! Glee! It's Harj Kardeck!"

The door opened an inch, then swung wide. Felicity held a candle, shielding the wick from the breeze with a cupped hand; Glee carried a staff, which he set aside as he said, "Harj! Welcome! What brings you—"

"Japhis," he said. "In the cart." He stepped back so they could come into the yard, then moved between them and his sister. "Wait."

The priests glanced at each other in the moonlight, and as they did, a moment of almost filial affection came to Harj. Glee's head was clean-shaven (he had been losing his hair when last Harj saw him). He was thinner than Harj remembered, and shorter too. Felicity's hair, newly flecked with gray, was loose, falling almost to her waist.

Harj said, "Japhis's hand was cut off. I wrapped the wrist as best I could with clean cloth." He raised his own hand to stop them from going to the cart. "But she broke the King's law. No one's to help her. I suppose I'm breaking the law by bringing her here, but—"

"Harj," Felicity said, gripping his shoulder.

Harj began to cry. "I don't know what to do! She's got a fever. She'll die, but—"

Glee shook his head. "We'll care for her."

"If anyone finds out . . ." Harj bit his lip and began again. "If they hear you helped her, they'll blind you."

"I know that," Glee said, going to the cart. "I taught you the local law, now, didn't I?"

They carried her into a tiny whitewashed room at the back of the house. While Glee cleaned and bound Japhis's arm, Felicity said, "She's lucky. No infection. With so little care . . ." She shrugged. "I don't see how. The God must have plans for her."

"Plans for her, maybe," Harj said. "Not for me. I'll leave tomorrow morning for Tyrwilka."

"She shouldn't be moved," Glee said from Japhis's bedside.

"I thought . . ." Harj looked away.

"Yes?" she prompted.

"I thought I'd become a Quester."

Glee glanced at him, and Felicity said, "Why? To seek something, or to flee something?"

Harj shook his head.

Felicity rested her hand on Harj's shoulder. "It doesn't matter. All we care is that you work to learn. No one will presume to judge you."

Japhis woke in a frustratingly familiar room. Light through a narrow window told her that the hour was shortly after dawn. A clean sheet covered her naked body, and she lay on a mattress much firmer than the bed in her manor. She was hot (though she could tell that the air was cool) and very tired, slightly wary, and in spite of all that, unaccountably comfortable. She knew the smell of the air and the sounds of morning birds. For a second, she thought she had fallen asleep in an unfamiliar room in her manor. She brought her right hand up to brush tangles of her hair from her eyes. The hand hurt, as if she had fallen on it. As it came before her face, she gasped and remembered.

She put her arm at her side and stared at the ceiling. She tried to flex her right fingers and felt as if she had succeeded, yet they did not grip the bed. The hand began to ache horribly.

She lifted it again. Her arm ended at the wrist. White bandages bound it in a parody of a First Caste headband.

She sat up and screamed, "Harj! Harj! Where are you?" She stopped herself before she added, "Where am I?" She thought this was a prison, then saw the room was too clean, the window too wide. Was she in a Tyrwilkan hospital? She remembered the amputation and the cauterization, then a boat or a cart that carried her through some storm. . . .

A priest ran into her room. She did not recognize him at first, then said, "Glee. You shaved your head."

He stopped and laughed, moving his hand across his pate. "Yes. Vanity, eh? Felicity thinks that should be my new name." When she didn't answer, he added, "You're hungry?"

Japhis nodded, suddenly aware that she was.

"I'll bring soup."

"Not turnip." She meant it as a question and a joke, but heard that her words were without inflection.

Frowning, Glee glanced at her. "No. Mushroom."

She nodded. "Good. I'm in your house."

"Yes. Harj brought you."

"Ah. Where is he?"

Glee's expression became sad, almost pitying. "Gone to Tyrwilka. He left several days ago."

She nodded once, then said, "Tyrwilka. Why?"

"To join our Order."

"No." Her voice was no louder than before, and she was glad it was no more expressive. "Why?"

"Because he knew you would be cared for here."

She lifted the stump of her arm, and smiled when Glee glanced at it, then away. "Cared for. That's good."

Her body healed surprisingly quickly. On the fourth day after waking, she walked around the house for exercise. On the sixth, she practiced left-handed sword techniques with an elm branch. Felicity saw her battling an oak and called, "Are you winning, Japhi?"

"Not yet," Japhis answered, speaking between her teeth while she hacked at the bark. "But I will."

She spent her afternoons reading in the front room. The Questers had twelve books besides a heavy *Teachings,* but she only read one: Varsiliyas's *Treatise on Demonology.*

Glee sat by her one day and said, "You still enjoy reading. That makes me glad."

"Enjoy? Not anymore. Not like when you taught us. But I'm grateful to you, Glee. Knowledge is the most useful weapon."

"Knowledge is what you make it, Japhi."

"I know. That's what I meant."

"But that's not what *I* meant." He sighed and left her to her reading.

One evening as Glee and Felicity and Japhis shared a glass of mead by the fire in the front room, Felicity said, "Japhis? You're planning something."

She smiled, almost as if they were visitors to her manor who had come to entertain her. "I can't stay with you two forever." She added sarcastically, "And I'm not ready to become a priest. I have to make plans."

"You're planning some form of revenge," Glee said sadly.

"Against Lessanor? Or the King, perhaps?" She laughed. "I'm not mad."

"No. But . . ."

"Yes?"

Glee looked away, and Felicity said, "You scream of demons in your sleep sometimes, Japhi."

"So? There are many kinds of demons in the world."

"We know," Glee said gently. "You should banish yours."

"You're right." She smiled.

"There's no reason to seek—"

Japhis touched his arm and shook her head. "Only fools and suicides would go hunting for demons, eh? Do I look like either?" She laughed so delightedly that Glee joined her, though Felicity only watched and frowned.

Her journey back through the woods of the Korz was frustratingly slow. She had not walked this trail since she had studied with the Questers. She found herself slowing at several forks to remember the old route. She saw a small pile of rocks, probably heaped by a village child in an idle moment, and remembered when she and Harj had constructed castles of stones and dirt. Once she tripped in a rut in the path and fell, reaching out to catch herself with the hand she no longer had.

She did not reach her former home until sunset. When she finally stood on a familiar rise, she dropped to her knees. The manor was all rubble and charred wood, the work of careless trespassers or jealous neighbors. She brushed a tear away with her bandaged wrist, then gasped, and finally cried freely. She buried her face in the ashes and battered the ground with her forearms. After several minutes, she let herself fall forward. Then, exhausted of all emotion save embarrassment, she looked up to see if anyone watched her. Her clothes were black and gray with caked soot, and she imagined herself as a dirty, pathetic thing. Dragging her sleeve across her face, she scowled into the woods. She saw no one. At last, she rose and began to search through the ruins of her home.

That night, a bonfire burned in the hills across the valley. The servants of the Demon of Korz Pass danced furiously to the rhythm he kept with the uprooted sapling that served as his staff, to the music he made by rustling its leaves like tiny bells. One shadow stopped dancing to cry, "Master! Master! An intruder!"

The bearded giant laughed. "Ah, Acorn, you've drunk too much of our good dew wine! Who could come so softly that the lord of the woods and the wind and the waste would fail to hear his approach?"

Japhis stepped forward, staying in the shadow of an oak bough. "Have you forgotten me so soon?"

The demon turned, and the dancers turned with him. He roared in delight and stamped his staff several times. "Japhis Kardeck! Have you come for another gift?"

"No," she said. "I've brought one for you." She thrust a knife out from her sooty poncho. Seeing it, the dancers shrieked and hurried behind the demon in mock terror. Japhis turned the knife slowly in her hand, and pale rays of moonlight darted from either side of its blade. The dancers covered their eyes. Several began to whimper. Japhis's face was as pale as her knife.

"Quiet, Acorn," the demon said. "Trust your master." To Japhis, he said, "A kitchen knife? I'm insulted."

She shrugged. "I found my dueling sword in the house. The heat had twisted it badly, and the hilt . . ." She smiled and lifted the knife higher. "Still. Can't you feel this? I learned the words from the Old Tongue to speak over an edged weapon." She walked around him to the far side of the fire, keeping the

blade between them. He turned as she moved, always facing
her. The dancers followed behind the demon to keep his
shadow company. Japhis said, "I've studied since we met."

"Education usually instills humility."

"I know two priests you should meet, demon. A shame you
never shall."

"Perhaps I will."

"Perhaps." She hesitated, then said, "You gave me incen-
tive to study." She held up the bandaged stump of her right
arm. In the crowd of dancers, someone snickered. The demon
motioned for silence, and the sound stopped. He watched
Japhis. "It led me to an interesting book." She lowered her
arm toward their fire. "It suggested . . . It suggested one fight
fire with fire." Her lips curled into a taut smile that did not
touch her eyes. The smile fled her face, and she plunged the
stump of her wrist into the coals.

Screaming did not lessen her agony. She fell backwards,
still shrieking. Sweat streamed from her skin. As the shadowy
forms of the demon's servants rushed toward her, Japhis bit
her teeth together and rocked to her feet. Crouched and panting, she waved the butcher knife. The dancers scampered behind the demon, and he chuckled.

Blue flames encased her bandages, yet the cloth did not
burn. Japhis tried to keep her face calm. A vein betrayed her
as it pulsed at her temple. She pulled a small terra cotta bottle
from her belt, holding bottle and knife in her hand. When the
dancers advanced again, she whispered, "Like the knife.
Same words. Shall I splash you?" They recoiled as if struck.
The demon guffawed, though Japhis could not tell if he
laughed at her or at his servants.

"Laugh all you will." Japhis broke the end of the bottle
against a rock to splash some of its contents over her bandages. Steam sizzled and rose, and Japhis gasped. "My
weapon," she whispered. The bandages were heavy on her
wrist, coated with the demon's gold, perhaps turned into
demon gold.

"I may frustrate your plans to fight me," the demon said
quietly. "It may be more amusing to leave you here."

"No. I'll never let you leave."

"You won't let me?" He pounded the leafy sapling against
the ground as he chortled, and the others joined as his chorus.

"No. I drew a circle around this place with my knife, and I whispered the words of binding. You can't leave. Even if I die here, I win." As the laughter ceased, she added, "No one will come to break the ring." She placed the clay bottle on the ground, dipped the blade of the knife into the ashes of the demon's fire, then set it before her and poured the rest of the purified water over it.

When she threw the empty bottle into the bushes, the demon said, "You humans have strange ways to show your thanks."

"I've nothing to thank you for."

"No? Three lumps of gold and seven years of good fortune."

"Your gold doomed me. Seven good years to make my fall worse. Even Harj left me."

"You doomed yourself, dear Japhis, if anyone did. Who made you accept my gift? Who told you how to use it?"

"You're trying to trick me!" She thrust the knife at him.

The demon stepped back, opening his arms in conciliation. "Ah, Japhis. You're still a fool."

She spat into his fire; a tiny gold nugget formed in the flames. "Fight me! You'll see who's the fool!"

"And what of my companions?"

"I . . ." Japhis had not considered them. "They . . . may leave." Watching warily, she erased a section of the circle with the flat of the gold-bladed knife. "One at a time. Not you."

The dancers looked at the demon. He nodded, smiling. The shadow called Acorn was the last to pass through, and Japhis drew the circle shut.

"There's hope for you yet," the demon said.

She hesitated. "Hope for what?"

"For letting the innocents go."

"They're not innocent if they follow you. But they're not guilty."

The demon laughed. "You come so close to understanding. You need more time in the world."

Without warning, Japhis swung her knife toward the demon's stomach. Firelight caressed its blade. The demon lifted his sapling, catching her weapon in its roots, and twisted. The knife spun from her grip in an arc that ended outside the circle she had drawn.

"No!" She punched at his waist with her gold-encased wrist.

"Yes." He caught her arm behind the stump's casing and lifted her above the ground. "You've much to learn, Japhis Kardeck." As he carried her outside her circle, she could not conceal her disbelief. The demon laughed. "For example," he said, "Asphoriel, the greatest of us all, penned Varsiliyas's *Treatise* one afternoon several centuries ago, filling it with minor truths and major lies to protect our kind. So let your first lesson be: Not all you learn is true." He laughed while she dangled in the air. "Go back to the world, Japhis Kardeck." He dropped her on the ground, and she fell painfully onto her side. "Do that, or die. I won't choose for you."

Still laughing, the demon called his servants together. They left her standing quietly in the dark.

In the morning, Japhis remained huddled by the cold ashes of the demon's fire. She looked about with weary eyes, then whispered, "You can hear me, demon. I know it." When he did not answer, she wondered whether he truly could hear, then decided it did not matter.

She found the knife in the light of the dawn, dried its golden blade, and stuck it into her sash. No one seemed to watch her, not even a squirrel. Feeling slightly foolish, she kicked through the demon's ashes and found a small gold nugget. Feeling more foolish, she said loudly, "I could kill myself to escape you, but you'd think that was your victory, wouldn't you? So I'll live, demon. Hear me? I'll live well, and be happy, and you'll have to know so long as you exist that there was one life you could not destroy. Hear me, demon! I promise it!"

With that final flourish, she stalked toward City Gordia to fulfill her vow. And the Demon of Korz Pass sent songbirds to sing along her path.

7

Amber Realities

Kromar the Thief severed the nightgaunt's neck with a last, wild sweep of his enchanted blade. New strength coursed into Kromar's body as his sword funneled the nightgaunt's life force into his soul. With renewed vitality came a smug certainty that the warriors' guild would award him several points in swordskill for the battle he had fought, and the thieves' guild might raise him an entire rank. Kromar turned, a wide grin on his handsome, swarthy features, expecting compliments or the embrace of Ardula, the half-naked harem girl he had rescued from the nightgaunt's chambers.

But no one waited at the edge of the clearing, where he had left Ardula to guard the gold he had looted from the nightgaunt's castle. Kromar spun about, soul-drinking weapon at the ready, and wondered what new challenge faced him. In the distance, a band of the nightgaunt's undead servants were carrying the fair Ardula toward Castle Dread . . . and in the opposite direction, armored goblins fled toward the Loathsome Caverns with Kromar's recently stolen booty.

He looked from the zombies to the goblin soldiers and back again. Ardula, slung over a decaying shoulder and clutched by a rotting hand, screamed, "Save me, Kromar, save me!" Her breasts jounced beneath her tiny metal bra, and her voice promised that she would reward him with anything he could think to ask or demand. Yet in the arms of waddling, burly goblins, his sacks of gold glistened under the bright moonlight.

Kromar hesitated, considering which group to pursue, which prize would mean more to him, whether he could defeat either group and if so, which opponents would win him more points with the guilds of High City. If he guessed wrongly, he might fail, or, far worse, die to be reborn a pauper with the lowest ranking in each guild. His decision held more moral ambiguity than at first appeared; the stolen gold would buy a dozen harem girls, but Ardula might be the daughter of a noble or a merchant, who would pay him very well for delivering her safely home.

Suddenly feeling simultaneously bored and unclean, Kromar said, "Exiting."

Hobie the Halfling, a waist-high, barefooted man in pseudo-medieval clothing, appeared in a puff of scentless smoke. "Thanks for visiting Treasure Realm!" Hobie said, wriggling his furry toes in his pleasure at seeing Kromar. "You were with us for thirty-three minutes! Come back soon!"

Hobie and the manicured forest disappeared. The Enter-Tech logo hung in the air before Kevin for an instant as he heard, "Off at one twenty-three A.M."

Prompt stood in a room that seemed to be the inside of a small sphere. The walls glowed red; the air smelled slightly of hot metal, though it felt cool on Kevin's skin. Prompt wore a silver gown that fell to the concave floor. "Disconnect?" she said.

He could not sleep, he knew, but he did not want to read or work. He considered visiting one of the sex adventure sections of the net, but he might as well have pursued Ardula, if that was all he wanted. Before he could decide, Prompt said, "You have a phone call."

"At one-fucking-thirty in the morning?"

"No," Prompt said. "At one-fucking-twenty-six in the morning."

Kevin glanced at her. "Someone alter your programming, or is your self-teaching mode giving you my sense of humor?" Before she could answer, he said, "Pretty damn poor sort of self-teaching, if so. Disconnect."

A pulsing red light on his eyelids met his return to his body and his room. The phone, in its late-night visual mode, blinked desperately. He reached over and said, "Yo."

"You know what that stupid bitch is doing?"

Still slightly disoriented, he sorted through the clues. The voice was feminine and husky, the accent was educated U.S. Southern, the tone was angry and impatient. "No, Gwen," he said, at last alert. "What's Janny doing?"

"She's dreaming on the jack. On the project. She's fucking dreaming on the fucking jack!"

"Gwen—"

"On the creator level, Kevin. She's letting her fucking subconscious—" He heard an inhalation, then: "Forget it. Sorry I called."

"No, wait!" he said, before she could disconnect. "Explain it, okay? I'm not sure—"

"Bitch would've never told us, if . . . Oh, all right. I found this city when I was checking the desert. Only it was completely empty, nothing but dusty marble buildings. All extremely pretty, but completely impractical. Like a city that'd been built as a monument and abandoned, like no one ever planned to live there. No toilets, no sewers. A lot of fountains, but the water came gushing out without any plumbing or underground streams or anything beneath them. Some of the buildings sat over the mouths of caves that were filled with bats. But there wasn't any thought to the ecology, nothing for the bats to live on—"

"What'd Janny say?"

"She said we could fix it up. Just like that, like it wasn't anything at all."

"We never talked about anything like—" He stopped himself, feeling as if he were betraying Janny by supporting Gwen. "We could make it a forgotten city, maybe, and patch up—"

"That's not the point! I told her we couldn't be putting in new crap at the last minute, just 'cause she thought it was neat. And she said she couldn't help that. She said she couldn't control her dreams."

"When did she start this?"

"A few days ago. Before the Tangled Lands test."

I made it real, he remembered Janny saying. Her voice had

been pleased and embarrassed and defiant. "Mad Dog must've known."

"Bastard did. Bastard helped her rig up a couch so she'd be comfortable sleeping with the jack in. They figured if they messed up the master copy of Janny's World, we'd just use the backup for the next day's work. But since they liked the results, they kept that version and didn't tell us. We've been making backups of the fucked-up thing Janny's dreaming. That's what we jacked into, when we did the Tangled Lands run. Bastards."

"They should've told us." Janny had shared this secret with Mad Dog and not with him. "No wonder you're pissed."

"Damn right. I'm walking."

"Say what?"

"Say I'm walking, Kev. I don't need this secrecy shit, mucking up our work while we're not watching. I got better things to do."

"Shouldn't we all talk?"

"We're all talking. I talked to Michael and Brian; they agreed. Now I'm talking to you. Who're you with?"

He brushed his fingers through his hair, as if stimulating his scalp would stimulate his brain. "Slow down, Gwen, please. Shouldn't the group get together—"

"There's no group, Kevin. There's Mad Dog and Janny sabotaging our work, and there's the rest of us just trying to make a decent living."

"And do something great, damn it! You were in Janny's World, you know what it's like!"

"I know," Gwen said, her voice abruptly gentle. "Wasn't going to work, though, y'know. Even before they pulled this shit, you could tell it wasn't going to work. Janny said that's why she did it, 'cause she thought it might be the only way to fix things."

"Maybe she's right. Maybe we can keep doing patchwork and rationalizations for—"

"She said herself she couldn't control her dreams! It's stupid, Kevin. The world's either going to be eaten by the Tangled Lands demons or by Janny's psychic demons, and either way, I'm out of the mess."

"She should've asked us first."

"Sure. And we would've told her she was crazy. She's

right about that much. So she and Mag Dog did this without us. Fine. Let them play now. There's not much left for any of us to do, anyway. The world's pretty much designed. If Janny and Mad Dog can deliver a workable draft to Omari, we're all rich. If they can't, well, we all got our advances, we go on to the next job. Let Janny live with her cute shit, that's all I say."

"I've got to talk to Janny." He heard himself and added, "And Mad Dog. I can't just decide like this. None of us should."

"You decide, Kev. I've already made up my mind. 'Night."

"G'night," he said reluctantly, and the dial tone sang in his ear.

He stalked from his tiny living room to his closet-sized kitchen, threw open the door of his refrigerator, and stared. He was not hungry. He opened the freezer. He was not hungry at all. He took out a pint of chocolate almond ice cream and took a clean spoon from his dish rack. He started to reach for a bowl from the dish rack too, then left it. He sat in the living room and began to eat. He was not hungry, but the ice cream was very, very good.

After his fifteenth or twentieth bite, he began to feel uncomfortably full. He returned the ice cream to the freezer, grabbed his jacket, and walked toward the Silver Socket.

Toxic Moxie was in·her usual place behind the bar. The crowd was small, typical for late-night Tuesdays. He saw no one he knew. There were a couple of Hitlers at one table, and he felt an anger that displaced his self-disgust. Then he smiled, thinking he was becoming too old and too concerned with symbols and ideals that had lost their meaning.

"Hi, Kevin. The usual?" Moxie's voice came through a speaker slightly behind him, and he almost turned toward it.

He shook his head. "Single-malt whiskey. Straight. Leave the bottle."

She frowned. "You've seen too many cowboy movies, Kevin. I didn't know anyone was making yuppie cowboy movies, though."

"I wanted jokes, I'd've gone to a comedy club."

"Right. Be glad your credit rating's good again. This one isn't on the house." She filled a shot glass with Glenfiddich, placed it in front of him, and turned away.

"The bottle, I said."

"This is a bar, not a package store, asshole."

Kevin laughed. "You treat all your customers so—" Then he said quietly, not sure whether she'd hear him and not caring, "Sorry, Mox."

"*Pas de problème, mon ami*. You want the bottle for the ambience, it'll cost the same as thirty shots, and you don't carry it out of here." He nodded, and she set it before him. "No wonder you're always broke."

"That's just more of the ambience."

"Omari cancel the project?"

"Not exactly."

"Bugs, then?"

He nodded glumly. "Bigger than the cockroach that ate New York."

Moxie made a sound as if she were about to choke, and her eyes opened to permit tears to pass.

"That's funny?" Kevin said, and then he smiled. "Yeah, well—"

"Not like you couldn't find work, Kevin."

"Wouldn't pay what we got in the hoary glory days."

"Still pays way better than most."

He downed the shot without commenting.

"If you're not drinking for taste," Moxie said, "you should get something cheaper. Or something more expensive."

"If people could get married for thirty seconds at a time, you and I'd have some great romances."

Moxie smiled. "Someone should set it up on the net. *Romanceland*. Something like *Treasure Realm* for people who'd like more than their hormones stimulated."

"Someone is—" He caught himself and finished, "Working on something like that. Most likely. Ten years from now, we'll all have surrogate lives in the worlds of our choice."

"Some people prefer reality."

Kevin laughed and lifted his drink. "Amber reality in cold, clear, heavy glasses, Mox. Cheap at any price."

"How've you lived as long as you have, Kevin Fikkan?"

He poured himself another. "By seeking reality in all of its forms, sweet Moxie."

"Avoiding 'em, you mean."

"Hey, how'll I avoid 'em if I don't know what they look like?" He took the neck of the bottle between his thumb and forefinger and cradled the shot glass with his middle, ring, and little fingers. "Time for some electronic reality, now." He wandered toward an empty table.

"When you're halfway through that bottle, I'm cutting you off!" Moxie said from a speaker above the table he was approaching.

"You're a lifesaver, Mox," he said. "But relax." He reached for one of the club's many dangling jack cords. "Maybe it's white noise time."

And maybe it's not, he thought, entering the interface. Prompt waited for him, as she always did. Her face was perfectly calm, perfectly understanding, perfectly Janny's. "Turn around," he said.

The room was large and dark; he did not look at it. He was aware of distant walls hung with thick drapery. The only illumination was a single lamp on the far side of a large oak desk. The floor was covered with an Indian rug that cushioned his steps as he moved closer to Prompt.

She wore a gray skirt and a gray jacket. Her shirt was a black silk turtleneck. Her boots were black English riding boots. A tiny bit of onyx set in silver decorated each ear lobe. The clothing was more formal than anything Janny ever wore. The room was nothing like any room he had ever seen Janny in. He did not question it. He had written the software himself; Prompt's environment would always be appropriate to his mood, or as closely appropriate as any psych program could provide.

Without hesitating, without showing any doubt or curiosity, Prompt turned to face the oak desk. Her narrow shoulders were relaxed, strong. He could smell her perfume now, a trace of jasmine in the air. In Janny's World, there would be other scents, human smells for Prompt and him, a faint smell for each thing in the room and a gestalt smell that was the room's odor.

His mouth was dry. He swallowed, then said, "Bend over."

Prompt leaned forward from the waist. Kevin reached out, placing his palm against the small of her back. He spread his fingers wide, feeling the muscles along either side of her spine, then withdrew his hand. He thought of the Glenfiddich and created a shot glass. He sipped once, then said, "Drop the skirt."

The gray skirt, untouched by Prompt's hands, fluttered to the floor. Her underwear was dark gray cotton, printed in black with a circuit board pattern.

"Very funny." He turned away from her, squeezing the shot glass and wondering how much it would hurt if he made it break in his hand.

"The aerodynamics were perfect."

"You're being thick," he said. He willed the shot glass to disappear.

"Yes," she agreed. "If you had continued, you would only have despised yourself more."

"You're no fucking shrink program! You do what I tell you!"

"Yes. I did."

He could not tell if he heard amusement or pleasure in her voice. He glanced back. The skirt hung smoothly from her waist.

She added, "I could provide any scenario you wished, of course."

"Then why didn't . . ."

"You gave no instructions. Nor did it seem—"

"Yes?"

"Psychologically sound," she finished, strangely as if she regretted not finding a gentler way to say it.

"You're good, Prompt. I've got to give you credit for that."

"What do you mean?"

"You're one hell of an AI. But that's all you are."

"Yes."

The words sounded silly as he said, "You don't have a soul."

"If I was programmed to believe in a religion, would I then?"

Kevin sat; a plush couch formed under him to catch him. He fell over sideways, laughing. "You and my father! Oh, God! If the two of you'd debate—"

Prompt did not join in his laughter. He almost ordered her to. When he stopped at last, he said, "Send a message to Frohn: 'Failure of Tangled Lands almost certain; how much silver for the fateful kiss? Love, Judas, Jr.'"

"Would you like me to send it tomorrow, after you've thought—"

"No advice, AI. Send it now."

"Yes. It's been received."

"Thank you. Is Janny on the net?"

"No."

"What about Brian Cohn?"

"Yes."

"Send: 'Yo, Bri. CO? Kevin.'"

Prompt abruptly became Brian, who was wearing a glowing white spangled jumpsuit with a high collar, open almost to his waist. He had added flesh to his stomach and jowls. His black hair hung in short bangs over his sweaty forehead and partway over his ears. "Sounds good," Brian said, and became Prompt again.

"CO," Kevin said, and he and Brian were suddenly on a brightly lit stage before hundreds or thousands of people. Brian appeared dressed as he had been when answering Kevin's message. Kevin shielded his eyes with one hand from the stage lights. "Is this necess—" Realizing that the people moving about on stage were a primitive video crew dressed in forty-year-old clothing, he laughed delightedly. "My God! You're the Henry the Eighth of rock 'n' roll!"

Brian frowned. "No, it's an Elvis Pres—"

"I know, Bri. Sorry. It's perfect. Have you worked up a Graceland yet?"

"Started to. Don't think I'll finish it. The food's boring, and the drugs just make you stupid. The only part that's really fun is shooting out TVs. Gwen talked to you?"

"Yeah."

"What do you think?"

"Someone ought to talk to Janny."

"I did. She didn't deny any of it. She said it was for the good of the project, and it was her world anyway."

"So you're just going to walk away from it?"

Brian shrugged, raising meaty shoulders toward his sweat-drenched sideburns. "I guess. It's not really like we're abandoning it. It's more like we're finishing early."

"Uh-huh."

"What's left to do? Michael's about done with his research, Gwen and I are about done with interface software, Mad Dog's been done with the customizing of the main computer for weeks now. . . ."

"It's just the Tangled Lands."

Brian nodded. "Which Janny and Mad Dog have tangled up hopelessly."

"Good intentions—"

"Count for something, sure. That's what I told Gwen. You can guess what she said they counted for."

"Shit fuckin' all?"

Brian laughed. "More or less."

"So that's it? The project splits up without a celebration, without sad farewells, nothing?"

"Michael's already accepted a job in Buenos Aires. Leaves tomorrow. You and Gwen and I'll get together again, of course."

"I know." Kevin rested his hand on Brian's shoulder, then jerked it away and flicked sweat from his fingertips. "Christ, Bri, you could be a little less authentic, y'know."

Brian drew himself up. "*Moi?* I have a reputation to maintain."

Kevin nodded. "Only thing I don't understand is, since we're in the net, why don't you look exactly like Elvis?"

"Oh, Kevin, Kevin, Kevin. I thought you had more faith. Anyone can imitate Elvis. I'm imitating an Elvis imitator."

Kevin shook his head. "You make me feel old, Bri."

"Are you drunk or something?"

"Not really. Why?"

"I don't know. You seem a little—" Brian's face wrinkled into a moue and smoothed. "I don't know."

"Me, neither. I'm going to talk to Janny."

"She's probably asleep."

"In her world, too, I'll bet. I think it's time for a visit. Want to come along?"

"I should get some sleep. Good luck."

"See you. Exiting."

He thought for a second that Prompt had reached Janny, for he was facing her. He stood in a dark hallway of seamless walls. A single light glowed over Janny, who slouched in a wicker chair. She wore a black and red kimono he had never seen before, tight copper pants, and cheap black tai chi shoes. He said, "Jan—"

"Name?" she said.

He understood immediately. "Kevin Fikkan."

"Password?"

"Scaramouche."

"What would you like?"

"To talk to Janny."

"She's not available."

"She's not jacked in, or she's not to be disturbed?"

"She's not available."

"Right. *Lands of Adventure*, then."

"That section is not available."

"I love artificial intelligence. I gave you my password."

"Your password permits access to the Laias-O'Neill bulletin board system."

Janny and Mad Dog had closed him out of the game. Perhaps they ordinarily changed the passwords for the project when they didn't expect any of the designers to visit. He could exit, phone Mad Dog, and find out. Mad Dog might be annoyed if he was sleeping, but that would be the proper thing to do.

"I still have access at the command level?"

"Yes."

He laughed. "Add an additional password for *Lands of Adventure*: 'Don't leave the key in the lock, kids.' Now, I want into *Lands of Adventure*."

"Password?"

"I really love AI's. Don't leave the key in the lock, kids." As he finished the sentence, he found himself in a clean, sparsely decorated room with oak paneling and wide windows that opened on rolling prairies. Janny's simulacrum now wore a long gray robe that was given shape by a thin white cord around her waist.

She said, "Welcome to the Lands of Adventure. Do you wish to play a particular character?"

"There any new candidates for solving the Tangled Lands scenario?"

"Yes."

"Sexes?"

"One male, one female, one neuter."

"God, not the last. Are they all physically fit?"

"Yes."

"I think the male, then." As the greeting room for Janny's World disappeared, Kevin thought he saw the AI smile.

Davin woke, coughing desperately. Something had disturbed his sleep, but he was not sure what. He felt momentarily displaced from his body, as if he were a stranger watching himself, and he was not pleased with what he saw. The intellectual displacement was a new sensation, or rather, an old sensation that had not visited him in years. The disgust was very familiar, and he knew the cure for both. He reached under the dirty rags that served as his pillow and closed his hands around a clay jug.

He smiled in anticipation, then glanced around to be sure he was alone. The alley was dark and still, lit by the faint glow of the approaching dawn. A three-legged dog nosed through a greengrocer's rotted produce near him. He and the dog had no other company than the gnats overhead. Davin's smile turned to a frown as he realized he did not recognize this alley. He must have taken a wrong turn in the night and finally found this safe and quiet place. That had happened before. He did not hurt any worse than he did on a good morning, so he knew he had not been beaten by youths and left here.

The dog trotted toward him, leaping from its one rear leg to its two front. Its tail wagged expectantly. Davin wondered how long a crippled thing could survive without friends or home. His guts clenched suddenly, from hunger or bad liquor, and sitting up, he waved his arm at the dog. "Hunh! Get! Damn dog!" The dog whined. Davin snatched a clod of horse dung and hurled it, missing the dog. It yelped anyway, and bounded toward the quiet street.

The nearest buildings were of whitewashed wood, two storeys tall with narrow, shuttered windows and steep roofs to shed snow. He was still in Tyrwilka, then. He had his worn moccasins, his pants and shirt and cloak. That was all he needed to know whenever he woke. That, and the contents of his stoppered clay jug.

Davin slid it carefully before him, trying not to shake it or weigh it in his palm. It was too light to be full, but he could not remember how much it weighed empty. He could not possibly remember how much it weighed empty, and surely he wouldn't have drunk all of it last night. He tried to remember what he had bought to fill it. His mouth tasted like curdled milk, leaving him without any clues.

If the begging had gone well, he might have bought mead or port. If the begging had gone adequately, ale or cider would have served him well enough. But if the begging had gone poorly, he would have gone to the back door of the Dancing Goat to beg the kitchen boy for the "leavings"—the dregs from the pail holding dirty mugs and pitchers when the tavern's public room closed. The leavings were adequate at night, when they were somewhat fresh and he had probably started the day with something finer to drink, something stolen or begged or taken in payment for a chore. But Davin hated to face the leavings in the morning, when his head ached and he was almost sober, and the smell of the warm mixture of beer and wine and strangers' saliva was enough to make him want to smash his jug against a wall . . . but never enough to make him do it.

With the slow elegance of ancient ritual, he reached out to uncork the jug. Beer, he prayed. Hoping for wine would be presumptuous, damning him to the leavings for sure. He did not let himself think the jug might be empty; if there were gods, surely they were kinder than that. The cork exited with a small explosion of air. As it slid free, Davin heard something, a sound of wood tapping lightly against earth or stone or wood. He suspected that he had heard this sound earlier, though fainter and from farther away. It had wakened him, or had come while he was waking.

He hurried to his feet. In the distance, a woman said, "It's a broken crate. I'll help you around—"

A man's voice interrupted. "There's no hurry. I can manage."

"I wish I knew what you were looking for."

"Me, too."

The voices approached from an intersecting alley. He could run into the street before they could see him, then wondered why he should, then realized they might steal his jug. Davin tipped it up for a quick sip, tipped it higher, finally tipped it all the way as he realized no gods loved him. A few bitter drops fell onto his outstretched tongue. They might have been warm wine.

He flung his arm downward, as if to hurl the jug from him, but kept his hold on its neck. "Unicorn buggering—"

Two priests in charcoal-gray robes stared at him from the intersection of alleys. He glared back, saying, "Dragon-turd eating. . . ."

"Surely that couldn't be—" The woman's eyes were wide and skeptical.

"I suspect he is." The man, resting on his ash staff, smiled at a point midway between Davin and his companion.

"Demon-fucking, priest-sucking hell!" Davin snarled, wanting words so foul they hurt these intruders, words that would make them know his unhappiness was infinitely greater than their smug good fortune, words powerful enough to send them scurrying like the dog.

The female priest, an attractive woman with short graying hair, shook her head as though he were an unruly child in her care. The man, bald and tan with pale eyes, laughed delightedly.

Had the laughter seemed malicious, Davin might have attacked them. "I'm not funny," he said, turning to go, beginning to forget them as he turned.

"I wasn't laughing at you," the man answered.

"Yeah?" Davin turned back and marched toward them. The woman touched her companion's shoulder, but the man did not raise his staff or step away. Davin said, "One of your gods tell you a joke, Niner?"

"Quester," the man corrected. "No, no joke, other than the one we inhabit."

"Ain't funny."

"That depends, my friend. What's the difference between a tragedy and a comedy?"

"A jug of beer." Davin came closer. "Half poured in my stomach and half poured over your head, that's a right uproarious comedy. Other way around, I'm likely to cry. Give me a copper, and I'll demonstrate comedy for you at the Roost." He grinned, not knowing if he seemed threatening or pitiful, and not caring.

"No, thanks," the man said. "Come to our temple, though,

and we'll give you more than money." His pale eyes did not follow Davin. The priest was blind.

Davin's humor faltered, but he forced it to return. The priest was clean and healthy and far too pleased with himself to deserve anyone's pity. "Copper's all I ask, friend. Just enough for a mug of breakfast."

"I think you're wrong," the woman told her companion. "This one's neither strong nor pure."

"Begging your pardon," Davin said laughing, "but if you think I'm not strong, there's something wrong with your nose. And I'm purely in need of a drink or a smoke, I am. Be kind to a fellow human in need, urm?"

"You don't want help," the woman said. "You just want pity."

"Don't need your pity," Davin snapped.

"Of course not," the woman said. "You have plenty of your own. You just need a copper or two to bolster it."

Davin looked at the ground, then began wandering toward the street. "Sanctimonious bastards."

"We can help you!" the woman called, her voice almost pleading.

"Yeah, prove it." Davin did not look back. "Give me some money." He recognized the street: Dream Makers' Way. The Mug and Mountain was nearby; the owner would give him a simple task or two, and fill his jug with her cheapest beer when he finished.

Something small and hard hit him just above his right shoulder blade. He swore, then looked down to see a thin copper coin embedded in the mud. He looked over his shoulder. The blind man was grinning. The woman said to the blind man, "Your grasp of the intricacies of human nature is invariably amazing."

"Did he stop?" the blind man asked, and then, "Did I hit him?"

"Yes, Glee," the woman said patiently. "Your ear is excellent."

"Hah!"

"Is it a pitching post you lack?" Davin stared at the coin at his feet. "Is that all I am to you rich, happy bastards?"

"It's not all you could be," Glee said. "Take the copper and leave us now, and you may never be anything more."

"Yeah, right." He scratched his head, and small flakes fell from his scalp onto the coin in the mud. The coin was a new Gordian copper with the Empress's profile on its face. That would buy him two jugs of cheap beer, or three of cider, since last year's apple harvest had been so good. "And if I come with you?"

The bald man reached into a bag slung at his side. He removed a gnarled translucent thing as long as a human forearm, but curved and tapering from a thick, cut end to a skewed point. Glee said, "Then you may have a chance to redeem yourself, Unicorn Rider."

8

The Principle of Fairness

"Out!" Kevin screamed. "Out, fucking now!" The priests and the alley disappeared. He felt disembodied, as though his soul were rushing on psychic winds to an unknowable destination. Behind him, Janny's voice dwindled infinitely, becoming constantly quieter than it could in the physical world, yet never becoming indistinct: "Thank you for visiting the Lands of Adventure, Kevin Fikkan. Return soon!"

Prompt appeared. The room was small and comfortable; Kevin did not notice it. Her clothes were simple and functional; he did not notice them either. Prompt said, "Do you—"

"Disconnect now!"

And he was at his table in the Silver Socket. His body shaking, he stood and stumbled backwards, knocking over his chair. Only a sharp tug at the back of his neck as the jack cable reached its normal extension made him fully aware of himself, and still he wanted to run, not caring how much safety length the jack cable had, not caring whether he tore the entire ceiling down or ripped the jack socket out of his skull.

A tall black man from a nearby table gripped Kevin's upper arms to reassure or restrain him. "Easy, Jack. You're out safe, whatever it was."

Moxie's voice came from an overhead speaker. "Kevin? You all right? Say something, please."

He made himself breathe deeply, feeling his chest and shoulders rise and slump as he panted. "It's fine," Kevin said, a little loud, a little angry, suddenly aware of too many eyes watching him. He twisted quickly, freeing himself of the tall man's grip. "No prob, okay?"

The man said guardedly, "Didn't seem that way."

"S'right." Hearing his tone at last, Kevin said, "Sorry. I'm just . . . a little shook, that's all. I'm fine." He reached behind him and pulled the jack plug.

"Well, you say so. . . ." The man nodded skeptically and rejoined friends at another table.

"Kevin?" Moxie said, her voice coming more softly from the speaker. "What happened?"

"Nothing, Mox." He refilled his shot glass, then threw the shot down his throat.

"Yeah. I can tell."

He glanced back at the bar. Moxie was sliding clean wine-glasses into the overhead rack. Her back was to him, but he had spotted the ceiling camera that had tracked him when he sat again. He poured another glass and saluted the lens. "Cheers."

"I wasn't kidding about cutting you off, Kevin."

"I paid for this bottle."

"So you'll have some private stock. The way your credit ping-pongs . . ."

"None of your affair, Mox."

He thought she would leave him alone then, but suddenly he heard: "Might help if you talked about it."

"Why? Hoping I got a little of what you got, maybe enough so there'd be another jackstar who lost his nerve?"

The speaker was quiet, then rattled slightly, just before Moxie's voice came through. "Don't you want friends?"

"I've got all I can afford."

"I don't know, Kevin. Sometimes I think you just want people to fuck and people to fuck over."

"And you were both, kid."

The speaker was silent even longer. "Funny. I didn't think I was the one crying into the phone in the middle of the night, begging—"

"I was trying to let you off easy."

Moxie laughed. "Right-o. And when you broke my new boyfriend's nose—"

"Just my way of saying it'd been fun while it lasted. I wanted you to think I still respected you."

Moxie laughed more. "Uh huh. And you let him beat you so I'd know you didn't think it meant too much."

"Well." His breathing was finally normal, his fear gone. He wished he could apologize to Moxie for being so harsh, but if he could, they might still be living together. "We were sixteen. What'd we know about life?"

"I don't know. Sometimes I think we knew a lot more then. We didn't play so many games to hide what we felt."

Kevin shook his head. "Sure we did, Mox. We just didn't play them nearly as well." He stood. "I ought to be going."

"Whatever."

Kevin stepped over to the table of the man who'd intervened. The man's companions, a heavy black woman with sparkling Neotrad cornrows and an Oriental Poseur dressed as a Lon Chaney Fu Manchu, seemed suspicious, but the black man's face was calm. Kevin smiled slightly. "Hey, sorry I was such an asshole. You did right."

The man nodded, his expression unchanging. "We got to look out for each other, Jack."

"I s'pose." Kevin made a small wave with his hand, a tiny turning of his wrist, and left them. He picked up his glass and the Glenfiddich as he passed his table, then set them on the bar near Moxie, who wiped the counter with lazy circular passes.

The bottle and the shot glass met the polyurethane surface more loudly than he intended, yet Moxie did not turn toward him. "Hey, Mox? You're happy with Linc?"

The back of her head bobbed once.

Kevin smiled, trusting that the video cameras would catch his expression or that she could decipher his sincerity from the tone of his voice, however it might seem filtered through her electronic perceptions. "I'm glad."

"Thanks."

"I'm straightening things out, Mox. I've got my money problems under control. I've made some important connections. It's blue sky from here on. Really."

"Blue sky? Sounds like into the ozone again, Kid Flash."

"Hey, I'm sorry about, about—" He grimaced, then finally said, "Hope I didn't upset anyone when I came off the jack. I was a little confused."

"Do tell?" She made a few more swipes at the clean counter.

"It was just, well, a program acting strangely. I thought it . . . meant something more, that's all."

"What do you mean?"

"I don't know. Nothing, I guess. You run into a funny coincidence and you think it means something."

She shrugged. "Maybe it does."

He laughed. "Get real, Mox."

She smiled. "And why should I get real when artificial's so much easier to clean?"

Davin knew the outside of the Questers' large temple on Empire Avenue; he had begged near it many times. The octagonal building stood three storeys tall, capped with a cone of slate shingles that rose above the temple's eight chimneys. A ramp on either side of the wide front steps led up to plain wooden doors and a simple marble façade. Narrow windows of translucent glass traversed each of the eight sides from foundation to roof. The stone walls surrounding the rear and side gardens were seven feet high, tall enough for privacy but not tall enough to inconvenience any healthy person who wished to pass over them.

Felicity, midway up the steps, turned and beckoned with a flicker of one finger. "Come in. Some of your questions will be answered immediately."

"Not all?"

"No. But at least you'll know which questions won't be answered, eh?"

"Urm." Davin wiped his mouth with the back of his grimy hand and followed the priests.

The door opened easily to Glee's touch. As he swung it wide on silent hinges, he said, "It's never locked."

"Eh." The entry room was large and clean and bare of furniture. Open doors to the left showed a small dining hall, and to the right, a vast, empty room that Davin suspected was for religious services. A spiral stairway before him climbed from the basement to the upper floors. The flagstones under his moccasins were dark granite, worn by the passing of generations of visitors. A cloth on one wall showed a field where wolverines and rabbits frolicked together, and hawks flew with gulls, and unicorns ran with cheetahs, and perhaps a hundred other wild and domestic animals existed together as if a truce had been called between hunter and prey. A smiling dark-haired woman towered over them. Davin pointed. "That's your god?"

"That's the God," Glee said, "if you refer to the tapestry. I wouldn't say we worship Her. We simply . . . recognize Her."

"Right." Davin did not try to hide his disdain.

A small and pudgy pale boy in a white robe ran in from the right, stared at Davin, then told Glee and Felicity, "They're waiting in the sun room."

Glee smiled broadly. "Thank you, Merry. We'll be there shortly."

The boy nodded and ran back the way he had come.

Davin laughed. "Do you all take clown names?"

"Davin," Felicity said, "is a very old Torionese name. It means 'of the swamp' or 'muck dweller.'"

Before Davin could speak, Glee said, "It's a common, human thing, to adopt new names to mark the beginning of a new life. We usually take the name of a priest who has died recently, though some of us invent new names. The exception is the Speaker for the Inner Circle, who is always called Serenity, to honor our first Speaker."

"The Speaker's your leader?"

"If we have one." Glee moved confidently toward the descending stairs. "Come. You'll meet him."

"The sun room's underground?"

"No. The baths are."

"I'm thirsty." Davin's headache grew steadily worse, and he knew the cure, though he would not plead for it. The Questers' cellar was probably full of wine and ale barrels.

"There'll be food and drink after you wash. Come."

He crossed his arms. "I'm clean enough for the best of you."

Felicity laughed. "You aren't clean enough to be buried in a dungheap."

Worry showed on the blind man's face in the instant before

Davin grinned. "I take your money, I take your orders." He held both hands before him. "O wash my sins from my soul, noble priests."

"From both soles," Felicity said. "And behind your ears."

He followed them quickly down the stairs, for he wanted to know the contents of their larder. To his disappointment, half the lower level seemed to lie beyond a closed door. To his pleasure, the door did not seem to be locked.

"This way," Felicity said, watching impatiently.

"Of course, of course!" He hurried after her. The dark, tiled hall was lit by the windows at the top of the basement walls. Felicity took his clothes and made him sit in a small steam room, then brought a bucket and made him scrub his hair and his body, then brought him to a small heated pool, where he almost fell asleep. Finally, he shaved and dressed in clean clothes much like the ones he had discarded, and Felicity brought him upstairs, where Glee rejoined them.

"Davin?"

"Yeah?"

"Ah!" Glee sniffed loudly and grinned. "If you tiptoed, I might not know when you entered the room, now."

"He looks better, too," Felicity said. "Younger than I thought."

Davin shook his head. "Old enough. And unless your mirror lies, I look like a fat white slug."

Glee shrugged. "Only you can change that."

Davin, surprised, said nothing. He had expected a polite lie from the polite priest. Too late, he wondered whether the priest meant Davin could change the way he looked or change the way he saw himself.

The priests took him to the back of the ground floor, where a small bright room faced gardens of low grass, trimmed bushes, and pruned trees. Thick red and blue and yellow mats were strewn about the room, and several wicker and cherry-wood chairs waited in each corner. A very old, very dark Southern man in a black robe sat cross-legged on a cushion. He nodded to them as they entered.

"Serenity," Glee and Felicity said, nodding in return.

Davin walked into the middle of the room, turned in a complete circle to see everything, and ignored the old man.

"The rowan is particularly beautiful this time of year." Serenity lifted his chin toward a young tree with clusters of berries the color of ripe tomatoes.

"Urm." He ignored the tree to stare at the old man.

"This," Glee said politely, "is Davin Greenboots. He has come to hear our offer."

"The first part of our offer," the old man corrected, coughing. Davin thought he recognized the cough: the Wasting Sickness. Serenity would be dead before spring. Did he know it?

"I could stand a drink," Davin said.

"Of course." The old man stood unsteadily, then hobbled to a low table and picked up a red shellacked tray with four blue porcelain cups and four golden wheat buns.

"Ah." Davin took a cup and drank. "That's tea!"

"Yes," Glee said. "Our own blend. We call it—"

"Ferret piss," Davin said.

"No. Our Own Blend," Glee finished, grinning.

"We will feed, clothe, and shelter you," the old man said, "for a month."

"And if I don't want that?"

"We will pay you three royals for each week that you stay with us. You may leave any time you wish, of course, but if you leave, you cannot return."

"Ah." Davin studied the priests' faces, and wondered if they ever let strong emotions show, or if they were capable of feeling them. "And I'll still be paid, if I leave?"

The old man nodded.

To hide his delight, Davin picked up his wheat bun and bit into it. The bun was stuffed with cheese and mushrooms. "This is good," he said. "Be good with beer."

"Undoubtedly," Felicity said.

"At the end of the month, you'll be offered an opportunity which could lead to honor, acclaim, and wealth, if you succeed. If you fail, it could lead to your death."

Davin shrugged. "So I'm expendable." He remembered Glee calling him Unicorn Rider in the alley. "How many bums have you offered this chance?"

"None," Glee said quickly. "You may be irreplaceable."

"Oh?" Why would they tell him they needed him, unless it was true and they were impossibly naive? If there was bargaining to follow, he had been given the stronger position, and that made no sense at all.

"Or we may have made the wrong choice," Felicity said, as quickly as Glee. "So we wait a month to see what you are."

"To see what you can become," Serenity corrected.

"Yeah, right." Davin's headache had returned. He touched his hand to his forehead, and felt sweat on his brow. The priests were dressed as warmly as he, yet they seemed comfortable. If he had not come here, he would not have his new clothes, but he already would have earned or begged his first beer and would be feeling infinitely better.

"There are three conditions," Serenity said, coughing into his hands. "You must study every day in our library."

"What things?"

"What you will. History, magic, demonology. We make suggestions, if you need them, but we cannot be sure what you'll need to know."

"I can read."

Serenity smiled. "Good. You must exercise, too. We will teach you. You will become fit."

"For what?"

"For anything. There are seventeen priests presently in this place. Among us, we have many skills."

Davin shrugged, wanting only for this conversation to end. He imagined taking his first week's wages to the Wanderer's Roost and telling the barkeep to keep his mug full for a month. "I can exercise."

"Good. The third and most important condition is that you end your addiction."

Davin almost spilled his tea. "My what?" He laughed.

The old man glanced at Felicity. "I am unclear in this language, still? Well, then. If you take a single taste of wine or mead or beer or any alcoholic drink, if you take one whiff of mirthweed or dreamflower or any narcotic substance, if you use any substance that increases your pleasure at the expense of your mind or body, we will pay you your wages and expel you instantly."

"For a single drink? You're mad." Davin stared, but none of the priests showed sympathy or understanding. He grew angry with himself, wondering why he had expected them to.

"If we thought you could take a single drink, we would not need to ask this of you."

"Why do you think I can't?"

"Have you tried to drink moderately?" Glee asked. "Some people cannot. If you're one of them—"

"Rot in hell," Davin said.

"I think that's an affirmative," Felicity said.

"There's no shame in becoming addicted," Glee said. "Only in remaining addicted. We will help all we can."

"Is that why you're doing this? To have someone around who'll make you feel superior?"

"No," Glee said.

Felicity inhaled loudly, and Davin looked and saw she was making herself say something she would rather not. "How could we ever feel superior to anyone? If we didn't have our weaknesses, we'd live in the world like normal people."

Davin sneered. "Want to be a happy little peasant on a happy little farm, working all day for a happy little master who'll work you until you die? Spare me your fantasies about normal people, old woman."

Felicity, her face impassive, looked toward the garden.

Serenity shrugged, a tiny lifting of the shoulders that set off his cough. "If you cannot indulge yourself moderately, you must quit entirely. The solution is simple, even if it is difficult."

"Simple?" Davin laughed, thinking of how much they asked and how little they offered.

The old man nodded. "Very simple. But very, very difficult."

Davin stood, then tossed back the rest of his tea as though it were his favorite beer. "You think I can't do it?"

Serenity gave his quick shrug. "We shall see."

"I know you can," Glee said in his soft, certain voice.

Felicity was silent. Her face, turned quickly away from Davin's gaze, told him that she knew he could not.

"Just watch me," Davin said, and his words sounded falsely heroic in his ears.

He could not study that afternoon; his eyes would not focus. He exercised in the large, open room with eight Questers, but he could not keep up with their drills and dances.

Without asking permission to go, he staggered to the cot he had been assigned and tried to sleep. Felicity brought soup and fruit juice to his bed; he ignored it. The next day might have been worse. He felt as if he could neither sleep nor stay awake, his throat hurt, his skull ached, his skin flashed from hot to cold and remained slick with sweat. He could not concentrate, which was hardly new to him, but the painful impossibility of focused thought was another symptom of this trial he did not have to face.

The priests had not lied when they said the front door was always open. On his second night in the Questers' temple, he tried the handle after the others had retired, then stood in the doorway, listening to the cries of distant nightbirds. What did he hope to gain by submitting to the priests' test? He rejected half a dozen answers. Smoke from neighboring chimneys drifted to his nose. He thought he could see the lights of the inns on Moonrise Lane from here, though he was not sure.

The priests were playing with him. They set his needs and his wishes and his pride—what little remained of that—against each other to lead him where they wished, and only the knowledge that he could leave any time kept him from leaving immediately. Whenever he thought he could stand no more, when he knew that no payment was enough to keep him sober, he had threatened to go, or had sometimes simply looked longingly at a door or a window. One of the priests invariably reminded him that the choice was his. Perhaps the freedom to leave was the only thing that kept him. Perhaps he wanted to know what task they would offer him. Perhaps he was as curious as the priests to see whether he had the strength or the need to become more than he had been. At last, he closed the front door and returned to his cot in the large, empty dormitory for visitors.

That night, he sweated and turned, and his old dreams returned. The giant black unicorn raced through a windy night, its eyes like dark mirrors, its horn like polished jet. It sought him, but he did not know if it wanted him for its rider or its prey. He woke shivering on his cot, needing comfort from his clay jug more than ever before. He slept fitfully for the rest of the night. In the morning, he realized that the dreams had never ceased after he abandoned his quest. He had only managed to forget them in his habitual drugged sleep, and now he was denied even that temporary relief.

He had let Felicity bring his dinner to his cot on the first two nights, but on the third day, he felt stronger. He exercised, and though he did not work as strenuously as the priests, he did not stop until they did. He read in the library, and while he could not concentrate on any serious works, a collection of folk tales about the Tangled Lands amused him for several hours. Serenity paused by his chair, looked at the book, then nodded approvingly. Against his will, Davin felt a sense of accomplishment that lasted until he joined the priests at their long common table.

Merry, the plump boy, carried a tray of cups along the table, passing one to each person with a quick, "Your tea, Delight," or "Your mineral water, Serenity." When he came to the woman next to Davin, he said, "Your wine, Mirth," and handed her a cup.

Davin stood, knocking his low chair onto its back. "What's this? You won't let me drink, and then you drink in front of me?"

"I like a cup now and then," Mirth said softly, her eyes cast downward.

"You do? Well, so do I, I'll have you know!"

"And who would've guessed?" Felicity asked.

"I'm sober," he said. "I've proven you were wrong. Haven't I?"

Serenity shrugged. "Have you?"

"Yes. So if anyone's going to have a drink when I'm around, I'm entitled to one, too."

"Ah." Serenity looked up. "And why is that?"

"Because it's not right!" Everyone watched him, and he felt suddenly foolish, which increased his anger. "It's rude!"

"Rude?" said Serenity. "But we have something for you, I'm sure."

"Grape juice," Merry whispered.

"Grape juice." Davin scowled at the boy. "Pour it in a bottle and bring it back when it's grown up."

A priest he did not know laughed; when Davin glanced at the woman, she looked away as if embarrassed.

"You won't ignore me! None of you'll ignore me!"

"That would appear to be true," Serenity said. "If we have

offended you, we apologize. But you cannot expect us to change our habits to suit your whims."

"My whims? It's not my whims we speak of! It's the principle of fairness!"

"Oh." Felicity nodded. "A fine principle."

"It's not fair," Serenity said slowly, "that Mirth can drink wine and you cannot?"

"Yes." His anger had seeped away, leaving him only his embarrassment, but he kept his tone gruff.

"Yes," Serenity agreed, and put his spoon into his soup as though the conversation were over.

"That's all you'll say?" Davin stared at each person at the table. "Any of you?"

"What more can we say?" Felicity said. "It's not fair. Are you strong enough to accept that?"

Davin turned to Serenity. "I'll take my pay, now."

"You have not finished your week," the old man said, coughing.

"Can you finish your week?" Felicity asked.

"I have just gone through—" He stopped, then said, "Are none of you aware of what I've endured in the last three days?"

"Yes," said the woman who had laughed when he made his small, angry joke about the grape juice. She lifted her cup. "Mine's tea. I know what it's like."

"And I," said a plump woman.

"And I," Glee said quietly.

"Yeah, right. You all know what it's like." Davin turned on the ball of his foot to depart. At the door, he paused. "I'll finish the week to show you how easy it is. Then you can find yourselves another fool for your fool's task, whatever it is."

Much later that night, Davin crept barefoot through the bare, silent halls to the central staircase and descended to the basement. He would stay the week, as he had promised. He would have his three royals, for he had already earned them. But he would make the rest of the week pass much more easily.

His eyes were slow to adjust to the faint, reflected moonlight, but at last, he could see the shape of the storeroom door. It opened as quietly as every other door in this well-kept building. The room beyond was darker than the hall, and he stumbled against a cabinet as he began to feel his way among boxes and cabinets and bins. A flash of light blinded him, and before he could adjust to the glare, he heard Felicity ask, "Thirsty?" She lay on a mat spread before a large wine keg. On the floor beside her was the lamp whose shutters had just opened.

"I was looking for the toilet." He blinked to see clearly again, and thought it was the stupidest lie he had ever made.

She nodded, sitting up. Her sleeping robe was a cloud of white, her gray hair a smaller one. "Many of our visitors have that difficulty. That's why the door at the end of the dormitory has a sign saying TOILET."

"Maybe I was looking for something wet. A fellow gets thirsty."

"Especially a fellow who's addicted to strong drink."

"I'm no addict! I'm . . . fond of a drink now and then, sure. I'm no addict."

"Well, that should be easy enough to prove," she answered. "Next to the toilet, there's a small washroom with clean water piped from Lake Tyrwilka. You might not have noticed it. The sign on the door says WATER."

"And if a fellow'd rather fancy a small taste of wine?"

"I won't stop you. We told you as much."

"Yes." There were several wooden cups on the counter, near the keg. He reached for one. "Join me?"

"I'm no addict."

"No. You're a burr up the butt, is what you are, old woman."

She nodded solemnly. "I take no credit. It's a gift."

He set his hand on the keg's wooden spigot.

"We will expel you if you take a single drink," Felicity said. "Serenity wasn't being rhetorical. Since that's the cost, I'd try the back room for our best wine."

He said in his friendliest tone, "This'll do. One drink won't hurt. Makes more sense to ease off—"

"How many times did you try to ease off, before we found you?"

He could count the tries, if he cared to. When the potter at Winterberry had threatened to dismiss him. When the potter at Winterberry did dismiss him. When the Little Falls potter had threatened to dismiss him. When the Little Falls potter did dis— He did not care to count the tries. "Ah, you're like the rest of them. But worse."

She shrugged.

"You won't stop me from drinking?"

"Never." She added sweetly, "That's against our principles. Be glad. If I made policy, you'd be nailed into an empty barrel until your need had gone, then kept chained until you were . . . somewhere with no temptations to distract you."

Davin laughed. "I suppose Serenity had you watch me because he knew you'd love to catch me."

"No," she said calmly. "I set myself to catch you because Glee believes in you."

"And you don't? You're brighter than the rest of this sexless bunch." He turned the tap, and grinned as dark wine splashed into the wooden cup.

"No again." Felicity's voice became quieter, and quicker. "I don't want to see Glee disappointed."

"That," Davin said, raising his cup to salute her, "is a damn shame."

"Before you drink," she said, her voice less assured, "tell me one thing." When he glanced at her, she added, "Please."

"And that is?"

"Why do you pity yourself so much?"

He almost laughed, but he caught himself, suddenly aware that he could slip from laughter to tears too easily. He lifted the cup toward his lips.

"Please," she repeated. "Not because you owe it to us, or anyone. I'd just like to know."

"It's none of your affair."

"Maybe not. But you're prepared to sacrifice so much for a taste of wine that I could give up in an instant."

He shrugged. "So could I."

"Then why don't you?"

"For what?"

"We can't tell you. Not until you prove you can stay sober and alert . . ."

"That's me," Davin said. "The noble warrior." The smell of the wine was sweet, tart, and tantalizing. He brought the cup close to his lips, and watched Felicity's eyes go wide. He lowered it, and she relaxed. He laughed, and raised the cup up and down, watching her track its motion, catch herself, and glare at him.

"Go on," she said suddenly. "Drink up!"

"Fine."

"That's what you want, isn't it? An excuse to feel sorry for yourself!"

She was so wrong that he almost drank. If he did, she would never listen to his explanation, and he realized that though he did not like her, he respected her. He lowered the cup, keeping it safely in his hand where she could not snatch it away. "I have enough excuses to feel sorry for myself, I assure you."

"Then why do you want another? Is it so everyone else will feel sorry for you? Is it so you'll have an excuse to never try to be anything more than what you are?"

He glared at her, felt his fingers squeezing the cup too tightly. "Do you really care?"

"No." She frowned. "But I don't understand why you don't."

He watched her, and saw that she would wait patiently for an answer he did not owe, to a question she had no right to ask. He set the cup untasted on the counter by the keg. "Oh, spare me this. I'm going to sleep."

"Thank you." Though he listened carefully, he had only heard sincerity in her voice. As he moved toward the stairs, she called softly, "The Order is hardly sexless."

He laughed his favorite, uncaring laugh. "Is that an invitation?"

"No. I'll leave the cellar unguarded from now on; you can come and go as you please. Glee will be happy that my whim to make my bed elsewhere has passed. But I thought it odd you should call us sexless, when Glee says you're still a virgin."

He swallowed. "That's my concern, old woman."

"Perhaps. I don't understand the Unicorn Riders' obsession with virginity, but I thought I should point out that since this is important to you, you should be proud of that, if nothing else."

"Save your compliments," Davin said, and climbing the stairs, he almost turned for the front door and Moonrise Lane. He continued climbing, thinking he would finish his week,

take his pay, and having proved all he needed to others and
himself, never be sober again.

On the fifth night, he returned to the cellar. The last two
days had gone well; he had even remembered an old trick and
thrown the woman who taught wrestling. He asked himself
why he returned to the basement now, what comfort the wine
would give him. He did not even think it would taste particularly good; it would satisfy a subtler, nameless desire.

He studied the barrel, weighing his strength and his need.
He had been sober for five days. The certainty that his joints
were impaled with needles had passed, and so had the head-
aches, yet he wanted to drink. One cup, he told himself, and
then he would creep upstairs and sleep. But how could he face
the priests again? He answered that easily: by lying to them.
But even if he fooled them, the act of lying would be an
admission that they were right, that he was an addict, that in
his own eyes he was inadequate.

Which had almost made him laugh, there in the cold,
damp cellar: he was inadequate. The unicorn knew the truth.
He had forgiven himself for killing it; that had either been
an instant's spite or an accident, and although he could
never know which, he could accept that he had committed
one horrible, youthful mistake. He could never forgive himself for trying to perfect his body and spirit, then offering
himself to the unicorn, only to see his life proved a failure
when she rejected him.

He filled one of the cups and wondered why he did this
now, when it would destroy the unknown second chance that
the Questers promised. In the darkness, some wine sloshed
onto his fingers. The resinous scent of the wines of Lyrandol
filled the room, more sweetly than the night before. The liquid
that had spilled was cool on his skin, and grew cooler as it
dried. He waited in the dark, his right hand gripping his mug,
his left hand resting on the wine tap. He had been sober for
five days; he would celebrate by getting drunk.

Glee would be sad. That he could face with ease. Felicity
would despise him. That he could also face—after a few
drinks, with ease. He would remember them when he was
sober. The solution was simple there, too. He would not let
anyone trick him into being sober again.

He looked around the cellar, then checked under its narrow wooden stairs. No one watched him. No one would interfere. Felicity had spoken honestly. The decision was his.

He wanted to cry. He could not decide what to do. If he did not drink, he would be surrendering to the wishes of others. If he drank, he would be surrendering to his need. He could not win. He smiled at the insight: He had known all along that he could not win; that was one of the many reasons he drank.

He felt foolish, standing alone in a dark cellar with a full cup of wine. At last, he carried it upstairs and pounded on the door to Glee and Felicity's room.

The door opened; a bald head was barely perceivable in the gloom. "What?" Glee asked. "Davin?"

"Here. I thought you might be thirsty."

The priest's hands closed on the cup. He smelled it, then said, "Oh." Glee's voice was thick with failure.

"Yeah. I wasn't."

"Oh!" the priest said with paternal pride.

"Will it ever get easier?"

"No. Sometimes it will get harder, and sometimes it will be no harder than this."

"Hell." Davin shaped the word carefully, and kept all his feeling from it.

"Oh, my poor child," Glee said, and embraced him.

He began to cry, though he did not know why. His nose and his eyes leaked onto the blind man's robe. His chest hurt, and he could not stop himself from making sounds like someone dying or giving birth. At last, he stumbled backwards, away from the priest.

"Why?" Davin asked. "That's all I want to know."

"Me, too."

Felicity watched from the room, her expression oddly kind. Davin wanted to turn and run, but he knew the only destination he could have was Moonrise Lane. He said, "You don't have answers?"

"We look for answers. For us, that's become an answer."

Davin dragged the sleeve of his shirt across his damp face. "Why?"

"Why what?"

"Why live?" he whispered.

"Because death is unavoidable. Why hurry to it?"

Davin turned toward the dormitory. "That's not enough of an answer."

"Then look for a better one," Glee called, and as Davin walked, he thought, *Look for an answer.* He did not know why it comforted him, but he knew he would sleep better tonight than he had in years.

9

Interesting Challenges

A flashing red light on Kevin's eyelids told him either that it was time to wake up, that he had a message waiting, or that he was sleeping on the roof on a police car. He did not remember setting an alarm. The softness under him felt like his own bed. He wiggled his ears once to activate his jack chip, and Prompt whispered, *Yes?*

Time? he thought.

2:37:14 p.m.

Oh, God. Do something about my hangover.

You have orange juice in the refrigerator. Drink several glasses. Fluids and vitamin C will—

Now, Prompt.

The headache diminished considerably as Prompt adjusted his perception of his body's needs. *Is that sufficient?*

All the way.

The headache disappeared. Prompt said, *May I remind you to drink—*

"Yeah, yeah." He rolled on his air bed to fumble at the headboard and find a jack cable. The dim bedroom was replaced with a small, bright office. Kevin wore a three-piece black suit flecked with tiny starlike lights that seemed to glow within the darkness of the suit, rather than on it. His shoes

127

glistened. His tie seemed to be crimson silk; his shirt, white cotton.

Glancing at himself, he said, "Who died?"

"No one. Dieter Frohn returned your call."

"Himself?"

"No. His AI."

"A-hah. The message?"

Hugo's plastic features filled a monitor that appeared on the far wall. Hugo said, "Mr. Fikkan, betrayal need not be measured in units of silver, unless you prefer it. We offer payment in gold or plutonium, dollars or yen, stock or real estate, art or antiques. When you tell us that *Lands of Adventure* has proven a failure, we will pay you twice your income last year, and offer ten business recommendations. In anticipation of your agreement, one-tenth payment has been made to your account in yen via a Tokyo broker; a friend remembered you in his will. We suggest you invest in Angel Pin Repairs, a very promising company involved in medical nanotechnological development."

The monitor disappeared with Hugo's image. Prompt said, "Mr. Frohn hopes to hear from you at your earliest convenience."

"Yeah, right. Let's do it."

The varying grays of the sky and the ground of the infinite plain that was Frohn's reception room had become shades of metallic blue; Kevin suspected they would be olive drabs the next time he visited. The air smelled of ozone. Some boringly innocuous Old Age music drifted from the direction of the pale sun on the horizon. Otherwise, the place had not changed. A designer undoubtedly had been paid well for this season's concept of an environment that would remind petitioners of their true relationship to the person they hoped to meet.

Hugo sat behind a floating dark blue oval plane that formed a desk top. He smiled, baring the smooth curve of white that served for teeth. "Mr. Fikkan. Welcome. I've alerted Mr. Frohn. He can see you now."

There was no handshake this time. That might mean they trusted him not to try to sneak any espionage programs into Enter-Tech memory. More likely, they assumed he only needed the one reminder that he was constantly under surveillance; their electronic watchmen were too sophisticated for him to hope to notice without state-of-the-art programs of his own.

Hugo walked beside him through the door to Frohn's office. Though expected, the dislocation programs left Kevin with a sense of vertigo that might have been more profound than before, perhaps because he expected it. The room was huge and almost bare; a low crystalline ceiling glowed overhead. Several Miro prints hung on royal-blue walls beside and behind Frohn. To Kevin's left, a wide window gave a view of pale green waters illuminated from above by shafts of light. A shark passed close to the window as Kevin glanced at it.

"Kid Flash!" said Frohn, rising from behind his desk and extending a many-ringed hand. Paisley patterns in yellow and brown swam within his shirt. Something was wrong with the program for his jeans; the weathered texture seemed painted on, no more natural in appearance than bleached or stonewashed denim. "How's it hanging?"

"In any direction you want." Kevin smiled to cover his suspicion that what he had meant as a joke had revealed his annoyance at surrendering control over the interface.

Frohn shrugged and grinned. "Hey, let me know, and you can have any size and direction you like."

"I'm fine," Kevin lied.

"Excellent." Frohn sat and waved toward a chair of aluminum and leather the color of clotting blood. As Kevin sat, Frohn put his fingertips together in Christian prayer book fashion. "So, Kid Flash. You say *Lands of Adventure* is dying."

He could tell Frohn he had changed his mind, he would spy no more for Enter-Tech, he would return their latest payment. Knowing he would not, he answered brusquely in hopes of ending this quickly. "Yes. The others learned that Janny and Mad Dog made modifications without consulting them. A bad move. Gwen is furious, Brian is extremely unhappy, and Michael's taken another job. Probably a job with a little more structure than this project had. He never did quite fit in."

"Their unhappiness'll kill the game?"

Kevin turned up his palm in stylized helplessness. "I don't know. Mad Dog claims he has working software that'll solve the game's memory requirements. He thinks we can tap the players' unused brain cells for extra short-term memory."

Frohn raised an eyebrow. "People have tried that before."

"What can I say? Mad Dog's confident."

"That's what bothered the others?"

"Not really. Janny's been dreaming on the programming level of the game and saving the results."

Frohn sat up, suddenly alert. "No one noticed?"

"Not exactly. Somehow, she and Mad Dog managed to keep Janny's World from becoming a surreal mess. At least, I think they have. It's creepy, how real the game seems now. Might be too real for people who're expecting light entertainment, but that's Omari's problem, not mine."

"And the Tangled Lands problem? Any breakthroughs there?"

"No. I suspect it's Janny's dreaming that's screwed it up. The original scenario probably required the players to accumulate a few magical doohickeys that would defeat the demons. But the way it is now, I don't think the solution's so simplistic. I'm not even sure one exists."

Frohn nodded. "So you don't think they'll succeed?"

Kevin looked down, shook his head. "No. I don't think they will."

"Even if the team gets back together?"

"Hard to say. Looks like Michael's gone, either way, but that hardly matters."

"He's irrelevant to the team?"

"Now he is. I mean, he came up with some nice bits for the world, but so far as the really creative work goes, he's irrelevant."

"Like you."

Kevin glanced up; Frohn, electronically inhaling from an electronic handrolled joint, was looking away, toward a window that looked down on the distant Earth from one of the L-5's, probably Satellite New Brazil. "Depends on how you see it," Kevin said. "Not too many people could've made the first run. Or the second."

"Ay-uh." Frohn released a gout of silver-blue smoke. "Care for a hit?"

Kevin shook his head. "You could mainline constantly here. A tap in one arm and an unending rush. Or you could forget the analogs and go hothead, direct to your pleasure centers."

"You could," Frohn said. "I'm on a splitter, m'man. You're my third conference just now; one more, and I'd have to go completely straight." He grinned, showing a gold tooth inlaid with a platinum skull. "Or completely mad." The joint disappeared from his fingers. "Did you hear Analog's new Master Tester is about ready for release? They did complete psych studies on all their resident jackstars, then created an AI composite. They say Master Tester's better than any of their humans."

Kevin shrugged. "Better than a company kid? My, my, my. It can find its analog ass with both analog hands?"

"Analog thinks the thing's ready to replace you, Kid Flash. No one'll have to buy insurance to protect an AI. No one'll have to pay it overtime. Had to happen sooner or later, you know. You outlast all the gunfighters, and the West goes civilized." Frohn smiled. "If it didn't, you wouldn't outlast 'em, eh?"

"What's this leading up to?" Kevin said, certain that he already knew.

"Means I want you to be smart enough to take a job with a winner, Kid Flash. Means I want you to kill *Lands of Adventure*."

"Why not wait?"

Frohn laughed. "Not much of a bonus for you if it happens by itself."

"It's kind of you to be looking out for me."

"No kindness in it. I want your team for Enter-Tech. Michael's already with us."

Kevin glanced at Frohn, then looked at the far window. A dead planet lay outside the window, its dust undisturbed by any atmosphere. Frohn still grinned as Kevin looked back. "You hired him?"

"Yep. Months ago."

The window was perfectly black. "You didn't tell me."

"No need. You agreed to talk, a position opened up in the development team, we let you talk and we filled the position."

"You can't get the game. Omari has first rights."

"Who wants the game?" Frohn tapped the table with a thick finger for punctuation. "You're not listening. I want the team. The game's a dead end. Too weird, too intellectual, a loser. The extrapolation programs are promising. The software to exploit the players' memory is very promising. That's what I want. If you salvage *Lands of Adventure*, Omari will have those things to use on other games or to lease to other companies. If you kill it, we will."

Kevin sat quietly while the window showed a storm of red dust raging beyond the room. "S'pose I just say no?"

Frohn shook his head. "Kevin, Kevin, Kevin. Do you think I want to announce you've been spying for us? Omari'd drop you immediately, no one else'd touch you, and Enter-Tech'd have to say *sayonara*, too. 'Cause if it was known that you liked to make midnight sales out the back door, no one in Enter-Tech would be comfortable working with you. This entire business should stay our little secret, don't you think?"

No, Kevin wanted to say, I never think. "Sure." He made himself grin. "Sure thing, Dieter. I'll kill *Lands of Adventure* for you." It would be no more than a mercy killing.

Mad Dog swung the door wide and held it open, showing the usual chaos of his apartment beyond him, releasing the usual plethora of confined human and electrical odors tinged with, perhaps, patchouli incense that had been burned to improve the mix. Something Celtadelic was playing loudly; Kevin thought he recognized Giant-Size Man-Thing. Mad Dog said, "I'll be damned. A rat came back."

"Easy, Mad Dog." Kevin touched his hand to his forehead. "Rough night, last night. I'm still recovering."

"Then enter, enter. Hell, I'm glad to see you." Mad Dog scooted his wheelchair back, then led Kevin toward Byte-henge, calling, "Sweet parts! Kid Flash's making a visit!" Without pausing, his voice returned to Mad Dog's usual too loud conversational level. "Gwen was so pissed, I figured you'd all cut and run by now."

"Sounds like she had call to, Mad Dog."

"Well . . ." He grinned and shrugged. "Maybe a little. But getting mad is one thing. Walking out's another."

"You talk to Brian?"

"Yeah. He said he didn't like it, but he had to stand by Gwen." Mad Dog paused. "Are he and Gwen . . .?" He made a circle with the thumb and middle finger of one hand, then he inserted the middle finger of his other hand and moved it back and forth.

Kevin attempted his best upper-class English accent. "Are you attempting to say 'fucking,' sir?"

Mad Dog looked bashful. "I didn't want you to think I was trying to impress you with the jargon, Kid."

"About what?" said Janny, coming from the kitchen. Her short hair was held back from her forehead with several clips, one with a silver head shaped like a quarter note, another a brightly enameled Minnie Mouse. She wore baggy khaki pants, a red UNIVERSAL EVERYTHING sweatshirt, socks in the colors of a coral snake, and no shoes. Kevin didn't think she wore makeup, but the irises of her eyes were light purple today.

He thought, *I love you*, and said, "Oh, just..." He shrugged.

Mad Dog said, "The Kid was talking about fucking. Wasn't that right? Fucking? I'm pretty sure it was fucking you were—"

"Mad Dog was wondering about Gwen and Bri," Kevin explained quickly.

Janny's lip quirked, and she rubbed Mad Dog's head. "Such a gossip."

Kevin nodded. "They're just good friends."

Janny said, "Now, as for Brian and Michael..." She looked from Kevin to Mad Dog, then laughed. "You didn't notice?"

"Oh," Kevin said. "Poor Bri."

"Oh?" Janny cocked her head to one side; Kevin wondered if she suspected what that look did to his mind and loins.

"Michael's gone to Buenos Aires. I didn't realize..." He shrugged. *Poor, poor Bri*, he thought. *No wonder he was playing Elvis last night. Did Michael tell him anything more than farewell when he left?*

"Thirsty?" Janny turned toward the kitchen. "There's coffee, o.j., carbonated sugar water in several flavors, grape juice—"

"Vitamin C," Kevin said, remembering that he was suffering from dehydration and vitamin depletion. "In any form. I was celebrating last night."

"Was she anyone we know?" Mad Dog asked.

Kevin shook his head.

"Hell, if you won't talk about it, I might as well fetch the drinks. Coffee, Jan?"

Janny nodded and smiled. As Mad Dog wheeled away, Janny said, "You look a little frazzled."

"Gets on the nerves. At least you're getting plenty of sleep."

Janny glanced guiltily at him. "Maybe I shouldn't've—"

"Done is done," Kevin said. "But why'd you try it? I thought the game was important to you."

"It is!" She glanced downwards. "But it was too... predictable. And the work was going too slowly. And—" She shook her head, her face and her tone shy and self-mocking. "I wanted to make it real. The Tangled Lands scenario was already a mess. And I realized that I was spending all of my time thinking about the world anyway. I woke up one morning, knowing I'd been dreaming about it. I must've been up for hours, trying to decide how to fix everything by the deadline. Wondering what effect dreaming would have on an artificial world." She looked up from under her pale lashes. "When Mad Dog finally got up, I asked him, figuring he'd laugh at me."

"And he thought it was an interesting challenge."

Janny nodded. "Yeah. He studied all the psych files Gwen and Bri used for the program that generates the game's new characters, then he went through everything he had on electronic interaction between people and smart programs. 'Cause that's what Janny's World is, ultimately, just a huge AI. And he decided we had enough of the world sketched in for it to be stable, if I didn't dream anything too weird. He wrote a program to yank me out if I did, like if I was suddenly naked in my eighth-grade geography class. Then I did a test run. It didn't work well the first couple of nights, so we always restored the backup before the rest of you jacked in. And then it seemed to work fine, so we kept that version as the master."

"Right before the last Tangled Lands run."

"Yeah."

"Thanks for fixing it for us."

Janny winced. "We would've told you when we were done. Really."

"When you were sure you'd succeeded."

"Yeah. But Gwen happened to notice that I'd been logged on overnight, and when I confessed, she blew."

He suspected the truth was more complicated than that, but essentially no different. "What's it like, dreaming on the jack?"

She smiled. "When I'm conscious on the programming level, I'm the AI's boss. But when I dream, I'm its conscience." She glanced at him, then away before he could muster sympathy or understanding, and began to chew at a hangnail on her right little finger. "You think I'm crazy."

"No."

"You think Mad Dog's crazy for helping me."

He laughed. "I know Mad Dog's crazy. If I hadn't been in, I would've thought you were crazy. I still think the whole thing's crazy, but it's—" He bit his lip, then said, "It's the best simulation I've ever experienced, even if it is gigascrewed."

She stood and took both his hands in hers. He thought that she needed sleep, that she was beautiful, that she intended to kiss him. He thought of his relationship with Frohn and Enter-Tech, and felt slightly ill. Janny said, "Thank you. You'll help me save it?"

"Oh, Christ, Janny, it's—" He turned away, but she caught his arm.

"You're good, Kevin. You could do it."

"How many times did I try?" The question was rhetorical; he had been six different adventurers who ventured into the Tangled Lands. Tival Ar, the most promising, had been defeated as easily as the others.

"You can't quit now. You're better than that." Janny's voice was quick, quiet, confident. "You know more about it, too. We've got a few days left till the deadline. We can keep trying—"

"Sometimes you have to cut your losses." He met her look and did not let himself feel a thing.

"No! Damn it, Kevin, you owe it to try!"

"To who?" He backed away from her, surprised by his anger and unable or unwilling to suppress it. "To you?"

"Yes." She nodded. "To all of us. Michael, Bri, Gwen, Mad Dog. We worked as hard as you. But you owe it to yourself most of all."

"Oh, c'mon, Janny. That's corny as hell."

She stalked up to him, grabbed his black silk pullover in both hands. "Don't give up so fast, Kevin Fikkan. You'll hate yourself if you do."

He glanced down at her grip and planned to say, *Don't stretch the fabric, okay*? Instead, he heard himself say, "I'll hate myself more if I fail."

"But you'll have tried! You'll have fought the good fight! Hell, you know the clichés better than I do, and that's not the point. Will you do it? For whatever reason? Please?"

He closed his eyes, then nodded once.

Janny's hands slid across his chest, releasing his shirt to grip his arms. "You're a good friend. Really."

"My!" said Mad Dog, returning with two tumblers and a coffee mug on a tray. "Getting cozy in here."

"Kevin's going to help," Janny said.

"'Course he is." Mad Dog set the tray on the footlocker in front of the sofa. Without looking at Kevin, he said, "You visited the game last night."

"Yeah." When Mad Dog glanced up, Kevin added, "You checked who logged on?"

"Uh huh."

"Why'd you change the password?"

Mad Dog's grin seemed a challenge. "I thought someone might get mad about what Janny and I'd done and pull something fast with Global Gaming or Enter-Tech."

"Ah." Kevin picked up a glass of grape juice and drank deeply.

"It's silly," Janny said. "No matter how mad Gwen got, she wouldn't do that. And Brian sure wouldn't."

"Yeah," said Mad Dog. "But what about Michael? We don't know much about him, huh? Who knows what kind of slimy thing he might try?"

"He's a nice guy," Janny said.

Kevin smiled to repress a wince. "I don't think you have to worry about Michael now."

"Well, better safe." Mad Dog lifted his cola to salute them both. "Still, I'm a lot happier knowing it's down to the two of you. Sometimes I think you're the only people I trust. Cheers."

"Cheers." Kevin raised his grape juice and wondered what he had done to his life.

"Cheers." Davin raised his grape juice and wondered what he had done to his life. His body still ached from a month of work and exercise, and though he had felt a momentary pride when he saw himself in the bathroom mirror that afternoon, he rarely spent more than an hour without wanting to walk through the front doors and buy wine or mirthweed from old friends whose names he had never learned. The Questers had paid him each week as they promised; his savings would let him live two months on Moonrise Lane without denying himself any of his former favorite pleasures.

"Cheers," Glee agreed, raising his cup toward Davin. Beside him, Felicity nodded and sipped her drink. The three were alone in the Questers' dining hall. An oil lamp dangled above the center of the long table; two others burned in niches in opposite walls.

"I didn't think you'd last the month." Shadows rippled across Felicity's face as she smiled.

Davin shrugged. "I'd've bet with you. Disappointed?"

"You're fishing for compliments."

"Yes," Davin agreed. "With a net."

She laughed. "Congratulations, Davin Greenboots. I'm proud of you." He stared at her, not expecting that concession and further surprised when she added, "I doubt I could've done it."

"Doesn't matter who else could've done it," Glee said. "What matters is that you did it."

Davin shook his head. Compliments embarrassed him, especially ones he did not deserve. "I had help."

"You can have all the help in the world, and it'll do you no good unless you're willing to help your helpers."

Davin started to nod agreement, then understood. "You're sending me away."

"Too much advice?" Glee asked.

"Yes."

"A bad habit. Whenever I feel like I'm speaking for the Order, I preen like a peacock. We're not sending you away. But it's time for you to decide what you'll do with your life."

Davin glanced at Felicity, then said casually, "Will I stay here, or will I go fight demons, you mean?"

Felicity stared. Glee's surprise seemed subtler; his mouth moved as if he would speak, then closed.

Davin laughed. "You didn't think I would figure it out?"

"Not at all," Felicity answered. "But we didn't think you'd stay if you did."

"Urm." Davin swirled the grape juice in his cup, watched the highlights from the lamp break on the black liquid's surface. "Figured it out on the third or fourth day, I think. You were hardly discreet. Get in shape, study magic, study demons. What was I to conclude?"

"So why'd you stay?" Felicity asked.

"After I realized it wasn't for payment or to prove you wrong about me being addicted? Because I didn't want to go back to what I was." Which was not half the truth, he knew, but was all the truth he cared to tell them.

Felicity reached across the table and covered his hand with hers, and squeezed.

"Thank you," he said quietly.

A moment's confusion flickered across Glee's face, then he smiled. "You can stay here, you know. Or you can go back into the world and rebuild your life. It would not be easy, but you know that already."

"And if I go into the Tangled Lands?" He thought they knew he had already decided to, but the question should be asked.

"We'll provide you with supplies and money. We'll arrange for you to meet your companions. If you come back, we'll give you a hundred gold Tyrwilkan royals."

"If I succeed, you mean?"

Glee snorted, an aborted laugh. "If you come back. Many do, you know. The humor of demons . . ." More somberly, he added, "Many kill themselves. Failure isn't easy."

"That's why you chose me? Figuring I knew how to live with failure?" Davin heard hints of self-pity and anger in his voice and tried, too late, to stifle them.

"No. We have ways of sensing what should be done. You may be one of the Three who can succeed, Davin."

"Ways? Mystic passes and magic crystals like the wizards in Gordian melodramas?"

"More like prayers and meditation and the contemplation of our dreams."

Davin smiled, keeping himself from sneering only because he had come to like these priests. "That's hardly enough to make me confident."

"Hardly enough to make any of us confident," Glee agreed. "But it's the best we've got."

"And you're the best we've got," Felicity added.

"Two others?" Davin asked, to make someone else the conversation's subject.

"Yes. A woman we knew, and—" She hesitated. "A representative of the unicorns."

Davin felt his eyes go wide, and narrowed them. "Oh."

"Perhaps that's why you were chosen," Felicity said. He could not tell if this was to comfort or warn him, and he wondered if they knew of the unicorn he had killed.

"The woman's a priest?"

Glee and Felicity laughed together in sudden, comfortable intimacy. "Japhis?" said Felicity. "Hardly."

"And the . . . representative? A unicorn?"

Glee shrugged. Felicity said, "Your guess may be better than ours."

"Ah. Will I be paid more than the hundred royals if I succeed?"

"We're not rich!" Felicity said.

Glee smiled. "If you save the world, you'll have the kind of fame that'll bring all the wealth you could want."

"True." He refilled his cup with grape juice. "I suppose it's rather petty of me."

"Hardly," Glee said. "It's difficult to imagine that this world we love could be destroyed, or that we can . . . or should . . . do anything to save it. So you think of this as a task, I imagine, and concentrate on what you can do when it's all over."

Davin nodded as if that were true, then realized that Glee could not interpret his silence. "Yes," he lied. He had seen a simpler truth than the priests had. Since killing the unicorn, he had been trying to find a way to die. What could be simpler or more elegant than venturing into the Tangled Lands?

10

The Grasp of the Past

The nurse at the front desk was a young Polynesian man with fluorescent facial tattoos in intricate, ancient patterns. Setting down a phone, he glanced at Kevin, taking in the uncombed hair, the round mirrored glasses in silver 1890's frames, the faded corduroy jacket, the rumpled black silk turtleneck, the paint-spattered metallic work pants, the torn black Keds. He frowned as he noticed the button Kevin had pinned to the jacket for this visit: LIFE'S A BITCH, AND THEN THEY WON'T LET YOU DIE. "Yes?"

The tone did not inspire Kevin to be polite. "I want to look at the hotheads."

"This isn't—" the nurse began, then caught himself. Kevin mentally finished the sentence: —a zoo. The nurse shook his head, and his tattoos changed from purple to scarlet. "Sorry. A long day. You have a relative in there?"

"I'm paying Wizciencki's room and board." A register was open on the desk before him, so Kevin picked up a pen and signed in: *Miserables, Les.*

"Ah. Visiting hours are over in about twelve minutes, you know."

Kevin bared his teeth in the semblance of a smile. "We get lost in conversation, you don't hesitate to interrupt us, hear?"

The nurse closed his eyes. "Eleven minutes. You can find it?"

"No prob." Earlier, Prompt had accessed the hospital map; now, the outline of an arrow was superimposed on Kevin's vision, pointing past the nurses' station toward an intersecting hall and skewing to the left.

He followed Prompt's arrow, passing a young girl with a robot leg who limped beside a very frail boy jacked into a gracefully moving exoskeleton. The boy was saying, " . . . hard to do, but if you can forget you're—" When Kevin reached the door at the end of the hallway, he hesitated, then shoved it abruptly with the flat of his hand and stalked in.

The initial sight was disappointing. He had seen it in photos and vids: a large room with subtle lighting, pastel walls, and light gray carpeting; forty beds, all occupied; no visitors. A window at the far end of the room gave a view of the hospital courtyard, but what did that matter? No one would appreciate it. Perhaps it was there for the relief of the hospital staff, so they could be reminded of the greater world while they tended the undead.

Prompt's arrow pointed toward the far end of the room, but Kevin ignored it. The patients were all young, most of them within a year or two of his age. They seemed to sleep peacefully. Their bodies were healthy, their expressions placid. Bald, thanks to hair inhibitors that made them easier to clean, garbed in identical blue hospital gowns that made them easier to dress, they seemed as sexless as mannequins. Their jacks were hooked to hospital monitors, serving their owners in ways their owners had never anticipated. Miscellaneous cables ran under clean white sheets, carrying commands and nutrients, removing information and wastes. The patients could be the crew of a starship in deep space, sleeping until they came to a bright new world.

The monitor screens above each bed gave names, but no handles. Armadillo Frisbee slept here, Kevin knew, but he had never seen her face and could not remember her real name. Something about a slender black man seemed familiar; the monitor confirmed that he was Tim Bradley, but knowing that, Kevin could see nothing that reminded him of the cheerful fat boy who had worked with him on *Alien Endgame*. Cynthia Kilgallen's name was familiar, but he knew she wasn't the

Frisbee and wondered if she might have been one of his
friends or lovers some years ago, or if he had only heard her
name mentioned in a conversation with strangers about people
who had gone hothead.

Rebecca Ann Wizciencki, born 11/4/89, admitted 7/10/07,
was 5'5" tall and weighed 109 pounds. The rest of the information on her monitor was medicalese which undoubtedly
meant that for someone assigned to the hothead ward she was
fine. Kevin looked from the monitor to the calm face and
wondered if she had been homely or attractive, happy or mis-
erable, clever or slow-witted. Blood pressure and heart rate
told so little about a person.

What color had her hair been? Her features, untouched by
emotion, could have been beautiful or forgettable, depending
on how she carried herself. What color were her eyes? He
wanted to pry apart her lids to see, but he could not make
himself do it. He imagined her suddenly rising at his touch,
her face wild, her hands tearing at his flesh. He wanted to
touch her cheek, to know this was a real person and not a
well-made simulacrum, but he could not make himself do
that, either. It would be a kind of rape. Because she could not
notice it, he would be the only victim of his act.

The room smelled faintly of disinfectant, and that was
probably deliberate, probably chosen with the wall color because it was soothing with its connotations of conscientious
people cleansing the world of dirt, bacteria, and evil. Instru-
mental music came softly from unseen speakers, a tune his
mother often played that Kevin almost recognized, something
written by Prince or the Beatles or another of the better late
twentieth-century composers. The air moved discreetly
through the room at a comfortable 72 degrees Fahrenheit. The
sleepers could find worse places to spend the rest of their
lives.

He wanted to roll a patient out of its bed and lie there, eyes
closed, half-covered by a crisp white sheet. It would be so
easy to arrange to become one of them.

The door opened behind him, but he did not bother to turn
around. Someone had come to see that all the visitors left
promptly on the hour. If he did not look around, he might
have another minute to compose himself before he left. He did
not want to speak to anyone, or to hear anyone speak. He

would have turned and gone instantly, but he did not want to see anyone capable of seeing and judging him.

Something made him glance again at Rebecca Ann Wizciencki's monitor. It read: "Visitors: 2."

He whirled. A man of thirty-five or forty years stood by the door, staring at him. In any other setting, Kevin would not have recognized him. His hair was thinner and shorter than it had been in the photo, his glasses were fashionably oversized now, he had grown a goatee and added twenty or thirty pounds of weight, mostly to his stomach. He wore a tweed jacket and a loose tie instead of a football jersey, and the only thing in his hands was a black vinyl briefcase. But Kevin could superimpose tears on the man's cheeks and a battered toy bunny in his hands.

"I'm sorry," the man said, his voice kind. "I didn't mean to startle you. I— There are hardly ever visitors here."

"S'all right." He knew he should leave. He should leave as quickly as he possibly could. He looked past Rebecca Ann Wizciencki's father and began to walk toward the door.

"You don't have to go." The man moved slightly, enough so that Kevin would have to turn sideways to pass him. "I can be alone with her in a roomful of visitors."

"S'okay."

As Kevin came close, the man said, "Did you know her?"

"No." Because that felt too much like a lie, Kevin added, "Not really," then wished he had been clever enough to say nothing, or something smarter. Her father had seen him studying her, but he could have said that he was visiting Tim Bradley and just happened to be looking around when he came in. What business of the father's was it, anyway? He wanted to step around him and leave, but there was something desperate in the father's expression that made Kevin say, "I wish I had."

"I come here every night, after work." The man smiled sadly. "Well, almost every night. I tell myself she's dead, even if her body's still alive, but I can't make myself believe it. Her sister gets mad when I mention Becky Ann. She thinks I'm some sort of ghoul to visit her so often. Do you?"

The man's crazy, Kevin thought, but whose fault was that? "No." He shrugged. "I'm here."

"Not every night."

"No."

"Last year, I only came three or four times. Her sister hadn't gone off to school, then, so I was busier, and I knew the hospital would call if something changed. But it never does."

"No." No hothead had ever found his way back from his premature visit to heaven or hell. People studied the problem, and found it interesting, and learned more about mind and brain, and the hotheads continued their unknowable dreams.

"Her mother never comes here. She left me a year after Becky Ann's accident. It's hard on a family, something like that."

"Yeah. I'd imagine." Kevin glanced at the door. "Visiting hours must be about over."

The man shook his head. "They're kind, here. Especially for visitors to this ward, where the machines take care of everyone. We've probably got another five minutes or so before anyone'll come to chase us away. Did you go to school with Becky Ann?"

There would have been no point in denying he was visiting her; her father may have already noticed "Visitors: 2" on her monitor, and had certainly seen that he had signed in as her guest. The false name had been a silly joke, but now Kevin was glad he had written it. "We, ah, met on the net. You know, visiting a section and noticing a message someone had left, that sort of thing."

"Yes." The man smiled absently. "Becky Ann loved the net. Her mother and I saved for years to pay for her jackware. It was that or an Ivy League school. She chose the jackware. I suppose it was the practical decision. Wave of the future, and all."

Wave of the past, and all, Kevin thought. How do I tell you that? People are building smarter interfaces every day. Ten years from now there'll be total body suits that anyone can slip into, and the suit'll provide the body with all the illusions and all the analogies that the jack presently provides the mind. And the suit'll be twice as safe and half as expensive as jack operations. "Yes, I suppose it is."

The man held out his hand. "Tom Wizciencki."

Kevin took it and smiled. "Miserables. Les. A net handle." *A net handle, but not one that's mine,* he thought.

"Net handles." Tom Wizciencki nodded. "Becky Ann was

Honey Bunny. Did you read any of the *Honey Bunny* books?"
As Kevin shook his head, Wizciencki continued. "She loved
them. I understood that. Happy people in a happy world
where the worst things are innocent misunderstandings that
are cleared up in a few pages. Who couldn't understand that?"

Kevin shrugged.

"Becky Ann's world wasn't happy, Les. Not sad, mind
you, but her brother died when she was six. A drunken driver,
it's an old story. And she wasn't popular. She had a weight
problem." Wizciencki made a half-laugh. "No more. They use
the jacks to exercise them, every day. Puppets on electronic
strings. If she recovered, she'd be so proud of the way she
looks."

"I s'pose," Kevin said. "I didn't really know her all that
well. I should prob—"

"But even though I understood why Becky Ann became
Honey Bunny and spent so much time on the net, I never
approved. It's running from reality. It's dishonest, somehow. I
suppose she could tell what I felt. That probably just made her
go on the jack more often." Wizciencki looked at Kevin, almost as if he would cry. "The thing I never asked is, who did
it hurt? I thought it hurt her, that she should learn to deal with
the real world more effectively, but did it really matter?"

"I don't know, Tom." Kevin glanced away, looking for a
clock or a nurse or someone or something that he could use as
an excuse to leave.

"You're a part of that world, Les. You must've thought
about these things."

Kevin shook his head quickly. "I'm not much on self-
analysis."

"Aren't you?" Wizciencki pointed at his daughter. "When
you're here, at the very least don't you wonder if you'll end
up like Becky Ann?"

Sometimes he wanted to end up like Becky Ann. He
shrugged. "Some people are lucky, some aren't."

"And that's all?" Wizciencki stared at him. "That's all you
can say?"

"I wish" —*it had never happened, I'd never been born, we
all lived in Honey Bunny's happy world*—"there was something I could say to make it better. I've got a good friend
here." He heard what he'd just said. "Besides Becky Ann.

And I had another friend who rejected her jackware. They operated to remove it, but her entire brain..." Kevin grimaced. "A couple of friends have their senses all screwed up, though they get around. Maybe they're lucky, compared to Becky Ann, but..."

"But they have to live with it every day?" Wizciencki finished.

Kevin nodded.

"So do I. So does Becky Ann's mother, and her sister, who found her drooling, sitting in her own urine. And her grandfather who called Becky Ann his best friend." Wizciencki's voice faltered. "I haven't seen her fiancé in over a year, so I don't know how he's doing now. They hadn't chosen a date, but they wanted to be married in a submarine. Isn't that crazy?" Wizciencki smiled as tears came to the corners of his eyes. "Her mother took Becky Ann's dog to California." He suddenly gasped, his body shaking as he finished, laughing and crying simultaneously, "Her goldfish died! Her goddamn goldfish died!"

There must be hundreds of hidden cameras in the ward. Someone must be watching them. Someone must have noticed Wizciencki's anguish. Kevin put his hand on Wizciencki's arm and whispered, "I'm sorry."

Wizciencki dropped his briefcase and grabbed Kevin's wrist with both hands. "You're sorry?" One hand released Kevin's wrist to snatch his mirrored glasses and fling them to the carpeted floor. "You're goddamn sorry?" Wizciencki let go of Kevin to stamp on the sunglasses with his brightly polished shoes. The glasses shattered as Kevin staggered backwards, trying to understand what had happened.

"Oh, God." Wizciencki crumpled cross-legged to the floor and covered his face with both hands. "Oh, God-god-god-god-god."

"Come help!" Kevin called to the hidden cameras and their hidden attendants. "Can't you see to come help!"

"She's not—" Wizciencki said, and then, "You're not—" and then, "Oh, Christ Jesus, you bastard." The blasphemy made no sense until Wizciencki looked up into Kevin's naked eyes. "I want to make you understand! Can't you understand? One stupid game ruined so many lives, and I want—" Wizciencki clutched at the air, trying to grasp something invisible to Kevin, and perhaps to Wizciencki, too. "I want to forgive you, but you lie about who you are and why you're here—"

Kevin stumbled backwards, away from the man.

"Oh, I knew you, Kevin Fikkan, I knew you all along. And my conscience tells me I should forgive you, that I have to forgive you if I'm ever to forgive myself—"

"I didn't—" Kevin began, not knowing what he didn't do, but knowing it was something he should have done.

"And you lie to me! And you try to weasel out of your responsibility, you rich, happy jackstar! You pay Becky Ann's bills, as if—" Wizciencki's voice grew calmer. "As if you're doing us a favor, keeping her alive when I couldn't even afford to do that, not here, anyway."

The hall door opened, admitting brighter light and two figures in white, lit from behind like angels of new technology. Wizciencki did not turn to look at them. "Maybe all you have to give is money," he said.

The people in white moved closer, each taking Wizciencki by the arm. One was the Polynesian nurse, the other a black woman in a doctor's coat. "Come along, Tom," the doctor said.

Wizciencki stood with their aid, but did nothing to acknowledge their presence. "Maybe you can't give anything until you've given all your money."

"Get some sleep," the nurse said to Wizciencki. "Come back tomorrow." He watched Kevin, and Kevin could not tell if there was pity or disgust on his tattooed face. "Becky Ann'll be all right." In his words was the knowledge that Becky Ann might be all right for eighty years or more.

"Maybe I'll talk to my lawyer," Wizciencki told Kevin. "Maybe we'll take more of your money. Maybe if we took it all, you could find out who you are." Suddenly, Wizciencki almost spat. "Miserables! Do you know what misery is? Do you—"

The doors closed behind Wizciencki as his escorts took him into the hall. Kevin stood alone in the hothead ward. Turning to leave, he said softly, "Stupid bastard. Stupid pathetic bastard."

Felicity walked into the village of Foxhome early in the afternoon of a cool day of gentle winds and low gray clouds.

The community consisted of twenty or thirty cabins that stood at a bend of the Fastwater. Felicity was not sure, but she thought there were several new buildings since she had last passed this way. Small children and dogs played as equals in the central lane. Cats and older people watched from the shade of low porches. A manure cart, driven by a slouching youth in a shapeless wool hat, approached and passed her on its way to the village's fields; the driver tipped her hat respectfully to Felicity and said nothing.

One child noticed the Quester and pointed, and the children all darted aside to stand whispering by the side of the lane. Felicity smiled, wanting to tell them to continue their game and knowing they would only stare until she was out of their sight. When she stopped before the largest home, a cabin of indigo logs with whitewashed shutters, porch, and door, one of the biggest children came cautiously forward. Felicity wasn't sure, but she thought this was a boy; the children were almost indistinguishable in dusty unbleached woolen smocks and tangled hair that hung to their shoulders.

"Wanting to ferry the Fastwater, Lady? My mum and da' have—"

"No," Felicity said.

"Come to see the mayor, then?"

"This is still her house?"

"Yes, Lady." The child pointed at one window. "That's glass! From Tyrwilka. You can see right through it! Mayor says it's made out of sand, but I can't see through sand. Can you?"

Felicity glanced at the child, then patted its bare shoulder and walked toward the front porch. The lawn to the right of the gravel path lay fallow, but the lawn to the left was a carefully tended garden of herbs and vegetables, dotted with marigolds to discourage insects and wild roses for no discernible purpose save beauty.

Felicity rapped at the front door twice with her staff. After a moment, the door swung wide, silent on oiled leather hinges, and a stout, one-handed woman stood in the doorway. "Felicity," she cried, flinging her arms wide to embrace the Quester. When they separated, Japhis said, "Look at you!"

"Me?" Felicity frowned. "Tired old woman. But you! The prosperous matron—"

"Fat old woman, you mean." Japhis laughed. "Oh, come in, come in, it's good to see you! What's it been? Six years? Seven?"

Felicity grunted an acknowledgment, then nodded, swatted once at her dark, dusty robe, and followed. The large central room was open to the rafters, with sleeping or storage lofts to either side. The tall, narrow windows admitted sunlight that reflected on whitewashed cupboards and plaster walls. Wicker chairs, two tables, a loom, and a cedar chest had been pushed against the wall so that eight or ten children, older and cleaner than those in the lane, could sit cross-legged on the sanded maple floor. A brick oven gave warmth, as well as the smell of birch burning and bread baking. To one side of the oven was a shelf with several books. Hanging from a hook on the wall on the opposite side was a kitchen knife with a golden blade, and from the same hook, what appeared to be a plain golden cup on a leather strap.

Japhis strode to the center of the room and announced, "This is Felicity, she's a Quester and a friend of mine, and that's all any of you little pry-secrets need to know. I hereby declare a half-holiday. School is adjourned!"

"You shouldn't—" Felicity began, setting her staff and shoulder bag near the door.

"I should," Japhis said, then added more quietly, "You didn't come visiting without Glee to hear me teach letters, the Gordian trade tongue, or the history of the bad King Yenzla." The latter sentence was lost in the children's cheers. Japhis called, "I expect each of you to fill your slate with an essay about teachers who spoil their charges by granting unannounced holidays!"

"Yes, Mayor," the children answered in unison.

"Then you may go."

The children left quickly, bowing to Japhis and Felicity as they passed. Felicity used the time to study Japhis. She was heavier than Felicity remembered, though her stride was still sprightly. The naked stump of her right arm was smooth and brown, almost as if a hand had never been there. He face was lightly lined from age or weather, her hair had dulled somewhat, and she squinted as if she did not see as well as she once did, but Felicity thought she had never seen Japhis happier.

"Tea?" Japhis asked.

"Please."

As Japhis poured warm tea from a green ceramic pot into two matching cups, Felicity said, "How's Villel?"

"Happy enough, though he wishes I'd let someone else be mayor."

"Oh?"

Japhis raised her cup in salute. "He thinks the village takes too much of my life. He thinks he and I and Lizelle should be freer of duty, to have time to do nothing, to travel. . . ." She smiled. "He'd go crazy, and so'd I. I think he just wants more children, but I say one's enough. He wants another, he can carry it in his stomach this time."

They laughed together, and Felicity regretted her mission.

"Here, sit," Japhis said, pushing an orange cat from a chair near the brick oven. "That's Underfoot. Lizelle thinks we should name it Underbutt."

"How is she?"

"Underfoot? Oh." Japhis pursed her lips. "Lizelle. I don't know. She seems strange for an eight-year-old, but then, children are strange at any age, and adults worse, eh? She'll sit about doing nothing at all for hours if I don't give her a task, and she's much too fond of her ability to lie."

"That's not good."

"No," Japhis agreed. "But I don't think it's bad, either. Villel thinks if we indulge her, she'll grow out of it." Japhis set her cup aside. "Why'd you come? Not to hear about my cat or my child, I'm certain."

Felicity placed her cup beside Japhis's. "No. We need you."

"You and Glee?"

"No. The Order."

Japhis snorted and shook her head. "I'm hardly the sort of priest you want. Harj is happy enough in City Gordia. One Kardeck should be enough for you."

"It's not so simple, Japhis. You know the prophecy about the Tangled Lands?"

"Three must go and one will die? Sure."

"We think you're one of the Three."

For a moment, Felicity thought Japhis had not heard her. Japhis was watching the cat asleep on its back in a spot of sunlight, with its legs outspread as if it had been dropped from the top of World's Peak. Then she lifted her cup and sipped, and returned the cup to the table. Still watching the cat, she said, "I can't go."

"You must."

"You can't ask me."

Felicity swallowed. "I must."

"Why didn't Glee come?"

"Because of his blindness."

Japhis glanced at her. "He travels well enough with company."

"Because he did not want to remind you that he lost his sight because he helped you, after you'd lost your title and your lands. He didn't think it was fair to make that part of your decision."

Japhis's eyes flicked to her wrist and back to Felicity. "But you don't mind reminding me."

"Of course I mind it!" Felicity breathed deeply. The Order should have sent someone far more skilled in diplomacy. "Glee doesn't hold you responsible. Nor do I. I blame him for insisting that if anyone must be punished, he would take full responsibility. But if you still feel responsible . . ."

Japhis finished the thought: "I could agree to go to ease my conscience."

"I don't care why you agree, Japhis. But you must. It's the world we speak of."

Japhis nodded slowly. "You're sure I'm one of the Three?"

"No. But the Inner Circle is sure. Glee is sure. That's enough."

"Could you wait for another champion?"

"Of course. But we might wait forever. And we know the demons grow stronger every day they remain in our world. The Tangled Lands grow more every day."

"They won't reach the mountains for centuries."

Felicity shrugged. "Perhaps a century. You and I'll be dead. Lizelle may be dead. But do we abdicate responsibility simply because we can?"

"I don't care about fancy sentiments, Felicity. This is my home."

"Yes. You should protect it."

Japhis shook her head. "I'm no one's champion, Felicity.

I'm Lizelle's mother and Villel's mate and Foxhome's mayor. You're asking me to leave all three?"

Felicity nodded.

"To go unprepared into the Tangled Lands."

"Glee went. He was one of the three Gordian brothers who went forty years ago. He'll tell you what he learned—"

"He failed," Japhis said quietly, looking down.

"Yes. You haven't."

"I tried to defeat a demon once. The Korz Demon, after you cared for me, after this." She held up her wrist. "I failed there."

"You were young and unprepared."

"Now I'm old and unable."

Felicity stood, her patience exhausted. "Hear yourself, girl! You're not old, and you're not unable! I'd go myself if the damn signs said I might win, but they don't, so all I can do is convince you!" She closed her eyes and felt herself breathing quickly. When she opened them again, Japhis was staring at the knife on the wall. "Please," Felicity said. "Don't make me fail in this."

"I have duties," Japhis said. "We're going to irrigate new lands this summer. It'll double our harvest. I'm the only one who has the time and the desire to teach the children. My daughter needs me. Villel..." She shook her head slowly. "Villel and I could be apart, but why should we? Because you believe some silly prophecy, you're asking me to throw away a good life for a stupid death?"

Felicity raised her hands, wanting to grab Japhis and shake her until she saw the limits of her vision. But the issue was not one of vision, it was one of faith. Felicity let her hands fall to her sides. She could do nothing but continue to reason, though she had to appeal to something greater than reason to win. "I've always thought of you as my daughter. It's presumptuous, I know. But—"

Japhis stood, her face sad and surprised, her arms reaching out. "Oh, Felicity, I—"

"No!" Felicity stepped back. "I don't want—" She began again. "I'm not here because of an obligation to the Questers or to Glee. I'm here because I love you and our world. I don't know if you can succeed. But I know no one else can. Even if you fail, you may be able to return, like Glee, with the knowledge that you tried."

"It's too much." Japhis shook her head. "You ask too much."

"Then I've failed?"

"Felicity, I wish . . ."

"I've failed." Felicity nodded. "Glee should've come."

"No!" Smiling sadly, Japhis said, "No, it wouldn't have mattered. I owe you so much for the past, and I may owe so much to the future, but don't I owe something to the present, too? Futures change, Felicity. You can't know what the demons want, or who might come along to deal with them. But it's not me. I'm sorry."

"I am, too." Felicity turned toward the door.

"Could you stay?"

"Would it change anything?"

"No."

Felicity shrugged. "I'm out of arguments, but I've nothing else worth saying. It's a long walk back." She reached for her traveling bag and staff.

"Felicity?"

She turned. Japhis stood in the center of the room, a prosperous middle-aged woman in her cheery, attractive home.

After a moment, Japhis said, "Would you do differently?"

"If I were you? Would you change your mind, if I said I would?"

Japhis smiled. "No."

Felicity nodded once. "Give up everything I loved because a crazy old woman said I could save the world? No, probably not." She slung the bag onto her shoulder. "But for the sake of the world, I wish I would."

11

Acts of Love

Kevin sat in the middle of the Reading Room. He had modeled it after the auditorium of Radio City Music Hall, and sometimes he peopled it with thousands of spectators. Today, he sat alone in the shadows, watching public messages from his favorite subject forums scroll in giant letters across the screen. He had abandoned the Civil War section of the U.S.A. forum and begun to browse Japanization when Prompt, in a silver usher's uniform, appeared beside him and handed him a phone. Placing it to his ear, he heard Prompt's voice through the receiver: "Private. CO? J. Laias."

Not Prompt's voice. Janny's. He could not think what to say.

"Or are you busy?" The difference between Janny's voice and Prompt's was not one of tone or pitch, but of emotion. Janny's had a reluctance, a politeness, that could have been a mask for shyness. "Call me later, if so. J. Laias."

"Private," he sent back. "No. CO sounds great. Now? Kid Flash."

"Now. J. Laias."

Laias CO, he thought, and flickered out of the Reading Room.

Janny waited on a featureless beige plane, illuminated by

154

a dim haze of light. She wore loose black coveralls that undu-
lated as though she were a tiny planet and they were a turbu-
lent sea of black oil. Her head, hands, and feet were bare.
When she moved, her hair floated as if she were underwater.
Her eyes were brown, a little lighter than her hair.

He arrived in faded copper jeans, a turtleneck of silver
mesh, and black canvas-and-rubber sneakers fastened with
blood-red laces. "Janny?"

She laughed and indicated herself with an inward flick of
her fingers. "Who else would show up looking like this?"

Prompt, he thought in answer, but he only shrugged.

Yes? Prompt whispered.

I didn't call— Wait. That's really Janny?

Jennifer Krystal Laias. Yes.

Thanks. "It's good to see you. I mean, away from *Lands*."

"Well . . ." She looked at the horizon, toward the seam of
blank ground and blank sky, then glanced back at him.
"There's nothing left to do with the game, I think. Except fix
it."

He nodded, wondering why she had called him and not
daring to mention that for fear she would leave. "I thought
you'd be getting some sleep. Before the big run."

"I thought you'd be, too. But I noticed you in the net." She
looked away, avoiding his eyes. "System's instructed to
tell me when people I like are jacked in."

"Ah." To say something, anything, he said, "I used to do
that, but not anymore. It got distracting, having people's
names announced while I was doing stuff. Reading messages,
playing games. Like that."

"Ditto. There's only a few people I keep on my notification
list."

"Oh?" He felt himself begin to blush, and, to cover,
changed his clothes to those of a wealthy eighteenth-century
European nobleman. He bowed with an extravagant flourish;
white lace swirled nicely from the sleeve of his gold silk
jacket. "Milady's too kind."

She smiled, suddenly in a gown and coiffure worthy of
Marie Antoinette, and curtsied. "Milady's a sucker for guys
with nice legs."

"Do tell?" He flickered into sixteenth-century white tunic

and black tights, and then back to metallic jeans and turtle-neck. "I get embarrassed."

Janny laughed. "Silly boy. What would you've done if I'd said you had a nice ass?"

He switched to a white Greek chiton and sandals, then, blushing, back to the jeans.

Janny shook her head. "You're such a tease."

"You like that—" He bulked himself into a tanned, mus-cled beachboy in a tiny red bathing suit, then let his forearms and jaw swell, his chest and upper arms grow impossibly thin. A sailor's cap appeared on his bald head, and a corncob pipe in his mouth.

"Oh, Popeye!" Olive Oyl, in yards and yards of a billow-ing 1930s bathing suit, tucked her chin and batted her huge eyes at him.

"Uh . . ." Kevin returned to his earlier form in his earlier clothes.

Olive Oyl became Janny again, who touched his arm. "Too silly?"

"Yes," he said. "No, not really. I just—" He shrugged, glancing at his feet.

"You seemed to be enjoying yourself."

He looked at her, held her gaze, and nodded. "A little too much."

"Oh."

He swallowed, then said, "Are your eyes really brown?"

She nodded.

"Why the contacts, all the time?"

"Brown's so boring."

"Are you kidding? You've got great eyes."

She turned into a leering cartoon wolf. "The better to see you with, my dear."

He almost became a Howard Pyle Red Riding Hood, but decided that would make him extremely uncomfortable, what-ever Janny might think of it. He said, "Janny?"

The wolf nodded, then said, "Oh," and became Janny again.

Trying to sound perfectly casual, Kevin said, "What're we doing?"

"I don't know." She spoke as calmly as he hoped he had sounded. "I like you."

"I like you," he replied, seconding an unspoken proposition.

"I don't want to hurt Mad Dog."

Kevin looked away, then put a remorseless sun high in a naked blue sky. White sands, bright and barren, stretched to the horizon in every direction. "Uh huh."

The surf of a sea that was not of his making roared beside them. Gulls cried overhead; a cottage of bamboo and thatch stood in the dunes nearby. "But I do like you," Janny said, placing a hand on his chest. He felt her begin to alter his electronic reality, and, wanting to trust her, he did not resist. Their clothes disappeared.

He could misunderstand, if he wanted to, and they could go swimming as any friends might. He put his arms around her waist. Her scent was of salt and roses. Her skin was very warm under his hands; the curves of her back were paradoxically soft and firm, infinitely delightful. He glanced at the cottage and back into her bare brown eyes. "You want to go in?"

She laughed and nodded. "Beaches are badly overrated, m'dear."

He grinned, kissed her lightly on the lips, then held her away from him. He wanted to ask her any number of questions, but could only make himself ask one. "It doesn't matter, here?"

She shook her head, and her hair brushed his shoulders. "It always matters, Kev."

"Good," he said, and picking her up, carried her toward the open door of the cottage.

A fan of brass and wood turned lazily in the rafters above them. Its hum reminded Kevin of Bytehenge, and he considered asking Janny what had inspired it. The bed and armchair were of varnished wicker. Photos of smiling aviators and ancient airplanes were on the wall, along with primitive wooden masks and spears with barbed bone points. The cottage seemed a construct from black-and-white films of the early twentieth century, when romantic Caucasians could flee civilization's responsibilities, only to find love and purpose with a fellow Caucasian romantic. If he wanted nothing more than fun, Kevin would have created a cheerful houseboy to hurry into their bedroom, offering good liquor with a Hollywood Third-Worlder's bad English.

Instead, he pushed down the coarse cotton sheets, which felt too warm on his body, and looked at Janny's torso. She brought her arm across her breasts, saying, "I probably should've made a lot of little fixes—"

"No way." He kissed the back of her wrist and tugged it gently from her chest, draping her hand on his shoulder. "You're gorgeous."

"You're incorrigible."

He lifted his eyebrows high. "So what're you waiting for? Encourage me."

She touched his nose with the tip of her forefinger and wiggled it from side to side, then giggled. "Are you this exuberant off the jack?"

"You could find out."

Her head shook in a tight, fast pattern. "We shouldn't."

"Shouldn't've done this, either."

"It was just once." Her tone was almost pleading, but she seemed to be trying to convince herself, not him . . . or so he told himself. "Like Oscar Wilde said. The only way to resist temptation is to give in to it."

"You're not tempted to meet again? Just on the jack, maybe?" He touched her sternum, which was slick with sweat. "I won't be too pushy, but—" He realized what he had said, and laughed. "No. I'll be pushy as hell."

Her expression remained serious. "I've got to think about it, Kev."

"Don't get"— He stroked her right nipple with his forefinger —"too cerebral."

She swatted the back of his hand lightly, but he saw she was annoyed. He moved his hand down to her stomach as she said, "If all I wanted was neural stimulation, I would've jacked into a sex channel."

"Sorry."

"Well—" She shrugged, then kissed his nose. "Let's try to keep this light, okay? Mad Dog and I get, oh, impatient with each other, but it doesn't mean we're through. And even if we are, I don't want to leap from him to you, just to have someone around."

He nodded solemnly. "Yeah. I have a Freud Four, too.

Maybe my therapy AI should check with your therapy AI. Maybe they could have an affair for us."

"Kevin."

He heard the warning and nodded. "You're right. We'll keep it light." He canceled the gravity and gave her a gentle shove.

She shrieked and laughed, snatching at the sheet as she drifted toward the open window. The sheet, which was not tucked in, had no observable effect on her trajectory. She reached for the upper windowsill to anchor herself, so he made the wall swing open on silent hinges, as if the cottage were concealment for a missile silo in a bad vid plot. She laughed again, saying, "You bastard!"

A cloud drifted across the sun, which must have been her doing, to reduce the glare in her eyes as she floated. He created a crimson and white Flash Gordon flying suit for himself, with a bronze jetpack and a silly silver pistol at his hip, and launched after her. When he came close, she snapped her fingers, and his archaically futuristic outfit shredded into a cloud of feathers. They drifted together toward the sky.

A globe of warm air enclosed them as the planet of blue waters and yellow sand dwindled into a bright dot against stars and black space. The bedsheet still partially draped them, perhaps because it reminded them of the cottage. Kevin imagined they must look like skinny Rubens angels and smiled, thinking this was one of the rare, perfect moments that he would happily prolong forever.

"I really should go off-line," Janny said.

Mad Dog's waiting up, Kevin realized. He considered making them appear in a cheap motel room, but Janny might not think that was funny. Before he could decide, he felt Janny act. They were standing in an airport departure lounge. They wore conservative traveling clothes, and anonymous people scurried by, ignoring them. Kevin laughed, and Janny smiled proudly. "Well." She reached to hug him farewell.

"The game's important to you," he said, partly because he didn't want her to leave and this was the first topic that he could think of, partly because he wanted to hear her say that it didn't matter, that he could sell out *Lands of Adventure* to Enter-Tech with only a modicum of guilt.

"Of course," she said in surprise. "Isn't it to you?"

"It's fun. But it's a job, too."

She shook her head, fluffing the cloud of her hair. "Not to me."

"It's a chance to prove yourself?"

She smiled. "Janny Laias, project director for *Lands of Adventure*?"

He nodded.

"It was, when I started. But now it's the world that's important." She looked bashful. "I'm its God. I didn't think that meant anything, before I started dreaming in there, but now it's like I'm sharing my soul with every character the main program creates. The world's more real than I am."

"Ah."

"I feel guilty about it, sometimes. Maybe things with Mad Dog wouldn't have gotten so strange if I wasn't so obsessed with *Lands*."

"Maybe you wouldn't be so obsessed if things hadn't gotten strange with Mad Dog."

She shook her head. "I don't know. Maybe the more you love, the more you can love. But there's only so much time, even on-line in fast-time. And there's the game, there's my family, there's Mad Dog, there's my friends . . ." She smiled at him. "And there's you. I don't—" She bit her lip, then said quickly, "I don't like a lot of responsibility, Kevin."

"Me, neither." He held both hands up in the air. "I promise you, Janny, no pressure."

She nodded, then squinted suspiciously. "If you shut down the atmosphere, I'll make sure we both explode."

He smiled. "Damn."

After a moment, she said, "You're thinking about something."

He nodded, then made himself laugh. "No, not really. I was just wishing I had something to feel proud about, the way you feel about *Lands*."

She frowned, and gripped his upper arms as if to shake him. "It's your work, too. Even if the whole thing crashes with the Tangled Lands, it'll have been a great experiment. But it's not going to crash. When we save it, trust me, you'll feel proud. Not everyone gets to save a world." She hugged him then, and said, "We should get some sleep. See you tomorrow." After a quick kiss, she disappeared from the airport. No one noticed. After a moment, he exited, too.

Prompt, in a silver jumpsuit, said, "Function?"
"Don't look like Janny anymore. Or sound like her."
"What should I seem to be?"
"A cat. With Groucho Marx's voice."
"And his mannerisms?"
"Good God, no. Exiting."

He sat at a table in the Silver Socket, with his forearms resting on a wobbly table of clear lucite embedded with tiny toy cars and plastic soldiers. A chrome red jack cable, already disconnected, was in his right hand and a mug of Leinenkugel's was in his left. A partially eaten bratwurst sat next to his beer. The room smelled faintly of stale cigarette smoke, alcohol, and North American fried food, the Thursday night special. The Socket was perhaps half-filled with silent customers, all plugged into shiny metallic ceiling cables. He liked the bar when people were talking, and he liked jacking here, where he could come off-line and see something besides his small apartment. But when everyone was jacking, he invariably imagined that the inhabitants of the hothead ward had been propped about the room.

He drank half his beer, walked to the phone, jammed in his credit card, and punched a number from memory. Someone answered on the second ring: "Urm?"

"Bri?" Kevin said. "I wake you?"

"No." Brian made a quick, high-pitched laugh. "Not exactly."

"Oh. Sorry to interrupt."

"S'right. Important?"

"Well . . ."

"That means yes?"

"Yes," Kevin admitted. "Want to get some coffee, or something?"

"You need to talk."

"Well . . ."

"I do hope you're more communicative in person. C'mon over and I'll put the pot on."

"Thanks."

"S'right. You remember the new address?"

"I think so."

"Good. Give me twenty—" Kevin heard a distant slap and a laugh, and, delivered away from the speaker, Brian's "Do you mind? No, of course you don't," followed by, "Uh, an hour, okay?"

"'Kay. Bye." Kevin hung up the pay phone and looked around the Silver Socket. Moxie, without turning toward him, lifted her hand in what might have been a wave, so he nodded toward her, then stuck his credit card back into the phone.

Gwen answered on the first ring. "H'lo"

"Hi, it's Kevin."

"Kevin! How're you?"

"A little drunk."

"Ah. What's wrong?"

"Nothing much."

"Uh huh. That's why you phoned."

"No. I wanted to know if you'd reconsider working on Janny's World."

"Um. She ask you to ask me?"

"No. I don't know if she's thought past solving the Tangled Lands problem. There'll be lots of tweaks to do, then."

"If you solve the Tangled Lands."

"No prob. Janny and I go in tomorrow. We'll just keep playing it until we win."

"Until you lose, you mean."

"No. Whenever we get stuck, we'll just revert to the back-up and try again. It may take a while, but it'll be a breeze."

"If there's a solution."

"Yeah," he admitted.

"Who's playing the third?"

"You. If you're willing."

He listened to a long silence, then Gwen laughed. "You got balls, son. I told you—"

"You were pissed. That's cool. I think the game's salvage-able. I think Janny might've even made it a little more inter-esting when she dreamed on the design path." He hesitated, wanting a simple way to explain something he did not understand.

"Just say it, son."

"You'll think I'm crazy."

"You're a goddamn jacker, Kev. 'Course you're crazy. What do you mean, more interesting?"

"It's the psych programs that Mad Dog used, or maybe it's Janny's dreams, or maybe it's both, but the thing's more than a game."

Gwen snorted. "Knew that. Told Omari that was a feature."

"No. I mean, it's more than the chance to live in a fantasy world. The computer's creating analogs for the players. At least, it did for me."

"That's also what it's supposed to do, son."

"No. I mean, direct analogs, not just player characters. Like, I've fucked things up gigabad—" He continued quickly so she wouldn't ask what he meant by that. "So the program gave me a character who's fucked things up gigabad. A character who's got a second chance to make things right, at a time when I wanted a second chance. Scared me when it happened, but now it's kind of encouraging."

"You're saying the program's given you a message?"

"Not exactly. But a chance to look at things differently, to realize it might not be too late to change."

"Be depressing as hell if your character blows his second chance, won't it?"

"Well, yeah."

"And maybe you're feeling better because other things are going well?"

"Like what?"

"Like the game not being as screwed as we'd feared—"

"We don't know that for sure," Kevin said. "But it looks a lot better from the inside than I expected. I thought it'd be Salvador Dali meets the Brothers Hildebrandt, or worse. But it's consistent. Weird, but consistent."

"Okay. I'm glad to hear that. For your sake." Gwen snorted. "Hell, for everyone's sake." More gently, she said, "Things are going better, Kev?"

He nodded, realized she could not see that, and said, "Yeah. I think so. Really."

"Then don't read too much into a stupid fucked-up computer game, okay?"

"It's not stupid."

"Fine. Don't read too much into a smart fucked-up computer game, okay?"

He laughed. "Thank you, Gwendolyn."

"Don't sweat it. Someday I'll call you up in the middle of the night with a mystical revelation, and you can be patient with me."

"Deal. You'll run the third in the game?"

He waited; at last, she said, "Sure. The new job doesn't start for a week. Janny asks me, I'll run the third. Starting early?"

"You damn betcha. It may take a while."

"Shit. Okay. The crack of noon, then."

"Good. See you." He hung up the receiver and returned to his table. He ignored the bratwurst, took a couple of drinks of the beer, then decided to walk to Brian's.

The autumn air was cool and sobering. As he walked under the street lights, he watched storefront display windows and remembered the last part of his conversation with Janny. No promises had been made, nor should they have been, but he felt calm and confident and capable. He would save the game for her, regardless of the cost. And if he succeeded, perhaps she would save his life.

The Inner Circle gathered on the roof of the Questers' temple to hear Felicity's report. The morning was clear and windy; a herd of clouds like fat white sheep scurried across the sky toward the Cities of Man. Tyrwilka's cedar shingles and red clay tiles reflected sunlight like five thousand tiny pools of water, mimicking the distant brightness of Lake Tyrwilka. Serenity sat cross-legged on a thin pillow with his eyes closed, appreciating the heat on his lids, attempting to meditate while he waited for his fellows to settle about him.

When the roof was quiet, he opened his eyes. Eight humans and a clip-eared Elf in black robes sat to either side of him in the circle. Felicity faced him. Her long gray hair was tied behind her neck, and her robes were still dusty from her travel. The lines of her face might suggest contentedness to someone who did not know her, but he knew what he would hear before he asked, "Her answer?"

"No," Felicity replied, and looked down.

"You bear no blame."

"I did not succeed."

"You did all you could."

He did not mean it as a question, but she said, "Yes."

"Then you bear no blame."

"How can we succeed?" Her voice sounded unusually young and desperate.

"By continuing," he answered with more certainty than he felt, and turned to the Elf. "Are there any other candidates?"

"No." The Elf's precise Gordian was beautiful to hear. Her eyes were the pale blue of the southern horizon at sunrise on a cloudless day. "These seem to be the last who could make a Three." She hesitated. "Our studies suggest this is the last year in which they might become a Three."

"As do ours," Serenity admitted.

"If there will be other candidates, they come in years far after ours. No wizard of Faerie can sense hope of future saviors. Can any human mage?"

"No."

"Perhaps that only means these Three may yet act."

"You know the third, then?"

The Elf shook her head; hair as light in color and weight as a dandelion puff rippled about her shoulders. "The unicorns know, but they run and do not tell. The First of Unicorns has said that if the two go, the third will join them."

"It's hardly comforting," Glee said from his place beside Felicity.

"It's enough," Serenity answered. "Davin will go?"

"Yes," Glee said. "He is not . . . resolute. But he will go. I think he'll find he's stronger than he believes."

"We can hope." Serenity turned to a tiny, balding Gordian woman. "The preparations are complete?"

The Gordian nodded, then rocked forward to raise a red cloth from a small bundle on the tiles before her. An intricately carved wand of bone lay on a pillow, with a black leather holster beside it. The wand was as long as a human forearm, and tapered from a thick handgrip to a sharp, curved point. "The horn that the unicorns sent us. I included as many protective runes from as many traditions as I could remember when I worked it, though I doubt any will add to its potency." She reached into a pocket of her robe, then brought out three circles of the same yellow bone, each dangling from a leather cord. "I made necklaces from the excess. Japhis may have her own defenses, and I trust the third will, too, but these might give each of the Three some extra advantage."

"Will any of this help?" asked a tall, middle-aged man whose ruddy hair was braided in the fashion of the North. He was the youngest of the Circle. Sometimes his impatience exasperated Serenity, sometimes it delighted him.

Serenity shrugged. "The unicorn's horn symbolizes purity and truth. The demons are corruption and lies given form and power. The horn may not help in battle, but it might help the Three see past the demons' illusions." He glanced at Felicity. "Japhis still has her defenses?"

"The knife and the wrist-case? Yes. But she doesn't have the spirit."

Serenity glanced at the Elf. "We are not wrong?"

She moved her head confidently from side to side. "I do not believe it." Then her mouth quirked in indecision or repressed pain. "If we are wrong about Japhis, we are wrong to do anything."

"Perhaps we are." The Northern man glanced at the Elf. "Faerie has retreated to the far side of the mountains we call The Wall. Humanity retreats from the Tangled Lands, too, if not so quickly or so far."

"It is caution, not cowardice," the Elf said carefully.

The Northerner shrugged. "That does not matter. My point is that the world is large. Perhaps demons and humans and elves could all exist here. Perhaps we can grant the demons the lands they need—"

"Until when?" The small Islander's voice was quick and shrill and angry; her calm face seemed a mask over her fury. "Until this world is theirs, and we must make our way to the moon? Will the demons stop then? Will the Tangled Lands follow us beyond the world? If we die and do not stop the demons, will they conquer the afterworld next?"

"You cannot know," the Northern man said.

"Exactly." She nodded once in quick satisfaction. "So we must stop them, so we will know."

Serenity raised a hand before the Northerner could respond. "We've all resolved to act. The only question remaining is how to carry out our resolve."

"Did you offer her money?" the Gordian sculptor asked Felicity.

Felicity looked at the blind priest beside her, who seemed to sense her discomfort. Glee reached for Felicity's wrist, squeezed it, and said, "Japhis has had wealth. She treasures subtler things now."

"Her family?" asked the Northern man.

"Her home," Glee answered.

The Elf smiled. "Ah."

"We could offer money to her people, then," the Gordian suggested. "We could give something to her family or her village."

"Her family prospers," Felicity said. "So does her village."

"I have met her mate," Glee added. "If she went without him, he would follow."

"Three cannot be four," the Elf said.

Felicity's face flickered in exasperation, but Serenity merely agreed, "No."

"If the prophecy is wrong?" the Islander asked.

"It's not." Very simply, without pride, the Gordian woman explained. "I called a demon once, and questioned it. It claimed to understand the prophecy no better than we do, but it claimed to believe it."

"Perhaps the demon lied," the Northern man suggested.

"Then we know nothing," Serenity said. "Then there are neither rules nor hope."

"Why would they submit to binding, if there are no rules?" the Gordian woman asked. "Why would the Tangled Lands grow so slowly, if the demons could take whatever they wanted?"

"The God made order when She made the world." The Islander looked around the Circle. "We may not know the Pattern, but even demons are bound by it."

"Or so we assume," Serenity said. "So we must assume." He turned to the Elf. "You trust the unicorns regarding the third?"

"That there is a third?" She nodded. "Unicorns do not lie. That the third could succeed?" She shrugged. "Who knows a unicorn's whim?"

Serenity sighed. The morning was beautiful. The Inner Circle were his true family. He would enjoy this day as best he could, in contemplation and conversation. "Tell Davin to leave for Foxhome and the Tangled Lands tomorrow. I'll depart then, too, but I'll travel faster than he."

The Elf glanced toward him. "Oh?" Her tone was wonderfully casual; a human actor might not master it in a lifetime. One thin eyebrow plucked in an Elfin arch lifted almost imperceptibly.

He smiled at her. "Japhis will be ready to accompany him, when he arrives in Foxhome."

"Ah." The Elf's nod was as subtle as her raised eyebrow. Perhaps Serenity looked for approval in her expression, but he thought he saw respect.

Serenity left the next dawn without saying goodbye to anyone. He took one of the Order's best bottles of wine, then used the language he had almost forgotten to transport himself from a Tyrwilkan basement to the woods near Foxhome. He arrived in a cloud of smoke and dust and swirling leaves. The smoke was customary to impress watchers; Serenity included the effect from habit. He did not expect or want watchers. The dust and swirling leaves proved that his skill had decreased since he had joined the Questers. He coughed as he stumbled out of the accidental whirlwind, then swatted most of the leaves and dust from his hair and robes.

He found a clearing on a low hill that let him look over the village where Japhis Kardeck lived. A haze hung above the Fastwater and around the cabins closest to the river. Tendrils of smoke, no darker than the haze, rose lazily from almost every home. A few people and many animals scurried about; Serenity heard occasional human voices mix with those of pigs and goats and chickens to create a music that was rustic and comforting.

He had left a village much like this one to join the Questers. His farm had been prosperous, and in his way, he had loved his wife and children, but he had needed more profound truths than pleasant existence. His family had never understood that there were times when all solutions were painful.

He placed his wine bottle on the ground, then took a vial from his pocket. The glass had been melted at the neck to seal in a clear liquid, but when Serenity spoke again in the First Tongue, the clear liquid disappeared. He dug up a clump of grass, placed the empty vial in the hole he had created, and stomped the heel of his boot onto it, breaking the glass and driving the fragments deep into the dirt. That done, he replaced the clump of grass. When it had been tamped back into the ground, the earth appeared never to have been disturbed.

From the same pocket that had held the vial, he removed a smooth gray oval stone wrapped in a handkerchief. Lifting the folds of the handkerchief, he spoke a third time in the odd syllables of the True Language, and the world shimmered about him. He peered into the stone. Its atoms seemed to evaporate as a picture formed within its depths.

He recognized Japhis Kardeck's house from Felicity's description. He waited. A small, dark-haired girl of six or seven ran into the house with a basket that probably held this morning's eggs. She must be the daughter, Lizelle. Half an hour later, the small girl left again, now wearing a red cloak, followed immediately by Japhis Kardeck in a cloak of the same red dye. Serenity looked up from the stone to the road that led from Foxhome.

Japhis and Lizelle called at several houses, gathering seven or eight adult villagers, all bundled in cloaks of various hues. To Serenity's unaided eye, they were only a band of shadows that walked toward the village fields, but when he looked back into the scry stone, he could see each of them distinctly. Lizelle was thin, darker than her mother, and somber-faced; she ran ahead and waited for the group to come near, then ran farther ahead. Japhis's attention stayed with the villagers. Serenity could see her speak, but could not hear her words. She seemed to be explaining the morning's work, and periodically gestured excitedly from the fields toward the river.

When the road had taken Japhis and her company beyond Foxhome and the hill where Serenity waited, he looked again into the stone. No one had left Japhis's house, or entered it. Serenity stood awkwardly, dropped the stone into his pocket, picked up his wine bottle, and walked into the village.

He did not hesitate before Japhis's house; its appearance within the scry stone was sufficient to assure him of his destination. He stepped onto the porch, rapped briskly, and waited.

The stout man who opened the door was not young, though he was obviously less than half Serenity's age. His height and visage were not remarkable, but his features were pleasant and his simple woolen clothing was clean. A sprinkling of gray showed in his brown hair, but not in his beard. He frowned at the priest, saying, "Yes?"

"Villel Mayorsmate?"

The man nodded. "So I'm known."

"I'm called Serenity, of the Order of the Quest. May I come in?"

Villel's squint moved from Serenity's face to a point beyond his shoulder, then back again. He shrugged. "As you will. I doubt you've a harness needing mending, or a belt to commission."

Serenity smiled a little, shook his head, and stepped into the cabin's living room. "I don't have work for you, but I have an offer."

"Oh?" Villel glanced at the bottle Serenity carried.

"It regards Japhis."

"She told me one of you'd been by. Had a mad proposition, she said." He gestured toward the fireplace. "Something to drink? The kettle's on."

Seeing a stool by the wall, he moved it out and sat. "We want Japhis to be one of the Three."

Villel squatted on the edge of the raised lip of the hearth. "Eh. That madness."

"Why do you say—"

"Where are they, these demons you talk of?" Villel waved both arms. "When do they come here to the borderlands?"

"You've heard—"

"Ten thousand stories." Villel nodded and grinned, and Serenity saw that Villel was still a handsome man, with a charm that seemed only a little self-conscious. "Who'd believe them all?"

"You don't think the demons exist?"

Villel laughed. "Not at all. But I have my doubts concerning prophecies about the Three, and even if they're true, Japhis isn't meant by them."

"Oh?"

"She's had an unusual life, but she's not an unusual person."

Serenity turned his head dismissingly. "I could quibble, but I'll grant that. What makes you think—"

"She's my woman!" Villel stabbed his forefinger at Serenity. "I know her!" He shook himself, as if shaking away his anger. "Why do you come to me, anyway?"

"Perhaps you could convince her."

"To leave her home and duties on some mad mission?"

"To save the world."

Villel stared at Serenity, then rocked back and laughed.

Serenity said, "We could pay you."

Villel's smile said he was humoring a madman. "How much?"

Serenity reached into his pocket and withdrew a pouch. While Villel watched, he untied the pouch and spilled coins on the hearth.

"Twenty royals? That's hardly—"

Serenity sighed. "Ten times that, if it'll make a difference."

Villel's features smoothed themselves into a mask of calm. After a long moment, he said, "You're paying me to give up my woman. To send her off to the demon lands, to die or be enslaved. . . ."

Serenity nodded. "Or to succeed."

Villel stroked his beard several times. "If I asked for a hundred times that?"

Serenity nodded again. "For the world, any price is cheap."

Villel turned toward a window. Beyond the thick glass, a young man and young woman, laughing together, passed in the lane with wooden rakes on their shoulders. Villel's brow furrowed. He moved his chin as if to speak, then finally said, Fifty thousand royals."

"Twenty is the best we could do."

"I thought you said—"

Serenity made himself smile. "Any price would be cheap. Twenty thousand would be possible, though the Order might never recover from such a price."

Villel raised an eyebrow.

"But we would pay it," Serenity said.

"Eh."

"We could not get it all to you at once."

"How quickly?"

"Five thousand now. Five thousand each month for the next three months."

"No," Villel said softly.

"That's all we can pay."

Villel laughed. "I believe you."

"And if we'd had the fifty thousand?"

Villel snorted. "Not even then, I pray."

"You're sure?" Serenity asked hopefully.

"Yes. Sure too there'll be times I'll regret this, but I'm sure. She's a good woman."

"So I believe." Serenity lifted his bottle of Lyrandol. "I'd brought this to celebrate success, but there's no reason to waste it."

Villel grinned. "That was forethoughtful. You were so sure I'd agree?"

"I thought I might want the wine," Serenity said carefully, "no matter what you answered." His sentence was punctuated by the tiny explosion of the freed cork.

Villel grabbed two green ceramic cups and held them out. "Wouldn't you despise me, if I'd agreed?"

Serenity shook his head. "Not at all. I'd pity you."

"Heh." Villel's humor seemed shaken, but not entirely displaced. "What of you, in that case? You came expecting to find my price. Or did you hope to fail?"

"I don't know." Serenity filled both cups, and the room smelled suddenly of wine and resin. "In either case, I'd despise myself."

"Do you?"

Serenity nodded.

"Poor man. This is what your belief has brought you to? Backroom bribery?" Villel gulped half his cup. "'S good. Lyrandol?"

Serenity sipped his own wine. "Yes. Small consolation." He sipped again, then refilled Villel's cup.

"Japhis said you Questers did not believe in intervening in the world's affairs. That's just your public face?"

"No. We do not believe in intervening needlessly."

"Ah." Villel downed his second cup of wine. "This is the best I've ever drunk."

Serenity nodded. "I'm glad you like it. But now I must apologize. I've poisoned you."

Villel frowned, then laughed. "You should give me poison like this every day."

"I'm serious. You'll die in ten minutes or so."

Villel grunted and glanced at Serenity. "I'm not amused."

"I wouldn't expect you to be." Serenity finished his wine, then refilled both their cups.

"No." Villel stood unsteadily. "I shouldn't get drunk. There's work to be done. I appreciate your wine, but not your whim—"

"No whim," Serenity said.

"Ah." Villel stumbled toward the door. "The Lyrandol's more potent than I thought." He seized the door latch. "I'll ask you—" He tugged furiously. "I'll ask you to—" He took the latch in both hands and wrenched; the door shivered but did not budge. "What—"

"I've sealed us in." Serenity stood. "It is magic. There's nothing you can do."

Villel stalked toward Serenity. "This is my home, priest. You have no right—"

"I know. Nor did I have any right to poison you, yet I did."

Villel's moustache twitched into a smirk. "Poison? Because I refused your offer?"

"It made no difference, whether you refused it or not."

Villel stared. "You're serious."

Serenity nodded.

Villel clutched his stomach, then said hesitantly, "I don't feel anything."

"It's a kinder poison than many I might have used. You'll fall asleep, then die."

"And then your magical barrier goes away?"

"Yes."

"You're serious," Villel repeated. "You've killed me—"

"Yes. For what it's worth, I'm sorry. Truly."

"You're sorry? You're sorry?" Villel laughed and threw himself back onto his seat on the edge of the hearth. He covered his face with both hands and gasped. "It's because of her."

"Not exactly." The conversation had taken a turn that Serenity did not understand. "It's just . . . simplest, this way. If I was wiser, or had more time, perhaps I could have found another solution."

"I love her." Villel dropped his hands. His eyes were wet with tears. "She loves me."

"I know."

"Does Japhis know?"

Serenity thought the poison had already affected Villel's reasoning. "I acted on my own. I couldn't burden anyone else with the responsibility."

"No." Villel leaned forward, catching Serenity's knee in a thick, strong hand. "About Lizelle and me."

"About—"

Villel's grip tightened. "Does she?"

Serenity squinted, and then, understanding what Villel must mean, he turned away. A doll made of rags and yarn lay in the corner. It wore a tiny red cloak. Serenity did not want to speak, but he made himself say, "No."

"Thank you," Villel said, his voice still weak. "I wouldn't hurt her. I wouldn't hurt either of them."

"You already—" Serenity checked himself. It did not matter; Villel would not be able to harm either of them, now. He felt an instant of angry vindication, as if the God had revealed this to him so he would know he had done the right thing. And that was followed by a sad disgust with himself. "I'm sorry," he whispered. "She'll never be able to forgive you. Even if she wants or needs to, she won't be able to."

"I don't understand," Villel said.

Serenity shook his head. "Perhaps someday, when she's older, she won't blame herself. Perhaps that'll be enough."

"What're you—"

"Nothing. Nothing you could understand in the minutes that remain." He had meant to be cruel, but he did not feel better when Villel began to blubber into his hands. He tried to see the strong man with compassion, but the image of the small, somber girl kept imposing itself. Perhaps Villel had been taught to be what he was, or perhaps he had learned this on his own, but in either case, Villel was an adult. The only definition that Serenity accepted was that adults were people who took responsibility for their actions.

If Serenity wanted to think himself an adult, he must do the same. "This has nothing to do with Lizelle. You're dying so Japhis will go to the Tangled Lands."

Villel's face soothed itself somewhat as self-pity gave way to confusion. "Japhis? Why would she—"

"She loves you." Serenity glanced at the man, then away. Children ran in the lane, tossing a muddy leather ball from hand to hand. "Don't ask me to explain why. She'll think the demons slew you, to get at her. And so she'll go into the Tangled Lands, to avenge you."

"Why'd she think that?"

"They'll find our untouched bodies in a house with doors and windows latched from within. What other enemies does she have, who would slay her husband and the Speaker of the Questers?" When Villel turned toward him, Serenity nodded. "Obviously, I came and convinced you that Japhis should go. Obviously, the demons killed us both. If she doesn't think of this, the Questers will, and they'll convince her. She'll need an answer. That one's simple enough."

"You're mad."

Serenity shook his head, then shrugged. "I don't know if it matters."

"You'll die too, then."

"The price I pay for what I've done." Serenity refilled their cups. "Drink up. It'll hurry this." He spoke a last time in the magician's tongue and sent the empty wine bottle far away, to the bottom of the deepest canyon of the Sunset Sea.

"Why'd you do that?"

"So there will be no clues. You've drunk more than I; you'll pass out first. I'll rinse our cups, then pour a bit of tea into the bottom of each." Thinking of the girl and Japhis's cat, Serenity added, "Then no one will be poisoned accidentally. And no one will find a more reasonable explanation for our deaths, either."

Villel closed his eyes. "And if I'd accepted your money?"

"I'm not sure. Perhaps I could have killed you in better conscience, then, but I doubt it. I think you would've had to die. If you sent her away, she might not go to the Tangled Lands. Now she'll hurry there."

"And if I'd fought you? Could I have made you cure me? Would I have found an antidote on your body?"

Serenity smiled. "I still exercise. And I am a magician. Trust me. You've done all you could have done, Villel."

Villel smiled back at him. "And more than I should have." He saluted Serenity with his cup, then drained the wine.

12

Dark Pursuer, Dark Prey

"Bri?" The entryway to Brian's condo was as spare and as bright as a spaceship's airlock. Kevin wondered if undesirables could be locked in here or gassed unconscious for the police. He tried to look prosperous and invited. "It's me."

"Damned informative." Brian's voice was followed by the inner doors swinging wide. Kevin walked into a lobby of low marble benches, burnished metal ashtrays, and a huge abstract mural in innocuous colors. Several uninspired brass clockwork nudes frolicked in tired imitation of youthful exuberance on the rim of a shallow pool filled with giant goldfish. The lobby existed to be passed through; he did.

An elevator with plush tan carpet and a faint odor of cigar smoke brought him to the thirty-seventh floor and a tiny entry room equipped with a leather-covered bench and a coat rack. Feeling as if he had entered a second, more exclusive elevator, he looked for a doorbell. The wooden door opposite him opened before he found one. Brian, smiling, wore a crimson silk robe, blue- and white-striped cotton pajamas, and leather slippers the color of mahogany. His hair was short and ruffled; a few strands fell over his forehead.

"Nice." Kevin pointed vaguely at Brian's chest. "Cary Grant?"

Brian glanced down, frowned, shook his head. "My bathrobe."

"I meant—" Kevin began, then saw Brian's grin. "Har-de-har."

Brian stepped back from the door. "Welcome to my house. Enter freely and of your own will." He grinned again.

"S'right. I gather you've already had your victim for the night." As Brian nodded smugly, Kevin stepped into a living room done primarily in shades of cream, accented by natural cherry woodwork. The far wall was entirely of glass, showing city lights extending to a distant horizon. Kevin whistled. "No wonder you moved. You've got the whole floor?"

Brian nodded. "There's no success like excess."

The furniture included sofas and chairs and low tables in bizarre, elongated shapes that were undoubtedly ergonomic when occupied. "High modern?"

"I think of it as Bowwow House." Brian continued through the living room and turned a corner, circling the elevator. "It's great for parties, but the sitting room's cozier."

"Uh huh." The sitting room, perhaps as large as Kevin's apartment, was dominated by brown leather chairs and dark green wallpaper. "In this place, you probably don't even have cozy closets." As Brian began to frown, Kevin said, "Joke, son. This is great."

Brian smiled and made a small bow. "Thank you. Cappuccino sweet, medium, or bitter?"

"In a cup with a handle is all I ask."

"Coming up." Brian started for the kitchen.

Kevin followed. "What, did you have to shoot the servants?"

"One does not shoot one's servants. One has one's servants shoot each other."

"Ah."

"I do have someone in to clean twice a week."

"Must be nice."

Brian shook his head. "It's embarrassing. I think the old rich are used to being cared for, but it makes me feel like I'm incapable, or lazy."

"I know what you mean," Kevin agreed. "Fortunately, I am incapable and lazy." Brian's laugh surprised him.

Most of the kitchen was so modern and utilitarian that

Kevin felt as if he had walked onto a set for an interior design show. At the far end, beneath a window, stood a wooden table and four wooden chairs painted with white enamel. Brian brought out two brown porcelain mugs, one chipped, that clashed with the slate-blue walls, which Kevin found vaguely consoling. He sat at the table while Brian played with the cappuccino machine.

Brian handed him a mug. "So, what do you want to talk about?"

"*Lands*. We're going to save it."

"Think you can?"

Kevin sipped his coffee. "Think we better. It's a shame to shit-can it when we're so close."

"Omari might not put it on-line, even if we fix it. It's . . . not what they're expecting."

"Fuck Omari. I want to do it for Janny."

"Janny."

Kevin nodded.

"I thought she and Mad Dog—"

"They're breaking up." Seeing Brian's surprise, he amended, "Well, they're having problems. And she and I, uh—"

"This is more than theoretical?"

"Yeah."

"Oh." Brian nodded sympathetically. "Sounds messy."

"Mad Dog doesn't know."

"Sounds extremely messy. Someone's going to tell him?"

"I don't know. We haven't worked it out yet." Kevin held his mug between the palms of both hands and stared at the head of milk froth and cinnamon. "I wish he wasn't crippled."

"Why? So you could have a nice manly fight over Janny? It never works that way."

"I know. I don't even know she'll leave him."

"You think he's got an advantage, being crippled? That that'll make her stay with him, 'cause she'll feel sorry for him?"

Kevin glanced at Brian. "Maybe."

Brian shook his head. "I don't think people stay with any-one solely out of pity. They might tell themselves that pity's why they stay, but we all lie to ourselves. And no one lies to us better than we do."

Kevin raised an eyebrow. "That from a fortune cookie or a video?"

Brian shrugged. "Okay, no generalizations. Janny's tough. She won't stay with someone out of pity, I don't think. I say that to encourage you, shithead, not to point out that if she stays with Mad Dog, it's because she prefers him."

"Thank you, Miss Lonelyhearts."

Brian smirked. "Hey, I'm cheaper than a Freud Four, and infinitely more tolerant."

"Yeah, well. So are you willing to come back to the project?"

"I don't know, Kev. I'm signing with Enter-Tech next week."

"There shouldn't be much more work left. Hell, there won't be any work for you if we don't save the Tangled Lands. But if we do, it'll need a few tweaks and cosmetic fixes to look less like a beta test and more like a version that's ready for release." While Brian hesitated, Kevin added, "Gwen's agreed. She'll do the Tangled Lands run with Janny and me."

Brian grinned. "Yeah? If you and the main designer can't beat it, no one can. And Gwen's certainly a better third than Michael or me." He nodded. "Sure, I can do it, if we can get it done this week. . . ."

"By Monday. Juan Takeda says we got to have it by deadline, or he'll lose all the support at Omari. He says they're really gung-ho on *ESPeeper*; the rest of the department think the fantasy craze won't last."

Brian nodded. "If the games don't get more interesting, they're probably right."

The kitchen door creaked slightly as it opened. "Oh, God, can't we escape games anywhere?" said Michael Hong. His queue fell over a red terry cloth robe. His legs and feet were bare.

"We didn't wake you?" Brian said, almost apologetically.

As Michael shook his head, Kevin said, "Up long?"

Michael looked at him, and his expression seemed perfectly alert. "Long enough to hear you're trying to salvage *Lands*."

Kevin shrugged. "Janny hasn't given up."

"I thought you had better things to do." Michael glanced at

Brian. "I thought we all had better things to do."

Brian laughed. "Oh, a few more days on the project won't hurt. If we get *Lands* going and it's a hit, you and I could take a nice long vacation. Maybe I won't accept Enter-Tech's offer after all."

"*Lands* is quite a gamble," Michael said dubiously. He placed his hand on Brian's shoulder and looked at Kevin. "Don't do anything foolish."

"Speaking of vacations," Kevin said, "I thought you were going to Buenos Aires."

"A change of plans." Michael sat in the chair beside Brian. "It seemed best to stick around here, until things were stable."

Brian smiled at Michael. "I'm glad."

Kevin nodded. "Yeah. It's sure great."

Michael smiled contentedly at him. "Is there any more work for me with *Lands*?"

Kevin shook his head. "I don't think so. I think everything's taken care of."

"You can handle it?"

Kevin nodded.

Michael's smile remained, polite and apparently effortless. "I'm glad. I hope you're right."

"So do I," Kevin said. "So do I." Michael would report to Frohn soon, perhaps tonight. Did that make any real difference in his plans? He thought not. He lifted his cup and returned Michael's smile. "I guess none of us'll know until after the Tangled Lands run, will we?"

When Lizelle was afraid that she might tell someone a secret she could never tell, she would hide until she felt stronger. Sometimes she swam to Gull Rock. This was forbidden, for Gull Rock was far from Foxhome, and a drowning swimmer's cries would never be heard. Sometimes she climbed the Mother Oak. This was forbidden because the Mother Oak was sacred to the priests of the Nine, and only priests and the First Caste were allowed near it. Sometimes she stole bread and cheese from her family or a neighbor and ate until she felt ill. And sometimes, as on this sunny autumn afternoon, she ran through the woods in search of the Godlings' Copse.

Her chest ached. Her breaths came as gasps. She thought

she might die if she did not rest and she knew she would want to die if she did. When she ran as fast as she could, the secret trailed behind her. If she slowed, it would embrace her, and then she would feel as though she could never be clean again.

Her hard, bare feet found safe footing on the deer trail. Her dark hair streamed behind her. Her breathing became steady and calm as her legs found a rhythm that soothed her. She raced past oaks and elms and pines, and saw their branches reaching for her, missing her. Sometimes she ducked beneath a limb and sometimes she leaped a puddle or a log. Sometimes she smiled, glad that the secret was forgotten, then frowned at the source of her pleasure and ran harder.

She heard the baying of hounds on a hunt. She stopped and whirled, lifting herself on tiptoe and raising her arms as if she thought she could fly, and stayed in that pose for a long moment, denying inertia and gravity both. Fear made her heart race faster than exertion had. Then she laughed, partly in relief, partly at herself. The sound had been nothing like the howling of wolves. The day was too bright and she was too close to Foxhome for any but the most desperate of predators. And the odd thought that she was the prey was even funnier. She knew the sound of the highborns' dogs. Her father had often said that the First Caste were kind masters to her people —kind because they took their taxes each year and left the villagers alone. That had always made Villel laugh with ugly pleasure.

The memory brought her too close to the secret. She ran on.

The deer trail paralleled the river shore. Other paths crossed it, where humans or animals went in search of drink. She heard that the hunters' course brought them closer to her, and she wondered if this was chance, or if their game was seeking water. She slowed her run to a lope. She wanted to see the quarry, but she did not want to come between the pack and the prey. At best, she would be laughed at. At worst, she would be cursed, and her mother would be told of her intervention, and Japhis would bow to the teller, and when that noble or that servant of the First Caste had gone, Lizelle would be beaten. Apologies would come later, and they would be worse than the beating.

The dark horse burst into the path like a creature from the

Demon Lord's realm. Lizelle saw it, and wondered why she had not heard it, and wondered why she was not diving into the brush to avoid it. The baying and yelping and shouting of the pursuers was far enough away that she had not expected to be interrupted so soon. She would be trampled; she could never evade the onrushing animal. It was taller and more magnificent than any horse she had ever seen. It seemed perfectly black except for a splotch of white on its brow. During the instant that her death galloped toward her, she even had time to wonder if the horse had escaped from a noble and to think that it deserved to be free, whatever the price of its freedom.

It swerved around her. She turned to watch the stallion go, and was less surprised that she lived than saddened that it would leave. She noted the strong curve of its chest, its taut belly, its high shoulders. Its tangled mane flew in the breeze of the stallion's making. Did the hunters follow to catch it or to kill it?

Come back, she thought without hesitation. *Oh, please, come back!*

As the stallion wheeled to face her, something touched Lizelle's mind like a soft nose nuzzling her palm. *Why?*

Her dark eyes opened wide as she sorted through half-formed thoughts. She wanted to ask the stallion if it had somehow spoken to her, but it *had* spoken to her, so she said the only thing that could justify her interruption. "I'll help you. If I can."

What price? No emotion came with the mental voice. Only the stallion's heavy breathing told of its urgency.

"Price?" The cries of the hunters grew louder, which meant she would have to act immediately if she could act at all, but her body still remembered that only an instant ago a wild stallion had been about to trample her, and her mind still struggled with the fact that somehow a horse spoke to her.

The stallion stepped carefully closer to her, as if it did not want to startle her. *Be strong.*

"I am strong," she whispered uncertainly.

Then all will be well.

The hounds were first to burst into the trail. They circled Lizelle and the dark stallion, and their yips and barks grew more delighted and more urgent. Lizelle's fear made her snatch up a stick and hit at one, but it danced back. She remembered her father saying, "Dog's not smart like us, girl. Kick one hard in the head, and it'll go down. Remember that, if you're scared. You can outthink anything with four legs. Remember that, and you can outthink most things with two."

But there were too many of them, maybe eight, maybe twelve; she couldn't tell because they kept circling and leaping, never attacking and never letting her or the horse get away. And they weren't mongrels like the hut-dogs of Foxhome. These were lean gray hunting hounds whose muzzles and shaggy coats hinted at a wolfish heritage. These were the property of a First Caste. To damage a First Caste's possession was to die.

Be calm, the stallion said. *They do not attack.*

"I got eyes," Lizelle replied.

Yes, the stallion said. *Four, now.*

Three hunters galloped onto the trail, and the dogs barked louder to impress their masters. Several small, wiry men in the black headbands of the Second Caste ran alongside the riders. One of these shouted, "Back! Back, back, you sons of the Wolf!"

The dogs turned toward the newcomers and quieted. The three riders watched, one on a bay, one on a palomino, one on a sorrel. Their saddles and bridles were gaudy things of red leather and brass, green leather and gold, blue leather and bright steel. Their kilts and boots and jackets were dyed to match their gear, and all three young nobles had the short haircuts of Gordian officers, though none wore the Empress's uniform. The dye of the blue rider's leather was a lighter hue than that of Gordia's banner. He and the green rider carried throwing spears in their right hands.

Lizelle felt tiny and dirty and stupid before the richly dressed men, so she straightened her shoulders and raised her head as high as she could.

"What's this?" said the slimmest, a blond boy in red, the only one without a javelin. "A Woods Elf, come to interfere with our hunt? Shall we show it what we think of Elves?" The boy swept out a sword and held it away from his body, as if to swat at Lizelle with the flat of the blade. She staggered backwards, forgetting her hauteur.

The blue rider, a dark boy with the beginnings of a black moustache, struck the blond across the chest with the shaft of his spear. "It's one of the serfs. One of *my* serfs. Leave it be."

The blond said, "Damn you, Uyor," without particular pain or embarrassment. He glanced at the front of his jacket, sheathed his sword, and began readjusting the folds and laces of his clothing. "I could tell what it was. But it's gotten in our way. We might chase it for a while. The servants could lead the horse away."

"We haven't taken the horse yet," said the third rider, a smaller boy in green, whose features resembled Uyor's. "No wound. You must've missed it." He dropped the butt of his spear into a saddle quiver and lifted a lariat from a hook beside the quiver.

The blond frowned at the stallion, then smiled at his companions. "And I'm glad, even if I lost my spear. Would've been a waste of a fine mount."

As the three nobles talked, the two dog tenders gathered the hounds and bade them sit beneath a tree.

"Fight's gone from it," said the blond, without looking up to hear the black stallion's snort.

"Out of the way, girl." Uyor kneed his horse closer. "You might be trampled."

Lizelle glanced at the dead leaves at her feet, afraid that she would be unable to speak, then mumbled, "He's mine."

"What's that?" said the blond with quiet amusement.

"He's my horse!" Seeing their surprised faces, she added, "Lords," and looked again at the ground.

"He was free in my woods," said Uyor, stroking his thin moustache.

"And bears no brand," said the blond boy. "Would you claim a horse that was not yours, girl?"

"No, Lord."

Be careful, the horse said in its strange way.

"We could go to the village," the youngest boy suggested. "And ask someone there if this was true."

"We could simply take it," said the blond.

"I'm no thief," said Uyor. "And you, Mavrion?"

Mavrion smiled very politely. "Of course not." Then he laughed. "We're nobles of Gordia. Who would call us thieves?" When neither of the darker boys laughed, Mavrion said, "The girl is one of your serfs, Uyor. If the horse can be said to be hers, it is yours, eh? It's too damned fine to drag a plow."

True, Lizelle heard.

Uyor glanced indecisively at his companions. "I suppose so."

"So claim it, geld it, and break it to the saddle. Why wait?" Uyor smiled. "All three, here and now?"

The priest, the horse said, with such force that Lizelle repeated, "The priest," before she knew what she said.

Mavrion laughed. "What priest?"

"This priest." The voice, quick and harsh and oddly accented, came from behind the riders. As they turned to see who had come, Lizelle thought of running, and heard, *No point. If the priest cannot help, the riders would follow.*

The man who stepped into the trail was small, dark, and stout. His hair and his beard had been trimmed very short; his face was so weathered that he might have been an ancient young man or a youthful old one. Nothing about him suggested priest. He wore a mud-brown cloak over a green jacket, blue trousers, and soldier's black boots. A canvas pack lay on his back, but his only potential weapon was a long hunting knife sheathed at his right hip. His forehead was bare.

"Priest?" The blond, Mavrion, laughed. "Too proud to wear a peasant's casteband? Or too cowardly to wear a mercenary's?"

The man did not seem to have heard. He stared at the horse with an intensity that frightened Lizelle, who had only seen that look on drunks and madmen.

"Used to be death not to wear your casteband," the youngest boy said. "Now it's just a whipping." He whirled the end of his lariat.

Uyor touched the back of his hand. "No, Conoy."

"It's not for fun," said Mavrion reasonably. Then he grinned. "It's our duty. We could have the servants hold him." The dog tenders watched from under the tree, but made no move to come forward.

The traveler walked between the nobles' horses, approaching Lizelle and the dark stallion.

"Hold there!" Mavrion called.

The man and the stallion studied each other with a quiet intimacy that made Lizelle envious. The man reached up and touched the horse's brow, saying softly, "Who would dare—"

"That's my cousin's!" Conoy's words were emphasized with a strike from his lariat, catching the dark man's shoulder. "You haven't—"

Conoy's sentence died as the man whirled. "Young lords, forgive me! I am an admirer of . . . horses."

"You are a priest?" Uyor asked cautiously.

"Yes." The man reached into the collar of his jacket and pulled out a large circle carved from bone that hung from a leather cord. "A Quester."

"Ah," said Mavrion, sneering. "And for what do you quest?"

Uyor shook his head. "They have a temple in City Gordia. The Empress recognizes them."

"He's been disrespectful!"

The man looked at each of the three riders, then at Lizelle and the stallion and seemed to speak to them. "Forgive me if I seemed so. In this company, I am wondrously respectful."

"You're not dressed like a priest," Conoy said.

"I'm more of an apprentice."

"Do you have any other proof?" asked Mavrion. "Anyone might carve a bit of bone and hang it about his neck."

"True." The man smiled. "Any three fools might tie white bands around their heads and pester passers-by with questions."

Mavrion frowned. "They'd be fools indeed, for they could not play that game long in Gordia. It's not wise to play any games here, old man."

"True?" The traveler turned to Lizelle. "Is that really true?"

"If the First Caste say so."

The man nodded. "Well, then. No games."

"You would do well to leave," Conoy suggested.

"If that's advice," the man answered, "I regret that I'm too thick to take it. I understand that I'm involved in this matter?"

"Tell them," Lizelle said quickly, "'bout the horse. That it's mine. They want it!"

The man glanced at her. His lips twitched with pain or amusement. "The horse . . . is hers."

"And who are you to say this?" asked Conoy.

"I am Davin Greenboots, once of Torion and most recently

of Tyrwilka, young lords." The man made a lavish bow that almost made Lizelle laugh.

"And she?" asked Conoy, twitching a thumb at Lizelle.

"Lizelle," she answered. "Of Foxhome."

"And the horse?"

"Horse?" she repeated, suddenly confused.

"Yes. Surely it has a name."

Name? asked the stallion. *This one is this one, that one is that. How can a name identify the nature of an intelligent entity? If one is intelligent, one's nature is always changing.*

"Darkwind," Lizelle stammered, desperate to answer.

Darkwind? the stallion said skeptically. *Glorious Salvation, perhaps, or The One Without Fleas, or—*

"Darkwind," Lizelle repeated firmly, then saw that the repetition had made the nobles more suspicious, and the traveler more amused.

"I don't think—" Mavrion began, but Uyor interrupted in kinder tones. "And if we ask in Foxhome, will they say Darkwind is Lizelle's horse?"

"No," she said. "He's a secret. For my ma. I been training him."

"You obviously had no money to buy him," Mavrion said. "So you stole him—"

"No!"

"—or found him, in which case, he belongs to your master." Mavrion indicated Uyor, who seemed bored or uneasy with the entire matter. "Which is it?"

"Neither. The priest give him to me." She glanced at Davin, praying the man would agree.

"Did you?" asked Conoy, as if he believed the story but could not understand why anyone would give a fine horse to a village girl.

Davin nodded. "You wouldn't doubt me?"

"Yes!" Mavrion reached for his sword.

Uyor laughed and caught Mavrion's arm. "They may be lying, but their story'll stand up in trial, without evidence to the contrary. The horse gave us a good chase. Now let's find new entertainment."

Mavrion winced, then grunted agreement. The dog tenders rose as the three nobles wheeled their horses; neither Conoy nor Mavrion acknowledged Davin and Lizelle, but one of the

tenders grinned at them as he followed his masters. Before
leaving them alone, Uyor turned in his saddle to salute them
both with a lift of his javelin.

"You didn't say your last name," the apprentice-priest said
when the riders had gone.

"Yes, Lord." She moved closer to the horse.

"I told you mine. Surely yours isn't any sillier."

She shrugged, and heard the horse say, *Names never define
one.*

"You are—"

"Villelschild," she mumbled.

"Oh?" The man squatted so that they were of the same
height. His eyes were the color of mahogany. "The name's
familiar."

"He died. Yesterday."

"I'm sorry."

She shrugged and stroked the horse's neck. "Darkwind,"
she said, thinking, *You're beautiful and strong and kind.*

So this one is, the horse agreed. *Yet that one saved this
one.*

Didn't the priest?

The priest helped that one save this one. It is not the same.

Davin gripped her shoulder and turned her to face him.
"Japhis Kardeck's man? Dead?" She winced and nodded. He
released her hand, saying, "Sorry, Lizelle," but he seemed to
be thinking of other things. After a moment, he said, "Why
were you here?"

"Just running."

"A whim?" She nodded, and he nodded too, saying, "I
heard the hunt, and wandered off the road. I almost didn't, but
I thought I could ask someone how far it was to Foxhome,
or. . ." He shook his head. "I don't know. That you should be
here is a bit of a coincidence, but that the . . . horse should be
here, too . . ."

*This one called the priest, but the priest cannot hear like
that one can. This one sought the priest. This one and the
priest are two of the Three.*

"The Three?" she asked.

Davin came so close that she almost turned to run. "You
know about the Three?"

"N-no."

"Then why—" He looked at Darkwind.

The horse nodded.

Davin pointed at Lizelle. "And her?"

The horse moved its head from side to side in an exaggerated denial.

"Japhis, then? Like the priests thought?"

The horse nodded.

"We must find her." Davin started back for the road to Foxhome. Lizelle and Darkwind looked at each other, then followed.

That one is troubled.

The priest?

No. The girl.

"Oh," Lizelle whispered.

What has that one done?

A part of the secret came into her memory. "No!" she yelled.

Davin turned back. "Lizelle? What's wrong?"

"Nothing," she whispered. "Sorry. I stepped on a stone. A sharp one."

"I could take a look...."

She shook her head. "It's all right. Really."

It is not, Darkwind said.

It is!

When they regained the old road, Davin said, "Much further to Foxhome?"

"No."

"I could carry you on my shoulders if your foot's bothering you."

"S'right."

Several villagers walked a few hundred yards in front of them, also heading toward Foxhome, but Lizelle did not call out to them. They would ask questions, and she did not want to talk with anyone. She would have left Davin and Darkwind, if there was not a mystery here that involved her.

This one is a unicorn.

Oh? Don't have no horn.

The horn was cut off.

You got no hands to cut with.

Unicorns have servants. The priest was one.

Davin? He cut your horn?

No. One of his teachers, at the request of the First Among Unicorns.

I seen goats with their horns cut off. Leaves a stump. You just got a white spot.

Magic was used.

Oh. Who's the First Among Unicorns?

This one's sire.

Why's he called that?

Because there is a speaker for all animals. For ants and elephants and fingerfish and catfish and hummingbirds and hawks. All animals.

The secret was almost forgotten. *Why?*

Because the God who made all beings will someday judge Her creations. The speakers answer for their kind.

There a First for people?

Undoubtedly.

Who?

This one does not know.

Who's your ma?

The First Among Horses.

You're not no unicorn, then. She felt betrayed. *You're some kind of mule.*

Darkwind whinnied, and Lizelle recognized that as laughter. She thought, *What's so damn funny!*

That one.

I'm not no mule.

What is that one, then?

A girl.

Ah. That one's parents were girls?

You're stupid. It's not the same.

True. This one understands about sex. This one knows that one's sex. This one wants to know what that one is.

Oh. I'm a Foxhomer. A Gordian.

Were both of that one's parents Foxhomers and Gordians?

No, she admitted, then added, *You snuck that out of my mind!*

Yes.

Don't do it again!

This one cannot control what that one thinks so loudly. But this one will respect that one's privacy.

Good. They walked on. Lizelle wondered if Darkwind

spoke the truth, but he said nothing when she wondered that, so she decided that he must have. She said, *I s'pose if you had a horn, you were a unicorn.*

Thank you.

Not one now.

Then what is this one now?

Lizelle giggled. *Darkwind.*

The horse nodded. *That's answer enough.*

After a moment, Lizelle thought, *I have a secret.*

Only one?

One big one.

Yes?

"I wished my father would die," she whispered. "And he did."

That one should be content, then.

"My father!" she repeated.

So? If that one wished for a barn of oats, would this one never hunger?

You don't understand. She was sorry she had confided in Darkwind, but did not know how to take her secret back.

True. A human may not understand a unicorn, but a unicorn knows its own mind. A human confuses everyone, including itself.

I don't understand.

Then these two are siblings in ignorance.

Lizelle laughed. *You're funny.*

Someone was waiting on a rock by the common field, a quarter-mile away from the bright cabins of Foxhome. The shape was unrecognizable: a stout person wearing a cape and a backpack. Strangers were rare enough in Foxhome; Lizelle studied the silhouette, wondering if this might be one of Uyor's company. There was no horse, but that might mean this was a servant. As they came closer, Lizelle became uneasy, knowing something was wrong. When she finally realized that the person's red cape was not just any red cape, she gasped and ran ahead of Davin and Darkwind.

"Ma!" she cried, burying her head into her mother's stomach as she threw her arms around her waist. Japhis returned the hug. "What're you doing, Ma? We can't go nowhere! We got to stay here!"

"Shush," Japhis whispered, her breath warm on Lizelle's ear. "You're not leaving home."

"You are?"

Japhis placed her hands on either side of Lizelle's head. Her palms were rough on Lizelle's cheeks, but she did not mind and hardly noticed. When Japhis nodded, Lizelle cried, "No, Ma, no! You can't!"

Japhis shook her head. "I must. You'll be all right. Your aunt'll take care of you."

"Lemme come."

"You can't."

Lizelle blinked to keep from crying, and nodded. *Ma hates me.*

Japhis said, "I'll come back as soon as I can."

Lizelle nodded again.

Japhis looked up, and Lizelle realized that Davin and Darkwind were near.

Japhis stated, "You're Davin."

"Yes," Davin answered with a hint of diffidence or embarrassment.

"I'm Japhis. Serenity and my man were found dead in our house yesterday. I buried 'em both last night." Japhis's voice was perfectly calm.

"I'm sorry."

"Glee came this morning. Not in person. His spirit body. He wanted to know why Serenity hadn't returned."

"What happened?"

Lizelle turned in her mother's embrace so she could watch both adults. Their voices were low and quiet, and there was a long pause between each person's statements so neither would interrupt the other. The careful consideration made her far more nervous than loud interruptions would have.

"Demons killed them. Nothing else could've. Maybe they wanted me. Maybe they wanted to harm me. I don't know. I'm ready to go now."

"We don't have to set out right away. I thought it'd take a day or two to convince you, and another for you to put your things in order."

Japhis barked a laugh. "All in order, Quester. My man's buried, my daughter's turned over to his sister, my village duties have been taken by a stupid, frightened man who'll

undo ten years of work before I return. If I return. Let's go."
Japhis released Lizelle and stood.

"Ma!" Lizelle cried. "Ma, don't—"

"Be tough," Japhis said. "When I was your age, my
brother and I were orphans. We made it alone for years."

You had your brother, Lizelle thought. *Who've I got?* "All
right, Ma."

Japhis bit her upper lip, then said, "I'd take you if I could,
'Zelle. But you're safer here."

Adults always made excuses. It seemed to be a rule.

"I love you," Japhis said.

Lizelle nodded. Adults always said they loved you when
they did something cruel.

Japhis nodded, too.

"She could follow a little ways," Davin said. "If she
wanted."

Japhis glanced at him. "Half a mile, maybe. If she
wanted."

"S'right," Lizelle said quickly.

Darkwind asked, *Does that one know what it means, to be
carried by a unicorn?*

You're not no unicorn.

*To lose a horn is not to stop being a unicorn. Does that one
know what it means, to be carried?*

Only good people are carried, she answered, her mental
voice like the faintest whisper. *Everyone knows.*

This one would carry that one, if that one wished.

She did not know what to say.

"Do you want to come?" Davin asked. "Just a little ways,
to see us off?"

Studying the dirt so no one could see her face, she nodded.

Darkwind knelt awkwardly beside her, settling back onto
his haunches, then lowering his forelegs in a motion so obviously alien to him that she wanted to scream at him to stop.
Mount, he said, and as Davin and Japhis stared, Lizelle
scrambled onto his back. *Cling tightly,* he said, standing, and
for a moment, she felt like the future was her friend.

"Is it safe?" Japhis asked Davin.

Davin laughed. "It'd better be. He's the third."

"A horse?"

"Look closer. The shape of the legs, the pattern of the hair around his hooves—"

"No horn."

"Someone cut it."

"Who?"

Davin shrugged. "It'll call less attention to us, now."

"It's so large!"

"I think it's a unicorn mule. Half horse, most likely. Unicorns are terribly inbred; the new blood's undoubtedly responsible for this one's size. I wonder if it's sterile?" Davin glanced at Lizelle, then reached up to touch her cheek. "What's wrong?"

Nothing was wrong. How could she tell him that was why she was crying?

These Three must go to save the world, Darkwind said. *No one else can come, no matter who that other might be.*

Ma wasn't lying, then?

No.

She'll come back?

This one can't know. This one hopes so.

And you?

Darkwind leapt forward; Lizelle clung more tightly to his mane and laughed.

This one hopes so.

13

Desperate Deeds

"Hey there, hi there, ho there, you're as welcome as can be," sang Mad Dog's doorbell at Kevin's touch. Mad Dog's voice, muffled through the painted metal door, followed: "Coming, Mother!" The door opened, and a gorilla in a wheelchair looked up at Kevin, then down the hall. "You're not my mother," it said, and began to close the door.

Kevin sighed. "Very funny, Mad Dog." He caught the door and followed Mad Dog into the loft. Someone had burned sausages for breakfast. Something Celtadelic played in the background, sounding like the Boys of the Loo covering an old song with a refrain like "I think we're a clone now." Someone turned the music down as they approached Byte-henge through the clutter of recent acquisitions. Kevin considered asking what Mad Dog planned to do with half of a rusty suit of armor, a gas-powered hedge trimmer with a broken blade, and a carton of LOLLYPOPS—ASSORTED, but then he thought better of it.

Mad Dog, pulling off the gorilla mask, called, "Gang's all here!"

Gwen and Janny stood by a rack of vinyl and laser disks, selecting music for the day. Gwen's metallic dreadlocks matched the synthetic red fur that hung from the snaps implanted in her skin, covering the front of her body from toes to neck and leaving her back entirely bare. Janny wore reflective black coveralls, much like the ones she'd appeared to wear in the interface. Brian, in a red and yellow jumpsuit like a spaceman's uniform from an ancient film, and Michael, in a conservative blue suit, white shirt, and red tie, sat near each other on the faded blue couch.

Gwen said, "The Kev!" and lifted him off the floor in an embrace of smooth fur and smoother muscle.

"Uh, Gwen—"

Grinning, she set him down again. "I'm glad we're all together again. It wouldn't have happened without you."

"Yeah . . ." Kevin shrugged, looking at Michael and Brian, who smiled at him. He wished Michael would give a hint of his plan, and was only consoled by the knowledge that Michael was certainly wishing Kevin would do the same.

"We had to be here," Michael said innocently. "For your moment of glory."

"Uh huh." Kevin grinned at Brian. "Hair's all wrong for Buster Crabbe. Needs gel, or something."

Brian shook his head, and his bangs fell over his eyebrows. "Poseur's passé. Everything's Future Revival now."

"Everything." Gwen laughed and ruffled Brian's hair. "Oh, yes. 'Bout three people in town and maybe six in Argentina are already doing Future Rev."

"If it's got a name, Bri, it's already passé." Regretting the statement even before Brian frowned, Kevin added, "Though I sure haven't noticed it yet. You've probably got a month before the rest of the world catches on."

Janny circled the footlocker, which was crowded with cups, bowls of potato chips, and several stacks of tapes in various formats. She said "Kevin" very quietly, and gave him a quick kiss on his right cheek. Her contacts were holograms of eagles in flight. The effect was of fierce, tiny birds flying from her pupils; her irises were the blue of the sky in the country on a clear afternoon. Wisps of cloud seemed to drift across them. He could not look into her eyes for long; he doubted anyone could. Feeling very stupid, he realized that might have always been her intention.

Mad Dog still wore the furry arms of the gorilla suit under his green ULTIMATE POSEUR!—POSING AS MYSELF tee shirt. He watched them with a bitter expression that faded as Kevin glanced at him. Mad Dog could not suspect. Surely he only had a headache, or was annoyed that he would have to entertain or ignore people working on something he had finished with. *Brian and Michael are finished for now, too.* Kevin asked, "What're you guys going to do while we make the run?"

Brian shrugged. "I thought I'd go on-line and read some messages, or something. I brought a book. Michael and Mad Dog're going to play chess."

Kevin nodded. Perhaps that was why Mad Dog was annoyed. Michael was the only person Kevin knew who could beat Mad Dog two games out of three.

Brian said, "We wanted to be around to cheer when you guys finish."

Mad Dog said, "Make it fast, okay?"

"And if we blow it?" Gwen asked. "Unlikely though that may be?"

Brian smiled. "Then I'll call Enter-Tech and tell 'em to draw up our contracts, starting immediately."

"Oh, boy." Kevin ignored Michael's look.

"Coffee?" Mad Dog asked.

"Not if we're jacking right away." Kevin glanced at Janny, who nodded.

"Everyone gone wee-wee?" Mad Dog said.

"Yes, Mad Dog," Gwen said sweetly, then asked Janny, "So what's the plan?"

The six looked at each other. Janny said, "The game's halted where the Three meet for the first time. The backup copy's at the same point. If we decide the present game's screwed, we quit and restore the game from the backup. And we keep going until we win, or go mad."

"No prob," Gwen said. "We're already mad."

"Well, then." Kevin took his usual place by the big Kimoda 700, picked up a jack cord, and began to recline his chair. "Shall we jack?"

"We could talk a little about strategy," Gwen said. "Like, do we have one?"

Janny moved to her chair, opposite Kevin's. "Since we don't know what to expect, I don't know what to suggest. Except maybe that you should take a fairly passive approach.

We're running the three characters most likely to succeed.
Their instincts should be good. We don't want to screw them
up."

"Passive." Gwen took the seat between Kevin's and
Janny's and sneered at a jack cable. "Why not let the fucking
program play its fucking self?"

Mad Dog laughed. "Did, of course. On automatic. One
thousand and one plays. Lost every time. Now you get to start
from the same point and see what you can add. And since I
seem to be your cruise director, I'll have pizza and coffee
ready whenever you jack out."

"Till the game is won?"

"You bet."

"Hope we win it fast, then. I'd hate to lose my weakness
for pizza." Gwen picked up a cable, placed its tip against the
back of her skull, and snapped it in, crying, "Flame on!"

Kevin looked at Janny. She might have smiled as their eyes
met. Tiny eagles flew directly toward him from a field of
blue, and he remembered, *Brown, like bitter chocolate*.

"Hawk-a-a-a!" Kevin yelled with a grin. As he slipped
into the interface, he heard Brian laugh, and Janny say,
"Would a little reverence be too much to— Yeah, I suppose
so. *Wacka-ding-hoy, kemo sabe!*"

A Tenniel Cheshire Cat met him in the interface. "Function?"

"That's a cat?" Kevin laughed. "I was expecting something
more traditional."

The Cheshire Cat became a yellow construction Caterpillar. "You never specified the kind of cat."

"You're fun, Prompt. Lands of Adventure, please."

The long-haired woman who looked like Janny waited in a
castle courtyard. She wore white fur boots and a white leather
gown belted with a golden chain. "Welcome, Ke—"

"Player specifications for communication abilities."

She nodded, reached into a pocket and withdrew a scroll.
Kevin was pleased; it seemed perfectly natural that she should
have been carrying the scroll, and if it had only been created
after he had asked for it, the act of creation was too subtle for
him to notice.

Scanning the scroll, he noted that Davin Greenboots was fluent in Torionese (Native Language), Gordian (Trade Language), and Tyrwilkan (Acquired Language). Davin's command of the First Language was minimal; apparently the Questers had taught him a few simple commands. Kevin wanted to bump Davin up to a master magician, but he was reluctant to introduce changes that would make the character inconsistent with his established past. *Lands of Adventure* was sufficiently unstable that any discrepancy which the program could not rationalize might unravel all their work. If this run were an ordinary game, he might make Davin latently telepathic, which would explain why the ability had never manifested itself before, but Kevin planned a more drastic, less honorable change that made telepathy superfluous.

"Enable direct communication between players at the player level." He and Janny had not decided if they would allow player consultation in the finished form of *Lands of Adventure* (Janny did not want it; he thought it should be available as a choice for beginners), but it would be useful now.

"Done."

"Has Janny enabled the pause option?" There would be no pause option for players in the finished game, when customers would come and go and the game would continue. The option had to remain at the design level, in case the game needed to be taken off-line and altered slightly before Omari put it back on the net.

"Yes."

"Then send me in."

The air was clean and cold, tinged with distant wood smoke, decaying leaves, and the subtle promise of rain later in the evening. His shirt and cloak felt coarse, but comfortable. The weight at one shoulder was his pack; at his hip, a long traveler's knife. The road, a bed of mulch, was soft under his moccasins as Davin Greenboots walked with a woman he did not know and something that was more than a horse. Lizelle and Foxhome were behind them, well beyond sight or hearing. He, Japhis, and Darkwind might be the only three living things within a mile. Several slate-colored juncos flew overhead to disprove him, and a squirrel chittered as if to say that

was the stupidest thought it had ever heard. Davin's feeling of
solitude did not depart.

(Kevin: Janny? Gwen? You in?)

(Janny: 'Bout time you showed up.)

(Gwen: It's weird.)

(Kevin: 'Course it's weird. You're a horse. Horse-oid?)

(Gwen: No. It's stranger than it should be. Like I'm here in
spectator mode, rather than player. Or something.)

(Janny: Worry about it later. Things are happening.)

(Kevin: Yeah. And I'm about to encourage them.)

(Janny: Don't—)

(Kevin: Trust me.)

(Gwen: I hate it when he says that.)

Davin stopped by the side of the road. "Not dark yet,"
Japhis stated without slowing, without looking back. Sunset
was at least two hours away.

"Something I need to show you." Davin tried to keep himself calm, and tried not to think about what he was doing, and
wanted to laugh or cry because trying to seem innocent would
be sufficient to alert Darkwind, if the creature could read his
mind as easily as it had seemed to read the girl's. It ambled
ahead of them, nibbling at tall grass and leaves that had not
yet changed color.

"What?" Japhis glanced back long enough to throw the
word over her shoulder.

Davin, removing his pack from his back and digging
through its contents, walked forward. "It's in here somewhere. Darkwind, this is important to you, too. The Questers
gave it to me."

The beast turned, studying him with the dark mirror of one
eye. Then, with something like resignation, it stopped in the
center of the road.

(Kevin: What's it thinking?)

(Gwen: It's curious, mostly. But there's something
else. . . .)

"There are several things to interest you, in fact." Davin
tossed Japhis one of the necklaces that the Gordian Quester
had given him.

She reached across her body with her left hand to catch it.
Her grunt might have been an expression of annoyance with
him for throwing it, or merely an expression of the effort in

turning suddenly. She held it up and said, "Nice. I like bone carving. A sailor's work?"

Darkwind peered at Japhis's necklace as Davin came close enough to touch the stallion's flank. "If you admire that," Davin said, "you'll adore this." He drew the wand of unicorn horn from his pack. Darkwind's head swung about quickly, in horror or fear, and in that instant, Davin brought the point of the wand against Darkwind's throat.

The creature reared to lash the air with ebony hooves. Japhis reached for Davin's wrist, crying, "What're you doing!"

Davin dropped his pack to push Japhis away with a stiff left arm. Her breast was soft under the heel of his hand, and she gasped. "I know what I'm doing," he said, not knowing if it was true, not daring to turn from Darkwind to see how Japhis reacted to his words. He kept the wand aimed at Darkwind's belly. The creature's hooves were meant to threaten, not kill. As soon as Davin saw that, Darkwind twisted and dropped to all fours to race away.

(Janny: Oh, Kevin, if you've fucked up . . .)

Davin leaped for Darkwind. He managed to get one arm around Darkwind's neck and dug his free hand into the creature's mane. It turned to nip at him as he scrambled onto its back. His legs clenched its flanks, but it would throw him in a second, he knew. He raised his right arm high, ready to drive the wand into Darkwind's side.

(Janny: Kevin!)

"No," someone said. The voice was deep, musical, and strange. What had been a black stallion, half unicorn and half horse, had become a giant man with skin the color of oak bark. Davin, clinging to the giant's back with his left hand entwined in the giant's hair, felt frightened and foolish. The giant's fist enclosed Davin's forearm; Davin's hand and the unicorn wand protruded uselessly beyond the grip of fingers as thick as saplings.

(Kevin: Gwen?)

(Gwen: Not a clue. You and Janny are on your own.)

Davin screamed when the huge hand twisted. He let go of the giant's hair, and realized that was what he was meant to do. He hung helplessly before the giant, and it laughed. Its eyes were milky spheres with burning coal at their core. Its teeth were mossy rocks as big as a large man's fist. Its hair and beard were a tangle of copper wire; its kirtle, a garment of living ivy.

"Korz Demon!" Japhis's golden knife was in her left hand, but she shook the stump of her right arm at the creature.

The demon smiled and, setting Davin roughly on the ground, bowed to her. "Japhis Kardeck. I'm proud of you."

It had forgotten the unicorn wand. Davin drew the shaft back by his ear to throw it at the giant's throat, but the giant looked at him and shook its head. "No need, Davin Greenboots. I am on your side now, without reservations." It chuckled, and its beard withdrew into its skin as the shape of breasts formed beneath the kirtle. Davin recognized the huge woman from Korz Pass. It nodded. "I'm proud of you, too."

Davin bit his lip, trying to think of a response. "I found one of the boys' spears in the woods before I found you and Lizelle. Bushes were broken as if something had passed that way, but the trail ended with the spear. The point was covered with blood. So was the ground, where something large had fallen."

(Janny: Oh.)

(Kevin: I . . . Davin . . . wasn't sure what to do. But this was one way to test the unicorn wand.)

The demon grinned. Its body grew slimmer, until only its height and its unnatural eyes showed that this was not a pre-pubescent human.

Japhis looked at Davin. "It's a demon," she said harshly. "It tried to destroy my life once. I don't know what it's done with the third, nor do I care."

The demon laughed. "I am the third. Now."

(Janny: You understand that, Gwen?)

(Gwen: No. I can't read it at all. It's like I'm in pure spectator mode. I'm not linked to anyone's point of view now.")

(Janny: Where's Darkwind?)

(Gwen: Present, I think, but unconscious or drugged. I can't sense anything specific, not even dreams.)

"Circle around it." Japhis moved away from Davin. "We can trap it between us."

"Oh?" The demon stroked its chin. "Or have I trapped you?"

"Ignore it." Japhis held herself in a traditional fencer's

stance: her side to the demon to present it with the narrowest target, the knife chest-high where she could parry high or low with ease.

If the demon intended to kill them, it could have attacked them much earlier. Davin weighed the wand in his hand. "What happened to the unicorns' third?"

"I saved him," the demon answered.

"Save us in the same way," Japhis said, "and your kind'll take the world." She skipped forward, extending the knife in a thrust. As the demon reached for her, she twisted the blade upward, slicing its hand as she stepped backwards. It grimaced. Thick drops of blood like black oil fell onto the dirt of the road. As it stared at its mortality, Japhis lunged.

"Wait!" Davin called.

(Kevin: Who's being impetuous, now?)

(Janny: It's a demon, or it's a bug in the program. In either case, Lands treats it as a demon. The sooner we get rid of it, the sooner we get to the Tangled Lands.)

Japhis's knife slid beneath the demon's sternum. It cried out, a sound like thunder, and its form shimmered, as if it hoped to escape in another shape. Still a giant human youth, it fell to its knees. It reached for Japhis with open, helpless hands. "I meant . . . well." It looked from Japhis to Davin. "Truly." Its wince was a tiny thing, as if it had noticed the wrong silverware set out for a dinner party. "Silly humans." It might have smiled then.

Its chest shook, as if it were trying to learn how to cry, then it fell forward without a sound. It shriveled, like a fragile thing put too close to heat, and was gone. Darkwind lay in its place. The stallion's chest had been pierced; blood surged from his wound. He breathed once, looking at them as his eyes became unseeing globes of jelly.

Japhis, dropping her knife, went to the stallion's side. "Dead," she whispered. "How—"

"It's over." Davin stared at her, wanting to make her understand what she had done. When he saw that she already understood, he began to pity her.

"We've got to do something!"

"What? Elf magicians don't know the words to restore life. Who else might?"

"I thought—" She stood, looking down the road to Fox-home.

"It's over," Davin repeated. He put his hand on her shoulder to guide her, and they began the short walk back to the village. Were it ten thousand miles away, Davin thought, it could never be sufficiently far. But he would have wine or beer or mead when he arrived. Alcohol could not console him, but it would be an adequate substitute for consolation.

(Kevin: Exit?)
(Janny: Exit.)
(Gwen: Exit.)

The three sat at a table on a hillside pavilion, looking down at a gleaming, vaguely medieval village. Kevin and Janny wore clothes like those on their bodies in Bytehenge; Gwen seemed to be a beast-woman covered in red hair.

"I'm sorry," Janny whispered.

Gwen clapped her on the back. "Hey, don't worry about it. The more mistakes we make, the more we learn."

Kevin smiled. "That's not too comforting. I don't want to be the perpetual undergraduate."

"No. You're right." Janny looked at them both; her eyes were brown. "I wanted it to be real, but I didn't expect—"

"The death?" Kevin asked.

"Not just that. Poor Japhis. She thought she hated the demon, but when I pushed her to kill it . . ."

"So, we jack out extremely early for pizza, or we try again?" Gwen asked.

"Again," Kevin said.

"Again," Janny agreed.

The air was clean and cold; his shirt, coarse; his pack and his knife, significant weights on his body; the road, soft under his moccasins. Déjà vu quickly shifted from unsettling to bor-ing for Kevin, but Davin Greenboots walked the Elf King's Road for the first time with his new companions. Kevin's boredom fled as Davin's mistrust of Darkwind grew. When three juncos flew overhead and a squirrel called its annoyance, Kevin suggested that Davin act.

The duel between the Three proceeded much as it had be-fore. Kevin could have asked the program whether there were differences, but he did not perceive any. Davin's threat to Darkwind forced the Korz Demon to reveal itself, and he and Japhis kept it trapped between the wand of unicorn horn and the knife of demon gold. Davin asked, "What of the unicorns' third?" and Kevin watched closely.

"I saved him," the demon said.

"Save us in the same way," Japhis said, skipping forward, "and your kind will rule the world." She thrust, the demon reached, her blade twisted, and blood as viscous as oil fell from the demon's hand onto the road.

"Wait!" Davin called.

(Kevin: Stop her! Before she kills it again!)

"Why?" Japhis answered.

(Janny: It's a warning, nothing more. Japhis needs to prove something, to the demon and to herself. But Davin'd better give her good reasons to let it live a while.)

Davin shrugged. "It could've escaped by now, if it wanted to. Turned into a bird or something similar. Or it could've attacked us earlier."

"You could've exposed it earlier, too."

"Didn't know if I should, with others around. Wasn't sure of the best way to test it."

The demon smiled. "You wouldn't have killed me without a test? I am grateful."

Davin shook his head and lifted the wand to remind the demon that he had not decided to free it. Japhis blocked it from continuing down the Elf King's Road; he blocked it from retreating. "Was there a third?"

The demon laughed. "There's a prophecy. Of course there's a third."

"What happened to it?"

"The noble boy killed it."

Davin nodded. "Then we might as well go home."

Japhis's blade dropped slightly, then came as quickly back to the ready. "What?"

"No need," the demon said. "The boy killed it, but it did not die."

"You love this nonsense," Japhis said, addressing the demon.

It grinned. "My humor. Yes. Imagine this. A man and a unicorn converge on a village, where the Three will convene.

Highborn boys go hunting near the village. Demons, who watch the world for the promised Three, direct the hunt toward the unicorn by false sounds and shadows, until the hunters pursue true, mortal prey. When a boy throws, the demons see that neither wind nor foliage deflect his spear."

"Your work," Japhis said.

The demon shook its head. "My siblings. I only watched. Outside the Tangled Lands, we must act in tiny, circumspect ways."

"There's no point in talking to it," Japhis told Davin.

"That's true," the demon replied. "But there's point in accepting my company. Continue to imagine. The spear flies to prick the unicorn's heart. But this is no common beast; it is the child of strength and speed and glory, who was to carry one of the Three to the heart of the Tangled Lands, where Demon's Gate stands open. The spear is not deep in its side, not so deep that death entered with the spear, yet deep enough that life would soon depart."

Japhis grunted. "It's dying. Continue."

The demon shrugged. "It leaps and runs, outdistancing the hunt for moments, perhaps for minutes. Were it whole, it would run still, and no mortal hound or horse would ever stay its course. In a copse of evergreens, it crashes to its side and lies panting.

"I occupy it then, before the last contraction of punctured lungs and failing heart. See me as mist, settling upon the dying beast. I fill its body with myself. Perhaps I destroy it then, for I learn each tiny part of it and remake it, exactly as it had been before the boy slew it. The unicorn stands, whole and healthy, where it had lain. An unwanted weapon marks the site of its death. It retraces its route, so the hunt will not find proof of its death. When the hunt sees it, it leads them away."

"It?" asked Davin. "Or you?"

"It," the demon answered. "It is reborn, or perhaps, its death is undone. The demon is an observer in its skull, little more. The unicorn runs for the village, its destination, and knows it can leave the hunt far behind. It must become part of the Three. That is its concern. That is its only concern."

Davin glanced at Japhis. "Then it encountered the girl, Lizelle."

One corner of the demon's mouth lifted in a kind smile. "Yes. It would have trampled her. She was an obstacle between it and its goal. I suggested it avoid her, and it did. When she called to it, I suggested it stop. The hunters could be evaded again, if necessary, but the girl's mind intrigued me."

"You were the unicorn, then," Davin said.

The demon shook its head. "I could affect its decisions. It thought those decisions were its own, so perhaps I affected its mind indirectly. Perhaps I have made it kinder, or at least more curious. But I was not it."

"Where is it now?" Japhis asked.

The demon's laugh filled the woods. "Where are we? I can say *here*, but what does that mean?"

Japhis flicked the knife's point closer to the demon. If it backed up any farther, it would impale itself on Davin's wand.

The demon smiled and shrugged. "It is within me. Perhaps you can understand its present nature that way. Darkwind is a perfect memory that can be given form whenever I choose."

"Restore it, then," Davin said. "And go away."

The demon chuckled. "Would you have unicorn steaks for dinner? If you want the living Darkwind, you must have us together, unicorn and secret observer. Else you will have an immortal demon and a unicorn in its death throes."

Japhis narrowed her eyes at the demon. "We won't be Three, then."

The demon lifted both hands to show its open palms. "What does the prophecy demand? Three physical selves, I think. If I restore Darkwind to you, and you do not force me to manifest myself in another shape, there will be Three, as all have hoped. If I had not acted as I did, there might never be Three."

"Will you . . . restore Darkwind again, if something else happens to him?" The idea made Davin uneasy, though he was not sure why. "Or would you restore us?"

"No." The demon's amusement continued. "The Three must face the demons. Now, that's possible. One of the Three must die when that happens. Now, that is possible, too. I will not restore the one who dies, whoever it might be. I dare not."

"Why do you care?" Japhis asked.

The cast of the demon's face changed. Weariness or sadness tinged its smile. "May we sit? Or talk as we walk?"

Davin glanced at Japhis. She nodded, and the two humans backed away from the Korz Demon. Japhis sheathed her knife; Davin walked over to the pack he had dropped. From its top protruded the wand's black holster, so he sheathed the wand, then tucked it and its holster into his belt. Throwing the pack over his shoulder, he said, "Walk?"

"Walk," Japhis agreed.

(Kevin: It's gotten complicated.)

(Gwen: It's been complicated.)

(Kevin: Does the backup start before Darkwind dies?)

(Janny: You want to try to save Darkwind from the hunters?)

(Kevin: Yeah.)

(Janny: I doubt it. None of our characters are near Darkwind then.)

(Gwen, laughing: 'Cept me!)

(Janny: Even with your help, Darkwind probably couldn't avoid a spear guided by demons. And how do we know the Korz Demon's story is true?)

(Gwen: You can control the demons on the design path, can't you?)

(Janny: Maybe. It'd be tricky. They're integral to the Tangled Lands scenario. I try to force the demons in ways they don't want to go—)

(Kevin: The whole program goes into meltdown.)

(Janny: Maybe. It's not worth the risk, not yet, anyway. I suppose we could quit this run and try to keep the next one simpler.)

(Kevin: I don't know. I've always liked complicated.)

(Janny: You don't say. All right. The game continues.)

(Kevin: Hey, we may be doing right. Sometimes complicated problems require complicated solutions.)

Their shadows stretched out before them, in the places where the forest left the Elf King's Road open to the sky. The demon had dwindled to human size, and the flames in its eyes had banked themselves. Its appearance of defenselessness heightened Davin's doubts. He said, "Why should we trust you?"

The demon shrugged. "What did the Questers tell you about us?"

To Davin's look, Japhis made a gesture of indifference. He said, "That you're not supposed to be present in our world. That centuries ago, a magician made a pact with Asphoriel, and in return for the Demon Lord's aid, the magician built Demon's Gate, which lies at the heart of what are now the Tangled Lands. So long as the gate is open, you can manifest yourself in the world. The longer the gate is open, the stronger you become. But if the gate closes, you must return to the demon realm, or die."

The Korz Demon clapped its hands. "Bravo! You are an excellent student, Davin Greenboots. What do you make of me?"

"There are renegade demons," Japhis said softly, before Davin could answer, "or loners. They inhabit quiet places in the world, and amuse themselves as they can."

The demon clapped again, more loudly. "Excellent! Such am I." It bowed to Japhis, then to Davin, and the leaves of its kirtle rustled as if a sudden wind had touched them.

"You would help us," Davin said.

The demon nodded.

"Against your fellows."

The demon nodded again.

"To amuse yourself."

The demon nodded a third time. "Everything I do, I do to amuse myself. But there is another reason. Tell me, Japhis Kardeck, of the difference between the Tangled Lands and the homes of the solitary demons?"

Japhis glanced at Davin, and he thought that this was the first time he had seen her surprised. Her eyes, he noted, were very dark, and she had a small mole near the outer corner of her right eye. She said, "I've never heard anything about the homes of the lone demons, other than that they're far from cities or the Tangled Lands."

"Does that suggest something to you?" the demon asked. "That we do not all remake your world to our whim?"

"It does not make me like you," she said quickly. "Or trust you."

The demon smiled. "Nor should it. But I have lived in your world for centuries. I love the barren places, the wild lands, the creatures that live and die without sense of purpose, or care of one—"

"You would help us," Japhis said, "because you like trees and furry animals?"

It nodded with an expression that might have been embarrassment. "Yes."

"You would save us—"

"No." The demon's voice became fiercely calm. "I would save this world. If I could save it and all humankind died, I would not care." It smiled. "But be pleased. In this case, humanity and the world will be preserved or destroyed together."

"There are other demons who think as you do?" Davin asked.

"Not so extremely, I think. There are few of us who live outside of Asphoriel's realm, and we are not inclined to work together. Even if we were, there is only one way to check the Demon Lord's expansion. When Demon's Gate closes, all demons must flee this world. Which means I will lose the thing I've acted to save."

Japhis watched the demon with something like sympathy, but when she noted Davin's gaze, she shook her head. "You tell me a demon can love?"

It smiled. "I tell you that I will preserve Korz Valley. Perhaps it is only another of my jokes, but if so, this joke will be on Asphoriel, Lord of Demons."

14

Quiet Days

On the first night of the journey to the Tangled Lands, Davin and Japhis cooked rice and red beans over a fire while building a shelter from fallen woods, saplings, and a tarp from Davin's pack. Their conversation consisted of simple things: "Hand me that." "I'll wash up." Later, they slept awkwardly, back to back, fully dressed. Darkwind stood guard under a nearby tree. It rained heavily during the night. By morning, their clothes and their gear might as well have been pitched into a pond. Japhis had kept the fire going, so they huddled around it to breakfast on tea, dried fruit, and cold sausage while their clothes grew warm on their bodies. Davin made a few attempts to talk: "Should be warmer later." "At least we've got provisions." Japhis answered with a grunt of agreement or an occasional "True."

Early that afternoon, they came to a traveler's inn, The Dancing Ferrets, and bought bread, cheese, dried lentils, pepper, and a bag of oats for Darkwind. They learned that a local farmer had horses for sale, so they purchased two, a dappled mare and a chestnut gelding which Japhis named Blotch and Noballs. Because Davin was spending the Questers' money, he did not dicker for a better price. The farmer felt so guilty that she gave them two used but serviceable saddles, two bridles, and two worn and faded horse blankets.

The horses were stolid, healthy creatures that would win no races, though they kept a steady pace. Noballs tended to shy at sudden movements; Davin thought that perfectly understandable. Blotch sometimes stopped to see if Japhis had ridden far enough, but she walked on contentedly whenever Japhis nudged her flanks and clucked. Darkwind paid little attention to the horses. He would precede them and Davin would call him back, thinking people would remember a riderless horse leading mounted beasts. This happened several times before Davin realized that it did not matter if people noticed them. Only the demons cared that they were coming, and who could hide from demons? After that, Darkwind stayed several lengths ahead of Japhis, and Davin rode slightly behind her.

They spent the next night in separate rooms at an inn called The Dancing Badgers. Davin, on seeing it, scowled and said, "Half the inns we pass are Dancing Somethings. It's true some people dance at inns, but it seems to me The Fucking Bunnies would be more appropriate." When Japhis laughed, he blushed.

At dinner, the serving boy asked if he wanted ale or wine. He looked at Japhis, then told the boy to bring him cow's milk. When the boy frowned, he added, "My stomach's upset," and cursed himself for needing a false explanation.

It rained all the next day, so they remained at The Dancing Badgers. After breakfast, Japhis sat by the hearth and watched the flames. Davin fed and brushed Darkwind, Blotch, and Noballs.

"I'm tired," he told Darkwind as he combed the stallion's mane. Darkwind watched him without any hint of emotion. "Can you talk to me like you talked to the girl?" Still Darkwind said nothing, or if he did, Davin could not hear him. "I assume the demon can hear me as well as you can." Darkwind did not nod or shake its head.

"Could the demon return, just for a while? We could talk about human things, or demonly ones." Darkwind looked out of his stall, where the rain fell through thick gray swashes of light.

"I suppose not. I suppose it'd further endanger our chances

of making the prophecy come true if one of the Three was gone from the world, even for a little while."

Darkwind nodded.

"I suppose that's why the demon couldn't turn itself into a dragon and carry us to the Tangled Lands, saving us from this unending, senseless, damned—" He heard his anger and checked himself, then grabbed the edge of the stall's inner wall and shook it, scaring Blotch and Noballs. He released the wall and slumped to the ground. After a minute, he began to pick at the splinter in his palm, all he had gained from his show of anger. Darkwind came near, but Davin ignored him. Darkwind bashed his muzzle against Davin's neck. Warm, moist breath and cold, wet nostrils met the skin beneath Davin's ear, and he laughed.

That afternoon, passing by Japhis's door, he thought he heard someone crying in her room. He remembered all that Japhis had left behind, and his own self-pity in the stable embarrassed him. He stood in the hall, then walked on. He begged a small ball of clay from the inn's cook and worked it into a stallion that stood proudly on its rear legs. The cook let Davin bake it in his own oven after Davin promised to clean any mess he made. The serving boy, giggling, brought the clay stallion on a tray with Japhis's dinner, and all the diners applauded, thinking this must be the one-handed woman's birthday. She smiled, her face flushed surprisingly red, and patted at tears with the loose sleeve at her right wrist.

The next morning, Davin saddled Noballs, but when Japhis went to throw her saddle on Blotch's back, Darkwind whinnied and stamped. Soon they understood that he was willing to carry one of them. "So the other rider can switch between Blotch and Noballs, to make better time?" Davin asked.

Darkwind nodded, so Japhis saddled him. He tossed his head when she tried to put a bridle on him. She smiled, then put the bridle into the saddlebag, saying, "I suppose it makes as much sense for me to wear this as you."

When she mounted, Davin repressed his envy. Even if Darkwind was half a horse and had no horn, the beast was a unicorn amazingly like the one in Davin's dreams. The envy faded as he realized that if Darkwind was a unicorn, he proved by carrying Japhis, a mother, that the unicorns' concept of purity encompassed far more than virginity. Davin's last bit of pride had been in keeping his virginity through the worst of his trials, and now that seemed a silly, bitter thing.

While they rode, he considered his life and wondered what purpose it had. Then he smiled at his foolishness. The Questers had given him a purpose greater than any he had dreamed of as a child. Whether the Three won or lost, that purpose would end in the Tangled Lands. Japhis had her daughter and her village to return to. Darkwind had the company of the unicorns. One of the Three must die battling demons; it might as well be him.

They covered ground much more quickly than before, he noticed. Had Darkwind consented to be ridden because of Davin's outburst in the stable?

The fourth day brought them within an hour of City Gordia, as close as they would come to Gordia's capital before turning north. Their inn, The Dancing Crickets, was almost entirely occupied by the Empress's soldiers. Japhis and Davin had to share a small, drafty room at the back of the inn. They went to sleep as they had on their first night in the woods, with their backs turned to each other, each clutching the edge of a thin blanket stretched taut over them. When Davin woke at dawn, he was lying on his back, and Japhis slept with her head on his shoulder. He did not move until she opened her eyes twenty minutes later. Then he snored once, blinked, and said, "Uh? Time 'o ge' up a'ready?"

They rode for two days through farmlands northwest of City Gordia and stayed with farmers. One night, Davin and Japhis slept on the floor of a single-room cabin with nine other humans, three dogs, seven puppies, a goat, and a cat. The next night, Japhis had the bedroom that had belonged to the farmer's daughter, who had married and moved away. Davin stayed in the barn with Darkwind and the horses. If they were truly Three, it was appropriate for him to share quarters with the strange stallion. The thought did not console him. He fell asleep thinking of Japhis, warm and alone in a wide, soft bed.

The skies were cloudless for those two days. The winds were almost warm, as if summer hoped to recapture the land from autumn. The Three traveled along fields and through small woods, along streams and a lake shore. Japhis sang old songs in a rough, pleasant voice, and Davin found himself talking about his life with the Unicorn Riders, something he had never discussed in detail with anyone. He asked her about her hand, and was told of an earlier life that Japhis did not miss. They talked about Lizelle, and the girl's hope to join a circus, and how Japhis hoped she and her daughter could become closer. She talked about Villel, and Davin wondered if Japhis had loved Villel until his death, or if she had only thought she had, then suspected that she was wondering the same thing. The spate of confidences seemed to embarrass them both. They rode in silence for the rest of the afternoon.

On the seventh night, they came to River Gordia, which marked the end of the farmlands and the beginnings of the plains. They stayed at an inn whose sign showed two grotesque catfish. "Dancing?" Japhis asked. "Or spawning? I don't think I want to know." They took two rooms, as usual. After dinner, Davin lay awake in his, and finally dressed again. He stepped onto the balcony. Below, a group of cattle herders played a card game; their laughter might have kept him awake. He stood before Japhis's door, not daring to knock. He remembered the time he had heard her crying, and wished she would cry now, because then he would dare. He had no excuse for his cowardice. The worst she could do was send him away.

He did not know when he first thought she was attractive. She was a stocky, middle-aged, one-handed woman with a weathered face and a quiet, almost grim manner that was rarely broken by humor or grief. He remembered when he first recognized that she was desirable. After he saw his virginity as a withered and ludicrous burden, he saw Japhis as an acceptable route to an indulgent end. Standing there, he did not know if he wanted to risk destroying their camaraderie by propositioning her. She was a mature woman, suffering from the loss of her man. Offering himself now might seem an insult. Far worse, if she accepted, she would discover he was an ignorant and bitter adolescent in the skin of an experienced man. He could not imagine any consequences of visiting her that would not be ugly or embarrassing, or both.

At last, he turned away. He stopped again in front of his door, then continued down the hall. If he could not sleep, he might as well have company. Descending the stairs, he felt something like comfort in familiar surroundings. The room smelled of wood smoke, mirthweed smoke, and spilled beer.

Drunken laughter with a Gordian plains accent was remarkably like drunken laughter from native Tyrwilkans. One of the herders picked out a dancing tune on a four-stringed, short-necked banjo, and Davin smiled, knowing he had made the right choice.

The serving man separated himself from the people watching the card players and asked Davin what he would have. He considered tea and milk, then realized he had decided when he turned from Japhis's door. "Beer." The serving man grinned. Japhis expected to leave early the next morning; a mug or two would help Davin sleep more soundly. He would be better company for her.

He woke the next morning on his bed in the room on the upper floor. His head ached and his body felt feverish. His mouth tasted as though he had vomited. When he looked at his shirt, he knew that he had, and had then made the feeblest attempt to clean himself. The door to his room was open. Someone was looking in. Someone had spoken to him; that was why he was awake when he should be mercifully unconscious.

Japhis was the shadow in his doorway. He could not see her face. She had said his name, he thought. He might even have answered her with a groan. He brushed his hand across his face to make the drunken Davin go away and the sober one appear. "J'phis. Yeah. I'm awake. I'm sorry. I need a—" His stomach lurched, and he could not speak for fear that he would vomit in front of her.

"How much money is left?" Her voice was frighteningly calm.

"Money?" He blinked, trying to understand why that was important.

"They said you were gambling with the herders. How much money is left?"

"Oh." He remembered something of the night then, sitting and laughing with long-haired men and women of the plains. He felt in his shirt pocket, but did not find his pouch. His pants lay on the chair beside his bed. He grabbed them and patted the pockets. At first, he thought the pouch was not there either, then frowned, trying to comprehend what the soft thing in his right pocket could be. Its shape and size was something like a banana peel, but its texture was of leather. Understanding, he whispered, "Oh."

Japhis whirled as people began to yell outside. "Godlings," she said, and left.

He fell back onto the bed, wanting to sleep, but the commotion continued. He sat up, and the room reeled. It stopped, so he stood and dressed. He splashed water from a basin onto his face and his shirt. Downstairs, the common room was empty, except for a serving girl. He ordered a beer and told her he would pay for it when they paid for their rooms. He raised the mug to his lips, drained half, then wandered to the front door to see what was happening.

The herders were on horseback, chasing a dark, saddleless horse around the inn's corral. They rode well, laughing and yelling, and Davin grinned. The sun hurt his eyes, but as he adjusted to the morning glare, he looked more closely. Blotch and Noballs were among the horses being ridden. Darkwind was the horse they chased. He suddenly felt horribly sober.

Japhis stood midway between the inn and the corral. She turned, looked at Davin, glanced at the mug in his hand, and said, "Congratulations. You gambled away Darkwind."

He dropped the mug and, squatting in the dust by the side of the inn, began to cry.

She walked up to him, shading him from the sun. "What do we do now, Davin? How do we save the world now?" If her voice had been angry or sneering, it would have been less painful. Her words held weariness and disillusionment, nothing more.

He spoke between gritted teeth. "I think we pause for a conference."

Kevin and Janny and Gwen sat at an oval table with a silver top in an oval room with silver walls. They wore black business suits; at each throat, a thin black strip slashed vertically from collar to sternum through an inverted triangle of white. Gwen's dreadlocks were matte black, like their suits. Janny's bobbed hair glistened as if it had been oiled.

Janny cleared her throat. "I—"

Gwen said, "What the hell happened? One minute I'm being a happy horsey in my stall, and the next, a bunch of cowboy Arabs are trying to rope me, and you two are just watching as if it didn't matter!"

"Not us," Janny said. "Japhis and Davin."

"Yeah, fine fucking distinction. What's happening? What do we do?"

"I'm sorry," Kevin said softly. "I blew it."

Gwen's voice became quiet and sympathetic, as if she had never been angry. "What do you mean?"

"I got drunk. I mean, Davin got drunk. I was bored—" Horny, he thought, but forcing Davin to enter Japhis's room would have been like forcing him to rape someone. "—and I thought I'd just have a beer or two before going to sleep."

"He gambled away our money and our horses," Janny explained. "Including Darkwind."

"How could you?" Gwen sounded horrified, almost as if she would cry. "Darkwind's . . ." She moved her hand as if she might catch the right words from the air.

"I didn't know!" Kevin slammed his hands down on the smooth table top, and his palms stung. He slid his hands back, then lifted them in a gesture of surrender. "I didn't know. Davin was tempted to have a drink or two. I decided he should. I thought I could make him stop."

"You couldn't?"

"I don't know. He didn't want to. I didn't want to." Kevin swallowed, then admitted, "I didn't try. I didn't realize how dangerous it was."

"Nice going, Kev," Gwen said.

He shrugged and glanced at Janny. "Some boy wonder, huh?"

Her eyes were the same brown as Japhis's. She reached across the table to pat his hand. "Hey, you only sold the third. You didn't kill him."

He nodded and smiled as if he felt much better. "Yeah, well. We start over?"

"Couldn't we just kill the cowboy Arabs?" Gwen asked.

Kevin shook his head. "This isn't *Treasure Realm*, Gwen. First, by local law, they think they own Darkwind, and we don't have anything to use to buy him back. Second, there's a lot more of them than us."

"Okay," Gwen said. "Once more, from the top. Let's do the next one right, okay?"

Janny said, "That's a thought. Exiting."

"Exiting."

"Exiting."

It only took an instant to realize that nothing had happened, but Kevin could not tell how much subjective time passed before he said, "What the—"

Gwen stood and stared at the ceiling. "Exit!"

"This is . . . very strange," Janny said.

"You're both experiencing this?" Gwen said cautiously. "I haven't gone hothead?"

"Maybe we've all gone hothead," Janny suggested.

"Maybe one of us has gone hothead, and the other two exited," Kevin said. "I hope I'm one of the ones who exited."

Gwen laughed. Janny glanced at them both, then smiled. She said, "Okay. If you two are here, I'm not crazy and the computer hasn't shut down. Which means we've run into some weird bug in *Lands'* pause mode—"

"Which I doubt very much," Kevin said. "It would've shown up earlier."

"Or someone's in the game on the programming level."

"Mad Dog?" Gwen said. "That's—"

The far wall became a large 3-D screen, filled by Mad Dog's giant, disembodied head. His eyes were closed. His limp blond hair floated about him as if he were underwater.

"Mad Dog?" Janny said.

His eyes, pale blue and bloodshot, flicked open. Kevin thought Mad Dog stared at him, then realized that Janny and Gwen must think the same thing.

"Hey, Hound Dog!" Gwen called. "A joke's a joke, but trapping us in here isn't funny."

"Hello." Mad Dog's voice seemed insanely calm. "You may wonder why I've called you here."

"No shit," Gwen said.

"Look, Mad Dog," Janny said. "Don't do this. It won't solve any of our problems, you know."

After a moment of silence, Mad Dog continued. "Now you may stop wondering. I am the great and powerful Oz, but there's no way for you to reach the man behind the curtain." He nodded. "That's a joke."

"Very funny," Gwen said to Kevin.

"And this is a recording, in case any of you haven't figured it out yet. In real time, I am—" His voice became inhumanly low, a painful rumbling: "—talking very slow." It returned to something like a normal speed. "And having lots of fun, so don't you worry about me, kiddies. And don't worry about yourselves, either. I haven't trapped you in there. Mad Dog isn't that kind of asshole. What kind of asshole is he, you may ask. And you'll know after you've heard me out."

His eyes closed; he seemed very tired when he opened them again. "The first thing you should know is that I erased the backup copy of *Lands of Adventure*. The second thing you should know is that I've disconnected *Lands* from the net, so you can't call anyone for favors or try to do anything clever on the jack. The third thing you should know, or that I should remind you of, is that you're making the present run at maximum computer speed. Which means that if you jack out into real time to make a new backup, the present game will finish without you, well before you could possibly make the new backup. At best, you'd end up with a backup of a thoroughly bugged program which would be of no use to anyone. I hope I've been sufficiently clear, because you don't have the option of seeing this message again."

He grinned, baring yellow teeth. "What kind of asshole am I? I am the kind who's giving you one chance to return to a game that you wanted to quit, and try to win it. Isn't that sweet of ol' Mad Dog? Just save the Tangled Lands scenario on this run, and *Lands*'ll run fine. You'll have time to jack out and make as many backups as your little hearts could ever desire. All you have to do is win the present game. Easy, no?"

Mad Dog's head turned, as if to look in a room next to theirs, then faced them again. "Sorry to do this to you, Gwen. You're just an innocent bystander in the whole business. Unless you've been fucking Janny, too, and Michael managed to keep that secret." He sneered. "But you, Kevin Kid Fucking Flash, and you, my sweet little Janny, fucking under ol' Mad Dog's nose while ol' Mad Dog busts his balls on a project to make you backstabbers rich—"

"Oh, Mad Dog," Janny whispered.

"Christ," said Gwen.

Mad Dog laughed. "Well, happy gaming, boys and girls. I hope you don't lose too quickly. I want you to treasure this experience, since it'll be your last time in *Lands*." The corner of a giant lip twisted into a false frown of sympathy. "Oh, you won't have anyone to pat your backs when you come out. I'm off to the Silver Socket. As for the boys, Michael was all heartbroken about his little slip-up, as if he thought the Mad Dog could have his feelings hurt. Brian made me promise not to do anything rash before he took Michael home, and you can see that I haven't." He raised an eyebrow. "Rash would've been trashing both copies and letting you blame me for the project getting shit-canned. But Mad Dog's no credit-hound. Now when you lose, you can blame yourselves, too. Cheerios."

The screen became a wall again.

Gwen said gently, "I'm sorry. . ."

"Forget it," Janny said.

Kevin put his hand on her arm. "I'm sorry he learned like this."

She shook his hand off. "You told Michael."

"No. Brian."

"Same thing."

"I didn't know! I didn't—" He shrugged and looked away.

Gwen clapped him on the shoulder. "Ain't love grand?"

Janny glared at Gwen, then closed her eyes and shook her head. "Poor Mad Dog."

"You think he meant it?" Kevin asked.

"'Course he meant it." Janny looked at the far wall. "We've got to get back in the game. We've got to save it."

Kevin nodded. "No prob. We'll do our best."

Gwen made a fist and raised it high. "All for one, and one for all!"

"It's not a game," Janny said quietly. "Don't you see that? It was supposed to be a game, and we can manipulate it like a game, so we think it's a game. But it's not a game. It's a world, and we've got to save it."

"Sure, Janny." Kevin looked at Gwen and thought that Janny worked too much and slept too little. She would be fine when the game was finished. Everything would be fine after the game was finished. He gripped Janny's shoulders and felt them thin and strong under his hands. When she looked up, he said, "Mad Dog's just made sure we'll all work a little harder. We'll save it."

She smiled. "Oh, Kev. You're so sincere."

Gwen laughed, and Kevin blushed. "Back into the game?" he asked.

"Back into the game," Janny agreed.

He was squatting in someone's shadow. He smelled wood smoke and cow manure, heard people yell and horses race. The roughness at his back was the plank wall of the inn. Japhis stood before him. He shook his head, wishing it would clear, and pushed himself upright. "Darkwind!" he yelled. "C'mere!"

The stallion turned toward them. A lariat snaked above Darkwind's head as he slowed; it fell onto the dusty floor of the corral as he launched himself toward Davin. A high fence of log rails stood between them. For a moment, Davin thought Darkwind would kill himself against it, or more impossibly, burst it apart, but Darkwind leapt, clearing the highest rail by several inches. The mounted cowherders stared, then one cheered, and the others joined in.

Darkwind stopped a few yards short of Davin and Japhis. Davin stepped forward, reaching to stroke Darkwind's nose, and stumbled. Japhis braced him with her right forearm and whispered, "Careful."

"I'm sorry," Davin said. "I can't undo what I've done, but maybe I can salvage something."

"Maybe you'd better." Japhis looked toward the corral.

The herders, twelve or fourteen men and women, all lean and dark and long-haired, rode toward them. The men wore shaggy moustaches. Both sexes dressed in hooded brown jackets and baggy brown pants with high boots; only their bright sashes and horse blankets differed from rider to rider. A man in the lead said, "A fine horse I won last night! I'm almost sorry to take him from you!"

"I told you that we'd gamble for my horses." It was not a question, though Davin did not know the answer.

The man nodded.

"Did I say how many?"

"There was no need. We notice people's horses. This one was your prize."

"I didn't mean this one."

The dark man frowned. He wore a saber at his hip, as did most of his people. Japhis's golden knife must still be upstairs. Davin was not sure whether he still owned his hunting knife, but it would not matter, even if he had it in his belt. The man pointed at Darkwind. "He's not a horse?" His people laughed, but he did not.

"I don't think of him as a horse. He's half unicorn. Feel his brow."

"Uh." The man threw one leg over the front of his saddle and slid to the ground, then sauntered toward them. When he reached for Darkwind's forehead, Davin was afraid the stallion would back away, but Darkwind lowered his neck. The herder stroked the star on Darkwind's brow. "A tiny bump does not a unicorn make."

"Then I'll prove he's wiser than a horse. Darkwind! Am I a drunken fool? Be honest."

Darkwind studied Davin, then nodded extravagantly. The herders laughed. A small woman on a pinto said, "You've trained it to some signal."

"No. Darkwind, face them, not me." Darkwind turned. "It's not my favorite view," Davin said, and the herders laughed again.

"Maybe you deserve it," Japhis whispered.

Davin addressed the skeptical woman. "He cannot see me. I'll be quiet. Tell him to do something, and see if he obeys."

The woman made a quick sound like a laugh. "Horse. Kiss me."

The man riding next to the woman nudged her. "Always the new thrill." They smiled at each other.

Darkwind walked slowly toward the mounted woman and stood beside her pinto. "He comes to my voice," she said, shrugging. "So? A clever—"

Darkwind reared. The woman did not flinch. She patted her pinto to calm it, and Darkwind touched his nose to the woman's cheek.

"It must be a trick," said another woman.

"What proof can I give you?" Davin asked. "He cannot talk, but he understands. Will you—" He let the sentence die, seeing that the herders stared at Darkwind.

Davin thought the stallion pawed the dirt with its front right hoof because he was angry, then understood.

Japhis pointed, saying nothing.

On the ground, in rough Gordian letters, was scrawled, "What horse writes?"

The woman on the pinto rode beside Darkwind and read the message aloud. The herders crowded around to stare at the dirt.

At last, the man who seemed to be their leader laughed and leaped back onto his gray mare. "I've seen more graceful writing," he said, and Darkwind snorted. "But none that's more persuasive," the man concluded, saluting the black stallion, and Darkwind nodded to him.

"Thank you," Davin said.

The leader stroked one corner of his moustache with his index finger. "You will not tell me now that you did not think of your gold as gold?"

Davin sighed. "No. I could tell you that I did not think."

The herders grinned. "Ah, you were good company!" The leader wheeled his gray. "But we've cattle to drive to City Gordia. I bid you farewell, bold gambler!"

"Farewell," Davin said, and Japhis, turning to go back into the inn, seconded him.

As they stepped inside, Japhis said, "Blotch may be happier with a few horses besides Noballs around, and I never had time to become fond of Noballs. Besides, walking will be good for you. After watching you for a couple of days from Darkwind's back, I might even be able to forgive you."

Davin spent the day chopping and stacking wood to repay the innkeeper for their stay. Japhis sat nearby, watching him work. After ten or fifteen minutes, she began to clean and mend her gear, then did his that afternoon because, she told him, she was bored; he should not interpret this as kindness or pity. That night, Japhis slept in the loft of the innkeeper's barn, and Davin slept on hay near the door. In the morning, Davin chopped more wood. At last, the innkeeper smiled and said she was satisfied. Davin, Japhis, and Darkwind left Catfish Inn at noon on the ninth day of their trip.

They had no more money for inns, but there were no inns in the plains. They traveled across low hills of long grass for several days without seeing anyone. After the first day in the plains, Darkwind carried their packs and Davin and Japhis walked beside him, heading constantly into a cold wind from the north. They ate dried foods and the occasional rabbit or quail that Davin killed with a sling.

On their third day in the plains, he told her that he could not drink.

She nodded. "Who would have guessed?"

"Anyone but me," he answered, not daring to look at her.

"Oh." They continued for several minutes, and she asked, "Why did you, then? When you were tempted, that night, why didn't you just come talk to me, instead?"

He began to laugh helplessly. The lines of her face furrowed more deeply in puzzlement, and at last she began to laugh because he did.

Late that afternoon, they came upon the cowherders' village, a cluster of tents that sheltered children, older adults, and a few cripples. Davin offered to work in exchange for food and a night's lodging, and was pleased that Japhis offered, too. The herders laughed and took them in, saying they would rather have guests than servants.

The next morning, as the Three moved on, they saw a dark shape traveling toward them from the north. Davin suggested they avoid it, but Japhis asked what it mattered who they met outside the Tangled Lands. Bandits would have a hard fight for tiny gains. Besides, she wondered who would journey from the demons' holding.

The shape proved to be a small covered wagon, drawn by two mules and guided by a gray-haired woman in a paint-spattered jacket. "Hello!" Japhis called.

"How'd you do?" The wagoneer reined in her mules, took her pipe from her mouth, and smiled. "Off to see the Tangled Lands?" Her accent was Torionese, and Davin, to his surprise, felt a pang of something like homesickness.

Davin and Japhis glanced at each other, then nodded to the woman.

"It's beautiful this time of year," the woman said. "But when winter comes, I always go south. Someday I'll bring fuel and food enough to stay until spring."

"You visit the Tangled Lands?" Davin asked in surprise.

The woman nodded. "I paint them." When she looked at their faces, she laughed. "From outside the border, of course!"

"Oh," said Davin.

"Are you poets? Essayists? Or simply travelers?"

"Travelers," said Japhis with a nod. "Why do you ask?"

"Just curious. You obviously don't carry paints or boards, and I doubt you'd try to drag back sculptures with just one horse and yourselves."

"No. We're—" He had never said it to anyone, and he wondered why it sounded silly to him. "We're a Three."

"A Three? Oh. The horse?"

"Half unicorn."

"Hmm." She looked at them and said nothing for a moment. "Not suicides? The Tangled Lands attract too many suicides."

"No!" Japhis's vehemence startled Davin, then he remembered Lizelle and understood why Japhis would consider the suggestion obscene.

"He really is half unicorn." Davin pointed at Darkwind's star. "It was cut."

"A Three," the woman said. "I thought they'd finished with Threes."

"You say that," Japhis said, "as if you wished we weren't going to try."

"Oh, I hope you try." The painter nodded deeply. "I hope you succeed. But I'll be sad, too. They're beautiful, the Tangled Lands."

"They threaten us all!" Japhis said.

The woman shrugged. "Beauty has no ties to purpose. Will the demons die if you succeed?"

"You care?" Davin's surprise came because he had worried about that point, and had thought he was alone.

"They're fellow artists, in their way."

"Oh. They shouldn't die. When Demon's Gate begins to close, they'll all rush through to the other side before the Gate slams shut."

"Ah." The woman squinted. "May I paint you?"

Davin and Japhis glanced again at each other. "Us?"

"You're heroes, you know. I could share my food, and maybe spare a blanket, if you'd give me two hours. I can finish your portrait from memory, later."

"Heroes?" Davin said, and the woman clearly did not understand why he and Japhis began to laugh.

On the fourth night in the plains, under their new blanket,

Davin and Japhis made an end of Davin's virginity. Afterwards, he said, "It seems . . . anticlimactic."

She nudged him. "It usually gets better. Patience is important."

Much later, lying together, they noticed light flicker on the northern horizon like lightning, but they heard no thunder. For several hours the next afternoon, the northern sky was dark, but if it was a storm, it did not move toward them.

That night, they repeated themselves, beginning to learn each other's likes and weaknesses.

In the north, the dance of light reappeared on the horizon. Davin began to suspect it proclaimed the nearness of the Tangled Lands. He did not ask what Japhis thought. So long as he could, he would appreciate their journey and ignore their destination.

The next day, their sixth in the plains, the northern sky was as black as moonless night. Stars shone within the huge shadow. They formed constellations that Davin had never seen.

"The Tangled Lands," Japhis said.

That night they made love.

15

Demon's Gate

Davin, Japhis, and Darkwind stood on a low hill, facing a warm wind that smelled impossibly of garlic and jasmine. Behind and to their right were the plains they had crossed. To their left was a forest of young trees, where a fire had burned fifteen or twenty years before. Before them lay the Tangled Lands.

"If I don't survive," Japhis said, "tell Lizelle I loved her."

Davin nodded.

Within the Tangled Lands' borders, the ground appeared to be a mat of ochre things that moved like grasses blown in ten thousand directions or like a sea of snakes crawling endlessly over each other. Davin thought he could see the border expanding, creeping slowly and inexorably onward. Above the Tangled Lands, the air, shimmering and electrical, pulsed as if to the beat of an unseen heart, as though the Tangled Lands were a single creature that mindlessly consumed their world.

"If you can, give her my knife and the wrist-case. That's not much of an inheritance, but they should be worth something."

He nodded again. "Japhis?"

"Yes?"

"If I die, send word to Torion. There's a tiny county called

Greenboots far to the southwest. My family's still there, I believe. Send to the head of Family Greenboots."

"You're highborn?"

"We had the right to wear white silk castebands. We didn't have the wealth. It's a very unimportant county. And I left when I was small."

"What should I tell them?"

"That I lived and died . . . as best I could. And I remembered my family with love." He shrugged. "You can keep my belongings. Give them to Lizelle, perhaps."

Japhis's mouth quirked into a smile. "Heroes."

He shook his head. "Don't do anything heroic. Your daughter needs you. Maybe the prophecy's wrong. Maybe we'll all live."

Japhis nodded and stroked Darkwind's neck. "If we fail, I'd rather win."

(Kevin: I've been thinking. You two should jack out.)

(Janny: That's nice. Forget it.)

(Gwen: Stick to what you're good at, Kev.)

(Kevin: Look, I'm not being a macho twit. Or if I am, I'm trying to be a nice macho twit. I haven't said anything 'cause so far, if one of your characters'd died, the safeties probably would've pulled you out. But the Tangled Lands scare me. Something happens to your character in there, and you might have serious problems jacking out.)

(Janny: You talking hothead?)

(Kevin: I don't know. Maybe. Hell, you might go hothead just by crossing the border. We don't know what rules still apply on that side. Maybe none of them do.)

(Gwen: C'mon, Kev. You warned me before I went in as Tikolos Ar. You weren't half so worried then.)

(Kevin: I didn't know Janny had been dreaming on the design path, then.)

(Janny: Look, I'm sorry I didn't—)

(Kevin: S'right. If you'd known how dangerous it was, you probably wouldn't've done it. And I'm not saying you shouldn't've. I'm just saying it's dangerous. Okay?)

(Janny: Okay.)

(Kevin: Somebody's got to go in to change the odds so the Three have a chance of winning. But that doesn't mean we all have to.)

(Janny: How do we know whose character needs help? Maybe they all do.)

(Kevin: Maybe the program's hopelessly screwed no matter what we do.)

(Janny: Maybe. But I'm the God of this world. I'm going in.)

(Kevin: I'd rather you didn't.)

(Janny: Your concern's noted, Kevin. But I'm going in. If it'll comfort you any, Mad Dog may've made a mistake that'll help us. We can still change characters within the game.)

(Gwen: So? We're already running the only three characters that're useful.)

(Janny: As long as I'm the program God, I've got access to the demons through the design path.)

(Kevin: No!)

(Janny: I could run a demon just like I run Japhis. Maybe. Any edge we can get—)

(Kevin: Maybe you should just buy yourself a hothead rig and save some time, too.)

(Janny: Huh?)

(Kevin: Superimpose your mind on a buggy subroutine like a demon? Forget it, please.)

(Janny: Okay. But I'm still going in as Japhis.)

(Kevin: Gwen? You crazy, too?)

(Gwen: Nope. Just stupid, son. Can't protect stupid people from themselves.)

(Kevin: Fuck. All right. Will you two be extremely careful? I care, y'know?)

(Gwen: If this won't be a breeze, you best be worrying 'bout your own ass, white boy. *Kiss*)

(Janny: 'Cause we can't watch it for you. It's too distracting. *Hug*)

(Kevin: *Blush* I'm shutting up now. You two embarrass me no end.)

(Gwen: Wouldn't want to do that. It's the cutest little end that I—)

(Kevin: Bye!)

"It is beautiful," Davin said. "The painter was right."

Japhis glanced at him. "If the demons were content with a few acres . . ."

The Tangled Lands extended to the northern and the east-

ern horizons. Japhis pointed at a cluster of monolithic structures so black that their shapes were hard to perceive. "Think
that was Sandiston? I hear some of its people still travel
through the South, seeking a new home. I hear the North-
landers are moving west, and they've had skirmishes with the
Empress's troops. The Empress justifies her expansion by
saying Gordia must grow before the Tangled Lands, not die
within it." Japhis shrugged. "There was a lake by Sandiston.
Good fishing, I hear. I wonder what the demons made of it."

"You hear a lot."

She glanced at him, then smiled and lifted the gold cup that
covered the stump of her wrist. "I got in the habit of knowing
what the noble and the rich intended to do."

She had been grimmer all morning, since she first donned
the gold wrist-case and strapped on her golden knife. He
wanted to ask if she regretted their last days of intimacy, but
he did not dare.

Darkwind snorted and trotted downhill. Japhis squeezed
Davin's hand, released it, and unsheathing her golden knife,
followed Darkwind. Davin nodded to himself, then withdrew
the unicorn wand from the holster in his belt. He wished he
had thought to ask the Korz Demon if the wand was made
from Darkwind's horn or from the horn of the unicorn Davin
had killed. He hoped that it was neither.

He expected some form of resistance when he passed the
border, but he stepped from familiar fauna onto foreign as
easily as stepping onto a rug. The light was brighter and more
diffuse within the Tangled Lands. The air might have been
warmer, but Davin was not sure. The brown grass writhed
under his moccasins and around his ankles, but it did not cling
or offer resistance. It was shorter than the prairie grass, and
easier to walk through. An eerie wailing came from the distant
black monoliths. Davin wondered if that was music, or the
noise of demonic machinery, or the cry of something so
strange that it had no human equivalent.

It would be too easy to lose their way on this odd, featureless plain. He looked over his shoulder to fix the hill beyond
the border as a landmark. Expecting to see the gray sky of his
world and the low hill with its two bare pine trees, he saw
instead a mirror that extended like a wall as high as he could
see. "Japhis! Darkwind!"

In the mirror, Davin gaped and Japhis glared. Where Dark-wind stood in the Tangled Lands, the Demon of Korz Pass watched in its form of the giant woman in a leafy kirtle. Japhis must have seen something in the mirror, too, for she whirled toward Darkwind and lifted her knife. The stallion seemed puzzled and paced awkwardly backwards. In the mirror, the Korz Demon smiled with . . . amusement? Respect? Resignation? Triumph?

The Tangled Lands, Davin thought. What can we trust? He looked at the wand in his hand. Can we trust ourselves?

"Japhis! The demons would gladly set us against each other!"

Darkwind nodded; so did the Korz Demon in the mirror.

"Are we trapped?" Japhis called.

Davin stepped close to the mirror and stretched out his hand. The unicorn wand passed through the mirror as if one or the other were immaterial. "I don't know. Should I try it?"

"All of us or none of us should," Japhis said. She offered her right wrist to him, and when he gripped it, she lay her knife and left arm across Darkwind's back.

When they stepped through the mirror, they stepped into the same landscape they had left: ochre grasses, distant mono-liths, inhuman wailing. Behind them rose the mirror. Davin said, "Did we go somewhere else? Or were we . . . reflected back into the same place?"

"Tangled Lands," Japhis said, as if that were explanation enough.

"Are you confused?" The voice could have been male or female. Davin could not see its source; it came from the air, as if the Tangled Lands spoke to them. "That's to be expected. Would you return freely?" A golden door appeared in the mir-ror, then swung wide, admitting a cool breeze that carried prairie smells. The hill with two bare pines lay beyond. "Or would you be ejected?"

"Neither," Japhis answered, looking all around them. "Thank you."

Something blossomed from the brown grass at Davin's feet. It sprouted as tall as he before he could blink. Davin stumbled back, and saw that he looked at a young man made entirely of black and yellow flowers. The flower-man's eyes were closed; his body did not move. The petals that formed his clothing made a long Gordian robe that had not been fashionable in two hundred years. The young man smiled as if dreaming something wondrous. He swayed, perhaps to a breeze, and smelled of dandelions and camphor. "This one came to die," said the air. "And this we chose to do. Perhaps he has his wish. Shall we grant the same to you?"

"No," Japhis repeated. "Thank you. We have not come to die."

"Are you Three? Or are you four? If you leave, will there be more?"

Davin looked at Darkwind. If the stallion reacted to "four," Davin could not see it.

"No more," said Japhis. "Be glad. Where's Demon's Gate?"

"Have the Tangled Lands a heart? Will you search in every part? Does nothing have a center? Can you exit once you enter?"

"No games!" Japhis cried. "Come out!"

"A shame." The flower-man withered into dust dispersed by a sudden wind. In his place, an orange block of stone shot from the earth, throwing dust and clods of dirt onto Davin and Japhis. Twice the height of a human, it towered above them. Its head, a rough block with distorted human features, was as long as its torso. Its arms and legs, tiny for its size, remained folded against its body. "I doubt that you can win." The mirror disappeared, and their world was visible beyond the Tangled Lands' border. "You may go out as you came in."

"No." Japhis raised her golden blade.

The orange demon's head turned with the sound of stone grinding on stone to regard Davin.

"No." The unicorn wand seemed weightless and fragile in his hand.

The grinding resumed, and the orange demon faced Darkwind.

The stallion snorted derisively and shook his head with broad, mane-tossing sweeps.

The orange demon grinned with a horrible grinding. Orange sand fell from its jaws. "Let the game begin. May the purest player win."

The mirror returned, separating them again from their world. At that moment, the demon's arms and legs elongated, shafts of stone driving forward, too quickly to avoid. One fist lashed toward Davin, one toward Darkwind, both heels toward Japhis.

An instinct he did not recognize made Davin parry with the wand. The demon's arm became a jet of sand that sprayed the ochre grasses. Darkwind butted his head against the demon's other fist. Orange stone met the white star of Darkwind's brow, and orange sand spattered the stallion. Japhis's gold knife flicked from side to side, blocking both of the demon's feet and transforming them also to powder.

Four new limbs replaced those the demon had lost. It applauded with its tiny hands.

"Wizard's War!" Davin called, fearing the physical duel could continue until they were all exhausted.

"Choose a game to match your skill. If one bores me, three I'll kill."

"Davin?" Japhis asked.

"Wizard's War!" he repeated, and said to Japhis, "There's a chance. Glee spent hours with me before I left Tyrwilka."

"Many hours!" The demon laughed. "Mighty mage! Demons race before his rage!"

"Davin . . ." Japhis said.

He constructed the phrase of the First Tongue in his mind, then labored to pronounce it properly. Japhis winced at his slowness, but he paid no attention. If speed mattered, he could never win. Midway through his sentence, the orange demon broke in with a harsh ejaculation, then chuckled. Davin finished as if the demon had never interrupted.

The orange stone giant shrieked and burst like a dandelion puff in a tornado. The unicorn wand vibrated in Davin's palm, then the demon's voice came from the air. "Nooooo!"

Darkwind and Japhis both looked at Davin, both cocking their heads to question him without speaking.

He laughed. "I spent afternoons with Glee, trying to learn what he knew from being a Three with his brothers. Thelog Ar played Wizard's War with a demon, and lost because the demon always negated his command before he could finish it. I've been thinking about solutions all the way here."

"So what'd you do? Japhis asked.

"I said, 'In the unicorn wand, this demon shall—' That's when the demon cried, 'Not!' to cancel my spell. So I finished it, '—not be bound.'" Davin smiled. "If only my grammar teacher knew how well I'd mastered the double negative."

"You've won," the air said. "Bravo. Free me, and freely go."

Japhis said, "If you'll take us to Demon's Gate, we'll free you."

"No," the demon answered.

Davin shrugged. "What now?"

Darkwind crossed to Davin's side and dipped his head to take the unicorn wand in his teeth. Davin hesitated, thinking of the Korz Demon and still mistrusting it, wondering if this had all been a ploy to unarm them in the Tangled Lands. He had no idea what else they could do. He released the wand.

Darkwind lifted his head, then dropped the wand onto the writhing ochre grass. Davin reached for it, but Darkwind's hoof covered the wand before Davin could touch it. The wand creaked ominously as Darkwind pressed it into the ground, and the trapped demon's voice rang in the air. "Asphoriel, Lord of Demons, is lord of Demon's Gate. I'll send you to Asphoriel. Let him decide your fate."

Darkwind took his hoof from the wand. Davin, picking it up again, glanced at Japhis and Darkwind. "Good enough?"

Darkwind nodded, and Japhis shrugged. "I hope this Asphoriel doesn't like rhyme."

Davin repeated the memorized phrase from the magician's tongue: *"In the unicorn wand, this demon shall not be bound."*

The air spoke: "Thank you."

Something burst like a thunderclap, and the Three stood in a canyon of murky crystalline structures which gave a dark purple light and a smell like turpentine, tangerines, and musk. A humid heat brought sweat immediately to Davin's brow and neck. Above them stretched a starry, unfamiliar sky. At the far end of the canyon, a silver frame outlined an open door. Davin could not guess its scale. "Demon's Gate?" he asked, throwing back his cloak and unbuttoning the throat of his jacket.

Darkwind nodded as a pale glow like a firefly appeared between them and the shining silver door. Perhaps it approached them quickly, perhaps it grew quickly larger; Davin could not tell in the strange purple light. It took the form of a naked man surrounded by fire. His hair was long and pale; his eyes were blue stars behind the flames that flickered along his skin.

(Kevin: It looks like Mad Dog!)

(Gwen: Huh. Not the body, but the face.)

(Janny: I don't—You're right. Must be an effect of dreaming on the jack—my subconscious mind having too much fun.)

"Welcome," said the burning man. "None have come this far before." He bowed. "I am Asphoriel, called the Demon Lord. You know I cannot let you pass."

"But you'll give us the chance to pass," Davin said, wondering at the source of his confidence. "Because you can't resist a game. And playing for the Tangled Lands would be the greatest game of all."

Frowning, the Demon Lord nodded. "And the game will be—" He smiled. "Escape!"

The crystal walls of the canyon began to close on them. The air whined, a high, painful note that made thought difficult.

"Bastard!" Japhis cried. She leaped forward, extending her knife for the Demon Lord's breast, but he shriveled himself into a bright coal that disappeared before her golden blade came near his flames.

Several of the crystal structures slid behind and before them, shutting them off from Demon's Gate or whatever might lie at the opposite end of the canyon. Davin braced himself against one high crystal block in the hope that making the attempt to stop the wall's advance would be sufficient to stop it. He knew as soon as he tried that he had no chance. His moccasins slid on the slick floor. Davin struck the walls with the unicorn horn, and rolled it across their surface, and still they closed on them. The surface of the walls was like polished diamond. They offered no grip, and would not shatter or slow under Japhis's blade or Darkwind's hooves.

(Janny: I'm switching from Japhis to Asphoriel.)

(Kevin: No!)

(Janny: Can you think of a way to win in the game's terms?)

(Kevin: No, but—)

(Janny: Switching now.)

(Kevin: Janny!)

(Janny: Relax. I'm back with Japhis.)

(Kevin: Any luck?)

(Janny: I can ride Asphoriel fine, as an observer. But I can't make him do anything. He doesn't have any conflicting desires to play against each other. He doesn't care if we live, and he doesn't want us to reach Demon's Gate.)

(Gwen: You don't say.)

"Come back!" Japhis called. "We haven't a chance!"

The red glow appeared high above their heads. "Will you concede now? Death is sometimes necessary, but it rarely satisfies us. I offer the same conditions that my servant did."

"This isn't fair!"

"Oh?" Asphoriel laughed. "And why should a game be fair?"

"If it isn't, it's not a game!"

The Demon Lord remained quiet for so long that Davin thought he would not speak again. Their remaining room was a square of perhaps five paces to a side when Asphoriel said, "I'm much more interested in your surrender than your death."

"I'm sure." Japhis dropped her knife onto the ground and sat cross-legged. Davin stared at her, then shrugged and sat also.

"You acknowledge defeat, then?" Asphoriel asked.

The sides of the square dwindled to four paces. Darkwind had to twist his neck and curve his body to stand within its confines. Davin's sweat had nothing to do with heat or humidity.

Japhis said, "I think the only way to win this game is by seeing that it can't be won."

"If you can't win, you've lost."

"No." Their available room must have been less than three paces to a side. Darkwind sat on his haunches, and Davin and Japhis waited side by side, damp shoulders touching. She smelled of sweat and leather, and Davin inhaled deeply, thinking it a fine last scent to breathe.

"Many have died playing games with demons," Asphoriel said patiently. "Will you be among them?"

"They died while losing," Japhis called. "We've won."

Asphoriel's laughter made the tiny space seem smaller.

Japhis said, "If there's another way for us to win, tell us
and kill us! That would be fair." So little room remained that
Darkwind stood on his hind feet and rested his front hooves
against the crystal walls. "You can't, because we've won!"

"You will not claim victory when you're a stain on the
floor of my court."

"You want a stain," Japhis yelled, "to remember that you
failed?"

Laughter filled the dark canyon, and the walls retreated.
"Only this game," Asphoriel said. "Which was on my terms,
and my terms were that you would live to play another game.
What game's worth letting you stand before Demon's Gate?"

Again, a confidence filled Davin that he did not understand. "A game that proves you deserve to be the Demon
Lord."

"I am the Demon Lord. That's proof enough."

"If you're afraid to play against me, I suppose you'd have
to believe it."

Asphoriel appeared in front of Davin. His flames were
warm on Davin's skin, but they did not burn, and Davin did
not flinch. With agonizing reluctance, Asphoriel said, "I will
play any game."

"And you'll let us close Demon's Gate?"

"And I'll let you try to close Demon's Gate."

"You won't oppose us in any way?"

"No."

Davin smiled. "Good enough. Let's play Demon's War."

Asphoriel stared in something remarkably like human as-
tonishment, then shrugged. "Certainly. I'll turn you into a
statue of wood, and you'll remain a statue of wood. It will be
a very short game, and I'll win more easily than I have ever
won before, but if this is what you wish . . ."

"No." Davin kept his tone conversational. "Share your
power. Make me your equal at magic so we'll play skill
against skill, imagination against imagination."

"We would never be equals. I have had my power as long
as the world has existed. You have your short mortal life to
draw upon for knowledge, and little experience even with
awkward human magics."

Davin smiled. "Are you afraid?"

"I'm curious. You ask for fairness, and settle for this?"

"There's no perfect fairness. Give me the chance to start as your equal, and I'll play you."

"Very well. Three conditions. You have the power for as long as the game lasts. You cannot use the power outside the Tangled Lands. You cannot use the power on Demon's Gate."

Japhis touched Davin's arm. "You insist on going first?"

"I thought of it first."

She held his gaze, then nodded. "Be careful." The side of her wrist slid down his arm in what might have been a caress.

He turned to Asphoriel. "How do we begin?"

"Give me your hand." Asphoriel held out his arm. Flames writhed and leaped on his open palm. Swallowing deeply, Davin took the Demon Lord's burning hand.

Kevin, as intellect without form, felt Davin's panic when Davin's body and world disappeared, but he soothed Davin with suggestions he would give to any mind-wars novice. Or perhaps, Kevin thought, he soothed himself with familiar suggestions. Then he told himself to think about the game, not about questions of being and identity. If he lost, he might subjectively have eternity to ponder being and identity, or he might objectively have no time at all.

"Body," he told Davin, and Davin remade his physical form. From outside, it was an ugly parody of a man, but from within, it was Davin as he saw himself.

"War ground," he told Davin, and Davin placed their body in an empty arena with golden sands to fight on and a blue sky above.

"Protection," he ordered, and Davin encased their body in a full suit of shining steel armor.

Something tore through their body's right arm, and they dropped the sword that had been created with the armor. The naked, burning Asphoriel stood on the sands of the arena with a longbow in his hands. A crowd, beautifully detailed, filled the arena's seats with their presence and its air with their applause. A hot sun burned overhead; a few wisps of cloud trailed across the sky. Warm liquid coursed down the arm of Kevin and Davin's body. Kevin felt the body going into shock, and Davin going into panic. Davin understood that what he believed was real, and that he could not win against

Asphoriel, the greatest manipulator of reality his world had known since the God had shaped it.

Kevin overrode Davin to heal their arm and create a thick wooden wall to hide behind for a moment's respite. If they survived, Davin would rationalize this as best he could. He might think it part of Asphoriel's magic, that he began to react properly without thinking about it.

The wooden wall burst into flame. Kevin almost smiled, thinking that Asphoriel's imagery was too limited, and then screamed when flames erupted about him. His armor began to melt, his flesh to burn. The crowd went wild.

He flooded the arena and its spectators with cold sea water, and took a small, guilty pleasure in the contortions of the drowning audience. He coated himself in a silver reflective skin, impervious to pressure, atmosphere, or temperature, and looked for Asphoriel.

The Demon Lord remained a nude human, surrounded now by blue flames instead of red. It floated comfortably through the waters. Its voice spoke in Kevin's skull: *You play well for a human, but you can never play well enough.*

Something seemed to explode in Kevin's brain. He screamed. In the canyon that served as Asphoriel's court, Japhis embraced Davin's writhing body and tried to stroke his brow to comfort him. A message came from Janny: "Don't die for me, Kevin, please, God, don't!" And from Gwen: "Jack out, Kev! It's not worth it!"

He turned himself into a phantom—cool, translucent, and immaterial—and set off a hydrogen bomb at Asphoriel's feet. The flood waters boiled and evaporated; the arena became molten, radioactive slag.

Asphoriel's voice returned: *Thank you for challenging me, Davin Greenboots. I am enjoying this. Shall we make it more interesting?*

They hovered above the canyon of purple crystals. To either side, dark spires extended infinitely. Below, in the canyon, Japhis cradled an immobile Davin, and Darkwind nudged Davin's limp torso with his nose. Kevin sensed Asphoriel nearby, though he did not know how he knew it. He suspected that Asphoriel wanted him to know. He said, "They're not part of our game."

"They're not players in our game," Asphoriel answered.
"True. They're pieces."

A red glow surrounded Darkwind. The stallion whinnied
and reared, struggling against it. Kevin thought of a blue protective sphere enclosing Darkwind, preserving his life, and the
sphere appeared, but Kevin could sense that it would not hold.
In a strength of will against will, Asphoriel was the stronger.

"Gwen! Jack out now!" Kevin called.

"The game—" she began.

A second red glow formed around Japhis. She released
Davin and stood to slash wildly, futilely, about her with the
gold knife. Kevin demanded a second sphere to enclose her
and strained at both defenses, thinking them indigo, thinking
them opaque, thinking them impenetrable.

A crack formed in Darkwind's sphere, and Japhis's began
to quiver.

"I can't hold it!" Kevin called. "You've both got to jack
out!"

"Never!" Janny answered. Japhis still swung the gold
blade, but she stumbled as if sick or blind.

"If you jack out, I can keep fighting! If you don't—"

Darkwind dropped to his knees. Kevin felt the stallion's
labored breath, sensed his falling vision, knew Darkwind was
falling into unconsciousness and there was nothing Kevin
could do to save him. "Now, Gwen! Or you're hothead!"

As Darkwind's heart made a last, weak beat, Gwen called,
"Good luck! Exiting!"

The stallion lay on the slick crystal floor like a broken toy.
Japhis reeled about the canyon, still fighting her untouchable
foe. Her skin flushed bright red, and she stumbled.

"Janny, exit!" Kevin begged. "Now!"

"No. Save it. Must save it."

He did not know if she was talking to him or to herself, but
he knew he could not convince her. He made the sphere
around her blue-violet, then black, and still he felt it shatter-
ing. His personal mental defenses slipped as he strained to
reinforce those around Japhis. He felt Asphoriel's psychic tendrils began to touch his memories and emotions, but he could
not block the Demon Lord from his mind and save Japhis
from dying.

He was failing again, failing as he always did, failing

Janny, his parents, the pink bunny in the hothead ward, his teachers, his friends, himself. How many times could he fail? He could not save a character in a game. Japhis would die like Darkwind, and Demon's Gate would remain open. The Tangled Lands would consume Janny's World, and Omari would never put *Lands of Adventure* on the net.

Janny might go hothead, and he could not save her.

At last, one consolation rose from his despair. He could go hothead himself, with a wish. When his body was found, everyone would know that they had failed him.

"No!" he screamed, and dropped all of the barriers that kept Asphoriel out of his mind. He could feel the Demon Lord's pleasure as it seeped into him, sifting through him and through Davin for a memory or a fear that it could use to end this game.

Kevin touched Darkwind's heart, starting it again, then thrust everything that was Davin's life and everything that was his own into the Demon Lord's mind.

Two contradictory strings of code struggled to superimpose themselves on Asphoriel's essential nature. The Demon Lord fled back into its physical self to preserve its existence, and Davin returned to his body in Asphoriel's court.

"Janny?" Kevin asked.

"Better," she answered. "Sorry, but . . ."

"You have to see it through. I understand."

"Thanks for saving me."

He felt a phantom kiss on his nonexistent cheek, and he smiled with insubstantial lips.

"Gwen's out?" Janny asked.

"Yeah. Probably would've lost you both if she hadn't gone. I saved Darkwind, though. If Mad Dog hadn't fucked with the game, Gwen could jack back in now."

He sensed something from her that he interpreted as a shrug. "It's almost over," Janny said. "The two of us'll have to see it through."

Davin lay on the cool crystal floor, with Japhis cradling his head in her lap. She said, "Oh, Davin, I thought you'd died!"

He did not understand what had happened, but he remembered one impossible thing clearly. "I won?"

"You won." Asphoriel stepped aside with a flourish of one

burning arm. "There stands Demon's Gate. Close it if you can."

"You won't try to stop us?" Japhis asked, helping Davin to stand. Darkwind waited nearby as if he had never fallen.

"Of course not. I promised. I'll take you there, in fact." The Demon Lord smiled. "That does not mean you'll succeed." He clapped his hands, and they stood at the base of Demon's Gate.

The silver gate towered above them. Davin could not guess its height; looking up at the sheer, silver surface, he was reminded of mountain cliffs.

Asphoriel stood behind them. "Well?"

"Well," said the Demon of Korz Pass, appearing in Darkwind's place. It wore the form of the androgynous youth dressed in a kirtle of leaves. Its laughter seemed full of earthly things, of birdsongs and waterfalls and squirrels' cries.

Asphoriel stared. "I did not expect—"

"You promised!" Japhis said, lifting her golden knife.

"Yes," Asphoriel answered, more gently.

The Korz Demon placed its shoulder to the huge door, and the door began to move without a sound. Davin guessed that the arc they must follow before the door closed in the Gate was a quarter of a mile or more.

The Korz Demon seemed to find its task effortless. It strolled, pushing the door before it, and laughed.

"You'd betray us?" Asphoriel asked calmly, following the Korz Demon.

"I would frustrate you."

"To save this world?"

"Yes."

Davin and Japhis, apparently forgotten, trailed behind the demons.

"You'll never see it, once the Gate closes. Not unless a human magician summons you as its servant."

"I'll remember it."

Asphoriel laughed. "Remember it with the Gate open."

"I'll remember that I saved it."

"Ah." Asphoriel nodded. "And how will you remember that when you're dead?"

"You cannot kill me, Asphoriel. Or you never would have let me leave the Tangled Lands to live in the wilds."

"Kill you?" Asphoriel chuckled, and Davin thought the two demons might be something like siblings. "Why bother, when you intend to kill yourself?"

"Do I?"

"Indeed." Asphoriel nodded and said solemnly, "I, Asphoriel, banish you from my realm on pain of death. Hear me, my subjects?"

The sound was like an avalanche as uncountable voices echoed within the canyon: "Yes, Lord." "Yes, Lord." "Yes, Lord." Davin covered his ears, and saw Japhis do the same, and still the voices rang within his head, as loud as before: "Yes, Lord." "Yes, Lord." "Yes, Lord."

"If you stand without the closed Gate, you'll die immediately. If you stand within the closed Gate, your fellow demons will kill you immediately. Will you close the Gate now?" Asphoriel asked. "If you do not, I will return you to my favor."

The Korz Demon did not speak. Its face was unusually solemn.

"What value do you place on your life?" Asphoriel asked. "Would you give an immortal life for a mortal world?"

The Korz Demon shrugged. "Ask what value I place on this world."

Asphoriel laughed again. "I've defined that value. Will you pay it?"

The huge door might have been half-closed. Its movement ceased. "I think..." the Korz Demon said, and Davin saw their failure in the Korz Demon's hesitation. "...I will." And the Demon continued to close the immense Gate, more quickly than before. Davin sighed his relief.

"Very well," Asphoriel said. "Can we share this world? I would happily grant you a tenth. That should be land enough to support the local life."

The Korz Demon began to run. Asphoriel floated beside him, still speaking. Davin and Japhis ran after them, but quickly fell behind, unable to hear the demons' conversation.

At last, Davin caught Japhis's hand and slowed. "I think our part is done."

Japhis shook her head. "It hasn't closed."

(Kevin: So, the game'll finish on its own. Funny. I thought we'd have to see the final act through, somehow.)

(Janny: We will. Take care of yourself.)

(Kevin: Huh?)

(Janny: The Korz Demon wasn't quite willing to die. Tempted, yes, but not willing. I'm in it now.)

(Kevin: Jesus! Get out, Janny! Before the Gate closes!)

(Janny: If I switch back, it won't close the Gate.)

(Kevin: I—)

(Janny: It's that simple.)

(Kevin: You're going to go hothead for a stupid game.)

(Janny: For a world.)

(Kevin: A game.)

(Janny: Let's not argue, okay? Not now. I'll try to shift when the Gate closes.)

(Kevin: You won't make it. Not if it dies then.)

(Janny: I know. I'll still try.)

(Kevin: Oh, shit, Janny, please—)

(Janny: My choice, Kevin. Don't make it harder.)

(Kevin: What about us?)

(Janny: I don't know. It might've been fun. It might've never happened. I like you, Kevin. Hell, I love you like . . . well, not like a brother! Like a . . . good friend. Be a good friend, Kevin.)

(Kevin: Is it Mad Dog?)

(Janny: I wouldn't kill myself because Mad Dog got upset. Tell him I'm sorry he learned this way. Tell him not to blame himself. It wouldn't have made any difference, anyway.)

(Kevin: Why not?)

(Janny: The prophecy. I'm the third.)

(Kevin: God, Janny, don't—)

(Janny: Goodbye, love.)

A hot wind tore at Davin's and Japhis's back as they ran toward Demon's Gate. Above them, the strange sky grew darker. The crystalline ground shook as though the world would tear itself apart, and when Davin looked up, unnatural shapes hurled themselves through the air, a mad swarm of the bizarre and the improbable that flew toward Demon's Gate. To either side of Davin and Japhis, slabs of purple light broke away from the ground and joined the swarm overhead. The sky screamed in a cacophony of incompatible voices, and the tortured ground threw Davin and Japhis down onto its rough surface, where they huddled together.

It ended silently. They crouched on bare sand instead of dark crystal. A cool breeze rolled over them. The sky was a winter's gray that promised rain, but might continue to promise it for several days.

There was no sign that Demon's Gate or the Tangled Lands had ever been.

Prompt met Kevin as a Persian cat. She leapt into his arms, and he held her, petting her for a long time. At last, he said, "Has Janny Laias jacked out of *Lands of Adventure*?"

"No," Prompt answered.

"Is she . . . doing anything in there? Anything at all?"

"No."

He nodded. "Not Groucho Marx's voice anymore," he said. "Try . . . the star of *Casablanca*. The female one."

"Is this adequate?"

"Perfect," he said, and began to cry.

Sometime later, he said, "*Lands of Adventure*." The long-haired Janny met him, but he expected that. She wore a white robe; the room seemed to be a marble and granite entryway to a palace. He did not look closely. He said, "Design path," before she could speak, and heard Janny say, "Certainly, Kevin Fikkan."

It should have further saddened him when he became the world. His last hope was that Janny had switched to the design path in time and passively observed her world before jacking out. If that had been the case, he would not have been allowed access to this level; only one person at a time could run the design path.

Instead, he felt something like pleasure, something like glory. He was a world, and for all its flaws, it was a healthy, growing world. He was a grain of sand on a beach by a lake in Gordia. He was an evergreen high on World's Peak. He was a caterpillar in the Dawn Isles and an antelope in Bakh and a bear in the Northlands and a small girl among the Hrotish wanderers and an old man in Tyrwilka and a young Elf woman in Castle Thramering. He was the First Among Ants and the First Among Dragons. He was even, in a place that somehow existed beside the world, a demon who hoped for another chance to take the world but had no way to act.

The world's lore lay before him, to read or to change as he pleased. Something called his attention in a way he did not understand to something that was an anomaly in the version of the world that had existed before the Three closed Demon's Gate. It was not an anomaly in this version of the world.

The history of the God who had made the world had grown, among the few people who knew it. After She made everything that was, She divided Herself into an infinite number of portions and gave everything that was and everything that will be a part of Herself, so the World could be real and not Her illusion.

He was Japhis Kardeck and Davin Greenboots.

She pointed with her chin toward the south. "If we make it to the herders' camp, we can probably get supplies for the trip home. I can sell the knife, if I have to."

He nodded. Something moved in the distance, where Demon's Gate had stood. He stared, disbelieving, then yelled, "Darkwind!" The stallion, still carrying their packs, galloped up to them. He bashed his head against Davin's chest, and Davin staggered backward, laughing. Japhis hugged Darkwind's neck, and Davin said, "I thought you were dead!"

Darkwind neighed.

"Maybe that's why the Korz Demon was willing to do it," Japhis said, unsure of the source of her guess but sure of its truth. "Maybe, as Demon's Gate closed, the Korz Demon turned itself back into Darkwind."

"The prophecy?" said Davin.

"Two will live and one must die. If it ever turns itself back into the demon, it'll die. If it stays Darkwind, it'll die when Darkwind does." Japhis laughed. "Or maybe the prophecy's so much nonsense. What's it matter?"

"Not a damn thing," Davin answered. Taking her hand, they began the long walk south, and home.

"Exiting," Kevin whispered. And as he slipped from the design path, he thought he felt Janny's insubstantial kiss on his intangible cheek.

CLASSIC SCIENCE FICTION AND FANTASY

__DUNE Frank Herbert 0-441-17266-0/$4.95
The bestselling novel of an awesome world where gods and adventurers clash, mile-long sandworms rule the desert, and the ancient dream of immortality comes true.

__STRANGER IN A STRANGE LAND Robert A. Heinlein
0-441-79034-8/$4.95
From the *New York Times* bestselling author—the science fiction masterpiece of a man from Mars who teaches humankind the art of grokking, watersharing and love.

__THE ONCE AND FUTURE KING T.H. White
0-441-62740-4/$5.50
The world's greatest fantasy classic! A magical epic of King Arthur in Camelot, romance, wizardry and war. By the author of *The Book of Merlyn*.

__THE LEFT HAND OF DARKNESS Ursula K. LeGuin
0-441-47812-3/$3.95
Winner of the Hugo and Nebula awards for best science fiction novel of the year. "SF masterpiece!"—*Newsweek* "A Jewel of a story."—Frank Herbert

__MAN IN A HIGH CASTLE Philip K. Dick 0-441-51809-5/$3.95
"Philip K. Dick's best novel, a masterfully detailed alternate world peopled by superbly realized characters."
—Harry Harrison